HONOR IN A CORNER

Honor's dark eyes locked unflinchingly with Santino's, but even as they did, she kicked herself mentally for losing her temper, for she saw the sudden rage flashing in the depths of his glare. She'd kept her voice level and even, but the entire tone of her answer had been well over the line. No one would ever be able to prove it, but she and Santino both knew she'd done it to get some of her own back, and his florid complexion darkened angrily.

"I assume you know the penalty for insubordination," he grated. She said nothing, and his color darkened further. "I asked you a question, Snotty!" he barked.

"I'm sorry, Sir. I was unaware that it was meant as a question. It sounded like a statement."

She could hardly believe it even as she heard her own voice say it, and she sensed Senior Chief Shelton and his work party behind her, watching it all. What was *wrong* with her? Why in heaven's name was she goading him back this way?

"Well, it wasn't one!" Santino snapped. "So answer me!"

"Yes, Sir," she said. "I am aware of the penalty for insubordination."

"That's good, Snotty, because you just bought yourself a locker full of it! Now get out of my sight. Go directly to your quarters and remain there until I personally tell you differently!"

"Yes, Sir." She came to attention, saluted crisply, turned on her heel, and marched off with her head high while the man with the power to destroy her career before it even began glared after her.

WORLDS OF HONOR #3

CHANGER OF WORLDS

DAVID WEBER

WORLDS OF HONOR #3: CHANGER OF WORLDS

A Baen Books Original

Baen Publishing Enterprises
P.O. Box 1403
Riverdale, NY 10471
www.baen.com

ISBN: 0-7434-3520-6

Cover art by Carol Heyer

First paperback printing, February 2002

Library of Congress Cataloging-in-Publication Number 00-051939

Distributed by Simon & Schuster
1230 Avenue of the Americas
New York, NY 10020

Production by Brilliant Press
Printed in the United States of America

CONTENTS

Ms. Midshipwoman Harrington

David Weber

"That looks like your snotty, Senior Chief."

The Marine sentry's low-pitched voice exuded an oddly gleeful sympathy. It was the sort of voice in which a Marine traditionally informed one of the Navy's "vacuum-suckers" that his trousers had just caught fire or something equally exhilarating, and Senior Chief Petty Officer Roland Shelton ignored the jarhead's tone with the lofty disdain of any superior life form for an evolutionary inferior. Yet it was a bit harder than usual this time as his eyes followed the corporal's almost invisible nod and picked the indicated target out of the crowded space dock gallery. She was certainly *someone's* snotty, he acknowledged without apparently so much as looking in her direction. Her midshipwoman's uniform was immaculate, but both it and the tethered counter-grav locker towing behind her were so new he expected to hear her squeak. There was something odd about that locker, too, as if something else half its size had been piggybacked onto it, although he paid that little attention. Midshipmen were always turning up with oddball bits and pieces of person-alized gear that they hoped didn't quite violate Regs. Half the time they were wrong, but there would be time enough to straighten that out later if this particular snotty came aboard Shelton's ship. And, he conceded, she seemed to be headed for *War Maiden*'s docking tube, although that might simply be a mistake on her part.

He hoped.

She was a tall young woman, taller than Shelton himself, with dark brown, fuzz-cut hair, and a severe, triangular face which seemed to have been assembled solely from a nose which might charitably be called "strong" and huge, almond-shaped eyes. At the moment the face as a whole showed no expression at all, but the light in those eyes was bright enough to make an experienced petty officer groan in resignation.

She also looked to be about thirteen years old. That probably meant she was a third-generation prolong recipient, but recognizing the cause didn't do a thing to make her look any more mature. Still, she moved well, he admitted almost grudgingly. There was an athletic grace to her carriage and an apparent assur-ance at odds with her youth, and she avoided colli-sions with ease as she made her way through the people filling the gallery, almost as if she were per-forming some sort of free-form dance.

Had that been all Shelton had been able to discern about her, he would probably have put her down (provisionally and a bit hopefully) as somewhat above the average of the young gentlemen and ladies senior Navy noncoms were expected to transform from pigs' ears into silk purses. Unfortunately, it was not all that he could discern, and it took most of his thirty-four T-years of experience not to let his dismay show as he observed the prick-eared, wide-whiskered, six-limbed, silky-pelted Sphinx treecat riding on her shoulder.

A treecat. A treecat in *his* ship. And in the midshipmen's compartment, at that. The thought was enough to give a man who believed in orderly procedures and Navy traditions hives, and Shelton felt a strong urge to reach out and throttle the expressionlessly smirking Marine at his shoulder.

For a few more seconds he allowed himself to hope that she might walk right past *War Maiden* to the ship she actually sought, or that she might be lost. But any possibility of dodging the pulser dart faded as she walked straight over to the heavy cruiser's tube.

Shelton and the Marine saluted, and she returned the courtesy with a crispness which managed to be both brand new and excited yet curiously mature. She gave Shelton a brief, measuring glance, almost more imagined than seen, but addressed herself solely to the sentry.

"Midshipwoman Harrington to join the ship's company, Corporal," she said in a crisp Sphinx accent, and drew a record chip in an official Navy cover slip from her tunic pocket and extended it. Her soprano was surprisingly soft and sweet for someone her height, Shelton noted as the Marine took the chip and slotted it into his memo board, although her tone was neither hesitant nor shy. Still, he had to wonder if someone who sounded as young as she looked would ever be able to generate a proper snap of command. He allowed no sign of his thoughts to cross his face, but the 'cat on her shoulder cocked its head, gazing at him with bright, grass-green eyes while its whiskers twitched.

"Yes, Ma'am," the Marine said as the chip's data matched that in his memo board and confirmed Ms. Midshipwoman Harrington's orders and legal right to come aboard *War Maiden*. He popped the chip free and handed it back to her, then nodded to Shelton. "Senior Chief Shelton's been expecting you, I believe," he said, still with that irritating edge of imperfectly concealed glee, and Harrington turned to the senior chief and arched one eyebrow.

That surprised Shelton just a bit. However composed she might appear, he'd seen thirty-plus T-years of new-penny snotties reporting for their midshipman cruises, and the light in her eyes was proof enough that she was just as excited and eager as any of the others had been. Yet that arched eyebrow held a cool authority, or perhaps assurance. It wasn't the sort of deliberately projected superiority some snotties used to hide their own anxiety or lack of confidence. It was too natural for that. But that calm, silent question, delivered with neither condescension nor defensiveness, woke a sudden glimmer of hope. There might be some solid metal in this one, the senior chief told himself, but then the 'cat wiggled its whiskers at him, and he gave himself a mental shake.

"Senior Chief Petty Officer Shelton, Ma'am," he heard himself say. "If you'll just follow me, I'll escort you to the Exec."

"Thank you, Senior Chief," she said and followed him into the tube.

With the 'cat.

Honor Harrington tried conscientiously to keep her excitement from showing as she swam the boarding tube behind Senior Chief Shelton, but it was hard. She'd known she was headed for this moment for almost half her life, and she'd sweated and worked for over three-and-a-half endless T-years at Saganami Island to reach it. Now she had, and the butterflies in her midsection propagated like particularly energetic yeast as they reached the inboard end of the tube and she caught the grab bar and swung herself through into the heavy cruiser's internal gravity behind Shelton. In her own mind, that was the symbolic moment when she left His Majesty's Space Station *Hephaestus* to enter the domain of HMS *War Maiden*, and her heart beat harder and stronger as the sights and sounds and distinctive smell of a King's starship closed about her. They were subtly different somehow from those in the space station she'd left behind. No doubt that was her imagination—one artificial environment in space was very like another, after all—but the impression of differentness, of something special waiting just for her, quivered at her core.

The treecat on her shoulder made a soft scolding sound, and her mouth quirked ever so slightly. Nimitz understood her excited joy, as well as the unavoidable trepidation that went with it, but the empathic 'cats were pragmatic souls, and he recognized the signs of Honor Harrington in exhilarated mode. More to the point, he knew the importance of getting off on the right foot aboard *War Maiden*, and she felt his claws dig just a bit deeper into her uniform tunic's specially padded shoulder in a gentle reminder to keep herself focused.

She reached up and brushed his ears in acknowledgment even as her feet found the deck of *War Maiden's* boat bay, just outside the painted line which indicated the official separation between ship and space station. At least she hadn't embarrassed herself like one of her classmates, who had landed on the wrong side of the line during one of their short, near-space training missions! A part of her wanted to giggle in memory of the absolutely scathing look the training ship's boat bay officer of the deck had bestowed upon her fellow middy, but she suppressed the temptation and came quickly to attention and saluted the OD of *this* boat bay.

"Permission to come aboard to join the ship's company, Ma'am!" she said, and the sandy-haired ensign gave her a cool, considering look, then acknowledged the salute. She brought her hand down from her beret's brim and extended it wordlessly, and Honor produced the chip of her orders once more. The BOD performed the same ritual as the Marine sentry, then nodded, popped the chip from her board, and handed it back.

"Permission granted, Ms. Harrington," she said, much less crisply than Honor but with a certain world-weary maturity. She was, after all, at least a T-year older than Honor, with her own middy cruise safely behind her. The ensign glanced at Shelton, and Honor noticed the way the other young woman's shoulders came back ever so slightly and the way her voice crisped up as she nodded to the SCPO. "Carry on, Senior Chief," she said.

"Aye, aye, Ma'am," Shelton replied, and beckoned

respectfully for Honor to follow him once more as he led her towards the lifts.

Lieutenant Commander Abner Layson sat in the chair behind his desk and made an obviously careful study of his newest potential headache's orders. Midshipwoman Harrington sat very upright in her own chair, hands folded in her lap, feet positioned at precisely the right angle, and watched the bulkhead fifteen centimeters above his head with apparent composure. She'd seemed on the edge of flustered when he'd directed her to sit rather than remain at stand-easy while he perused her paperwork, but there was little sign of that in her present demeanor. Unless, of course, the steady flicking of the very tip of her treecat's tail indicated more uneasiness in the 'cat's adopted person than she cared to admit. Interesting that she could conceal the outward signs so readily, though, if that were the case.

He let his eyes return to his reader's display, scanning the official, tersely worded contents of her personnel jacket, while he wondered what had possessed Captain Bachfisch to specifically request such an ... unlikely prize when the snotty cruise assignments were being handed out.

A bit young, he thought. Although her third-gen prolong made her look even younger than her calendar age, she was only twenty. The Academy was flexible about admission ages, but most midshipmen entered at around eighteen or nineteen T-years of age; Harrington had been barely seventeen when she was admitted. Which was all the more surprising given what seemed to be a total lack of aristocratic connections, patronage, or interest from on high to account for it. On the other hand, her overall grades at

Saganami Island had been excellent—aside from some abysmal math scores, at least—and she'd received an unbroken string of "Excellent" and "Superior" ratings from her tactical and command simulation instructors. That was worth noting. Still, he reminded himself, many an Academy overachiever had proven a sad disappointment in actual Fleet service. Scored remarkably high on the kinesthesia tests, too, although that particular requirement was becoming less and less relevant these days. Very high marks in the flight training curriculum as well, including—his eyebrows rose ever so slightly—a new Academy sailplane record. But she might be a bit on the headstrong side, maybe even the careless one, given the official reprimand noted on her Form 107FT for ignoring her flight instruments. And that stack of black marks for lack of air discipline didn't look very promising. On the other hand, they all seemed to come from a single instance. . . .

He accessed the relevant portion of her record, and something suspiciously like a snort escaped before he could throttle it. He turned it into a reasonably convincing coughing fit, but his mouth quivered as he scanned the appended note. Buzzed the Commandant's boat during the Regatta, had she? No wonder Hartley had lowered the boom on her! Still, he must have thought well of her to stop there, although the identity of her partner in crime might also have had a bit to do with it. Couldn't exactly go tossing the King's niece out, now could they? Well, not for anything short of premeditated murder, at any rate. . . .

He sighed and tipped back his chair, pinching the bridge of his nose, and glanced at her under cover of his hand. The treecat worried him. He knew it wasn't supposed to, for regulations were uncompromising on that particular subject and had been ever since the reign of Queen Adrienne. She could not legally be separated from the creature, and she'd obviously gotten through the Academy with it without creating any major waves. But a starship was a much smaller world than Saganami Island, and she wasn't the only middy aboard.

Small jealousies and envies could get out of hand on a long deployment, and she would be the only person on board authorized to take a pet with her. Oh, Layson knew the 'cats weren't really pets. It wasn't a subject he'd ever taken much personal interest in, but the creatures' sentience was well-established, as was the fact that once they empathically bonded to a human, they literally could not be separated without serious consequences for both partners. But they *looked* like pets, and most of the Star Kingdom's citizens knew even less about them than Layson did, which offered fertile ground for misunderstandings and resentment. And the fact that the Bureau of Personnel had seen fit to assign *War Maiden* a brand new assistant tac officer, and that the ATO in any ship was traditionally assigned responsibility for the training and discipline of any midshipmen assigned to her, only deepened his worries about the possible repercussions of the 'cat's presence. The exec hadn't yet had time to learn much about the ATO, but what he had learned so far did not inspire him with a lively confidence in the man's ability.

Yet even the presence of the 'cat was secondary to Layson's true concern. There had to be some reason the Captain had requested Harrington, and try though he might, the exec simply couldn't figure out what that reason might be. Such requests usually represented

tokens in the patronage game the Navy's senior officers
played so assiduously. They were either a way to gain
the support of some well-placed potential patron by
standing sponsor to a son or daughter or younger relative, or else a way to pay back a similar favor. But
Harrington was a yeoman's daughter, whose only apparent aristocratic association was the highly tenuous one
of having roomed with the Earl of Gold Peak's younger
offspring for a bit over two T-years. That was a fairly
lofty connection, or would have been if it actually
existed, but Layson couldn't see any way the Captain
could have capitalized on it even if it had. So what
could the reason be? Layson didn't know, and that
bothered him, because it was a good executive officer's
job to keep himself informed of anything which might
affect the smooth functioning of the ship he ran for
his captain.

"Everything seems to be in order, Ms. Harrington,"
he told her after a moment, lowering his hand and
letting his chair come back upright. "Lieutenant
Santino is our assistant tac officer, which makes him
your OCT officer, as well. I'll have Senior Chief
Shelton deliver you to Snotty Row when we're done
here, and you can report to him once you've stowed
your gear. In the meantime, however, I make it a
policy to spend a few minutes with new middies when
they first come aboard. It gives me a chance to get
to know them and to get a feel for how they'll fit in
here in *War Maiden*."

He paused, and she nodded respectfully.

"Perhaps you can start off then by telling me—
briefly, of course—just why you joined the Service,"
he invited.

"For several reasons, Sir," she said after only the
briefest of pauses. "My father was a Navy doctor

before he retired and went into private practice, so I was a 'Navy brat' until I was about eleven. And I've always been interested in naval history, clear back to pre-Diaspora Earth. But I suppose the most important reason was the People's Republic, Sir."

"Indeed?" Layson couldn't quite keep the surprise out of his tone.

"Yes, Sir." Her voice was both respectful and thoughtful, but it was also very serious. "I believe war with Haven is inevitable, Sir. Not immediately, but in time."

"And you want to be along for the glory and the adventure, do you?"

"No, Sir." Her expression didn't alter, despite the bite in his question. "I want to help defend the Star Kingdom. And I *don't* want to live under the Peeps."

"I see," he said, and studied her for several more seconds. That was a viewpoint he was more accustomed to hearing from far more senior—and older—officers, not from twenty-year-old midshipwomen. It was also the reason the Royal Manticoran Navy was currently involved in the biggest buildup in its history, and the main reason Harrington's graduating class was ten percent larger than the one before it. But as Harrington had just pointed out, the looming war still lurked in the uncertain future.

And her answer *still* didn't give him a clue as to why Captain Bachfisch wanted her aboard *War Maiden*.

"Well, Ms. Harrington," he said at last, "if you want to help defend the Star Kingdom, you've certainly come to the right place. And you may have an opportunity to start doing it a bit sooner than you anticipated, as well, because we've been ordered to Silesia for antipiracy duties." The young woman sat even straighter in her chair at that, and the 'cat's tail stopped twitching and froze in the curl of a question mark. "But if you truly don't harbor dreams of glory, make it a point not to start harboring them anytime soon. As you're no doubt tired of hearing, this cruise is your true final exam."

He paused, regarding her steadily, and she nodded soberly. A midshipwoman was neither fish nor fowl in many respects. Officially, she remained an officer candidate, holding a midshipwoman's warrant but not yet an officer's commission. Her warrant gave her a temporary place in the chain of command aboard *War Maiden*; it did not guarantee that she would ever hold any authority anywhere *after* this cruise, however. Her actual graduation from the Academy was assured, given her grades and academic performance, but a muffed midshipman's cruise could very well cost her any chance at one of the career tracks which led to eventual command. The Navy always needed non-line staff officers whose duties kept them safely out of the chain of command, after all, and someone who blew his or her first opportunity to shoulder responsibility outside a classroom wasn't the person one wanted commanding a King's ship. And if she screwed up too massively on this cruise, she might receive both an Academy diploma and formal notice that the Crown did not after all require her services in *any* capacity.

"You're here to learn, and the Captain and I will evaluate your performance very carefully. If you have any hope of achieving command in your own right someday, I advise you to see to it that our evaluations are positive ones. Is that understood?"

"Yes, Sir!"

"Good." He gave her a long, steady look, then

produced a small smile. "It's a tradition in the Fleet
that by the time a middy has survived Saganami
Island, he's like a 'cat. Fling him into the Service
any way you like, and he'll land on his feet. That,
at least, is the type of midshipman the Academy *tries*
to turn out, and it's what will be expected of you
as a member of *War Maiden*'s company. In your own
case, however, there is a rather special complicat-
ing factor. One, I'm certain, of which you must be
fully aware. Specifically," he pointed with his chin
to the treecat stretched across the top of her chair's
back, "your . . . companion."

He paused, waiting to see if she would respond.
But she simply met his eyes steadily, and he made
a mental note that this one had composure by the
bucketful.

"No doubt you're more intimately familiar with the
Regs where 'cats aboard ship are concerned than I
am," he went on after a moment in a tone which said
she'd damned well *better* be familiar with them. "I
expect you to observe them to the letter. The fact
that the two of you managed to survive Saganami
Island gives me some reason to hope you'll also
manage to survive *War Maiden*. But I expect you to
be aware that this is a much smaller environment than
the Academy, and the right to be together aboard ship
carries with it the responsibility to avoid any situation which might have a negative impact on the
smooth and efficient functioning of this ship's company. I trust that, also, is clearly understood. By you
both."

"Yes, Sir," she said once more, and he nodded.

"I am delighted to hear it. In that case, Senior
Chief Shelton will see you to your quarters, such as
they are. Good luck, Ms. Harrington."

"Thank you, Sir."

"Dismissed," he said, and turned back to his data terminal as the middy braced to attention once more and then followed SCPO Shelton from the compartment.

Honor finished making up her bunk (with regulation "Saganami Island" corners on the sheets and a blanket taut enough to bounce a five-dollar coin), then detached the special piggyback unit from her locker and lifted the locker itself into the waiting bulkhead brackets. She grinned, remembering one of her classmates—from a dirt-grubber Gryphon family with no Navy connections at all—who had revealed his abysmal ignorance the day their first lockers were issued by wondering aloud why every one of them had to have exactly the same dimensions. That particular question had been answered on their first training cruise, and now Honor settled hers in place, opened the door, flipped off the counter-grav, and toggled the locking magnets once its weight had fully settled.

She gave it a precautionary shake, despite the glowing telltales which purported to show a solid seal. Others had trusted the same telltales when they shouldn't have, but this time they held, and she closed the door and attached the piggyback to the frame of her bunk. She took rather more care with it than she had with the locker, and Nimitz watched alertly from atop her pillow as she did so. Unlike the locker, which was standard Navy issue, she—or rather, her father, who had provided it as a graduation gift—had paid the better part of seventeen thousand Manticoran dollars for that unit. Which was money well spent in her opinion, since it was the life support module

which would keep Nimitz alive if the compartment
lost pressure. She made very certain that it was
securely anchored, then hit the self-test key and nodded in satisfaction as the control panel blinked alive
and the diagnostic program confirmed full function-
ality. Nimitz returned her nod with a satisfied bleek
of his own, and she turned away to survey the rest
of the berthing compartment known rather unroman-
tically as "Snotty Row" while she awaited Senior Chief
Shelton's return.

It was a largish compartment for a ship as small—
and as old—as *War Maiden*. In fact, it was about
twice the size of her Saganami Island dorm room. Of
course, that dorm room had held only two people,
her and her friend Michelle Henke, while this compartment was designed to house six. At the moment,
only four of the bunks had sheets and blankets on
them, though, so it looked as if *War Maiden* was
sailing light in the middy department.

That could be good or bad, she reflected, settling
into one of the spartan, unpowered chairs at the
berthing compartment's well worn table. The good
news was that it meant she and her three fellows
would have a bit more space, but it would also mean
there were only four of them to carry the load. Everyone knew that a lot of what any midshipwoman did
on her snotty cruise always constituted little more than
makework, duties concocted by the ship's officer
candidate training officer and assigned only as learning
exercises rather than out of any critical need on her
ship's part. But a lot more of those duties were anything *but* makework. Middies were King's officers—
the lowest of the low, perhaps, and only temporarily
and by virtue of warrant, but still officers—and they
were expected to pull their weight aboard ship.

She lifted Nimitz into her lap and ran her fingers slowly over his soft, fluffy pelt, smiling at the crackle of static electricity which followed her touch. He bleeked softly and pressed his head against her, luxuriating in her caresses, and she drew a long, slow breath. It was the first time she'd truly relaxed since packing the last of her meager shipboard belongings into her locker that morning on Saganami Island, and the respite was going to be brief.

She closed her eyes and let mental muscles unkink ever so slightly while she replayed her interview with Commander Layson. The exec of any King's ship was a being of at least demigod status, standing at the right hand of the Captain. As such, Layson's actions and attitudes were not to be questioned by a mere midshipwoman. But there'd been something, an edge she hadn't been able to pin down or define, to his questions. She tried once more to tell herself it was only first-day-aboard-ship nerves. He *was* the Exec, and it was an executive officer's job to know everything she could about the officers serving under her, even if the officers in question were mere middies. Yet that curious certainty which came to Honor seldom but was never wrong told her there was more to it than that in this case. And whether there was or not, there was no question at all that he regarded Nimitz's presence aboard *War Maiden* as an at least potential problem. For that matter, Senior Chief Shelton seemed to feel the same way, and Honor sighed.

It wasn't the first time, or the second, or even the twentieth time she'd faced that attitude. As Commander Layson had suggested, she was indeed fully conversant with what Navy regulations had to say about treecats and their adoptees in Fleet service.

Most Navy personnel were not, because the situation arose so infrequently. 'Cat-human bonds were vanishingly rare even on Honor's native Sphinx. The six-limbed arboreals were almost never seen off-planet, and they were even more uncommon in the Navy than in civilian life. Honor had done a little discreet research, and as far as she could determine, no more than a dozen or so current active-duty personnel of all ranks, including herself, had been adopted. That number was minute compared to the total number of people in the Navy, so it was hardly surprising that the 'cats created a stir whenever they did turn up.

Understanding the reason for the situation didn't change it, however, and Honor had been made almost painfully well aware that Nimitz's presence was regarded as a potentially disruptive influence by the vast majority of people who were unfamiliar with his species. Even those who knew better intellectually had a tendency to regard 'cats as little more than extremely clever pets, and an unfortunate percentage of humans never bothered to learn differently even when the opportunity presented itself. The fact that 'cats were unable to form anything like the sounds of human speech only exacerbated that particular aspect of the situation, and the fact that they were so cute and cuddly helped hone the occasional case of jealous resentment over their presence.

Of course, no one who had ever seen a treecat roused to fury could possibly confuse "cute and cuddly" with "harmless." Indeed, their formidable natural armament was another reason some people worried about their presence, even though Nimitz would never harm a human being except in direct self-defense. Or in Honor's defense, which he regarded as precisely the same thing. But people who'd never seen their lethality demonstrated had a pronounced tendency to coo over the 'cats and wish that *they* could have such an adorable pet.

From there, it was a short step to resenting someone else who did have one. Honor and Nimitz had been forced to deal with that attitude more than once at the Academy, and only the fact that the Regs were on their side and that Nimitz was a natural (and unscrupulous) diplomat had gotten them past some of the worse incidents.

Well, if they'd done it on Saganami Island they could do it here, as well, she told herself, and—

The compartment hatch opened with no warning, and Honor came quickly to her feet, Nimitz in her arms as she turned to face the unexpected opening. She knew the occupied light above the hatch had been lit, and opening an occupied compartment's hatch without at least sounding the admittance chime first was a gross infraction of shipboard etiquette. It was also at least technically a privacy violation which was prohibited by Regs except in cases of emergency. The sheer unexpectedness of it created an unaccustomed confusion in Honor, and she stood frozen as a beefy senior-grade lieutenant, perhaps seven or eight T-years older than her, loomed in the doorway. He was two or three centimeters shorter than Honor, with a certain florid handsomeness, but something about his eyes woke an instinctive dislike in her. Or perhaps it was his posture, for he planted both hands on his hips and rocked forward on the balls of his feet to glower at her.

"Don't even snotties know to stand to attention in the presence of a superior officer, Snotty?" he demanded disdainfully, and a flush of anger lit Honor's high cheekbones. His eyes gleamed at the sight, and she felt the sub-audible rumble of Nimitz's snarl through her arms. She tightened her grip in warning, but the 'cat knew better than to openly display his occasional dislike for those senior to his person. He clearly thought it was one of the sillier restrictions inherent in Honor's chosen career, but he was willing to humor her in something so important to her.

She held him just a heartbeat longer, concentrating hard for the benefit of his empathic sense on how important it was for him to behave himself this time, then set him quickly on the table and came to attention.

"That's better," the lieutenant growled, and stalked into the compartment. "I'm Lieutenant Santino, the assistant tac officer," he informed her, hands still on hips while she stood rigidly at attention. "Which means that, for my sins, I'm also in charge of Snotty Row this deployment. So tell me, Ms. Harrington, just what the hell are you doing *here* instead of reporting to me?"

"Sir, I was instructed to stow my gear and get settled in here. My understanding was that Senior Chief Shelton was—"

"And what makes you think a petty officer is more important than a *commissioned* officer, Ms. Harrington?" he broke in on her.

"Sir, I didn't say he was," she replied, making her voice come out calm and even despite her mounting anger.

"You certainly implied it if you meant to say his instructions were more important than mine!"

Honor clamped her jaw tight and made no response. He was only going to twist anything she said to suit his own ends, and she refused to play his stupid game.

"*Didn't* you imply that, Ms. Harrington?" he demanded after the silence had lingered a few seconds, and she looked him squarely in the eye.

"No, Sir. I did not." The words were perfectly correct, the tone calm and unchallenging, but the expression in her dark brown eyes was unyielding. Something flickered in his own gaze, and his lips tightened, but she simply stood there.

"Then what did you mean to imply?" he asked very softly.

"Sir, I meant to imply nothing. I was merely attempting to answer your question."

"Then answer it!" he snapped.

"Sir, I was told by Commander Layson—" she delivered the Exec's name with absolutely no emphasis and watched his eyes narrow and his mouth tighten once more "—that I was to remain here until the Senior Chief returned, at which time he would take me to formally report in to you."

Santino glared at her, but the invocation of Layson's name had at least temporarily stymied him. Which was only going to make things worse in the long run, Honor decided.

"Well here I am, Ms. Harrington," he growled after a long, silent moment. "So suppose you just get started reporting in to me."

"Sir! Midshipwoman Honor Harrington reports for duty, Sir!" she barked with the sort of parade ground formality no one but an idiot or an utter newbie would use aboard ship. Anger glittered in his eyes, but she only met his gaze expressionlessly.

It's really, really *stupid to antagonize him this way, girl!* a voice which sounded remarkably like Michelle Henke's chided in her head. *Surely you put up with enough crap at the Academy to realize that much!*

But she couldn't help herself. And it probably wouldn't matter that much in the long term, anyway.

"Very well, Ms. Harrington," he said icily. "Now that you've condescended to join us, suppose you accompany me to the chart room. I believe I have just the thing for you to occupy yourself with until dinner."

Honor felt far more nervous than she hoped anyone could guess as she joined the party assembling outside the hatch to Captain Bachfisch's dining cabin. *War Maiden* was only three days out of Manticore orbit, and she and her fellow midshipmen had been surprised, to say the least, to discover that the Captain habitually invited his officers to dine with him. It was particularly surprising because *War Maiden* was almost thirty-five standard years old, and small for her rate. Although the captain's quarters were indisputably larger and far more splendid than Snotty Row, they were cramped and plain compared to those aboard newer, larger ships, which made his dining cabin a tight fit for even half a dozen guests. With space at such a premium, he could hardly invite all of his officers to every dinner, but he apparently rotated the guest list regularly to ensure that all of them dined with him in turn.

It was unheard of, or almost so. But Captain Courvoisier, Honor's favorite instructor at the Academy, had once suggested to her that a wise CO got to know her officers—and see to it that they knew her—as well as possible, and she wondered if this was Captain Bachfisch's way of doing just that. But whatever the Captain thought he was up to, finding herself on the guest list was enough to make any snotty nervous, especially this early in the cruise.

She looked around as unobtrusively as possible as the Captain's steward opened the hatch and she followed her seniors through it. As the most junior person present, she brought up the rear, of course, which was only marginally better than being required to lead the way. At least she didn't have to be the very first person through the hatch! But that only meant everyone else could arrive, take their seats, and turn to watch her enter the compartment last of all. She felt the weight of all those senior eyes upon her and wondered if she'd really been wise to bring Nimitz. It was entirely proper for her to do so, according to Regs, unless the invitation specifically excluded him, yet she felt suddenly uncertain and ill at ease, afraid that her seniors might find her decision presumptuous. The uncertainty made her feel physically awkward as well, as if she had somehow reverted to the gawky, oversized horse she'd always thought herself before Chief MacDougal got her seriously interested in *coup de vitesse*. Her face tried to flush, but she ordered her uneasiness sternly back into its box. This evening promised to be stressful enough without borrowing reasons to crank her adrenaline, but she could at least be grateful that Elvis Santino wasn't present. Midshipman Makira had already endured this particular ordeal, and he *had* had to put up with Santino's presence.

At least her lowly status precluded any confusion over which seat might be hers, and she scarcely needed the steward's small gesture directing her to the very foot of the table. She settled herself into the chair as unobtrusively as she could, and Nimitz, as aware as she of the need to be on his best behavior, parked himself very neatly along the top of her seat back.

The steward circled the table, moving through the dining cabin's cramped confines with the grace of long practice as he poured coffee. Honor had always despised that particular beverage, and she covered her cup with her hand as the steward approached her. The man gave her a quizzical glance, but moved on without comment.

"Don't care for coffee, huh?"

The question came from the senior-grade lieutenant seated to her left, and Honor looked at him quickly. The brown-haired, snub-nosed officer was about Santino's age, or within a year or two either way. Unlike Santino, however, his expression was friendly and his tone was pleasant, without the hectoring sneer the OCTO seemed to achieve so effortlessly.

"I'm afraid not, Sir," she admitted.

"That could be a liability in a Navy career," the lieutenant said cheerfully. He looked across the table at a round-faced, dark-complexioned lieutenant commander and grinned. "Some of us," he observed, "seem to be of the opinion that His Majesty's starships actually run on caffeine, not reactor mass. In fact, *some* of us seem to feel that it's our responsibility to rebunker regularly by taking that caffeine on internally."

The lieutenant commander looked down her nose at him and sipped from her own cup, then set it precisely back on the saucer.

"I trust, Lieutenant, that it was not your intention to cast aspersions on the quantities of coffee which certain of your hard-working seniors consume on the bridge," she remarked.

"Certainly not! I'm shocked by the very suggestion that you might think I intended anything of the sort, Ma'am!"

"Of course you are," Commander Layson agreed, then looked down the length of the table at Honor from his place to the right of the Captain's as yet unoccupied chair. "Ms. Harrington, allow me to introduce you. To your left, we have Lieutenant Saunders, our assistant astrogator. To his left, Lieutenant Commander LaVacher, our chief engineer, and to your right, Lieutenant Commander Hirake, our tac officer." LaVacher, a petite, startlingly pretty blonde, faced Layson, who sat at Hirake's right, across the table. She and the Exec completed the group of dinner guests, and Layson gave a small wave in Honor's direction. "Ladies and gentlemen, Ms. Midshipwoman Harrington."

Heads had nodded at her as the Exec named each officer in turn, and now Honor nodded respectfully back to them. Not a one of them, she noticed, seemed to exude the towering sense of superiority which was so much a part of Elvis Santino.

Saunders had just opened his mouth to say something more when the hatch leading to the captain's day cabin opened and a tall, spare man in the uniform of a senior-grade captain stepped through it. All of the other officers around the table stood, and Honor quickly followed suit. They remained standing until Captain Bachfisch had taken his own chair and made a small gesture with his right hand.

"Be seated, ladies and gentlemen," he invited.

Chairs scraped gently on the decksole as his juniors obeyed the instruction, and Honor observed Bachfisch covertly as she unfolded her snowy linen napkin and draped it across her lap. It was the first time she'd set eyes upon the man who was master after God aboard *War Maiden*, and her first impression was one of vague dissatisfaction. Captain

Bachfisch had a thin, lined face and dark eyes which seemed to hold a hint of perpetual frown. In fact, he looked more like an accountant whose figures hadn't come out even than like Honor's mental image of the captain of a King's ship bound to suppress bloody piracy. Nor did his slightly nasal tenor seem the proper voice for such an exalted personage, and she felt an undeniable pang of disappointment.

But then the steward reappeared and began to serve the meal proper, which banished such mundane concerns quite handily. The quality of the food was several notches higher than anything which normally came in the way of a lowly snotty, and Honor dug in with a will. There was little conversation while they ate, and she was just as glad, for it gave her the opportunity to enjoy the food without having to worry about whether a mere midshipwoman was expected to contribute to the table talk. Not that there *was* much table talk. Captain Bachfisch, in particular, applied himself to his dinner in silence. He seemed almost unaware of his guests, and despite the gratitude Honor felt at being allowed to enjoy her meal in relative peace, she wondered why he had bothered to invite them in the first place if he only intended to ignore them. It all seemed very peculiar.

The dinner progressed from salad and an excellent potato soup through glazed chicken with sliced almonds, fluffy rice, stir-fried vegetables and sauteed mushrooms, fresh green peas, and crusty, butter-drenched rolls to a choice of three different desserts. Every time Honor glanced up, the steward seemed to be at her elbow, offering another helping, and she accepted with gusto. Captain Bachfisch might not match her mental image of a dashing and distinguished starship commander, but he set an excellent table. She hadn't tasted food this good since her last visit home.

The apple pie à la mode was even better than the glazed chicken, and Honor needed no prompting when the steward offered her a second helping. The man gave her a small, conspiratorial wink as he slid the second dessert plate in front of her, and she heard something which sounded suspiciously like a chuckle from Lieutenant Saunders' direction. She glanced at the assistant astrogator from the corner of her eye, but his expression was laudably composed. There might have been a hint of a twinkle in his own eyes, but Honor scarcely minded that. She was a direct descendant of the Meyerdahl First Wave, and she was well accustomed to the reactions her genetically modified metabolism's appetite—especially for sweets—drew from unprepared table mates.

But in the end, she was reduced to chasing the last of the melted ice cream around the plate with her spoon, and she sat back with an unobtrusive sigh of repletion as the silent, efficient steward reappeared to collect the empty dishes and make them magically vanish into some private black hole. Wineglasses replaced them, and the steward presented an old-fashioned wax-sealed glass bottle for Captain Bachfisch's inspection. Honor watched the Captain more attentively at that, for her own father was a notable wine snob in his own modest way, and she recognized another as the steward cracked the wax, drew the cork, and handed it to the Captain. Bachfisch sniffed it delicately while the steward poured a small quantity of ruby liquid into his glass, then set the cork aside and sipped the wine itself. He considered for just a moment, then nodded approval, and the steward filled his glass and then circled the table to pour for each of the guests in turn.

A fresh butterfly fluttered its wings ever so gently in Honor's middle as the steward filled her own glass. She was the junior officer present, and she knew what that required of her. She waited until the steward had finished pouring and stepped back, then reached for her glass and stood.

"Ladies and gentlemen, the King!" She was pleased her voice came out sounding so close to normal. It certainly didn't *feel* as if it ought to have, but she appeared to be the only one aware of how nervous she felt.

"The King!" The response sounded almost too loud in the cramped dining cabin, and Honor sank back into her chair quickly, vastly relieved to have gotten through without mischance.

There was a sudden shift of atmosphere around the table, almost as if the loyalty toast were a signal the diners had awaited. It was more of a shift in attitude than anything else, Honor thought, trying to put a mental finger on what had changed. The Captain's guests sat back in their chairs, wineglasses in hand, and Lieutenant Commander Hirake actually crossed her legs.

"May I assume you got those charts properly straightened out, Joseph?" Captain Bachfisch said.

"Yes, Sir," Lieutenant Saunders replied. "You were right, Captain. They were just mislabeled, although Commander Dobrescu and I *are* still a little puzzled over why someone thought we needed updated charts on the People's Republic when we're headed in exactly the opposite direction."

"Oh, that's an easy one, Joseph," Lieutenant Commander Hirake told him. "I imagine *War Maiden's* original astrogator probably requested them for her maiden voyage. I mean, it's only been thirty-six standard years. That's about average for turnaround on LogCom requests."

Several people around the table chuckled, and Honor managed not to let her surprise show as Captain Bachfisch's lined, disapproving face creased in a smile of its own. The Captain waved a finger at the tac officer and shook his head.

"We can't have you talking that way about LogCom, Janice," he told her severely. "If nothing else, you'll raise future expectations which are doomed to be disappointed."

"I don't know about that, Sir," Commander Layson said. "Seems to me it took about that long to get the emitter head on Graser Four replaced, didn't it?"

"Yes, but that wasn't LogCom alone," Lieutenant Commander LaVacher put in. "The yard dogs on *Hephaestus* actually found it for us in the end, remember? I almost had to demand it at pulser point, but they *did* find it. Of course, they'd probably had it in stores for five or six years while some other poor cruiser waited for it, and we just shortstopped it."

That drew fresh chuckles, and Honor's amazement grew. The men and women in the compartment with her were suddenly very different from those who had shared the almost silent, formal dinner, and Captain Bachfisch was the most different of all. As she watched, he cocked his head at Commander Layson, and his expression was almost playful.

"And I trust that while Joseph was straightening out his charts you and Janice managed to come up with an exercise schedule which is going to make everyone onboard hate us, Abner?"

"Well, we tried, Sir." Layson sighed and shook his

head. "We did our best, but I think there are probably three or four ratings in Engineering who are only
going to take us in intense dislike instead."

"Hmm." Captain Bachfisch frowned. "I'm a bit disappointed to hear that. When a ship's company has
as many grass-green hands as this one, a good exec
shouldn't have any trouble at all coming up with a
training program guaranteed to get on their bad side."

"Oh, we've managed *that*, Sir. It's just that Irma
managed to hang on to most of her original watch
crews, and they already know all our tricks."

"Ah? Well, I suppose that is a circumstance beyond
your control," Captain Bachfisch allowed, and looked
at Lieutenant Commander LaVacher. "I see it's your
fault, Irma," he said.

"Guilty as charged, Sir," LaVacher admitted.
"Wasn't easy, either, with BuPers hanging over my
shoulder and trying to poach my most experienced
people the whole time."

"I know it wasn't," the Captain said, and this time
there was no teasing note in his approving voice. "I
reviewed some of your correspondence with Captain
Allerton. I thought right up to the last minute that
we were going to lose Chief Heisman, but you finessed
Allerton beautifully. I hope this isn't going to cost the
Chief that extra rocker, though. We need him, but I
don't want him shortchanged out of the deal."

"He won't be, Sir," Layson replied for LaVacher.
"Irma and I discussed it before she ever resorted to
the 'essential to efficient functioning' argument to
hang onto him. We're two senior chiefs light in Engineering alone . . . and we're also going to be in Silesia
more than long enough for you to exercise your own
discretion in promoting Heisman to fill one of those
slots."

"Good," Bachfisch said. "That's what I like to see! Intelligent ship's officers effortlessly outsmarting their natural enemies at BuPers."

It was all Honor could do not to gawk at the changeling who had replaced the dour and unsmiling man in the chair at the head of the table. Then he turned from Layson and LaVacher and looked directly down the table at her, and this time there was a definite twinkle in his deep set eyes.

"I notice your companion has spent the entire meal on the back of your chair, Ms. Harrington," he observed. "I was under the impression that 'cats usually ate at the same time their people did."

"Uh, yes, Sir," Honor said. She felt a warmth along her cheekbones and drew a deep breath. At least his bantering with the more senior officers present had given her some opportunity to adjust before he turned his guns on her, and she took herself firmly in hand. "Yes, Sir," she said much more composedly. "Nimitz normally eats at the same time I do, but he doesn't do very well with vegetables, and we weren't sure what arrangements your steward might have made, so he ate in the berthing compartment before we came to dinner."

"I see." The Captain gazed at her for a moment, then nodded at his steward. "Chief Stennis is a capable sort, Ms. Harrington. If you'll be good enough to provide him with a list of foods suitable for your companion, I feel confident he can arrange an appropriate menu for his next dinner engagement."

"Yes, Sir," Honor said, trying unsuccessfully to hide her relief at the evidence that Nimitz's presence was welcome, and not merely something to be tolerated. "Thank you, Sir."

"You're welcome," Bachfisch replied, then smiled.

"In the meantime, is there at least something we can offer him as an after dinner snack while we enjoy our wine?"

"If Chief Stennis has a little celery left over from the salad, that would be perfect, Sir. 'Cats may not do well with most vegetables, but they *all* love celery!"

"Jackson?" The Captain glanced at the steward who smiled and nodded.

"I believe I can handle that, Sir."

Chief Stennis disappeared into his pantry, and Captain Bachfisch returned his attention to Commander Layson and Lieutenant Commander Hirake. Honor settled back in her chair, and the pleased buzz of Nimitz's purr vibrated against the back of her neck. If she'd been a 'cat herself, her own purr would have been even more pleased and considerably louder. She watched *War Maiden*'s captain chatting with his officers and felt a sense of ungrudging admiration. This Captain Bachfisch was a very different proposition from the formal, almost cold CO who had presided over the meal itself. She still didn't understand why he'd seemed so distant then, but she readily appreciated the skill with which he drew each of his officers in turn into the discussion now. And, she admitted, how effortlessly he had made a mere midshipwoman feel at ease in their company. His questions might be humorously phrased, and he might display an almost dangerously pointed wit, yet he had all of them involved in discussing serious issues, and he managed it as a leader, not merely as a captain. She remembered once more what Captain Courvosier had said about the need for a captain to know her officers, and realized that Bachfisch had just given her an object lesson in how a captain might go about that.

It was a lesson worth learning, and she filed it away carefully as she smiled and reached up to take the plate of celery Chief Stennis brought her.

". . . and as you can see, we have the Alpha Three upgrade to the emergency local control positions for our energy mounts," Chief MacArthur droned. The sturdy, plain-faced woman bore the hash marks of over twenty-five T-years' service on her sleeve, and the combat ribbons on her chest proved she'd paid cash to learn her weapons skills. It was unfortunate that she'd never mastered the skills of the lecture hall to go with them. Even though Honor was deeply interested in what MacArthur had to tell her, she found it difficult to keep from yawning as the dust-dry instruction continued.

She and Audrey Bradlaugh, *War Maiden*'s other female middy, stood in the number four inboard wing passage, peering over MacArthur's shoulder into the small, heavily armored compartment. It didn't offer a lot of space for the men and women who would man it when the ship cleared for action, and every square centimeter of room it did have was crammed with monitors, readouts, keypads, and access panels. In between those more important bits and pieces were sandwiched the shock-mounted couches and umbilical attachment points for the mere humans of the weapon crew.

"When the buzzer goes, the crew has a maximum of fifteen minutes to don skinsuits and man stations," MacArthur informed them, and Honor and Bradlaugh nodded as if no one had ever told them so before. "Actually, of course, fifteen minutes should give time to spare, although we sometimes run a bit over on shakedown cruises. On the other hand," the petty officer glanced back at her audience, "the Captain isn't what I'd call a patient man with people who screw up his training profiles, so I wouldn't recommend dawdling."

One eyelid flickered in what might have been called a wink on a less expressionless face, and despite herself, Honor grinned at the petty officer. Not that on-mount crew duties were the most humorous subject imaginable. Honor knew that, for she'd logged scores of hours in simulators which recreated every detail of the local control command position in front of her, and her grin faded as she envisioned it in her mind. Her excellent imagination pictured every moment of the shriek of the general quarters alarm, the flashing lights of battle stations, and the sudden claustrophobic tension as the crew plugged in their skinsuit umbilicals and the hatch slammed shut behind them while powerful pumps sucked the air from the passages and compartments around them. The vacuum about their armored capsule would actually help protect it—and them—from atmosphere-transmitted shock and concussion, not to mention fires, yet she doubted anyone could ever embrace it without an atavistic shudder.

Nimitz shifted uneasily on her shoulder as he caught the sudden edge of darkness in her emotions, and she reached up to rest one hand lightly on his head. He pressed back against her palm, and she made a soft crooning sound.

"If Chief MacArthur is *boring* you, Ms. Harrington," an unpleasant voice grated unexpectedly, "I'm sure we can find some extra duty to keep you occupied."

Honor turned quickly, shoulders tightening in automatic response, and her expression was suddenly a better mask than Chief MacArthur's as she faced Elvis Santino. It was obvious the OCTO had come quietly around the bend in the passage while she and Bradlaugh were listening to MacArthur, and she castigated herself for letting him sneak up on her. Now he stood glaring at her, hands once more on hips and lip curled, and she gazed back at him in silence.

Anything she said or did would be wrong, so she said nothing. Which, of course, was *also* the wrong thing to do.

"Well, Ms. Harrington? If you're bored, just say so. I'm sure Chief MacArthur has better things to do with her time as well. *Are* you bored?"

"No, Sir." She gave the only possible answer as neutrally as possible, and Santino smiled nastily.

"Indeed? I would've thought otherwise, given the way you're humming and playing with your little pet."

Once again, there was no possible response that would not give him another opening. She felt Bradlaugh's unhappiness beside her, but Audrey said nothing, either. There wasn't anything she could say, and she'd experienced sufficient of Santino's nastiness herself. But MacArthur shifted her weight, and turned to face the lieutenant. Her non-expression was more pronounced than ever, and she cleared her throat.

"With all due respect, Sir," she said, "the young ladies have been very attentive this afternoon."

Santino turned his scowl on her.

"I don't recall asking your opinion of their attentiveness, Chief MacArthur." His voice was harsh, but MacArthur never turned a hair.

"I realize that, Sir. But again with all due respect, you just came around the corner. I've been working with Ms. Harrington and Ms. Bradlaugh for the last hour and a half. I just felt that I should make you aware of the fact that they've paid very close attention during that time."

"I see." For a moment, Honor thought the lieutenant was going to chew MacArthur out as well for having the audacity to interfere. But it seemed even Elvis Santino wasn't quite stupid enough to risk making this sort of dispute with a noncom of MacArthur's seniority and in his own shipboard department part of the official record. He rocked up and down on the balls of his feet for several seconds then returned his glare to Honor.

"No matter how much attention you've been paying, there's no excuse for slacking off," he told her. "I realize Regs permit you to carry that creature with you on duty, but I warn you not to abuse that privilege. And stop playing with it when you ought to be concentrating on what you're here to learn! I trust I've made myself sufficiently clear?"

"Yes, Sir," Honor said woodenly. "Perfectly clear."

"Good!" Santino snapped, and strode briskly away.

"Lord! What *is* his problem?" Nassios Makira groaned.

The stocky midshipman heaved himself up to sit on the edge of his upper-tier bunk, legs dangling over the side. Honor couldn't imagine why he liked perching up there so much. He was shorter than she was, true, but the deckhead was too low to let even Nassios sit fully upright on his bunk. Maybe it was *because* she was taller than he was? As a matter of fact, Nassios was one of the shortest people aboard *War Maiden*. So did he spend so much time climbing around like a 'cat or an Old Earth monkey because it was the only way he could get above eye level on everyone else?

"I don't know," Audrey Bradlaugh replied without looking up from the boot in her lap. No names had been mentioned, but she seemed in no doubt about the object of Nassios' plaint. "But I do know that complaining about him is only going to make it worse if it gets back to him," the red-haired midshipwoman added pointedly, reaching for the polish on the berthing compartment table.

"Hey, let the man talk," Basanta Lakhia put in. The dark-skinned young midshipman with the startlingly blond hair lay comfortably stretched out on his own bunk. "No one's gonna be tattling to Santino on him, and even if anyone did, it's not against Regs to discuss a senior officer."

"Not as long as the discussion isn't prejudicial to discipline," Honor corrected.

Somewhat to her surprise, she'd found herself the senior of *War Maiden*'s midshipmen on the basis of their comparative class standings. That, unfortunately, only seemed to make matters worse where Santino was concerned, since her seniority—such as it was— pushed him into somewhat closer proximity with her than with the other middies. It also gave her a greater degree of responsibility to provide a voice of reason in snotty bull sessions, and now she looked up to give Makira a rather pointed glance from where she sat beside Bradlaugh at the table, running a brush over Nimitz's pelt. It was unusual for all four of them to be off-duty at once, but middies tended to be assigned to rotating watch schedules, and this time their off- watch periods happened to overlap. In fact, they had almost two more hours before Audrey and Basanta had to report for duty.

"Honor, you know I'd never, ever want to preju- dice discipline," Nassios said piously. "Or that any- thing *I* did could possibly prejudice it as much as *he* does," he added *sotto voce*.

"Basanta's right that no one is going to be carrying tales, Nassios," Audrey said, looking up at last. "But that's exactly the kind of crack that's going to bring him—and the Exec—down on you like a shuttle with dead counter-grav if it gets back to them."

"I know. I know," Nassios sighed. "But you've got to admit he's going awful far out of his way to make himself a royal pain, Audrey! And the way he keeps picking on Honor over Nimitz . . ."

"Maybe he thinks it's part of his job as our training officer," Honor suggested. She finished brushing Nimitz and carefully gathered up the loose fluff for disposal someplace other than in the compartment's air filters.

"Huh! Sure he does!" Basanta snorted.

"I didn't say I agreed with him if he did," Honor said serenely. "But you know as well as I do that there's still the old 'stomp on them hard enough to make them tough' school of snotty-training."

"Yeah, but it's dying out," Nassios argued. "Most of the people you run into who still think that way are old farts from the old school. You know, the ones who think starships should run on steam plants or reaction thrusters . . . or maybe oars! Santino's too young for that kind of crap. Besides, it still doesn't explain the wild hair he's got up his ass over Nimitz!"

"Maybe, and maybe not," Basanta said thoughtfully. "You may have a point, Honor—about the reason he's such a hard ass in the first place, anyway. He's not all that much older than we are, but if his OCTO worked that way, he could just be following in the same tradition."

"And the reason he keeps picking on Nimitz?" Nassios challenged.

"Maybe he's just one of those people who can't get

past the image of treecats as dumb animals," Bradlaugh suggested. "Lord knows *I* wasn't ready for how smart the little devil is. And I wouldn't have believed Honor if she'd just told me about it either."

"That could be it," Honor agreed. "Most people can figure out the difference between a treecat and a pet once they come face-to-face with the real thing, but that's hardly universally true. I think it depends on how much imagination they have."

"And imagination isn't something he's exactly brimming over with," Basanta pointed out. "Which goes back to what Honor said in the first place. If he doesn't have much imagination—" his tone suggested that he'd had a rather more pointed noun in mind "—of his own, he probably is treating us the same way his OCTO treated him. Once he got pointed that way, he couldn't figure out another way to go."

"I don't think he needed anyone to point him in that direction," Nassios muttered, and although she was the one who'd put the suggestion forward, Honor agreed with him. For that matter, she felt morally certain that Santino's behavior was a natural product of his disposition which owed nothing to anyone else's example. Not that she doubted for a moment that his defense, if anyone senior to him called him on it, would be that he was only doing it "for their own good."

"If he ever needed a pointer, he doesn't need one anymore, that's for sure," Basanta agreed, then shook himself. "Say, has anybody seen any of the sims Commander Hirake is setting up for us?"

"No, but PO Wallace warned me they were going to be toughies," Audrey chimed in, supporting the change of subject, and Honor sat back down and gathered Nimitz into her arms while the comfortable shop talk flowed around her.

She ought, she reflected, to be happier than she'd ever been in her life, and in many ways she was. But Elvis Santino was doing his best to keep her happiness from being complete, and he was succeeding. Despite anything she might say to the others, she was morally certain the abusive, sarcastic, belittling behavior he directed at all of them, and especially at her and Nimitz, sprang from a pronounced bullying streak. Worse, she suspected that streak was aggravated by natural stupidity.

And he *was* stupid. She only had to watch him performing as *War Maiden*'s assistant tac officer to know that much.

She sighed mentally and pressed her lips together, warning herself once more of the dangers inherent in allowing herself to feel contempt for anyone senior to her. Even if she never let a sign of it show outwardly, it would affect the way she responded to his orders and endless lectures on an officer's proper duties, which could only make things even worse in the end. But she couldn't help it. Her favorite subjects at the Academy had been tactics and ship handling, and she knew she had a natural gift in both areas. Santino did not. He was unimaginative and mentally lazy—at best a plodder, whose poor performance was shielded by Lieutenant Commander Hirake's sheer competence as his boss and carried by Senior Chief Del Conte's matching competence from below. She'd only had a chance to see him in the simulator once or twice, but her fingers had itched with the need to shove him aside and take over the tac console herself.

Which might be another reason he gave her so much grief, she sometimes thought. She'd done her level best not to let her contempt show, but he had access to her Academy records. That meant he knew exactly how high she'd placed in the Tactical Department, and unless he was even stupider than she thought (possible but not likely; he seemed able to zip his own shoes), he had to know she was absolutely convinced that she could have done his job at least twice as well as he could.

And that's only because I'm too naturally modest to think I could do it even better than that, she thought mordantly.

She sighed again, this time physically, pressing her face into Nimitz's coat, and admitted, if only to herself, the real reason she detested Elvis Santino. He reminded her inescapably of Mr. Midshipman Lord Pavel Young, the conceited, vicious, small-minded, oh-so-nobly born cretin who had done his level best to destroy her and her career at Saganami Island.

Her lips tightened, and Nimitz made a scolding sound and reached out to touch her cheek with one long-fingered true-hand. She closed her eyes, fighting against replaying the memory of that dreadful night in the showers yet again, then drew a deep breath, smoothed her expression, and lowered him to her lap once more.

"You okay, Honor?" Audrey asked quietly, her soft voice hidden under a strenuous argument between Nassios and Basanta over the merits of the Academy's new soccer coach.

"Hmm? Oh, sure." She smiled at the redhead. "Just thinking about something else."

"Homesickness, huh?" Audrey smiled back. "I get hit by it every so often, too, you know. Of course," her smile grew into a grin, "I don't have a treecat to keep me company when it does!"

Her infectious chuckle robbed the last sentence of

any implied bitterness, and she rummaged in her belt purse for a bedraggled, rather wilted stalk of celery. All of the midshipmen who shared Snotty Row with Honor had taken to hoarding celery almost from the moment they discovered Nimitz's passion for it, and now Audrey smiled fondly as the 'cat seized it avidly and began to devour it.

"Gee, thanks a whole bunch, Audrey!" Honor growled. "You just wrecked his appetite for dinner completely!"

"Sure I did," Audrey replied. "Or I would have, if he didn't carry his own itty-bitty black hole around inside him somewhere."

"As any informed person would know, that's his stomach, not a black hole," Honor told her sternly.

"Sure. It just *works* like a black hole," Basanta put in.

"I've seen you at the mess table, too, boy-oh," Audrey told him, "and if I were you, I wouldn't be throwing any rocks around my glass foyer!"

"I'm just a growing boy," Basanta said with artful innocence, and Honor joined in the laughter.

At least if I have to be stuck with Santino, I got a pretty good bunch to share the misery with, she thought.

HMS *War Maiden* moved steadily through hyperspace. The Gregor Binary System and its terminus of the Manticore Wormhole Junction lay almost a week behind; the Silesian Confederacy lay almost a month ahead, and the heavy cruiser's company had begun to shake down. It was not a painless process. As Captain Bachfisch's after-dinner conversation with Commander Layson had suggested, much of *War Maiden*'s crew was new to the ship, for the cruiser had just emerged from an extensive overhaul period, and the Bureau of Personnel had raided her pre-overhaul crew ruthlessly while she was laid up in space dock. That always happened during a refit, of course, but the situation was worse in the RMN these days due to the Navy's expansion. Every Regular, officer and enlisted alike, knew the expansion process was actually just beginning to hit its stride . . . and that the situation was going to get nothing but worse if King Roger and his ministers stood by their obvious intention to build a fleet capable of resisting the Peeps. The Government and Admiralty faced the unenviable task of balancing the financial costs of new hardware—and especially of yard infrastructure—against the personnel-related costs of providing the manpower to crew and use that hardware, and they were determined to squeeze the last penny out of every begrudged dollar they could finagle out of Parliament. Which meant, down here at the sharp end of the stick, that *War Maiden*'s crew contained a high percentage of new recruits, with a higher percentage of newly promoted noncoms to ride herd on them than her officers would have liked, while the personnel retention problems of the Navy in general left her with several holes among her senior petty officer slots. Almost a third of her total crew were on their first long deployment, and there was a certain inevitable friction between some members of her company, without the solid core of senior noncommissioned officers who would normally have jumped on it as soon as it surfaced.

Honor was as aware of the background tension as anyone else. She and her fellow middies could scarcely have helped being aware of it under any circumstances, but she had the added advantage of

Nimitz, and she only had to watch his body language to read his reaction to the crew's edginess.

The ship was scarcely a hotbed of mutiny, of course, but there was a sense of rough edges and routines just out of joint that produced a general air of unsettlement, and she occasionally wondered if that hovering feeling that things were somehow out of adjustment helped explain some of Santino's irascibility. She suspected, even as she wondered, that the notion was nonsense, nothing more than an effort to supply some sort of excuse for the way the OCTO goaded and baited the midshipmen under his nominal care. Still, she had to admit that it left *her* feeling unsettled. None of her relatively short training deployments from the Academy had produced anything quite like it. Of course, none of the ships involved in those deployments had been fresh from refit with crews composed largely of replacements, either. Could this sense of connections still waiting to be made be the norm and not the exception? She'd always known the Academy was a sheltered environment, one where corners were rounded, sharp edges were smoothed, and tables of organization were neatly adhered to, no matter how hard the instructors ran the middies. No doubt that same "classroom-perfect" organization had extended to the training ships homeported at Saganami Island, while *War Maiden* was the real Navy at last. When she thought of it that way, it was almost exciting, like a challenge to earn her adulthood by proving she could deal with the less than perfect reality of a grownup's universe.

Of course, Elvis Santino all by himself was more than enough to make any universe imperfect, she told herself as she hurried down the passage. The OCTO was in an even worse mood than usual today, and all of the middies knew it was going to be impossible to do anything well enough to satisfy him. Not that they had any choice but to try, which was how Honor came to find herself bound all the way forward to Magazine Two just so she could personally count the laser heads to confirm the computer inventory. It was pure makework, an order concocted solely to keep her occupied and let Santino once more demonstrate his petty-tyrant authority. Not that she objected all that strenuously to anything that got her out of his immediate vicinity!

She rounded a corner and turned left along Axial One, the large central passage running directly down the cruiser's long axis. *War Maiden* was old enough that her lift system left much to be desired by modern standards. Honor could have made almost the entire trip from bridge to magazine in one of the lift cars, but its circuitous routing meant the journey would actually have taken longer that way. Besides, she *liked* Axial One. *War Maiden*'s internal grav field was reduced to just under .2 G in the out-sized passage, and she fell into the long, bounding, semi-swimming gait that permitted.

More modern warships had abandoned such passages in favor of better designed and laid out lift systems, although most merchantmen retained them. Convenient though they were in many ways, they represented what BuShips had decided was a dangerous weakness in a military starship which was expected to sustain and survive damage from enemy fire. Unlike the smaller shafts lift cars required, passages like Axial One posed severe challenges when it came to things like designing in blast doors and emergency air locks, and the large empty space at the very core of the ship represented at least a marginal sacrifice in structural strength. Or so BuShips had decided. Honor wasn't certain she agreed, but no flag officers or naval architects had shown any interest in seeking her opinion on the matter, so she simply chose to enjoy the opportunity when it presented itself.

Nimitz clung to her shoulder, chittering with delight of his own as the two of them sailed down the passageway with impeccable grace. It was almost as much fun as Honor's hang glider back home on Sphinx, and his fluffy tail streamed behind them. They were far from the only people making use of Axial One, and Honor knew she was technically in violation of the speed limits imposed here under nonemergency conditions, but she didn't much care. She doubted anyone was likely to take her to task for it, and if anyone did, she could always point out that Santino had ordered her to "get down there double-quick, Snotty!"

She was almost to her destination when it happened. She didn't see the events actually leading up to the collision, but the consequences were painfully obvious. A three-man work party from Engineering, towing a counter-grav pallet of crated electronic components, had collided head-on with a missile tech using a push-pull to maneuver five linked missile main drive units down the same passage. It was a near-miracle no one had suffered serious physical injury, but there'd obviously been a fair number of bruises, and it was clear that the participants' emotions were even more bruised than their hides.

"—and get your goddamn, worthless pile of frigging junk out of my fucking way!" the missile tech snarled.

"Fuck you and the horse you rode in on!" the senior rating from the Engineering party snapped back. "Nobody ever tell you forward traffic to starboard, sternward traffic to port? Or are you just naturally stupid? You were all over the goddamn place with that piece of shit! It's a damn miracle you didn't kill one of us!"

She gave the linked drive units a furious kick to emphasize her point. Unfortunately, she failed to allow for the low grav conditions, and the result was more prat fall than intimidating. She sent herself flailing through the air towards the center of the passage, where she landed flat on her posterior on the decksole, without even budging the drive units, none of which did a thing for her temper. It did, however, have the effect of infuriating the missile tech even further, and he unbuckled from his push-pull and shoved himself off the saddle with obviously homicidal intent. One of the male Engineering ratings moved to intercept him, and things were headed rapidly downhill when Honor reached out for one of the bulkhead handrails and brought herself to a semi-floating stop.

"Belay that!"

Her soprano was very little louder than normal, yet it cracked like a whip, and the disputants' heads snapped around in sheer surprise. Their surprise only grew when they saw the fuzz-haired midshipwoman who had produced the order.

"I don't know who did what to whom," she told them crisply while they gawked at her in astonishment, "and I don't really care. What matters is getting this mess sorted out and getting you people to wherever it is you're supposed to be." She glared at them for a moment, and then jabbed a finger at the senior Engineering rating. "You," she told the woman. "Chase down those loose crates, get them back on the pallet, and this time get them properly secured! You and you—" she jabbed an index finger at the other two members of the work party "—get over there and give her a hand. And *you*," she wheeled on the missile tech who had just begun to gloat at his rivals' stunned expressions, "get that push-pull back under control, tighten the grav-collars on those missile drives before they fall right out of them, and see to it that you stay in the right heavy tow lane the rest of the way to wherever you're going!"

"Uh, yes, Ma'am!" The missile tech recognized command voice when he heard it, even if it did come from a midshipwoman who looked like someone's preteen kid sister, and he knew better than to irritate the person who had produced it. He actually braced to attention before he scurried back over to the bundle of drive units and began adjusting the offending counter-grav collars, and the Engineering working party, which had already come to the same conclusion, spread out, quickly corralling their scattered crates and stacking them oh-so-neatly on their pallet. Honor stood waiting, one toe tapping gently on the decksole while Nimitz watched with interest from her shoulder and the errant ratings—the youngest of them at least six standard years older than she—gave an excellent imitation of small children under the eye of an irritated governess.

It took a remarkably short time for the confusion to be reduced to order, and all four ratings turned carefully expressionless faces back to Honor.

"That's better," she told them in more approving tones. "Now I suggest that all of you get back to doing what you're supposed to be doing just a little more carefully than you were."

"Aye, aye, Ma'am," they chorused, and she nodded. They moved off—far more sedately than before, she suspected—and she resumed her own interrupted trip.

That went fairly well, she told herself, and continued her progress along Axial One, unaware of the grinning senior chief who had arrived behind her just in time to witness the entire episode.

"So, Shellhead," Senior Master Chief Flanagan said comfortably, "what d'you think of this helpless bunch of Momma's dirtside darlings now?"

"Who, me?" Senior Chief Shelton leaned back in his own chair, heels propped on the table in the senior petty officers' mess, and grinned as he nursed a beer stein. Not many were permitted to use that nickname to his face, but Flanagan had known him for over twenty standard years. More importantly than that, perhaps, Flanagan was also *War Maid*'s Bosun, the senior noncommissioned member of her company.

"Yeah, you," Flanagan told him. "You ever see such a hapless bunch in your entire life? I swear, I think one or two of them aren't real clear on which hatch to open first on the air lock!"

"Oh, they're not as bad as all that," Shelton said. "They've got a few rough edges—hell, let's be honest, they've got a *lot* of rough edges—but we're getting them filed down. By the time we hit Silesia, they'll be ready. And some of them aren't half bad already."

"You think so?" Flanagan's eyebrows rose ever so slightly at Shelton's tone, and the senior chief nodded. "And just who, if you don't mind my asking, brought that particular bit of praise to the surface?"

"Young Harrington, as a matter of fact," Shelton said. "I came across her in Axial One this afternoon tearing a strip off a couple of work parties who'd managed to run smack into each other. 'Tronics crates all over the deck, counter-grav pallet cocked up on its side, push-pull all twisted against the bulkhead, and half a dozen missile drives ready to slip right out of their collars, not to mention a couple of ratings ready to start thumping hell out of each other over whose fault it was. And there she stood, reading them the riot act. Got their sorry asses sorted out in record time, too."

Flanagan found it a little difficult to hide his surprise at the obvious approval in Shelton's voice.

"I wouldn't've thought she had the decibels for reading riot acts," he observed, watching his friend's expression carefully. "Sweet-voiced thing like that, I'd think she'd sound sort of silly shouting at a hairy bunch of spacers."

"Nah," Shelton said with a grin. "That was the beauty of it—never cussed or even raised her voice once. Didn't have to. She may only be a snotty, but that young lady could burn the finish off a battle steel bulkhead with just her tone alone. Haven't seen anything like it in years."

"Sounds like that shithead Santino could learn a little something from his snotties, then," Flanagan observed sourly, and it was Shelton's turn to feel surprise. In all the years he'd known Flanagan, he could count the number of times he'd heard his friend use that tone of voice about a commissioned officer on the fingers of one hand. Well, maybe one and half. Not that the senior chief disagreed with the bosun.

"Actually, I think he could learn a hell of a lot from Harrington," he said after a moment. "For that matter, he could probably learn a lot from all of them. If he could keep his own mouth shut long enough to listen to them, anyway."

"And how likely is *that* to happen?" Flanagan snorted.

"Not very," Shelton conceded. "The man does like to hear himself talk."

"I wouldn't mind that so much, if he weren't such a bastard," Flanagan said, still with such an edge of bitter condemnation that Shelton looked across at him with the first beginnings of true alarm.

"Is there something going on that I should be hearing about, Ian?"

"Probably not anything you don't already know about," Flanagan told him moodily. "It's just that he's such a total asshole. Hell, you're in a better spot to see the way he treats the snotties like dirt than I am, and he's not a lot better with his own tac people. Even he knows better than to piss off a senior noncom, but he came down like a five-grav field on his yeoman yesterday, for a screw-up that was entirely his own fault. You know I've got no use for any officer who beats up on his people when *he's* the one who screwed the pooch. Man's the most worthless piece of crap I've seen in an officer's uniform in years, Shellhead."

"I don't know that I'd go quite that far myself," Shelton said in a considering tone. "I've seen some pretty piss-poor officers, you know. Some of them could at least give him a run for his money. On the other hand, I don't think any of them were *worse* than he is." He paused for a moment, and looked quizzically at his friend. "You know, I think it's probably against Regs for two senior petty officers to sit around and badmouth a commissioned officer over their beer this way."

"And you don't see me doing it with anyone else, do you?" Flanagan returned, then grimaced. "Ah, hell,

Shellhead, you know as well as I do that Santino is the worst frigging officer in this ship. Come on, be honest. You're worried about the way he treats the snotties, aren't you?"

"Well, yeah," Shelton admitted. "I see a kid like Harrington—any of them, really, but especially Harrington—with all that promise, and there's Santino, doing his level best to crush it all out of them. I mean, it's one thing to be tough on them. It's something else entirely to ride them twenty-two hours a day out of sheer poison meanness because you know there's nothing in the world they can do to fight back."

"You can say that again," Flanagan said. "Not bad enough he's got the chain of command on his side, but they know he can flush their careers any time he damned well pleases if they don't kiss ass enough to make him happy."

"Maybe. But I've got to tell you, Ian, I don't know how much longer Harrington's going to put up with it." Shelton shook his head soberly. "I had my doubts when she turned up with that treecat of hers. First time I'd ever seen one onboard ship. I figured it was bound to make trouble in Snotty Row if nowhere else, and that Harrington might be full of herself for having it in the first place, but I was wrong on both counts. And the girl's got bottom, too. She's going to be a good one someday . . . unless Santino pushes her too hard. She's got a temper in there, however hard she tries to hide it, and Santino sticks in her craw sideways. One of these days, she's gonna lose it with him, and when she does . . ."

The two noncoms gazed at one another across the table, and neither of them any longer felt like smiling at all.

❖   ❖   ❖

"Tell me, Ms. Harrington," Elvis Santino said, "is it possible that by some vast stretch of the imagination you actually consider this a competently done job?"

The lieutenant stood in the weapon's bay for Graser Three, the second energy mount in *War Maiden*'s port broadside. He and Honor both wore skinsuits as Regs required, since the bay was sealed only by a single hatch, not a proper air lock. When the ship cleared for action, the bay would be opened to space, the emitter assembly would train outboard, and the powered ram would move the entire weapon outward until the emitter head cleared the hull and could bring up its gravity lenses safely. Honor had always been privately amused by the fact that modern energy weapons were "run out" like some echo of the muzzleloading cannon of Old Earth's sailing navies, but at the moment all she felt was a dull, seething resentment for her training officer.

Santino was in his favorite pose, hands propped on hips and feet spread wide. All he needed to complete the handsome HD star image was a bright sun to squint into, Honor thought derisively, and wondered yet again how he could possibly be unaware of the effect that sort of posturing was bound to have on the men and women under his orders. It was more than a merely rhetorical consideration at the moment, since six of those men and women—including SCPO Shelton—stood at her back in silent witness.

"Yes, Sir, I do," she made herself say levelly, and his lips drew back to bare his teeth.

"Then I can only say your judgment is suspect, Ms. Harrington," he told her. "Even from here I can see that the access panel is still open on Ram One!"

"Yes, Sir, it is," Honor agreed. "When we got it open, we—"

"I don't recall inviting excuses, Ms. Harrington!" he snapped. "Is or is not that access panel still open?"

Honor clamped her teeth and decided it was a good thing Nimitz wasn't present. The 'cat had no vac suit. As such, he was thankfully barred from this compartment and so unable to bristle and snarl in response to Santino's attitude.

"Yes, Sir, it is," she said again after a moment, exactly as if she hadn't already agreed it was.

"And you are, perhaps, aware of the standing orders and operating procedures which require all access panels to be closed after inspection and routine maintenance?" he pressed.

"Yes, Sir, I am." Honor's voice was clearer and crisper than usual, and a small tic quivered at the corner of her mouth. Something seemed to gleam for just an instant in Santino's eyes as he observed it, and he leaned towards her.

"Then just how the hell can even *you* stand there and call this a 'competent' job?" he demanded harshly.

"Because, Sir, Ram One has a major engineering casualty," she told him. "The main actuator must have developed a short since its last routine maintenance. There are actual scorch marks inside the casing, and stages one and five both show red on the diagnostic. As per standing orders, I immediately informed Commander LaVacher in Engineering, and she instructed me to open the main breaker, red-tag the actuator, and leave the access panel open until she could get a repair crew up here to deal with it. All of which, Sir, is in my report."

Her dark eyes locked unflinchingly with his, but even as they did, she kicked herself mentally for losing her temper, for she saw the sudden rage flashing in the depths of his glare. She'd kept her voice level and even, but the entire tone of her answer—and especially that last jab about her report—had been well over the line. No one would ever be able to prove it, but she and Santino both knew she'd done it to get some of her own back, and his florid complexion darkened angrily.

"I assume you know the penalty for insubordination," he grated. She said nothing, and his color darkened further. "I asked you a question, Snotty!" he barked.

"I'm sorry, Sir. I was unaware that it was meant as a question. It sounded like a statement."

She could hardly believe it even as she heard her own voice say it, and she sensed Senior Chief Shelton and his work party behind her, watching it all. What was *wrong* with her? Why in heaven's name was she goading him back this way?

"Well it wasn't one!" Santino snapped. "So answer me!"

"Yes, Sir," she said. "I am aware of the penalty for insubordination."

"That's good, Snotty, because you just bought yourself a locker full of it! Now get out of my sight. Go directly to your quarters and remain there until I personally tell you differently!"

"Yes, Sir." She came to attention, saluted crisply, turned on her heel, and marched off with her head high while the man with the power to destroy her career before it even began glared after her.

The hatch signal chimed, and Commander Layson looked up from his display and pressed the admittance button. The hatch slid open, and Lieutenant Santino stepped through it.

"You wanted to see me, Sir?" the lieutenant said.

Layson nodded, but he said nothing, simply gazed at his assistant tactical officer with cool, thoughtful eyes. His face was expressionless, but Santino shifted slightly under that dispassionate gaze. It wasn't quite a fidget, but it was headed in that direction, and still the silence stretched out. At last, after at least three full minutes, Santino could stand it no more and cleared his throat.

"Uh, may I ask why you wanted to see me, Sir?"

"You may." Layson leaned back in his chair and folded his hands across his midsection. He sat that way for several seconds, eyes never leaving Santino's face, stretching the lieutenant's nerves a bit tighter, then went on in a neutral tone. "I understand there was some . . . difficulty with Midshipwoman Harrington this afternoon, Lieutenant," he said at last, his tone very cool. "Suppose you tell me what that was all about."

Santino blinked, then darkened. He hadn't yet gotten around to reporting Harrington's gross insubordination, but obviously the girl had gone crying to the Exec over it already. Just a sort of thing she *would* do. He'd known even before the troublemaking, spoiled brat reported aboard what he'd have to deal with there, and he'd been grateful for the forewarning, even if it wasn't considered quite "proper" for an OCTO to have private, pre-cruise briefings on the snotties who would be in his care. She and her wretched pet and the special treatment they both got had certainly justified the warnings he'd been given about her. He could see the arrogance in her eyes, of course, the way she was not so secretly convinced of her superiority to all about her. That was one of the things he'd been determined to knock out of her, in the faint hope that he might somehow salvage a worthwhile officer out of her. Yet even though today's episode had dealt a death blow to that hope, he was still vaguely surprised that even she'd had the sheer nerve to go whining to the Exec after he'd confined her to quarters, which she knew perfectly well meant no com time, either. Well, he'd just add that to the list when he wrote her fitness report.

He blinked again as he realized the Exec was still waiting, then shook himself.

"Of course, Sir," he said. "She was assigned to a routine maintenance inspection of Graser Three. When I arrived to check her progress, she'd instructed her inspection party to fall out and prepared to sign off on the inspection sheet. I observed, however, that the access panel for one of the power rams was still open in violation of SOP. When I pointed this out to her, she was both insolent in attitude and insubordinate in her language, so I ordered her to her quarters."

"I see." Layson frowned ever so slightly. "And how, precisely, was she insolent and insubordinate, Lieutenant?"

"Well, Sir," Santino said just a bit cautiously, "I asked her if she thought she'd completed her assignment, and she said she did. Then I pointed out the open access panel and asked her if she was familiar with standard procedures and the requirement to keep such panels closed when not actually being used for inspection or repair. Her tone and manner were both insolent when she replied that she was aware of proper procedure. Only when I pressed her for a fuller explanation did she inform me that she had discovered a fault in the ram and reported it to Engineering. Obviously, I had no way to know that before she explained it to me, but once again her manner was extremely insolent, and both her tone and her choice of words were, in my opinion, intended to express contempt for a superior officer. Under the circumstances, I saw no option but to relieve her of duty pending disciplinary action."

"I see," Layson repeated, then let his chair come upright. "Unfortunately, Lieutenant, I've already heard another account of the discussion which doesn't exactly tally with yours."

"Sir?" Santino drew himself up and squared his shoulders. "Sir, if Harrington has been trying to—"

"I didn't say I'd heard it from Midshipwoman Harrington," Layson said frostily, and Santino shut his mouth with a click. "Nor did I say I'd heard it from only one person," the Exec went on with cold dispassion. "In fact, I have six eyewitnesses, and none of them—not one, Lieutenant Santino—describes events as you just did. Would you perhaps care to comment on this minor discrepancy?"

Santino licked his lips and felt sweat prickle under the band of his beret as the ice in the Exec's voice registered.

"Sir, I can only report my own impressions," he said. "And with all due respect, Sir, I've had ample opportunity to watch Harrington's behavior and attitude over the last eight weeks. Perhaps that gives me, as her training officer, somewhat more insight into her character than a petty officer and working party who haven't had the advantage of that perspective."

"The *senior chief* petty officer in question," Layson said quietly, "has been in the King's Navy for seven years longer than you've been *alive*, Lieutenant Santino. In that time, he's had the opportunity to see more midshipmen and midshipwomen than you've seen dinners. I am not prepared to entertain any suggestion that he is too inexperienced to form a reasonable and reliable opinion of Ms. Harrington's character. Do I make myself clear?"

"Yes, Sir!"

Santino was perspiring freely now, and Layson stood behind his desk.

"As a matter of fact, Mr. Santino, I asked Senior Chief Shelton to share the insight of his many years of experience with me some days ago when I began to hear a few disturbing reports about our officer candidates. As such, he was acting under my direct instructions when he gave me his version of your . . . discussion with Ms. Harrington. Frankly, I'm happy he was there, because this episode simply confirms something I'd already come to suspect. Which is, Mr. Santino, that you are clearly too stupid to pour piss out of a boot without printed instructions!"

The Exec's voice cracked like a whip on the last sentence, and Santino flinched. Then his face darkened and his lips thinned.

"Sir, I resent your implications and strongly protest your language! Nothing in the Articles of War requires me to submit to personal insults and abuse!"

"But the Articles *do* require Ms. Harrington and her fellow middies to submit to *your* personal insults and abuse?" Layson's voice was suddenly like silk wrapped around a dagger's blade. "Is that what you're saying, Mr. Santino?"

"I—" Santino began, then cut himself off and licked his lips again as he realized the Exec had set him up.

"Sir, the situations aren't parallel," he said finally. "Harrington and the other snotties are fresh out of the Academy. They're still learning that the world isn't going to stand around and wipe their noses for them. If I seemed—or if Senior Chief Shelton thought I seemed—abusive, I was simply trying to help toughen them up and turn them into proper King's officers!"

He met Layson's cold eyes defiantly, and the Exec's lip curled.

"Somehow I knew you were going to say that, Lieutenant," he observed. "And, of course, no one can prove you're lying. If I *could* prove it, I would have you up on charges so fast your head would spin. Since I can't, I will explain this to you once. I will explain it *only* once, however, and you had better by God be listening."

The Exec didn't raise his voice, but Santino swallowed hard as Layson walked around the desk, hitched a hip up to rest on it, folded his arms across his chest, and looked him straight in the eye.

"For your information, Mr. Santino, those young men and women are already King's officers. They are also in their final form at the Academy, true, and they're here for evaluation as well as training. But while they are here aboard this ship, they are just as much members of her company and King's officers as *you* are. This means they are to be treated with respect, especially by their seniors. A midshipman cruise is supposed to be stressful. It is supposed to put sufficient pressure on a midshipman—or woman— to allow us to evaluate his ability to function under it and to teach *him* that he can hack tough assignments. It is *not* supposed to expose any of them to abuse, to bullying, or to the unearned contempt of a superior officer too stupid to know what his own duties and responsibilities are."

"Sir, I have never abused or bullied—"

"Lieutenant, you've never *stopped* bullying them!" Layson snapped. "As just one example, the term 'snotty,' while universally accepted as a slang label for a midshipman on his training cruise, is not an epithet to be hurled contemptuously at them by their own training officer! You have hectored and hounded them from the outset, and I strongly suspect that it's because you are a coward as well as stupid. After all, who expects a mere midshipwoman to stand up to a superior officer? Especially when she knows that superior officer can flush her career right out the air lock with a bad efficiency report?"

Santino stood rigid, his jaws locked, and Layson regarded him with cold contempt.

"You are relieved as officer candidate training officer for cause, effective immediately, Lieutenant Santino. I will report that fact to the Captain, and he will undoubtedly select another officer to fill that slot. In the meantime, you will prepare all records on the midshipmen formerly under your supervision for immediate transfer to that officer. Further, you will take *no* action against Midshipwoman Harrington, any other midshipman aboard this ship, Senior Chief Shelton, or any member of Ms. Harrington's work party which I or the Captain could conceivably construe as retaliation. Should you choose to do so, I assure you, you will regret it. Is that clearly understood?"

Santino nodded convulsively, and Layson gave him a thin smile.

"I'm afraid I didn't hear you, Mr. Santino. I asked if that was clearly understood."

"Yes, Sir." It came out strangled, and Layson smiled again.

"Very good, Lieutenant," he said softly. "Dismissed."

Honor never knew exactly what Commander Layson had to say to Santino that afternoon, but the vicious hatred which looked at her out of Santino's eyes told her that it had not been pleasant. She and her fellow middies did their best—by and large successfully—to restrain their rejoicing when Commander Layson announced that Lieutenant Saunders would replace him, but it was impossible to fool anyone in a world as small as a single starship.

Conditions on Snotty Row improved both drastically and immediately. There was a tough, professional-minded officer behind Saunders' cheerful face, but Santino's mocking contempt was utterly foreign to the assistant astrogator. No one but a fool—which none of *War Maiden*'s middies were—would write Saunders off as an easy touch, but he obviously felt no temptation to hammer the midshipmen in his care simply because he could, and that was more than enough to endear him to them.

Unfortunately, it was impossible for the middies to completely avoid Santino even after Saunders replaced him. Tactics were one of the areas in which their training was most intense, which was why the assistant head of that department was traditionally the OCTO aboard any ship. The fact that Santino had been relieved of those duties—obviously for cause—was going to be a serious black mark on his record, which no doubt helped explain some of the hatred which so plainly burned within him. But it also made the change in assignments awkward for everyone involved. He might have been relieved as their training officer, but whatever the Exec and the Captain might have had to say to him in private, he had not been relieved of any other duties. Honor quickly noticed that Lieutenant Commander Hirake seemed to hand out a much higher percentage of their training assignments than had previously been the case, but it was impossible for any of them to report to Hirake without at least entering Santino's proximity. At least half the time, Santino was still the tac officer who actually oversaw their training sims, and none of them enjoyed it a bit when that happened. Nor did he, for that matter. He was careful to restrict himself to formalities, but the glitter in his eyes was ample proof of how difficult he found that. In some ways, it was almost hard not to sympathize with him. Given the circumstances of his relief, his contact with them as simply one more assistant department head was guaranteed to grind his nose into his disgrace. But however well Honor understood what he must be feeling, she, for one, was never tempted to feel sorry for him in the least. Besides, being Elvis Santino, it never occurred to him to blame anyone but Honor Harrington for what had happened to him, and despite anything the Exec had said to him, he was constitutionally incapable of hiding his hatred for her. Since he was going to feel that way whatever she did, she refused to strain herself trying to feel sympathy for someone who so amply merited his disgrace.

In some ways, it was almost worse now that he'd been relieved. Just as he was forced to stifle his fury at Honor on the occasions when their duties brought them into contact, she was required to act as if nothing had ever happened between them. Honor knew that there wasn't a great deal Layson could have done to decrease their contacts without far greater official provocation than Santino had given. Without stripping the man completely of his duties, there was no way to take him out of the queue. Certainly not without completing the lieutenant's public humiliation by absolutely confirming the reason he'd been relieved as OCTO in the first place. And there were times Honor wondered if perhaps Layson didn't have another reason for leaving Santino where he was. It was certainly one way to determine how she and her fellow middies would react under conditions of social strain!

For the most part though, she found herself blossoming and expanding as she was finally freed to throw herself into the learning experience a middy cruise was supposed to be. The fact that *War Maiden* arrived in Silesian space shortly after Santino's relief contributed its own weight to her happiness, although she supposed some people might have found it difficult to understand. After all, the Silesian Confederacy was a snake pit of warring factions, revolutionary governments, and corrupt system governors whose central government, such as it was, maintained its tenuous claim of rule solely on sufferance and the fact that the various unruly factions could never seem to combine effectively against it any more than they could combine effectively against one another. The casual observer, and especially the casual civilian observer, might have been excused for finding such an environment less than desirable. But Honor didn't see it that way, for the unending unrest was what had brought her ship here in the first place, and she was eager to test herself in the real world.

In a perverse sort of way, Silesia's very instability helped explain the enormous opportunities which the Confederacy offered Manticoran merchants. There was quite literally no reliable local supplier for most of the Confederacy's citizens' needs, which opened all sorts of possibilities for outside suppliers. Unfortunately, that same instability provided all manner of havens and sponsors for the privateers and pirates for whom the Star Kingdom's commerce offered what

were often irresistible targets. The Royal Manticoran
Navy had made its draconian policy concerning pirates
(the enforcement of which was *War Maiden*'s reason
for being here) uncompromisingly clear over the years.
The demonstration of that policy had involved quite
a few pirate fatalities, but the capture of a single
seven- or eight-million-ton merchantman could earn
a pirate crew millions upon millions of dollars, and
greed was a powerful motivator. Especially since even
the stupidest pirate knew that the Star Kingdom's navy
couldn't possibly cover the trade routes in depth and
that no one else—with the possible exception of the
Andermani—would even make the attempt.

That background explained why the Silesian Confederacy had been the RMN's main training ground
for decades. It was a place to blood fledgling crews
and starship commanders, gain tactical experience in
small-scale engagements, and expose Navy personnel
to the realities of labyrinthine political murkiness, all
while doing something useful in its own right—
protecting the Star Kingdom's commerce.

Still, the antipiracy effort was perpetually
undersupplied with warships. That had always been
true to some extent, but the steadily accelerating
buildup of the battle fleet had made it worse in recent
years. The increased emphasis on capital units and
the Junction forts, and especially on manning such
crew-intensive propositions, had reduced the availabil-
ity of light units for such operational areas as Silesia.

And there was a corollary to that, one which was
bound to affect HMS *War Maiden* and one Ms.
Midshipwoman Harrington. For if there were fewer
units available, then those which did reach Silesia
could expect to be worked hard.

✦   ✦   ✦

Honor stepped through the wardroom hatch with Nimitz on her shoulder. It had been late by *War Maiden*'s onboard clock when she went off duty, and she was tired, but she wasn't yet ready for bed. The heavy cruiser had made her alpha translation into normal space in the Melchor System of the Saginaw Sector shortly before the end of Honor's watch, and she'd had an excellent vantage from which to watch the process, for she was assigned to Astrogation this month. That was a mixed blessing in her opinion. It had its exciting moments, like the ones she'd spent backing up Lieutenant Commander Dobrescu during the approach to the alpha wall. Dobrescu, *War Maiden*'s astrogator, was Lieutenant Saunders' boss, and very good at his job, so there'd never been much chance that he was going to require Honor's assistance in a maneuver he'd performed hundreds of times before, but it had still been . . . not so much exciting as *satisfying* to sit in the backup chair at his side and watch the hyper log spin down to the translation locus. She still preferred Tactical to Astrogation—when Santino was absent, at least—but there *was* something about being the person who guided the ship among the stars.

Now if only she'd been any good at it . . .

Actually, she knew there was very little wrong with her astrogation in and of itself. She understood the *theory* perfectly, and as long as people would just leave her alone with the computers, she felt confident of her ability to find her way about the galaxy. Unfortunately, she was a midshipwoman. That meant she was a trainee, and to the Navy—including Dobrescu and Lieutenant Saunders (however satisfactory he might otherwise have been as an OCTO)—"trainee" meant "student," and students were expected to demonstrate their ability to do the basic calculations with no more than a hand comp and a stylus. And that was pure, sweat-popping, torment for Honor. However well she understood astrogation theory and multi-dimension math, her actual mathematical proficiency was something else altogether. She'd never been any good at math, which was all the more irritating because her aptitude scores indicated that she ought to excel at it. And, if people would just leave her alone and not stand around waiting for her to produce the right answer, she usually did come up with the correct solution in the end. For that matter, if she didn't have time to think about it and remember she was no good at math, she usually got the right answer fairly quickly. But that wasn't the way it worked during snotty-training, and she'd found herself sweating blood every time Dobrescu gave her a problem. Which was both grossly unfair—in her opinion—and stupid.

It wasn't as if Dobrescu or the astrogator of any other starship did his calculations by hand. The entire idea was ridiculous! That was what computers were for in the first place, and if a ship suffered such a massive computer failure as to take Astrogation offline, figuring out where it was was going to be the *least* of its problems. She'd just *love* to see anyone try to manage a hyper generator, an inertial compensator, or the grav pinch of a fusion plant without computer support! But the Powers That Were weren't particularly interested in the opinions of one Ms. Midshipwoman Harrington, and so she sweated her way through the entire old-fashioned, labor-intensive, frustrating, *stupid* quill-pen-and-parchment business like the obedient little snotty she was.

At least Lieutenant Commander Dobrescu had a sense of humor.

And at least they were now safely back into normal space, with only three dinky little dimensions to worry about.

It would have been nice if Melchor had been a more exciting star to visit, given how hard Honor and her hand comp had worked to overcome the dreadful deficiencies of her ship's computers and get *War Maiden* here safely. Unfortunately, it wasn't. True, the G4 primary boasted three very large gas giants whose orbital spacing had created no less than four asteroid belts, but of its total of seven planets, only one was of any particular interest to humans. That was Arianna, the sole habitable planet of the system, which orbited Melchor at nine light-minutes, over eleven light-minutes inside the star's hyper limit. Arianna was a dry, mountainous world, with narrow, shallow seas, minimal icecaps, and a local flora which tended to the drought-hardy and low-growing. It had been settled over two hundred standard years before, but the hardscrabble colony had never moved much above the subsistence level until about fifty years ago, when an Andermani mining consortium had decided to take advantage of the resource extraction possibilities of all those asteroids. The outside investment and subsequent discovery of an unusual abundance of rare metals had brought an unexpected boom economy to the star system and attracted more immigrants in less time than the Melchor system government could ever have expected. Unfortunately for the Andermani, the local sector governor had seen that boom primarily as an opportunity to fill his own pockets. That wasn't an uncommon occurrence in Silesia, and however angry the Andermani consortium's financial backers might have been, they could not really have been very surprised when the governor began muscling in on their investment. Bribery and kickbacks were a way of life in the Confederacy, and people like the Saginaw sector governor knew how to extract them when they were not offered spontaneously. Within ten years, he and his family had owned over thirty percent of the total consortium, and the original Andermani backers had begun selling off their stock to other Silesians. Within another ten, the entire mining operation had been in Silesian hands and, like so much else in Silesian hands, running very, very poorly.

But this time around, the majority of the stockholders seemed willing to at least make an attempt to restore their fortunes, and the Star Kingdom's Dillingham Cartel had been brought onboard as a minority stockholder, with all sorts of performance incentives, to attempt to turn things back around once more. Which, in no small part, explained *War Maiden*'s presence in Melchor.

Dillingham had moved in Manticoran mining experts and begun a systematic upgrade of the extraction machinery which had been allowed to disintegrate under purely Silesian management. Honor suspected the cartel had been forced to pay high risk bonuses to any Manticorans who had agreed to relocate here, and she knew from the general background brief Captain Bachfisch had shared with *War Maiden*'s company that Dillingham had seen fit to install some truly impressive defensive systems to protect their extraction complexes and Arianna itself. They would not have been very effective against a regular naval force, but they were more than enough to give any piratical riff-raff serious pause. Unfortunately, the Confederacy's central government refused to countenance privately flagged warships in its territorial space, so Dillingham had been forced to restrict itself to orbital systems. The ban on private warships was one of the (many) stupid policies of the Confederacy, in Honor's opinion. No doubt it was an attempt to at least put a crimp in the supply of armed vessels which seemed to find a way into pirate hands with dismal regularity, but it was a singularly ineffective one. All it really did in this case was to prevent someone who might have been able to provide the entire star system with a degree of safety which was unhappily rare in Silesia from doing so. The cartel's fixed defenses created zones within the Melchor System into which no raider was likely to stray, but they couldn't possibly protect merchant ships approaching or leaving the star.

Not that the Confederacy government was likely to regard that concern as any skin off its nose. The ships coming and going to Melchor these days were almost all Manticoran—aside from the handful of Andermani who still called there—and if the foreigners couldn't take the heat, then they should get out of the kitchen. Or, as in *War Maiden*'s case, call in their own governments to look after their interests. Of course, the Confederacy scarcely liked to admit that it needed foreign navies to police its own domestic space, but it had learned long ago that Manticore would send its naval units to protect its commerce whatever the Silesians wanted, so it might as well let Manticore pick up the tab for Melchor. And if the Star Kingdom lost a few merchant ships and their crews in the process, well, it served the pushy foreigners right.

Honor was scarcely so innocent as to be surprised by the situation. That didn't mean she liked it, but like anyone else who aspired to command a King's ship, she recognized the protection of the merchant trade which was the heart, blood, and sinews of the Star Kingdom's economic might as one of the Navy's most important tasks. She didn't begrudge being here to protect Manticoran lives and property, whatever she might think of the so-called local government that made her presence a necessity.

Despite all that, it was highly unlikely *War Maiden* would find anything exciting to do here. As Captain Courvosier had often warned, a warship's life was ten percent hard work, eighty-nine percent boredom, and one percent sheer, howling terror. The percentages might shift a bit in a place like Silesia, but the odds in favor of boredom remained overwhelming. Honor knew that, too, but she was still just a bit on edge and not quite ready to turn in, which explained her detour by the wardroom. Besides, she was hungry. Again.

Her eyes swept the compartment with a hint of wariness as she stepped through the hatch, but then she relaxed. A middy in the wardroom was rather like a junior probationary member of an exclusive club, only less so. He or she had a right to be there, but the tradition was that they were to be seen and not heard unless one of the more senior members of the club invited them to open their mouths. In addition, they had better be prepared to run any errands any of their seniors needed run, because none of those seniors were likely to give up any of their hard-earned rest by getting up and walking across the wardroom when there were younger and more junior legs they could send instead. In fact, the tradition of sending snotties to do the scut work was one of the Navy's longer-standing traditions, part of the semi-hazing which was part and parcel of initiating midshipmen into the tribal wisdom, and Honor didn't really mind it particularly. For the most part, at least.

But this time she was lucky. Santino was off duty, of course, or she wouldn't have been here in the first place, but Lieutenant Commander LaVacher, who, while an otherwise reasonably pleasant human being, had a pronounced talent for and took an unabashed delight in finding things for middies to do, was also absent. Lieutenant Saunders looked up from his contemplation of a book reader and nodded a casual welcome, while Commander Layson and Lieutenant Jeffers, the ship's logistics officer, concentrated on the chessboard between them and Lieutenant Livanos and Lieutenant Tergesen, LaVacher's first and second engineers, respectively, were immersed in some sort of card game with Ensign Baumann. Aside from Saunders' offhanded greeting, no one seemed to notice her at all, and she made a beeline across the compartment towards the waiting mid-rats table. The food in the wardroom was considerably inferior to that served in the officers' mess at normal mealtimes, but rated several more stars than the off-watch rations available to the denizens of Snotty Row. And perhaps even more important, from Honor's perspective, there was more of it.

Nimitz perked up on her shoulder as she spotted the cheese-stuffed celery sticks and passed one up to him, then snuck an olive out of the slightly limp looking bowl of tossed salad and popped it into her own mouth to stave off starvation while she constructed a proper sandwich for more serious attention. Mayonnaise, cold cuts, mustard, Swiss cheese, sliced onion, another layer of cold cuts, dill pickle slices, another slice of Swiss cheese, some lettuce from the salad bowl, and a tomato ring, and she was done. She added a satisfying but not overly greedy heap of potato chips to her plate to keep it company, and poured herself a large glass of cold milk and snagged two cupcakes to keep *it* company, then gathered up a few extra celery sticks for Nimitz and found a seat at one of the unoccupied wardroom tables.

"How in God's name did you put that thing together without counter-grav?"

She turned her head and smiled in response to Commander Layson's question. The Exec gazed at her sandwich for a moment longer, then shook his head in bemusement, and Lieutenant Jeffers chuckled.

"I'm beginning to understand why we seem to be running a little short on commissary supplies," he observed. "I always knew midshipmen were bottomless pits, but—"

It was his turn to shake his head, and Layson laughed out loud.

"What I don't understand," Lieutenant Tergesen said just a bit plaintively, looking up from her cards at the sound of the Exec's laughter, "is how you can stuff all that in and never gain a kilo." The dark-haired engineering officer was in her early thirties, and while she certainly wasn't obese, she *was* a shade on the plump side. "I'd be as broad across the beam as a trash hauler if I gorged on half that many calories!"

"Well, I work out a lot, Ma'am," Honor replied, which was accurate enough, if also a little evasive. People were no longer as prejudiced against "genies" as they once had been, but those like Honor who were descended from genetically engineered ancestors still tended to be cautious about admitting it to anyone they did not know well.

"I'll say she does," Ensign Baumann put in wryly. "I saw her and Sergeant Tausig sparring yesterday evening." The ensign looked around at the wardroom's occupants in general and wrinkled her nose. "She was working out full contact . . . with Tausig."

"With *Tausig*?" Layson half-turned in his own chair to look more fully at Honor. "Tell me, Ms. Harrington. How well do you know Surgeon Lieutenant Chiem?"

"Lieutenant Chiem?" Honor frowned. "I checked in with him when I joined the ship, of course, Sir. And he was present one night when the Captain was kind enough to include me in his dinner party, but I don't really *know* the doctor. Why? Should I, Sir?"

This time the laughter was general, and Honor blushed in perplexity as Nimitz bleeked his own amusement from the back of her chair. Her seniors' mirth held none of the sneering putdown or condescension she might have expected from someone like a Santino, but she was honestly at a loss to account for it. Lieutenant Saunders recognized her confusion, and smiled at her.

"From your reaction, I gather that you weren't aware that the good sergeant was the second runner-up in last year's Fleet unarmed combat competition, Ms. Harrington," he said.

"That he was—" Honor stopped, gawking at the lieutenant, then closed her mouth and shook her head. "No, Sir, I didn't. He never—I mean, the subject never came up. Second runner-up in the *Fleet* matches? Really?"

"Really," Layson replied for the lieutenant, his tone dry. "And everyone knows Sergeant Tausig's theory of instruction normally involves thumping on his students until they either wake up in sick bay or get good enough to thump him back. So if you and Doctor Chiem haven't become close personal acquaintances, you must be pretty good yourself."

"Well, I try, Sir. And I was on the *coup de vitesse*

demo team at the Academy, but—" She paused again. "But I'm not in the sergeant's league by a longshot. I only get a few pops in because he lets me."

"I beg to differ," Layson said more dryly than ever. "I hold a black belt myself, Ms. Harrington, and Sergeant Tausig has been known to spend the odd moment kicking my commissioned butt around the salle. And he has never 'let' me get a hit in. I think it's against his religion, and I very much doubt that he would decide to make an exception in your case. So if you 'get a few pops in,' you're doing better than ninety-five percent of the people who step onto the mat with him."

Honor blinked at him, still holding her sandwich for another bite. She'd known Tausig was one of the best she'd ever worked out with, and she knew he was light-years better at the *coup* than she was, but she would never have had the gall to ask to spar with him if she'd known he'd placed that high in the Fleet competition. He must have thought she was out of her mind! Why in the world had he agreed to let her? And if he was going to do that, why go so easy on her? Whatever Commander Layson might think, Honor couldn't believe that—

A high, shrill, atonal shriek cut her thought off like an ax of sound, and her sandwich thumped messily onto her plate as spinal reflex yanked her from her chair. She snatched Nimitz up and was out of the wardroom with the 'cat cradled in her arms before the plate slid off the table and the disintegrating sandwich's stuffing hit the decksole.

Lieutenant Saunders looked up from his displays and glanced at Honor over his shoulder as she arrived on the bridge, then flicked a look at the bulkhead chrono. It was only a brief glance, and then he gave her a quick, smiling nod as she crossed the command deck to him. Regs allowed her an extra five minutes to get to action stations, in order to give her time to secure Nimitz safely in his life-support module in her berthing compartment, but she'd made it in only thirteen minutes. It helped that Snotty Row was relatively close to the bridge, but it helped even more that she'd spent so many extra hours on suit drill at Saganami Island expressly because she'd known she'd have to find time to get her and Nimitz both cleared for action.

Not that even the amount of practice she'd put in could make it any less uncomfortable to make her skinsuit's plumbing connections that rapidly, she thought wryly as she settled gingerly into the assistant astrogation officer's chair. At the moment, Saunders occupied first chair in Astrogation, because Commander Dobrescu was with Commander Layson in Auxiliary Control. In fact, there was an entire backup command crew in AuxCon. Few modern heavy cruisers had auxiliary command decks, since more recent design theory regarded the provision of such a facility in so small a unit as a misuse of mass which could otherwise have been assigned to weapons or defensive systems. In newer ships of *War Maiden*'s type, an additional fire control position was provided at one end of the core hull instead, with just enough extra room for the ship's executive officer to squeeze into alongside the Tac Department personnel who manned it. But since *War Maiden* was an old enough design to provide an AuxCon, Captain Bachfisch had been able to create an entirely separate command crew to back up Commander Layson if something unpleasant should happen to the bridge.

Honor was delighted to be on the bridge itself, but because she was currently assigned to astro training duties, she'd drawn the assistant astrogator's duty here, while Basanta Lakhia filled the same duty for Dobrescu in AuxCon. The person Honor passionately envied at this moment was Audrey Bradlaugh, who sat beside Lieutenant Commander Hirake at Tactical. Honor would have given her left arm—well, a finger or two off her left hand, anyway—to sit in Audrey's chair, but at least she was luckier than Nassios. Captain Bachfisch had given Commander Layson the more experienced astrogator, but he'd kept the senior tac officer for himself, which meant Layson was stuck with Elvis Santino . . . and that Nassios had found himself stuck as Santino's assistant.

There were, Honor conceded, even worse fates than astrogation training duty.

She pushed the thought aside as she brought her own console rapidly online, and her amusement vanished and her stomach tightened when her astro plot came up and steadied. It lacked the detail of the tactical displays available to Hirake and Captain Bachfisch, but it showed enough for her to realize that this was no drill, for *War Maiden*'s arrival had interrupted a grim drama. The icon of a merchantman showed in her plot with the transponder code of a Manticoran vessel, but there was another vessel as well, the angry red bead of an unknown, presumably hostile ship less than four hundred kilometers from the merchie. The unknown vessel had her wedge up; the merchantman did not, and a jagged crimson ring strobed about its alphanumeric transponder code.

"Positive ID on the merchie, Skipper," Lieutenant Commander Hirake reported crisply. "I have her on my shipping list—RMMS *Gryphon's Pride*. She's a

Dillingham Cartel ship, all right. Five-point-five million tons, a pure bulk hauler with no passenger accommodations, and she's squawking a Code Seventeen."

An invisible breeze blew across the bridge, cold on the nape of Honor's neck as the tac officer's announcement confirmed what all of them had already known. Code Seventeen was the emergency transponder code which meant "I am being boarded by pirates."

"Range to target?" Captain Bachfisch's tenor was no longer nasal. It was clipped, cool, and clear, and Honor darted a glance over her shoulder. The Captain sat in his command chair, shoulders square yet relaxed, right leg crossed over left while he gazed intently into the tactical display deployed from the chair, and the dark eyes in his thin face no longer frowned. They were the bright, fierce eyes of a predator, and Honor turned back to her own display with a tiny shiver.

"Nine-point-three-one million klicks," Hirake said, and if the Captain's voice was crisp, hers was flat. "We don't have the angle on them, either," she went on in that same disappointed tone. "The bogey's already gotten underway, and we'll never be able to pull enough vector change to run him down."

"Do you concur, Astro?"

"Aye, Sir," Saunders said with equal unhappiness. "Our base vector is away from the merchie at almost eleven thousand KPS, Captain. It'll take us forty-five minutes just to decelerate to relative rest to them, and according to my plot, the bogey is turning well over five hundred gravities."

"They're up to just over five-thirty," Hirake confirmed from Tactical.

"Even at maximum military power, we're twenty gravities slower than that, Sir," Saunders said. "At normal max, they've got over one-point-two KPS squared on us, and they're accelerating on a direct reciprocal of our heading."

"I see." Bachfisch said, and Honor understood the disappointment in his tone perfectly. The pirate ship had to be smaller than *War Maiden* to pull that sort of acceleration, which meant it was certainly more lightly armed, as well, but it didn't matter. Their relative positions and base vectors had given the pirates the opportunity to run, and their higher acceleration curve meant the heavy cruiser could never bring them into even extreme missile range.

"Very well," the Captain said after a moment. "Astro, put us on a course to intercept the merchie. And keep trying to raise them, Com."

"Aye, aye, Sir." Saunders' quiet acknowledgment sounded much too loud against the bitter background silence of the bridge.

There was no response to Lieutenant Sauchuk's repeated hails as *War Maiden* closed on the merchantship, and the taut silence on the heavy cruiser's bridge grew darker and more bitter with each silent minute. It took over two hours for the warship to decelerate to zero relative to the merchantman and then overtake her. *Gryphon's Pride* coasted onward at her base velocity, silent and uncaring, and the cruiser was less than a minnow as she swam toward a rendezvous with her, for the whale-like freighter outmassed *War Maiden* by a factor of almost thirty. But unlike the whale, the minnow was armed, and a platoon of her Marines climbed into their skinsuits and checked their weapons in her boat bay as Captain

Bachfisch's helmsman edged his ship into position with finicky precision.

Honor was no longer on the bridge to watch. Bachfisch's eyes had passed over her with incurious impersonality while he punched up Major McKinley, the commander of *War Maiden*'s embarked Marine company, on the internal com and instructed her to prepare a boarding party. But then those eyes had tracked back to his assistant astrogator's assistant.

"I'll be attaching a couple of naval officers, as well," he told McKinley, still looking at Honor.

"Yes, Sir," the Marine's reply came back, and Bachfisch released the com stud.

"Commander Hirake," he said, "please lay below to the boat bay to join the boarding party. And take Ms. Harrington with you."

"Aye, aye, Sir," the tac officer acknowledged and stood. "You have Tactical, Ms. Bradlaugh."

"Aye, aye, Ma'am," Audrey acknowledged, and darted a quick, envious glance at her cabin mate.

"Come along, Ms. Harrington," Hirake said, and Honor stood quickly.

"Sir, I request relief," she said to Saunders, and the lieutenant nodded.

"You stand relieved, Ms. Harrington," he said with equal formality.

"Thank you, Sir." Honor turned to follow Hirake through the bridge hatch, but Captain Bachfisch raised one hand in an admonishing gesture and halted them.

"Don't forget your sidearm this time," he told Hirake rather pointedly, and she nodded. "Good," he said. "In that case, people, let's be about it," he added, and waved them off his bridge.

⬥   ⬥   ⬥

Hirake said nothing in the lift car. Despite *War Maiden's* age and the idiosyncratic layout of her lift shafts, the trip from the bridge to the boat bay was relatively brief, but it lasted more than long enough for conflicting waves of anticipation and dread to wash through Honor. She had no idea why the Captain had picked her for this duty, but she'd heard more than enough grizzly stories from instructors and noncoms at the Academy to produce a stomach-clenching apprehension. Yet hunting down pirates—and cleaning up the wreckage in their wake—was part of the duty she'd signed on to perform, and not even the queasiness in her midsection could quench her sense of excitement finally confronting its reality.

Lieutenant Blackburn's Second Platoon was waiting in the boat bay, but Honor was a bit surprised to see that Captain McKinley and Sergeant-Major Kutkin were also present. She'd assumed McKinley would send one of her junior officers, but she and Kutkin obviously intended to come along in person, for both of them were skinsuited, and the sergeant-major had a pulse rifle slung over his shoulder. Major McKinley didn't carry a rifle, but the pulser holstered at her hip looked almost like a part of her, and its grip was well worn.

The Marine officer's blue eyes examined the newcomers with clinical dispassion and just a hint of disapproval, and Hirake sighed.

"All right, Katingo," she said resignedly. "The Skipper already peeled a strip off me, so give me a damned gun."

"It's nice to know *someone* aboard the ship knows Regs," McKinley observed, and nodded to a noncom standing to one side. Honor hadn't seen him at first, but she recognized Sergeant Tausig as he stepped forward and silently passed a regulation gun belt and pulser to the tac officer. Lieutenant Commander Hirake took them a bit gingerly and buckled the belt around her waist. It was obvious to Honor that the Navy officer felt uncomfortable with the sidearm, but Hirake drew the pulser and made a brief but thorough inspection of its safety and magazine indicators before she returned it to its holster.

"Here, Ma'am," Tausig said, and Honor held out her hand for a matching belt. She felt both the major and the sergeant-major watching her, but she allowed herself to show no sign of her awareness as she buckled the belt and adjusted it comfortably. Then she turned slightly away, drew the pulser—keeping its muzzle pointed carefully away from anyone else—visually checked the safety and both magazine indicators and the power cell readout, then ejected the magazine and cleared the chamber to be certain it was unloaded. She replaced the magazine and reholstered the weapon. The military issue flapped holster was clumsy and bulky compared to the semi-custom civilian rig Honor had always carried in the Sphinx bush, but the pulser's weight felt comfortingly familiar at her hip, and Sergeant Tausig's eyes met hers with a brief flash of approval as she looked up once more.

"All right, people," Major McKinley said, raising her voice as she turned to address Blackburn's platoon. "You all know the drill. Remember, we do this by The Book, and I will personally have the ass of anyone who fucks up."

She didn't ask if her audience understood. She didn't have to, Honor thought. Not when she'd made herself clear in that tone of voice. Of course, it would have been nice if someone had told *Honor* what "the drill" was, but it was an imperfect universe. She'd just have to keep her eyes on everyone else and take her cues from them. And at least, given the Captain's parting injunction to Hirake and McKinley's response to it, she might not be the only one who needed a keeper.

The pinnace was just like dozens of other pinnaces Honor had boarded during Academy training exercises, but it didn't feel that way. Not with forty-six grim, hard-faced, armed-to-the-teeth Marines and their weapons packed into it. She sat next to Lieutenant Commander Hirake at the rear of the passenger compartment, and watched through the view port beside her as the pinnace crossed the last few hundred kilometers between *War Maiden* and *Gryphon's Pride*. The big freighter grew rapidly as they came up on it from astern, and the pinnace's pilot cut his wedge and went to reaction thrusters, then angled his flight to spiral up and around the huge hull.

Honor and Hirake were tied into the Marines' com net. There was no chatter, and Honor sensed the intensity with which the Marines fortunate enough to have view port seats, veterans all, stared out at the freighter. Then the pilot spoke over the net.

"I have debris, Major," he said in a flat, professional voice. "At your ten o'clock high position." There were a few seconds of silence, then, "Looks like bodies, Ma'am."

"I see them, Coxswain," McKinley said tonelessly. Honor was on the wrong side of the pinnace to lean closer to her port and peer forward. For a moment she felt frustrated, but then that changed into gratitude for the accident of seating that had kept her from doing just that. She would have felt ashamed and somehow unclean if Hirake and the Marines had seen her craning her neck while she gawked at the bodies like some sort of sick disaster-watcher or a news service ghoul.

"Coming up on her main starboard midships hatch, Ma'am," the pilot reported a few minutes later. "Looks like the cargo bays are still sealed, but the forward personnel hatch is open. Want me to go for a hard docking?"

"No, we'll stick to The Book," McKinley said. "Hold position at two hundred meters."

"Aye, aye, Ma'am."

The pilot nudged the pinnace into a stationary position relative to the freighter with the pinnace's swept wing tip almost exactly two hundred meters from the hull, and Sergeant-Major Kutkin shoved all two meters of his height up out of his seat. Lieutenant Blackburn was no more than a second behind the sergeant-major, and Kutkin watched with an approving proprietary air as the lieutenant addressed his platoon.

"All right, Marines, let's do it. Carras, you've got point. Janssen, you've got the backdoor. The rest of you in standard, just like we trained for it." He waited a moment, watching as two or three of his troopers adjusted position slightly, then grunted in approval. "Helmet up and let's go," he said.

Honor unclipped her own helmet from the carry point on her chest and put it on. She gave it a little extra twist to be sure it was seated properly and raised her left arm to press the proper key on the sleeve keypad. Her helmet HUD lit immediately, and she automatically checked the telltale which confirmed a good seal and the digital readout on her oxygen supply. Both were nominal, and she took her place—as befitted her lowly status—at the very rear of the queue to the pinnace's port hatch. With so many

personnel to unload, the flight crew made no effort
to cycle them through the air lock. Instead, they
cracked the outer hatch and vented the compartment's
air to space. Honor felt the pressure tug at her for
several seconds as the air bled outward, but then the
sensation of unseen hands plucking at her limbs faded
and her skinsuit audio pickups brought her the absolute silence of vacuum.

Corporal Carras—the same corporal, Honor realized suddenly, who had been *War Maiden*'s tube
sentry when she first joined the ship—pushed himself away from the pinnace. He drifted outward for
four or five meters, and then engaged his skinsuit
thrusters once he was sure he had cleared their safety
perimeter. He accelerated smoothly towards the
freighter, riding his thrusters with the practiced grace
of some huge bird of prey, and the rest of his section followed.

Even with their obvious practice it took time for
all of the Marines to clear the hatch for Hirake and
Honor, but at last it was their turn, and despite her
best effort to mirror the cool professionalism of
Blackburn's Marines, Honor felt a fresh flutter of
excited anxiety as she followed Hirake into the open
hatch. The lieutenant commander launched herself
with a gracefulness which fully matched that of the
Marines, yet was somehow subtly different. She sailed
away from the pinnace, and Honor pushed herself out
into emptiness in the tac officer's wake.

This far out, the system primary was a feeble
excuse for a star, and even that was on the far side
of the freighter. The pinnace and its erstwhile passengers floated in an ink-black lee of shadow, and
hull-mounted spotlights and the smaller helmet lights
of skinsuits pierced the ebon dark. The pinnace's

powerful spots threw unmoving circles of brilliance on the freighter's hull, picking out the sealed cargo hatch and the smaller personnel hatch which gaped open ahead of it, yet their beams were invisible, for there was no air to diffuse them. Smaller circles curtsied and danced across the illuminated area and into the darkness beyond as the helmet lights of individual Marines swept over the hull. Honor brought up her own helmet lamp as her thrusters propelled her towards the ship, and her eyes were bright. She cherished no illusion that she was a holo-drama heroine about to set forth on grand adventure, yet her pulse was faster than usual, and it was all she could do not to rest her right hand on the butt of her holstered pulser.

Then something moved in the darkness. It was more sensed than seen, an uncertain shape noticed only because it briefly occluded the circle on the hull cast by someone else's light as it rotated slowly, keeping station on the ship. She rotated her own body slightly, bringing her light to bear upon it, and suddenly any temptation she might still have nursed to see this as an adventure vanished.

The crewwoman could not have been more than a very few standard years older than Honor . . . and she would never grow any older. She wore no suit. Indeed, even the standard shipboard coverall she once had worn had been half-ripped from her body and drifted with her in the blackness, tangled about her arms and shoulders like some ungainly, rucked up shroud. An expression of pure horror was visible even through the froth of frozen blood caked about her mouth and nose, and the hideousness of her death had relaxed her sphincters. It was not simply death. It was desecration, and it was ugly, and Honor

Harrington swallowed hard as she came face-to-face with it. She remembered all the times she and Academy friends had teased one another, humorously threatening to "space" someone for some real or imagined misdeed, and it was no longer funny.

She didn't know how long she floated there, holding her light on the corpse which had once been a young woman until someone jettisoned her like so much garbage. It seemed later like a century, but in reality it could not have been more than a very few seconds before she tore her eyes away. She had drifted off course, she noted mechanically, and Lieutenant Commander Hirake was twenty or thirty meters ahead of her and to the right. She checked her HUD, and tapped a correction on her thruster controls. She felt a sort of surprise when her fingers moved the skinsuit gloves' finger servos with rocklike steadiness, and she accelerated smoothly to follow the tac officer through the blackness.

It was interesting, a detached corner of her brain noted almost clinically. Despite her horror, she truly was collected and almost calm—or something which counterfeited those qualities surprisingly well.

But she was very, very careful what else she let her helmet light show her.

". . . so that's about it, Sir." Commander Layson sighed, and let the memo board drop onto the corner of Captain Bachfisch's desk. "No survivors. No indications that they even tried to keep any of the poor bastards alive long enough to find out what *Gryphon's Pride* might've had in her secure cargo spaces." He leaned back in his chair and rubbed his eyes wearily. "They just came aboard, amused themselves, and butchered her entire company. Eleven men and five women. The lucky ones were killed out of hand. The others . . ." His voice trailed off, and he shook his head.

"Not exactly what our briefing told us to expect," Bachfisch said quietly. He tipped back in his own chair and gazed at the deckhead.

"No, but this is Silesia," Layson pointed out. "The only thing anyone can count on here is that the lunatics running the asylum will be even crazier than you expected," he added bitterly. "Sometimes I wish we could just go ahead and hand the damned place over to the Andies and be done with it. Let these sick bastards deal with the Andy Navy for a while with no holds barred."

"Now, Abner," Bachfisch said mildly. "You shouldn't go around suggesting things you know would give the Government mass coronaries. Not to mention the way the cartels would react to the very notion of letting someone else control one of their major market areas! Besides, would you really like encouraging someone like the Andermani to bite off that big an expansion in one chunk?"

"All joking aside, Sir, it might not be that bad a thing from our perspective. The Andies have always been into slow and steady expansion, biting off small pieces one at a time and taking time to digest between mouthfuls. If they jumped into a snake pit like Silesia, it would be like grabbing a hexapuma by the tail. They might be able to hang onto the tail, but those six feet full of claws would make it a lively exercise. Could even turn out to be a big enough headache to take them out of the expansion business permanently."

"Wishful thinking, Abner. Wishful thinking." Bachfisch pushed himself up out of his chair and paced moodily across his cramped day cabin. "I told the Admiralty we needed more ships out here," he said, then snorted. "Not that they needed to hear it from me! Unfortunately, more ships are exactly what we don't have, and with the Peeps sharpening their knives for Trevor's Star, Their Lordships aren't going to have any more to spare out this way for the fore-seeable future. And the damned Silesians know it."

"I wish you were wrong, Sir. Unfortunately, you're not."

"I only wish I could decide which were worse," Bachfisch half-muttered. "The usual sick, sadistic, murdering scum like the animals that hit *Gryphon's Pride,* or the goddamn 'patriots' and their so-called privateers!"

"I think I prefer the privateers," Layson said. "There aren't as many of them, and at least some of them pretend to play by some sort of rules. And there's at least a sense of semi-accountability to the government or revolutionary committee or whoever the hell issued their letter of marque in the first place."

"I know the logic." Bachfisch chopped at the air with his right hand. "And I know we can at least sometimes lean on whoever chartered them to make them behave—or at least to turn them over to us if they *mis*behave badly enough—but that assumes we know who they are and where they came from in the first place. And anything we gain from that limited sort of accountability on their part, we lose on the capability side."

Layson nodded. It didn't take much of a warship to make a successful pirate cruiser. Aside from a few specialized designs, like the Hauptman Cartel's armed passenger liners, merchantmen were big, slow, lumbering and unarmored targets, helpless before even the lightest shipboard armament. By the same token, no sane pirate—and however sociopathic all too many of them might be, pirates as a group tended to be very sane where matters of survival were concerned—wanted to take on any warship in combat. Even here in Silesia, regular navy crews tended to be better trained and more highly motivated. Besides, a pirate's ship was his principal capital investment. He was in business to make money, not spend it patching the holes in his hull ... assuming he was fortunate enough to escape from a regular man-of-war in the first place.

But privateers were different. Or they could be, at least. Like pirates, the financial backers who invested in a privateer expected it to be a money-making concern. But privateers also possessed a certain quasi-respectability, for interstellar law continued to recognize privateering as a legal means of making war, despite the strong opposition of nations like the Star Kingdom of Manticore, whose massive merchant marine made it the natural enemy of any legal theory which legitimized private enterprise commerce raiding. As far as Bachfisch and Layson were concerned, there was little if any practical difference between privateers and pirates, but smaller nations which could not afford to raise and maintain large and powerful navies adamantly resisted all efforts to outlaw privateering by interstellar treaty. Oh, they attended the conferences Manticore and other naval powers convened periodically to discuss the issue, but the bottom line was that they saw privateers as a cost-effective means by which even a weak nation could attack the life's blood of a major commercial power like the Star Kingdom and at least tie down major portions of its navy in defensive operations.

Bachfisch and Layson could follow the logic of that argument, however much they might detest it, but privateering as practiced in the Silesian Confederacy was a far cry from the neat theories propounded by the practice's defenders at the interstellar conferences. Breakaway system governments and an incredible variety of "people's movements" proliferated across the Confederacy like weeds in a particularly well-rotted compost heap, and at least half of them issued—sold, really—letters of marque to license privateering in the names of their revolutions. At least two-thirds of those letters went to out and out pirates, who regarded them as get-out-of-jail-free cards. Whereas piracy was a capital offense under interstellar law, privateers were legally regarded as a sort of militia, semi-civilian volunteers in the service of whatever nation had issued their letter of marque in the first place. That meant that their ships could be seized, but that they themselves were protected. The worst that could happen to them (officially, at least) was incarceration along with other prisoners of war, unless they had been so careless as to be captured in the act of murdering, torturing, raping, or otherwise treating the crews of their prizes in traditional piratical fashion.

That was bad enough, but in some ways the genuine patriots were even worse. They were far less likely to indulge themselves in atrocities, but their ships tended to be larger and better armed, and they actually did regard themselves as auxiliary naval units. That made them willing to accept risks no true for-profit pirate would consider running for a moment, up to and including an occasional willingness to engage light warships of whoever they were rebelling against that week. Which wouldn't have bothered the Royal Manticoran Navy excessively, if not for the fact that even the best privateers were still amateurs who sometimes suffered from less than perfect target identification.

The fact that some privateers invariably seemed to believe that attacks on the commerce of major powers like Manticore would somehow tempt those major powers into intervening in their own squabbles in an effort to impose an outside solution to protect their commercial interests was another factor altogether. The Star Kingdom had made it abundantly clear over the years that it would come down like the wrath of God on any revolutionary movement stupid enough to deliberately send its privateers after Manticoran merchant shipping, yet there always seemed to be a new group of lunatics who thought *they* could somehow manipulate the Star Kingdom where everyone else had failed. The Navy eventually got around to teaching them the same lesson it had taught their countless predecessors, but it was ultimately a losing proposition. That particular bunch of crazies would not offend again once the RMN crushed them, but a lot of Manticoran merchant spacers tended to get hurt first, and someone else would always be along in a year or two who would have to learn the lesson all over again.

And at the moment, the Saginaw Sector of the Confederacy (which just happened to contain the Melchor System) was in an even greater than usual state of unrest. At least two of its systems—Krieger's Star and Prism—were in open rebellion against the central government, and there were half a dozen shadow governments and liberation movements all boiling away just beneath the surface. ONI estimated that several of those insurrectionary factions had managed to open communications and establish a degree of coordination which had—yet again—taken the Confederacy's excuse for a government by surprise. Worse, The Honorable Janko Wegener, the Saginaw sector governor, was even more venal than most, and it seemed obvious to ONI that he saw the turmoil in his command area as one more opportunity to line his pockets. At the same time that Wegener fought valiantly to suppress the rebellions in his sector, he was raking off protection money in return for tacitly ignoring at least three liberation movements, and there was compelling evidence to suggest that he was actually permitting privateers to auction their prizes publicly in return for a percentage of their profits. Under the ironclad laws of cronyism which governed the Confederacy, the fact that he was a close relative of the current government's interior minister and an in-law of the premier meant Wegener could get away with it forever (or at least until the Confederacy's political parties' game of musical chairs made someone else premier), and the odds were that he would retire a very wealthy man indeed.

In the meantime, it was up to HMS *War Maiden* and her company to do what they could to keep some sort of lid on the pot he was busily stirring.

"If only we could free up a division or two of the wall and drop them in on Saginaw to pay Governor Wegener a little visit, we might actually be able to do some genuine good," Bachfisch observed after a moment. "As it is, all we're going to manage is to run around pissing on forest fires." He stared off into the distance for several seconds, then shook himself and smiled. "Which is the usual state of affairs in Silesia, after all, isn't it?"

"I'm afraid you're right there, Sir," Layson agreed

ruefully. "I just wish we could have started pissing on them by getting into missile range of the bastards who killed *Gryphon's Pride*."

"You and me both," Bachfisch snorted. "But let's face it, Abner, we were luckier than we had any right to count on just to recover the ship herself. If they hadn't wasted time . . . amusing themselves with her crew and gotten her underway sooner instead—or even just killed her transponder to keep us from realizing she'd been taken—they'd have gotten away clean. The fact that we got the hull back may not be much, but it's better than nothing."

"The insurers will be pleased, anyway," Layson sighed, then made a face and shook his head quickly. "Sorry, Sir. I know that wasn't what you meant. And I know the insurers would be just as happy as we would if we'd managed to save the crew as well. It's just—"

"I know," Bachfisch said, waving away his apology. The captain took one more turn around the cabin, then parked himself in the chair behind the desk once more. He picked up Layson's memo board and punched up the display to scan the terse report himself. "At least McKinley and her people cleared the ship on the bounce," he observed. "And I notice that even Janice remembered to take a gun this time!"

"With a little prodding," Layson agreed, and they grinned at one another. "I think the problem is that she regards anything smaller than a missile or a broadside energy mount as being beneath a tac officer's dignity," the exec added.

"It's worse than that," Bachfisch said with a small headshake. "She's from downtown Landing, and I don't think she and her family spent more than a day or two all told in the bush when she was a kid."

He shrugged. "She never learned to handle a gun before the Academy, and she's never actually needed one in the line of duty since. That's what Marines are for."

"Sergeant Tausig mentioned to me that Ms. Harrington seemed quite competent in that regard," Layson observed in a carefully uninflected tone.

"Good," Bachfisch said. "Of course, her family has a nice little freeholding in the Copper Wall Mountains. That's hexapuma country, and I imagine she grew up packing a gun whenever she went for a hike. Actually, I think she did quite well. At least she kept her lunch down while they recovered and bagged the bodies."

Layson managed to keep his eyebrows from rising. He'd known Harrington was from Sphinx, of course, but he hadn't known she was from the Copper Walls, so how did the Captain know? He looked at Bachfisch for a moment, then drew a deep breath.

"Excuse me, Sir. I realize it's not really any of my business, but I know you must have had a reason for specifically requesting that Ms. Harrington be assigned to us for her snotty cruise."

The sentence was a statement that was also a question, and Bachfisch leaned back in his chair and gazed steadily at his executive officer.

"You're right, I did," he said after a thoughtful pause. "Are you by any chance familiar with Captain Raoul Courvosier, Abner?"

"Captain Courvosier?" Layson's brow furrowed. "Oh, of course. He's the head of the Saganami Tactical Department, isn't he?"

"At the moment," Bachfisch said. "The grapevine says he's up for rear admiral on the current list. They're going to jump him right past commodore, and they'll probably drag him over to head the War College as soon as they do."

"I knew he had a good rep, Sir, but is he really that good?" Layson asked in considerable surprise. It was unusual, to say the least, for the RMN to jump an officer two grades in a single promotion, despite its current rate of expansion.

"He's better than that," Bachfisch said flatly. "In fact, he's probably the finest tactician and one of the three best strategists I've ever had the honor to serve under."

Abner Layson was more than simply surprised by that, particularly since that was precisely the way *he* would have described Captain Thomas Bachfisch.

"If Raoul had been born into a better family—or been even a little more willing to play the suck-up game—he would have had his commodore's star years ago," Bachfisch went on, unaware of his exec's thoughts. "On the other hand, I imagine he's done more good than a dozen commodores at the Academy. But when Raoul Courvosier tells me privately that one of his students has demonstrated in his opinion the potential to be the most outstanding officer of her generation and asks me to put her in my Snotty Row, I'm not about to turn him down. Besides, she's about due for a little offsetting career boost."

"I beg your pardon, Sir?" The question came out almost automatically, for Layson was still grappling with the completely unexpected endorsement of Honor Harrington's capabilities. Of course, he'd been very favorably impressed by her himself, but *the* outstanding officer of her generation?

"I said she's due for a career boost," Bachfisch repeated, and snorted at the confused look Layson gave him. "What? You think *I* was stupid enough to ask for Elvis Santino for my OCTO? Give me a break, Abner!"

"But—" Layson began, then stopped and looked at Bachfisch narrowly. "I'd assumed," he said very slowly, "that Santino was just a particularly obnoxious example of BuPers' ability to pound square pegs into round holes. Are you saying he wasn't, Sir?"

"I can't prove it, but I wouldn't bet against it. Oh, it could be innocent enough. That's why I didn't say anything about it to you ahead of time . . . and why I was so happy that he gave you ample grounds to bring the hammer down on him. The creep had it coming, whatever his motives may have been, but nobody who sees your report and the endorsements from Shelton and Flanagan could possibly question the fact that he was relieved for cause."

"But why would anyone want to question it in the first place?"

"Did you ever happen to encounter Dimitri Young?"

This time, despite all he could do, Layson blinked in surprise at the complete *non sequitur*.

"Uh, no, Sir. I don't believe I can place the name."

"I'm not surprised, and you didn't miss a thing," Bachfisch said dryly. "He was considerably before your time, and he resigned about the time he made commander in order to pursue a political career when he inherited the title from his father."

"Title?" Layson repeated cautiously.

"These days he's the Earl of North Hollow, and from all I hear he's just as big a loss as a human being as he ever was. What's worse, he's reproduced, and his oldest son, Pavel, was a class ahead of Harrington at Saganami."

"Why do I think I'm not going to like this, Sir?"

"Because you have good instincts. It seems that Mr. Midshipman Young and Ms. Midshipwoman Harrington had a small . . . disagreement in the showers one night."

"In the show—" Layson began sharply, then broke off. "My God," he went on a moment later in a very different tone, "she must have kicked his ass up one side and down the other!"

"As a matter of fact, she did," Bachfisch said, gazing speculatively at his exec.

"Damned straight she did," Layson said with an evil chuckle. "Ms. Harrington works out full contact with Sergeant Tausig, Sir. And she gets through his guard upon occasion."

"Does she?" Bachfisch smiled slowly. "Well, now. I suppose that *does* explain a few things, doesn't it?" He gazed sightlessly at the bulkhead, smiling at something Layson could not see, for several seconds, then shook himself back to the present.

"At any rate," he said more briskly, "Harrington sent him to the infirmary for some fairly serious repairs, and he never did manage to explain just what he was doing in the showers alone with her after hours that inspired her to kick the crap out of him. But neither did she, unfortunately, press charges against him. No," he said, shaking his head before Layson could ask the question, "I don't know why she didn't, and I don't know why Hartley couldn't get her to do it. But she didn't, and the little prick graduated with the rest of his class and went straight into the old-boy patronage system."

"And cranked the same system around to wreck Harrington's career." There was no amusement in Layson's voice this time, and Bachfisch nodded.

"That's Raoul's belief, anyway," the captain said, "and I respect his instincts. Besides, unlike you I did know Young's father, and I doubt very much that he's improved with age. That's one reason I have to wonder how we wound up saddled with Santino. North Hollow may not be Navy anymore, but he's got one hell of a lot of clout in the House of Lords, and he sits on the Naval Affairs Committee. So if he does want to punish her for 'humiliating' his precious son, he's in the perfect spot to do it."

"I see, Sir." Layson sat back in his chair, and his mind worked busily. There was even more going on here than he'd suspected might be the case, and he felt a brief uneasiness at the weight and caliber of the enemies his Captain appeared to be courting. But knowing Bachfisch as well as he did, he also understood perfectly. In many ways, there were actually two Royal Manticoran Navies: the one to which well-connected officers like Pavel Young and Elvis Santino belonged, where all that truly mattered was who was related to whom; and the one which produced officers like Thomas Bachfisch and—he hoped—Abner Layson, whose only claim to their rank was the fact that they put duty and responsibility before life itself. And just as the Navy of patronage and string-pullers looked after their own, so did the Navy of dedication and ability protect and nurture *its* own.

"Does Harrington know?" he asked. "I mean, know that Young and his family are out to get her?"

"I don't know. If she's as observant as I think she is—or even a quarter as good at analyzing interpersonal relationships as she is in the tactical simulator—then it's a pretty sure bet that she does. On the other hand, she didn't press charges against him in the first place, and that raises a question mark, doesn't it? In any case, I don't think a snotty cruise in the middle of Silesia is the best possible place and time for us to be explaining it to her, now is it?"

"You do have a gift for understatement, Sir."

"A modest talent, but one which has its uses," Bachfisch admitted. Then he picked up the memo board and handed it back to Layson. "But that's enough about Ms. Harrington for the moment," he said. "Right now, you and I need to give some thought to where we go from here. I've been thinking that it might be worthwhile to hang around here in Melchor for a while and use the system as a pirate lure, since this is the main magnet for our shipping at the moment. But if we do that too obviously, the local pirates—and probably Wegener—are going to get hinky. So what I was thinking was—"

Commodore Anders Dunecki replayed the brief message and clenched his jaw against the urge to swear vilely.

"Is this confirmed?" he asked the messenger without looking up from the display.

"Yes, Sir. The SN made the official announcement last week. According to their communique they picked off *Lydia* a couple of weeks before that, and Commander Presley is almost a month overdue." The nondescript man in civilian clothing shrugged unhappily. "According to the SN they took him out in Hera, and that was where he'd said he was planning to cruise with *Lydia*. We don't have absolute confirmation that it was him, of course, but all the pieces match too well for it to have been anyone else."

"But according to this—" Dunecki jabbed his chin at the holographic screen where the message footer was still displayed "—it was a heavy cruiser that nailed him." He paused, looking at the messenger expectantly, and the other man nodded. "In that case," Dunecki said, "what I want to know is how the hell the SN managed to run a ship that powerful into the area without our hearing about it. There's no way John Presley would have been careless enough to let a heavy cruiser sneak up on him if he'd known she was there to begin with. And he damned well ought to have known!"

The rage Dunecki had struggled to conceal broke through his control with the last sentence, and the messenger sat very still. Anders Dunecki was not a good man to anger, and the messenger had to remind himself that he was only the bearer of the news, and not the one responsible for its content.

"I didn't know Commander Presley as well as you did, Sir," he said carefully after a long moment of silence. "Or for as long. But I'm familiar with his record in the Council's service, and on the basis of that, I'd have to agree that he certainly would have exercised all due prudence if he'd been aware of the escalation in threat levels. Actually, as nearly as we can tell, at least two heavy cruisers, and possibly as many as three have been transferred into Saginaw in the last month and a half, and there are some indications that more will be following. Apparently—" he allowed himself a predatory smile despite the tension in Dunecki's cabin "—losses in the sector have gotten severe enough for the Navy to reinforce its presence here."

"Which is probably a good thing. Or at least an indication that we're really beginning to hurt them," Dunecki agreed, but his glass-green eyes were frosty, and the messenger's smile seemed to congeal. "At the same time," the commodore went on in the same chill tone, "if they're increasing their strength in-sector, it means the risks are going up for all of us . . . just like they did for Commander Presley. Which, in turn, makes timely intelligence on their movements more important than it ever was before. And that consideration is the reason I'm particularly concerned about Wegener's failure to warn us about this in time for *Lydia* to know she had to watch her back more carefully."

"He may not have known himself," the messenger suggested, and Dunecki snorted harshly.

"The man is Interior Minister Wegener's *nephew*, for God's sake! And he's Premier Stolar's brother-in-law, to boot—not to mention the civilian head of government and military commander-in-chief of the sector." The commodore grimaced. "Do you really think they'd send so many heavy units into his command area without even mentioning them to him?"

"Put that way, it does sound unlikely," the messenger agreed. "But if he knew about them, why didn't he warn us? Sure, we've lost *Lydia*, and a good chunk of our combat power with her, but by the same token we've also lost an equally good-sized chunk of our raiding ability. And that translates into a direct loss of income for Governor Wegener."

"If you were talking about someone placed lower in the chain of command, I'd be tempted to agree that he didn't know ahead of time," Dunecki said. "As you say, losing *Lydia* is going to cut into his revenue stream, and we've always known he was only in it for the money. But the fact is that no one in the Confed navy or government would dare send what sounds like a couple of divisions of heavy cruisers into his bailiwick without telling him they were coming. Not with his family connections to the Cabinet itself, they wouldn't! The only possible conclusion Stolar or Wegener's uncle could draw from that would be that whoever was responsible for withholding information distrusted the good governor, and that would be a fatal move career-wise for whoever made it. No, he knew about it and decided not to tell us."

"But why?" The messenger's tone was that of a man speaking almost to himself, but it was also thoughtful, as if his own mind were questing down the path it was apparent Dunecki had already explored.

"Because he's decided the time's come to pull the plug on us," Dunecki said grimly. The messenger looked up quickly in surprise, and the commodore chuckled. It was a grating sound, with absolutely no humor in it, and the expression which bared his teeth could scarcely have been called a smile.

"Think about it," he invited. "We've just agreed that we've always known Wegener was only in for the money. He certainly never shared our agenda or our ambition to achieve an independent Prism. For that matter, he has to know that we regard Prism as only the first step in liberating the entire sector, and if we manage that—or even look like we might come close to it—not even his connections to the Cabinet could save his job. Hell, they might actually go as far as throwing him to the wolves in a big, fancy inquiry or criminal trial just to prove how lily-white and innocent they themselves were! And greedy as he is, Wegener's also not stupid enough not to know that. Which means that he's always had some point in mind at which he'd cut off his relationship with us and do his damnedest to wipe out the Council and retake control of the system. From what happened to *Lydia* and what you're saying about additional reinforcements, it sounds to me as if we've been successful enough that he's finally decided the time is now."

"If you're right, this is terrible," the messenger muttered. His hands wrapped together in his lap, and he stared down at them, his eyes worried. "Losing the intelligence he's provided would be bad enough by itself, but he knows an awful lot about the Council's future plans, as well. If he acts on the basis of that knowledge . . ."

He let his voice trail off and looked back up at Dunecki.

"He doesn't know as much as he thinks he does." Dunecki's tone surprised the messenger, and his surprise grew as the commodore gave him a grim smile. "Of course he doesn't," Dunecki told him. "The Council has always known he'd turn on us the instant he decided it was no longer in his perceived interest to support us. That's why we've used him solely as an intelligence source rather than try to involve him in our strategic thinking or operational planning, and we've been very careful to use false identities or anonymous contacts whenever we dealt with him. Oh, he knows the identities of the public Council members from the independence government back in Prism, but so does everyone else in the star system. What he *doesn't* know is the identity of anyone else. And the only regular warships he knows we have are the ones he himself managed to 'lose' in our favor, like *Lydia*."

The messenger nodded slowly. The Council for an Independent Prism had been around for decades, and he'd been one of its adherents almost from its inception. But unlike Dunecki, he'd never been a member of the inner circle. He was confident that the Council trusted his loyalty, or they would never have assigned him to the duties he'd carried out for the movement, but he was also a realist. He'd known that another reason he'd been chosen for his various assignments was that the Council was willing to risk him because, in the final analysis, he was expendable. And because he was expendable—and might end up expended and in enemy hands—his superiors had always been careful to limit the information they shared with him, but he'd been active in the movement long enough to know that it was only in the last four or five years that the CIP had become a serious player even by the somewhat elastic standards of Silesia. What he didn't know were the ins and outs of how the organization had made the transition from an ineffectual fringe group to one which had managed to seize effective control of half a star system, but he knew Anders Dunecki and his brother Henryk had played a major role in that accomplishment. And although his commitment to the CIP's ultimate goal was as strong as it had ever been, he was no more a stranger to ambition than anyone else who had committed twenty years of his life to the forcible creation of a new political order.

Now he watched Commodore Dunecki with a carefully blank expression, hoping the time had come for him to learn more. Not merely out of simple curiosity (though he certainly was curious) but because the decision to share that information with him might be an indication that his longtime loyal services were finally about to earn him promotion to a higher and more sensitive level of the movement.

Dunecki gazed back at him impassively. He knew precisely what was going on in the other man's mind, and he rather wished that he could avoid taking the messenger any further into his confidence. Not that he actively distrusted the man, and certainly not because he faulted the messenger's obvious hope that he might finally be about to move beyond the thankless and dangerous role of courier. It was simply a matter of habit. After so many years of not letting the left hand know what the right hand was doing as a survival tactic it went against the grain to admit anyone any deeper into his confidence than he absolutely had to.

Unfortunately, like Anders, Henryk was out of the Prism System on operations. Dunecki knew he could have relied upon his brother to convince the Council that Governor Wegener's apparent change of attitude meant it was time to move to the next planned phase of operations. But in Henryk's absence, Dunecki was going to require another spokesman to make his case, and the messenger was all that was available.

"Wegener knows about the light cruisers and the frigates," the commodore said after a moment, "mostly because he and Commodore Nielsen were the ones who sold them to us in the first place." He watched the messenger's eyes widen slightly and chuckled. "Oh, I suspect that Nielsen thought he was simply disposing of them to regular pirates, but Wegener knew he was dealing with the CIP from the outset. After all, he was already taking a payoff from us to look the other way while we got ourselves organized in Prism, so there was no reason he shouldn't make a little more money off us by letting us buy a bunch of 'obsolescent' warships if Nielsen was willing to sign off on them for disposal. Of course, Nielsen told his Navy superiors that the ships had gone to the breakers, but I doubt any of them believed that any more than he did. Still, it's going to be at least a little embarrassing for Nielsen if any of his 'scrapped' ships wind up

being taken by regular Confed naval units, although
I have no doubt he has splendid paperwork to prove
that he sold them to ostensibly genuine scrap deal-
ers who have since disappeared after undoubtedly
selling the hulls to us nasty rebels.

"But we're pretty sure neither Wegener nor Nielsen
knows about the destroyers, and we *know* that they
don't know about *Annika*, *Astrid*, and *Margit*. We
bought the destroyers in the Tumult Sector, and
Annika, *Astrid*, and *Margit* came from . . . somewhere
else entirely."

He paused once more, watching the messenger's
face. The odds were that the other man had already
known everything Dunecki had just told him—except,
perhaps, for the fact that the newly created Prism
Space Navy's destroyers had come from Tumult—but
his expression indicated that he was beginning to see
previously unnoted implications in the information.

"The point," Dunecki went on after a moment, "is
that Wegener and Nielsen have probably based their
estimates of our strength on the units that they sold
us. They may have made some allowance for one or
two additional light units, but we've been very careful
in our discussions with our 'trusted ally' the Governor to make it plain that our only ships came from
them. We've even passed up two or three nice prizes
that Wegener had pointed us at because we didn't
have a vessel available to take them."

"Uh, excuse me, Sir," the messenger said, "but I
know that you and your brother have both taken
prizes. Doesn't that mean that they have to know
about *Annika* and *Astrid*, at least?"

"No," Dunecki said. "Henryk and I have taken
special precautions. Neither of us has disposed of any
of our prizes here in the Confederacy. We have

some . . . friends and associates in the People's Republic of Haven who've agreed to help out their fellow revolutionaries." The messenger's eyes narrowed, and the commodore chuckled once more. "Don't worry about it. The Legislaturalists are about as revolutionary as a hunk of nickel iron, but if it suits their purpose to pretend to support 'the People's struggle' as long as it's safely outside their own borders and they can make money on it, it suits our purpose just as well to have some place legitimate privateers can dispose of their prizes and repatriate their crews without questions being asked. It's just a pity that the Peeps aren't willing to help us out with additional ships and weapons, as well."

"So Wegener, Nielsen, and the Confed Navy all think that our naval strength is less than half as great as it really is," the messenger said slowly.

"More like a third," Dunecki corrected. "The ships they know about are all ex-Confed crap, just like their own units. Of course, they don't know about the system upgrades or the . . . technical assistance we've had in improving our missile seekers and EW capability, so even the ships they expect us to have are considerably more effective than they could possibly predict."

"I can see that," the messenger replied. "But does it really matter in the long run? I mean, with all due respect, Sir, even if we're in a position to inflict serious losses on Nielsen because they underestimate our strength, he's got the entire Silesian Navy behind him. You're probably right when you call them 'crap,' but they have an awful lot more ships than we do."

"Yes, they do. But that's where the other point you weren't cleared to hear about comes in." Dunecki leaned back in his chair and regarded the messenger coolly. "Haven't you wondered just how we

managed to get our hands on like-new destroyers and
heavy cruisers? *Andermani* destroyers and heavy
cruisers?"

"Occasionally," the messenger admitted. "I always
assumed we must have found someone like Nielsen
in the Empire. I mean, you and your brother both
have contacts in the Andy Navy, so—"

"In the IAN? You think there's someone in the *IAN*
who'd sell first-line warships on the black market?"
Almost despite himself, Dunecki laughed uproariously.
It took several seconds for him to get his amusement
back under control, and he wiped tears of laughter
from his eyes as he shook his head at the messenger. "I may have made it clear to captain in the IAN,
and Henryk may have been a full commander, but
trust me, the Imperial Navy isn't at all like the
Confeds! Even if there were someone interested in
stealing ships, there are way too many checkpoints
and inspectorates. No," he shook his head. "Henryk
and I did use contacts in the Empire to set it up,
but they weren't with the Navy. Or not directly,
anyway."

"Then who did you work with?" the messenger
asked.

"Let's just say there are a few people, some of them
from rather prominent Andie families, who were able
to stomach having their investment stolen by Wegener
and his family, but only until Wegener decided to
bring in another set of foreigners to take it over and
run it. That was a bit too much for them, and one
or two of them spoke to their prominent relatives after
Henryk and I spoke to *them*, just before he and I
came home to Prism. Which brings me to the point
I need you to stress to the Council when you get
home."

"Yes, Sir." The messenger straightened in his chair, his expression intent, and Dunecki looked straight into his eyes.

"The Andermani money people who made our ships available in the first place have just gotten word to me that the Imperial government is finally ready to act. If we can inflict sufficient losses on the local naval forces to provide the Emperor with a pretext, the Empire will declare that the instability in this region of the Confederacy has become great enough in its opinion to threaten a general destabilization of the area. And to prevent that destabilization, the Imperial Navy will move into Saginaw and impose a cease-fire, under the terms of which the Empire will recognize the Council as the de facto legitimate government of Prism."

"Are you serious?" the messenger stared at Dunecki in disbelief. "Everyone knows the Andies have wanted to move into the Confederacy for years, but the Manties have always said no."

"True, but the Manties are focused on Haven right now. They won't have the resources or the will to take on the Empire over something as unimportant to them as Saginaw."

"But what do the Andies get out of it?"

"The Empire gets the precedent of having successfully intervened to restore order to a sector of the Confederacy, which it can use as an opening wedge for additional interventions. It won't demand any outright territorial concessions—this time. But the next time may be a slightly different story, and the time after that, and the time after that, and the time after that . . ." Dunecki let his voice trail off and smiled evilly. "As for our sponsors, the one thing the Emperor's negotiators will insist upon is that Wegener, or whoever

Stolar replaces him with, revoke the trade concessions
Wegener made to the Manties in Melchor and regrant
them to the original Andy investors. So everybody gets
what they want . . . except for the Confeds and the
Manties, that is."

"My God." The messenger shook his head. "My
God, it might just work."

"It damned well *will* work," Dunecki said flatly,
"and it's what the Council has been working towards
for the last three years. But we didn't expect such
sudden confirmation that the groundwork had finally
been completed in the Empire, so no one back home
is ready to move. But coupling the word from my
Imperial contacts with what happened to *Lydia*, I
think we've just run out of time. If Wegener and
Nielsen are ready to begin moving against us rather
than working with us, we need to act quickly. So what
I need you to do is to go back to the Council and
tell them that they have to get couriers to Henryk
and to Captain Traynor in the *Margit* with instructions to begin all-out operations against the Confed
Navy."

"I understand, Sir, but I'm not sure they'll listen
to me." The messenger smiled wryly. "I realize you're
using me because you don't have anyone else available, but I'm hardly part of the inner circle, and this
will be coming at them cold. So what if they refuse?"

"Oh, they won't do that," Dunecki said with cold
assurance. "If it looks like they might, just tell them
this." He looked levelly at the messenger across his
desk, and his expression was grim. "Whatever they
may want to decide, *Annika* will commence active
operations against the SN one standard week from
today."

✧   ✧   ✧   ✧

"I still say there has to be a better way to do this."
Midshipman Makira sounded unusually grumpy, and
Honor glanced across the table and shook her head
at him.

"You have got to be one of the most contrary
people that I've ever met, Nassios," she told him
severely.

"And just what do you mean by that?" Makira
demanded.

"I mean that I don't think there's anything the
Captain could do that you couldn't decide was the
wrong way to go about it. Not to say that you're a
nit-picker—although, now that I think about it, someone whose disposition was less naturally sunny and
equable than my own probably would—but you do
have an absolute gift for picking up on the potential
weaknesses of an idea without paying any attention
to its advantages."

"Actually," Makira said in an unusually serious tone,
"I think you might have a point there. I really do have
a tendency to look for problems first. Maybe that's
because I've discovered that that way any of my surprises are pleasant ones. Remember, Captain
Courvoisier always said that no plan survives contact
with the enemy anyway. The way I see it, that makes
a pessimist the ideal commander in a lot of ways."

"Maybe—as long as your pessimism doesn't prevent you from having enough confidence to take the
initiative away from the bad guys and hang on to it
for yourself," Honor countered. Nimitz looked up
from his perch on the end of the Snotty Row table
and cocked his head in truly magisterial style as he
listened to his person's discussion, and Makira
chuckled.

"Not fair," he protested, reaching out to stroke the

'cat's ears. "You and Nimitz are ganging up on me again!"

"Only because you're wrong," Honor informed him with a certain smugness.

"Oh, no, I'm not! Look, all I'm saying is that the way we're going about it now, this is the only star system in our entire patrol area that we're giving any cover at all to. Now," he leaned back and folded his arms, "explain to me where that statement is in error."

"It's not in error at all," she conceded. "The problem is that there isn't an ideal solution to the problem of too many star systems and not enough cruisers. We can only be in one place at a time whatever we do, and if we try to spread ourselves between too many systems, we'll just spend all of our time running around between them in hyper and never accomplish anything at all in n-space." She shrugged. "Under the circumstances, and given the fact that the Star Kingdom's presence here in Melchor is pretty much nailed down, I think it makes a lot of sense to troll for pirates right here."

"And while we're doing that," Makira pointed out, "we can be pretty sure that somewhere else in our patrol area a merchantship we ought to be protecting is about to get its ass into a world of hurt with no one there to look out for her."

"You're probably right. But without detailed advance knowledge of the schedules and orders of every merchie in the entire Saginaw Sector, it's simply impossible for anyone to predict where our shipping is going to be at any given moment, anyway. For that matter, even if we'd had detailed schedules on every civilian ship planning on moving in our area at the time we left Manticore, they'd be hopelessly out of date by now, and you know it. And there aren't any such detailed schedules in the first place, which means every single Manticoran ship in Silesia is basically its own needle inside one huge haystack. So even if we were cruising around from system to system, the odds are that we'd almost certainly be out of position to help out the merchantship you're talking about. If we *were* in position to help, it could only be a case of sheer dumb luck, and you know that as well as I do."

"But at least we'd have a chance for dumb luck to put us there!" he shot back stubbornly. "As it is, we don't even have that!"

"No, we don't—we've got something much better than that: bait. We *know* that every pirate in the sector knows about the Dillingham Cartel's installations here in Melchor. They can be pretty much certain that there are going to be Manticoran ships in and out of this system on a semi-regular basis, not to mention the possibility that they might get lucky and actually manage to pull off a successful raid on the installations themselves, despite their defenses. That's the whole point of the Captain's strategy! Instead of chasing off from star system to star system with no assurance that he'll catch up with any pirates, much less pirates in the act of raiding our shipping, he's opted to sit here and set an ambush for anybody who's tempted to hit Dillingham's people. I'd say the odds are much better that we'll actually manage to pick off a few pirates by lying in wait for them than there'd be any other way."

"But we're not even showing the flag in any other system," Makira complained. "There's no sense of presence to deter operations anywhere else in the sector."

"That's probably the single most valid criticism of our approach," Honor agreed. "Unfortunately, the

Captain only has one ship and there's no way in the world to cover enough space with a single ship to actually deter anyone who can do simple math. What are the odds that *War Maiden* is going to turn up to intercept any given pirate at any given moment?" She shook her head. "No, unless the Admiralty is prepared to give the Captain at least a complete cruiser division to work with, I don't see how he can possibly be expected to create a broad enough sense of presence to actually deter anybody who's inclined to turn pirate in the first place."

"Then why bother to send us at all?" For the first time, there was a note of true bitterness in Makira's voice. "If all we're doing is trying to hold air in the lock with a screen door, then what's the damned point?"

"The same as it's always been, I suppose," Honor said. "One ship can't deter piracy throughout an entire patrol area the size of the Saginaw Sector—not in any specific sense, at least. But if we can pick off two or three of the scum, then the word will get around among the ones we don't get a shot at. At least we can make a few people who are considering the 'great adventure' as a career choice think about whether or not they really want to run the risk of being one of the unlucky ones. More to the point, the word will also get around that we're paying particular attention to Melchor, which may just remind them that the Star Kingdom takes a dim view of attacks on our nationals. I hate to say it, but in a lot of ways what we're really doing out here is encouraging the local vermin to go pick on someone else's shipping and leave ours alone."

"That's not what they told us back at the Academy," Makira said. "They told us our job was to suppress piracy, not just encourage it to go after merchies unlucky enough to belong to some poor sucker of a star nation that doesn't have a decent navy of its own!"

"Of course that's what they told us, and in an absolute sense they were right. But we live in an imperfect galaxy, Nassios, and it's been getting steadily less perfect for years now. Look," she leaned forward across the table, propping her elbows on it while her expression turned very serious, "the Navy only has so many ships and so many people, and important as Silesia is—and as important as the lives of Manticoran spacers are—we can only put so many ships in so many places. Back before the Peeps started conquering everything in sight, we could actually send a big enough chunk of the Navy off to Silesia every year to make a real hole in pirate operations here. But with so much of our available strength diverted to keeping an eye on the Peeps at places like Trevor's Star and Basilisk, we can't do that any more. We simply don't have enough hulls for that kind of deployment. So I'm sure that everyone at the Admiralty understands perfectly well that there's no way we can possibly 'suppress' piracy in our patrol areas. For that matter, I'd bet that any pirate who's not a complete imbecile knows that just as well as *we* do, and you can be absolutely sure that the Andies do!"

Nassios Makira tipped back in his chair, and his expression had gone from one that showed more than a little outrage to one of surprise. He knew that he and the other middies in *War Maiden*'s company all had exactly the same access to information, but it was suddenly apparent to him that Honor had put that information together into a far more complete and coherent picture than he ever had.

"Then why bother to send us?" he repeated, but

his tone had gone from one of challenge to one that verged on the plaintive. "If we can't do any good, and everyone knows it, then why are we here?"

"I didn't say we couldn't do any good," Honor told him almost gently. "I said that we couldn't realistically expect to *suppress* piracy. The fact that we can't stamp it out or even drive a significant number of the raiders out of any given area doesn't relieve us of a moral responsibility to do whatever we *can* do. And one of the responsibilities that we have is to protect our own nationals to the greatest possible extent, however limited that extent may be compared to what we'd like to do. We can't afford for the pirates—or the Andies—to decide that we'll simply write off our commitments in Silesia, however strapped for ships we may be. And when I said that what we're really trying to do is to convince pirates to go pick on someone else's merchant shipping, I didn't mean that we had any specific victims in mind. I just meant that our objective is to convince the locals that it's more unsafe to attack our shipping than it is to attack anyone else's. I know there are some people back home who would argue that it's in our true strategic interest to point the pirates here at anybody who competes with our own merchant marine, but they're idiots. Oh, I'm sure we could show some short-term gain if the pirate threat scared everybody looking for freight carriers in Silesia into using our merchies, but the long-term price would be stiff. Besides, once everybody was using Manticoran bottoms, the pirates would have no choice but to come after us again because there wouldn't be any other targets for them!

"Actually," she said after a moment, her tone and expression thoughtful, "there may *be* an additional advantage in pointing pirates at someone else. Everyone has relied on us to play police out here for the better part of a century and a half, but we're scarcely the only ones with an interest in what happens in Silesia. I'm sure that there have been times when the government and the Admiralty both did their very best to make sure that everyone else regarded us as the logical police force for Silesia, if only to depress Andy pretentions in the area. But now that we're having to concentrate on our own forces on the Peeps' frontiers, we need someone else to take up the slack out here. And I'm afraid the only people available are the Andies. The Confeds certainly aren't going to be able to do anything about it! So maybe there's an advantage I hadn't considered in persuading pirates to pick on Andy merchies instead of ours, if that's going to get the Andy navy involved in going after them more aggressively while we're busy somewhere else."

"Um." Makira rubbed his eyebrow while he pondered everything she'd just said. It made sense. In fact, it made a *lot* of sense, and now that she'd laid it all out, he couldn't quite understand why the same conclusions hadn't suggested themselves to him long since. But still . . .

"All right," he said. "I can see your point, and I don't guess I can really argue with it. But I still think that we could do more to convince pirates to go after someone else's shipping if we put in an appearance in more than one star system. I mean, if Melchor is the only place we ever pop a single pirate—not that we've managed to do even that much so far—then our impact is going to be very limited and localized."

"It's going to be 'limited' whatever we do. That's the inevitable consequence of only having one ship,"

Honor pointed out with a glimmer of amusement. "But like I said, I'm sure the word will get around. One thing that's always been true is that the 'pirate community,' for lack of a better term, has a very efficient grapevine. Captain Courvoisier says that the word always gets around when someplace turns out to be particularly hazardous to their health, so we can at least push them temporarily out of Melchor. On the other hand, what makes you think that Melchor is going to be the *only* place the Captain stakes out during our deployment? It's the place he's staking out *at the moment*, but there's no reason not to move his operations elsewhere after he feels reasonably confident that he's made an impression on the local lowlife's minds. I think the presence of the Dillingham operation here makes this the best hunting grounds we're likely to find, and it looks to me like the Captain thinks the same. But the same tactics will work just as well anyplace else there are actually pirates operating, and I'd be very surprised if we don't spend some time trolling in other systems, as well."

"Then why didn't you say so in the first place?" Makira demanded with the heat of exasperation. "You've been letting me bitch and carry on about the Captain's obsession with this system for days! Now you're going to sit there and tell me that the whole time you've actually been expecting him to eventually do what I *wanted*?"

"Well," Honor chuckled, "it's not *my* fault if what you've been letting yourself hear wasn't exactly what I've been saying, now is it? Besides, you shouldn't criticize the Captain quite so energetically unless you've really thought through what you're talking about!"

"You," Makira said darkly, "are an evil person who

will undoubtedly come to an unhappy end, and if there is any justice in the universe, I'll be there to see it happen."

Honor grinned, and Nimitz bleeked a lazy laugh from the table between them.

"You may laugh . . . for now," he told them both ominously, "but There Will Come a Day when you will remember this conversation and regret it bitterly." He raised his nose with an audible sniff, and Nimitz turned his head to look up at his person. Their eyes met in complete agreement, and then Nassios Makira's arms windmilled wildly as a gray blur of treecat bounded off the table and wrapped itself firmly around his neck. The midshipman began a muffled protest that turned suddenly into a most unmilitary— and high-pitched—sound as Nimitz's long, agile fingers found his armpits and tickled unmercifully. Chair and midshipman alike went over backwards with a high, wailing laugh, and Honor leaned back in her own chair and watched with folded arms as the appropriate penalty for his ominous threat was rigorously applied.

"Well, here we are," Commander Obrad Bajkusa observed.

One might have concluded from his tone that he was less than delighted with his own pronouncement, and one would have been correct. Bajkusa had an enormous amount of respect for Commodore Dunecki as both a tactical commander and a military strategist, but he'd disliked the entire concept of this operation from the moment the commodore first briefed him on it over six T-months before. It wasn't so much that he distrusted the motives of the commodore's Andermani . . . associates (although he *did* distrust

them about as much as was humanly possible) as that
it was Bajkusa's personal conviction that anyone who
screwed around with the Royal Manticoran Navy was
stupid enough that he no doubt deserved his Darwin-
ian fate. On the surface, Dunecki's plan was straight-
forward and reasonable, especially given the promises
of backing from the imperial Andermani court. So far
as logical analysis was concerned, it was very difficult
to find fault with the commodore's arguments. Unfortunately, the Manty Navy had a deplorable habit of
kicking the ever-living crap out of anyone foolish
enough to piss it off, and Obrad Bajkusa had no particular desire to find himself a target of such a kicking.

On the other hand, orders were orders, and it
wasn't as if the Manties knew his name or address.
All he had to do was keep it that way.

"All right, Hugh," he told his exec. "Let's head on
in and see what we can find."

"Yes, Sir," Lieutenant Wakefield replied, and the
frigate PSN *Javelin* headed in-system while the star
named Melchor burned steadily ahead of her.

"Well, well. What *do* we have here?"

Senior Chief Jensen Del Conte turned his head
towards the soft murmur. Sensor Tech 1/c Francine
Alcott was obviously unaware that she had spoken
aloud. If Del Conte had harbored any doubt about
that, the expression on her dark, intense face as she
leaned closer to her display would have disabused him
of it quickly enough.

The senior chief watched her as her fingers flickered back and forth across her panel with the unconscious precision of a concert pianist. He had no doubt
whatsoever what she was doing, and he clenched his
jaw and thought very loudly in her direction.

Unfortunately, she seemed remarkably insensitive to Del Conte's telepathy, and he swallowed a silent curse. Alcott was extremely good at her job. She had both a natural aptitude for it, and the sort of energy and sense of responsibility which took her that extra kilometer from merely satisfactory to outstanding, and Del Conte knew that Lieutenant Commander Hirake had already earmarked Alcott, despite her relative youth, for promotion to petty officer before this deployment was over. But for all her undoubted technical skills, Alcott was remarkably insensitive to some of the internal dynamics of *War Maiden*'s tactical department. The fact that she had been transferred to Del Conte's watch section less than two weeks earlier made the situation worse, but the senior chief felt depressingly certain that she would have been blithely blind to certain unpleasant realities even if she'd been in the same duty section since the ship left Manticore.

Del Conte glanced over his shoulder as unobtrusively as possible, then swallowed another silent expletive. Lieutenant Santino had the watch, and he sat in the command chair at the center of the bridge looking for all the world like a competent naval officer. His forearms rested squarely upon the command chair's arm rests. His squared shoulders rested firmly against the chair's upright back, his manly profile was evident as he held his head erect, and there was an almost terrifying lack of intelligence in his eyes.

Jensen Del Conte had seen more officers than he could possibly count in the course of his naval career. Some had been better than others, some had been worse; none had ever approached the abysmal depths which Elvis Santino plumbed so effortlessly. Del

Conte knew Lieutenant Commander Hirake was aware of the problem, but there was very little that she could do about it, and one thing she absolutely could *not* do was to violate the ironclad etiquette and traditions of the Service by admitting to a noncommissioned officer, be he ever so senior, that his immediate superior was a complete and utter ass. The senior chief rather hoped that the lieutenant commander and the Skipper were giving Santino rope in hopes that he would manage to hang himself with it. But even if they were, that didn't offer much comfort to those unfortunate souls who found themselves serving under his immediate command—like one Senior Chief Del Conte.

Alcott continued her silent communion with her instruments, and Del Conte wished fervently that Santino's command chair were even a few meters further away from him than it was. Given its proximity, however, the lieutenant was entirely too likely to hear anything Del Conte might say to Alcott. In fact, the sensor tech was extremely fortunate that Santino hadn't already noticed her preoccupation. The lieutenant's pose of attentiveness fooled no one on the bridge, but it would have been just like him to emerge from his normal state of internal oblivion at precisely the wrong moment for Alcott. So far, he hadn't, however, and that posed a most uncomfortable dilemma for Del Conte.

The senior chief reached out and made a small adjustment on his panel, and his brow furrowed as his own display showed him a duplicate of the imagery on Alcott's. He saw immediately what had drawn her attention, although he wasn't at all certain that he would have spotted it himself without the enhancement she had already applied. Even now, the impeller signature was little more than a ghost, and the computers apparently did not share Alcott's own confidence that what she was seeing was really there. They insisted on marking the icon with the rapidly strobing amber circle which indicated a merely possible contact, and that was usually a bad sign. But Alcott possessed the trained instinct which the computers lacked, and Del Conte was privately certain that what she had was a genuine contact.

Part of the problem was the unknown's angle of approach. Whatever it was, it was overtaking from astern and very high—so high, in fact, that the upper band of *War Maiden*'s impeller wedge was between the contact and Alcott's gravitic sensors. In theory, CIC's computers knew the exact strength of the heavy cruiser's wedge and, equipped with that knowledge, could compensate for the wedge's distorting effect. In theory. In real life, however, the wedge injected a high degree of uncertainty into any direct observation through it, which was why warships tended to rely so much more heavily on the sensor arrays mounted on their fore and aft hammerheads and on their broadsides, where their wedges did not interfere. They also carried ventral and dorsal arrays, of course, but those systems were universally regarded— with reason—as little more than precautionary afterthoughts under most circumstances. In this case, however, the dorsal arrays were the only ones that could possibly see Alcott's possible contact. The known unreliability of those arrays, coupled with the extreme faintness of the signature that had leaked through the wedge, meant that the contact (if that was what it actually was) had not yet crossed the threshold of CIC's automatic filters, so no one in CIC was so far even aware of it.

But Alcott was, and now—for his sins—Del Conte was, as well. Standing orders for such a contingency were clear, and Alcott, unfortunately, had followed them . . . mostly. She had, in fact, done precisely what she would have been expected to do if she had still been part of Lieutenant Commander Hirake's watch section, for the lieutenant commander trusted her people's abilities and expected them to routinely route their observations directly to her own plot if they picked up anything they thought she should know about. Standard operating procedure required a verbal announcement, as well, but Hirake preferred for her sensor techs to get on with refining questionable data rather than waste time reporting that they didn't yet know what it was they didn't know.

Del Conte's problem was that the lieutenant commander's attitude was that of a confident, competent officer who respected her people and their own skills. Which would have been fine, had anyone but Elvis Santino had the watch. Because what Alcott had done was exactly what Lieutenant Commander Hirake would have wanted; she had thrown her own imagery directly onto Santino's Number Two Plot . . . and the self-absorbed jackass hadn't even noticed!

Had the contact been strong enough for CIC to consider it reliable, *they* would already have reported it, and Santino would have known it was there. Had Alcott made a verbal report, he would have known. Had he bothered to spend just a little more effort on watching his own displays and a little less effort on projecting the proper HD-image of the Complete Naval Officer, he would have known. But none of those things had happened, and so he didn't have a clue. But when CIC did get around to upgrading their classification from sensor ghost to possible real contact, even Santino was likely to notice from the time chop on the imagery blinking unnoticed (at the moment) on his plot that Alcott had identified it as such several minutes earlier. More to the point, he would realize that when Captain Bachfisch and Commander Layson got around to reviewing the bridge log, *they* would realize that he ought to have been aware of the contact long before he actually got around to reporting it to *them*. Given Santino's nature, the consequences for Alcott would be totally predictable, and wasn't it a hell of a note that a senior chief in His Majesty's Navy found himself sitting here sweating bullets trying to figure out how to protect a highly talented and capable rating from the spiteful retaliation of a completely untalented and remarkably stupid officer?

None of which did anything to lessen Del Conte's dilemma. Whatever else happened, he couldn't let the delay drag out any further without making things still worse, and so he drew a deep breath.

"Sir," he announced in his most respectful voice, "we have a possible unidentified impeller contact closing from one-six-five by one-one-five."

"What?" Santino shook himself. For an instant, he looked completely blank, and then his eyes dropped to the repeater plot deployed from the base of his command chair and he stiffened.

"Why didn't CIC report this?" he snapped, and Del Conte suppressed an almost overwhelming urge to answer in terms which would leave even Santino in no doubt of the senior chief's opinion of him.

"It's still very faint, Sir," he said instead. "If not for Alcott's enhancement, we'd never have noticed it. I'm sure it's just lost in CIC's filters until it gains a little more signal strength."

He made his voice as crisp and professional as possible, praying all the while that Santino would be too preoccupied with the potential contact to notice the time chop on his plot and realize how long had passed before its existence had been drawn to his attention.

For the moment, at least, God appeared to be listening. Santino was too busy glaring at the strobing contact to worry about anything else, and Del Conte breathed a sigh of relief.

Of premature relief, as it turned out.

Elvis Santino looked down at the plot icon in something very like panic. He was only too well aware that the Captain and that asshole Layson were both out to get him. Had he been even a little less well connected within the aristocratic cliques of the Navy, Layson's no doubt scathing endorsement of his personnel file which had almost certainly accompanied the notation that he had been relieved as OCTO for cause would have been the kiss of death. As it was, he and his family were owed sufficient favors that his career would probably survive without serious damage. But there were limits even to the powers of patronage, and he dared not give the bastards any additional ammunition.

As it happened, he *had* noticed the plot time chop. Which meant that he knew that he—or at least his bridge crew, and for that matter, his own tactical personnel—had picked up the possible contact almost six full minutes before anyone had drawn it to his attention. He could already imagine the coldly formal, impeccably correct, and brutally blistering fashion in which Bachfisch (or, even worse, that ass-kisser Layson) would ream him out for not reacting sooner. The mental picture of that . . . discussion was the only thing which prevented him from ripping out Alcott's and Del Conte's lungs for having deliberately withheld the information. But Layson had already demonstrated his taste for using noncoms and ratings as spies and informants, and Santino had no doubt that the Exec would take gleeful pleasure in adding Del Conte's ass-covering version of what had happened to his own report. So instead of kicking their insolent and disloyal asses as they so richly deserved, he forced himself to remain outwardly oblivious to what they had conspired to do to him. The time would come eventually for the debt to be paid, yet for now it was one more thing he dared not attend to.

In the meantime, he had to decide how to handle the situation, and he gnawed on his lower lip while he thought hard. Del Conte—the disloyal bastard—was undoubtedly correct about the reason for CIC's silence. But if Alcott's enhancement was solid (and it looked as if it were) then the contact was bound to burn through CIC's filters in no more than another five to ten minutes, even with only the dorsal gravitics. When that happened, he would have no option but to report it to the Captain . . . at which point the fact that Alcott and Del Conte had officially fed him the data so much earlier would also become part of the official record. And the fact that they had deliberately concealed the report by failing to announce it verbally would be completely ignored while Bachfisch and Layson concentrated on the way in which he had "wasted" so much "valuable time" before reporting it to them. And Layson, in particular, was too vindictive for Santino to doubt for a moment that he would point out the fashion in which Santino had squandered the potential advantage which his own brilliantly competent Tactical

Department subordinates had won him by making such an early identification of the contact.

Frustration, fury, resentment, and fear boiled back and forth behind his eyes while he tried to decide what to do, and every second that ticked away with no decision added its own weight to the chaos rippling within him. It was such a *little* thing! So what if Alcott and Del Conte had picked up the contact six minutes, or even fifteen minutes—hell, half an hour!—before CIC did? The contact was over two and a half light-minutes behind *War Maiden*. That was a good fifty million klicks, and Alcott's best guess on its acceleration was only around five hundred gravities. With an initial overtake velocity of less than a thousand kilometers per second, it would take whatever it was over five hours to overtake *War Maiden*, so how could the "lost time" possibly matter? But it would. He knew it would, because Bachfisch and Layson would never pass up the opportunity to hammer his efficiency report all over again and—

His churning thoughts suddenly paused. Of course! Why hadn't he thought of it sooner? He felt his lips twitch and managed somehow to suppress the need to grin triumphantly as he realized the solution to his dilemma. His "brilliant" subordinates had reported the contact even before CIC, had they? Well, good for them! And as the officer of the watch, wasn't it his job to confirm whether or not the contact was valid as quickly as possible—even before the computers and the highly trained plotting crews in CIC could do so? Of course it was! And *that* was the sole reason he had delayed in reporting to the Captain: to confirm that the *possible* contact was a real one.

He caught himself just before he actually rubbed

his hands together in satisfaction and then turned to the helmsman.

"Prepare to roll ship seventy degrees to port and come to new heading of two-two-three," he said crisply.

Del Conte spun his chair to face the center of the bridge before he could stop himself. He knew exactly what the lieutenant intended to do, but he couldn't quite believe that even Elvis Santino could be *that* stupid. The preparatory order he'd just given was a classic maneuver. Naval officers called it "clearing the wedge," because that was exactly what it did as the simultaneous roll and turn swept the more sensitive broadside sensor arrays across the zone which had been obstructed by the wedge before the maneuver. But it was the sort of maneuver which only warships made, and *War Maiden* had gone to enormous lengths to masquerade as a fat, helpless, *unarmed* freighter expressly to lure raiders into engagement range. If this asshole—

"Sir, I'm not sure that's a good idea," the senior chief said.

"Fortunately, *I* am," Santino said sharply, unable to refrain from smacking down the disloyal noncom.

"But, Sir, we're supposed to be a merchie, and if—"

"I'm quite aware of what we're supposed to be, Senior Chief! But if in fact this is a genuine contact and not simply a figment of someone's overheated imagination, clearing the wedge should confirm it, don't you think?"

"Yes, Sir, but—"

"They're only pirates, Senior Chief," Santino said scathingly. "We can turn to clear the wedge, lock them in for CIC, and be back on our original heading before they even notice!"

Del Conte opened his mouth to continue the argument, and then shut it with a click. There was obviously no point, and it was even remotely possible that Santino was right and that the contact would never notice such a brief course change. But if the contact had them on a gravitic sensor which wasn't obstructed by a wedge, then *War Maiden* was at least nine or ten light-minutes inside its sensor range. At that range, even a brief change in heading would be glaringly obvious to any regular warship's tactical crew. Of course, if these were your typical run-of-the-mill pirates, then Santino could just possibly get away with it without anyone's noticing. It was unlikely, but it *was* possible.

And if the asshole blows it, at least my *hands will be clean. I did my level best to keep him from screwing up by the numbers, and the voice logs will show it. So screw you,* Lieutenant!

The senior chief gazed into the lieutenant's eyes for five more endless seconds while he fought with himself. His stubborn sense of duty pulled one way, urging him to make one more try to salvage the situation, but everything else pushed him the other way, and in the end, he turned his chair back to face his own panel without another word.

Santino grunted in satisfaction, and returned his own attention to the helmsman.

"Execute the helm order, Coxswain!" he said crisply.

The helmsman acknowledged the order, *War Maiden* rolled up on her side and swung ever so briefly off her original track, and her broadside sensor arrays nailed the contact instantly.

Just in time to see it execute a sharp course change of its own and accelerate madly away from the "freighter" which had just cleared its wedge.

❖   ❖   ❖

"I cannot *believe* this . . . this . . . this . . ."

Commander Abner Layson shook his head, uncertain whether he was more stunned or furious, and Captain Bachfisch grunted in irate agreement. The two of them sat in the captain's day cabin, the hatch firmly closed behind them, and the display on the captain's desk held a duplicate of Francine Alcott's plot imagery, frozen at the moment the pirate which the entire ship's company had worked so long and so hard to lure into a trap went streaking away.

"I knew he was an idiot," the commander went on after a moment in a marginally less disgusted voice, "but I figured he had to at least be able to carry out standing orders that had been explained in detail to every officer aboard."

"I agree," Bachfisch said, but then he sighed and leaned back in his chair. "I agree," he repeated more wearily, "but I can also see exactly what happened."

"Excuse me, Sir, but what *happened* was that the officer of the watch completely failed to obey your standing order to inform you immediately upon the detection of a potential hostile unit. Worse, on his own authority, he undertook to execute a maneuver which was a dead giveaway of the fact that we're a warship, with predictable results!"

"Agreed, but you know as well as I do that he did it because he knows both of us are just waiting for him to step far enough out of line that we can cut him right off at the knees."

"Well, he just gave us all the ammunition we need to do just that," Layson pointed out grimly.

"I suppose he did," Bachfisch said, massaging his eyelids with the tips of his fingers. "Of course, I also suppose it's possible his career will survive even this, depending on who his patrons are back home. And

I hate to admit it, but if I were one of those patrons, I might just argue to BuPers that his actions, however regrettable, were the predictable result of the climate of hostility which you and I created for Lieutenant Santino when we arbitrarily relieved him of his duties as OCTO."

"With all due respect, Sir, that's bullshit, and you know it."

"Of course I know it. At the same time, there's a tiny element of truth in it, since you and I certainly are hostile to him. You *are* hostile towards him, aren't you, Abner?"

"Damn right I am," Layson said, then snorted as the captain grinned at him. "All right, all right, Sir. I take your point. All we can do is write it up the way we saw it and hope that The Powers That Be back home agree with us. But in the meantime, we have to decide what we're going to do about him. I certainly don't want him standing any more watches unsupervised!"

"Neither do I. For that matter, I don't want him at Tactical, even if he's just backing up Janice. Bad enough that the man is a fool, but now his own people are helping him cut his own throat!"

"Noticed that, did you, Sir?"

"Please, Abner! I'm still a few years shy of senile. Del Conte knew exactly what would happen."

"I think that may be putting it just a bit strongly, Sir," Layson said cautiously. He'd hoped without much confidence that the captain might not have noticed the senior chief's obvious decision to shut his mouth and stop arguing with his superior. "I mean," the exec went on, "Santino specifically ordered him to—"

"Oh, come on, Abner! Del Conte is an experienced man, and he damned well shouldn't have let the fact that his superior officer is an unmitigated ass push him into letting that officer blow the tactical situation all to hell, no matter how pissed off he might've been or how justified he was to be that way. You know it, I know it, and I expect you to make very certain that Senior Chief Del Conte knows that we do and that if he *ever* lets something like this happen again I will personally tear him a new asshole. I trust that I've made my feelings on this matter clear?"

"I think you might say that, Sir."

"Good," Bachfisch grunted, but then he waved a hand in a dismissive gesture. "But once you've made that clear to him—and once you're sure that you have—that's the end of it." He pretended not to notice the very slight relaxation of Layson's shoulders. "He shouldn't have let it happen, but you're right; he did exactly what his superior officer ordered him to do. Which is the problem. When a noncom of Del Conte's seniority deliberately lets his officer shoot his own foot off that spectacularly, that officer's usefulness is exactly nil. And it's also the most damning condemnation possible. Even if I weren't afraid that something like this might happen again, I don't want any King's officer who can drive his own personnel to a reaction like that in my ship or anywhere near her."

"I don't blame you, Sir. And I don't want him in *War Maiden*, either. But we're stuck with him."

"Oh, no, we're not," Bachfisch said grimly. "We still haven't sent *Gryphon's Pride* home. I believe that Lieutenant Santino has just earned himself a berth as her prize master."

Layson's eyes widened, and he started to open his mouth, then stopped. There were two reasons for a captain to assign one of his officers to command a prize ship. One was to reward that officer by giving him a shot at the sort of independent command which might bring him to the notice of the Lords of Admiralty. The other was for the captain to rid himself of someone whose competence he distrusted. Layson doubted that anyone could possibly fail to understand which reason was operating in this case, and he certainly couldn't fault Bachfisch's obvious determination to rid himself of Santino. But as *War Maiden's* executive officer, the possibility presented him with a definite problem.

"Excuse me, Sir," the exec said after a moment, "but however weak he may be as a tac officer, he's the only assistant Janice has. If we send him away . . ."

He let his voice trail off, and Bachfisch nodded. Ideally, *War Maiden* should have carried two assistant tactical officers. Under normal circumstances, Hirake would have had both Santino and a junior-grade lieutenant or an ensign to back him up. The chronic shorthandedness of the expanding Manticoran Navy had caught the captain's ship short this time, and he drummed his fingers on his desktop while he considered his options. None of them were especially palatable, but—

"I don't care about shorthandedness," he said. "Not if it means keeping Santino aboard. Janice will just have to manage without him."

"But, Sir—" Layson began almost desperately, only to break off as Bachfisch raised a hand.

"He's gone, Abner," he said, and he spoke in the captain's voice that cut off all debate. "That part of the decision is already made."

"Yes, Sir," Layson said, and Bachfisch relented sufficiently to show him a small smile of sympathy.

"I know this is going to be a pain in the ass for you in some ways, Abner, and I'm sorry for that. But what you need to do is concentrate on how nice it will be to have Elvis Santino a hundred light-years away from us and then figure out a way to work around the hole."

"I'll try to bear that in mind, Sir. Ah, would the Captain care to suggest a way in which that particular hole might be worked around?"

"Actually, and bearing in mind an earlier conversation of ours, I believe I do," Bachfisch told him. "I would suggest that we seriously consider promoting Ms. Midshipwoman Harrington to the position of acting assistant tactical officer."

"Are you sure about that, Sir?" Layson asked. The captain raised an eyebrow at him, and the exec shrugged. "She's worked out very well so far, Sir. But she *is* a snotty."

"I agree that she's short on experience," Bachfisch replied. "That's why we send middies on their snotty cruises in the first place, after all. But I believe she's clearly demonstrated that she has the raw ability to handle the assistant tac officer's slot, and she's certainly a lot brighter and more reliable than Santino ever was."

"I can't argue with any of that, Sir. But since you've mentioned our conversation, remember what you said then about North Hollow and his clique. If they really did pull strings to put Santino aboard as OCTO and you not only relieve him of that duty, but then heave him completely off your bridge, and then take the midshipwoman they probably put him here specifically to get and put her into *his* slot—" He shook his head.

"You're right. That *will* piss them off, won't it?" Bachfisch murmured cheerfully.

"What it may do," Layson said in an exasperated

tone, "is put *you* right beside her on their enemies list, Sir."

"Well, if it does, I could be in a lot worse company, couldn't I? And whether that happens or not doesn't really have any bearing on the specific problem which you and I have to solve right here and right now. So putting aside all other considerations, is there anyone in the ship's company who you think would be better qualified as an acting assistant tactical officer than Harrington would?"

"Of course there isn't. I'm not sure that putting her into the slot will be easy to justify if BuPers decides to get nasty about it—or not on paper, at least—but there's no question in my mind that she's the best choice, taken strictly on the basis of her merits. Which, I hasten to add, doesn't mean that I won't make sure that Janice rides very close herd on her. Or that I won't be doing exactly the same thing myself, for that matter."

"Excellent!" This time there was nothing small about Bachfisch's huge grin. "And while you're thinking about all the extra work this is going to make for you and Janice, think about how Harrington is going to feel when she finds out what sort of responsibility we're dumping on her! I think it will be rather informative to see just how panicked she gets when you break the word to her. And just to be sure that she doesn't get a swelled head about her temporary elevation over her fellow snotties, you might point out to her that while the exigencies of the King's service require that she assume those additional responsibilities, we can hardly excuse her from her training duties."

"You mean—?" Layson's eyes began to dance, and Bachfisch nodded cheerfully.

"Exactly, Commander. You and Janice will have to

keep a close eye on her, but I feel that we should regard that not as an additional onerous responsibility, but rather as an *opportunity*. Consider it a chance to give her a personal tutorial in the fine art of ship-to-ship tactics and all the thousand and one ways in which devious enemies can surprise, bedevil, and defeat even the finest tactical officer. Really throw yourself into designing the very best possible training simulations for her. And be sure you tell her about all the extra effort you and Janice will be making on her behalf."

"That's evil, Sir," Layson said admiringly.

"I am shocked—*shocked*—that you could even think such a thing, Commander Layson!"

"Of course you are, Sir."

"Well, I suppose 'shocked' might be putting it just a tiny bit strongly," Bachfisch conceded. "But, seriously, Abner, I do want to take the opportunity to see how hard and how far we can push her. I think Raoul might just have been right when he told me how good he thought she could become, so let's see if we can't get her started on the right foot."

"Certainly, Sir. And I do believe that I'd like to see how far and how fast she can go, too. Not, of course," he smiled at his captain, "that I expect her to appreciate all of the effort and sacrifices Janice and I will be making when we devote our time to designing special sims just for her."

"Of course she won't. She *is* on her snotty cruise, Abner! But if she begins to exhaust your and Janice's inventiveness, let me know. I'd be happy to put together one or two modest little simulations for her myself."

"Oh, I'm sure she'll appreciate *that*, Sir."

✧   ✧   ✧

"It looks like you're right, Sir," Commander Basil Amami said. His dark-complexioned face was alight with enthusiasm, and Obrad Bajkusa forced himself to bite his tongue firmly. Amami was a more than competent officer. He also happened to be senior to Bajkusa, but only by a few months. Under other circumstances, Bajkusa would have been more than willing to debate Amami's conclusions, and especially to have tried to abate the other officer's obvious enthusiasm. Unfortunately, Amami was also Commodore Dunecki's executive officer. It was Bajkusa's personal opinion that one major reason for Amami's present position was that he idolized Dunecki. Bajkusa didn't think Dunecki had set out to find himself a sycophant—or not deliberately and knowingly, at any rate—but Amami's very competence tended to keep people, Dunecki included, from wondering whether there was any other reason for his assignment. Perhaps the fact that his XO *always* seemed to agree with him should have sounded a warning signal for an officer as experienced as Dunecki, but it hadn't, and over the long months that Dunecki and Amami had served together, the commodore had developed an almost paternal attitude towards the younger man.

Whatever the internal dynamics of their relationship, Bajkusa had long since noticed that they had a tendency to double-team anyone who disagreed with or opposed them. Again, that was scarcely something which anyone could legitimately object to, since the two of them were supposed to be a mutually supporting command team, but it was clear to Bajkusa in this case that Amami's statement of agreement with Dunecki only reinforced the conclusion which the commodore had already reached on his own. Which meant that no mere commander in his right mind was going to argue with them both, however tenuous he might think the evidence for their conclusion was.

"Perhaps I was right, and perhaps I wasn't," Dunecki told Amami, but his cautionary note seemed more pro forma than genuine, Bajkusa thought. The commodore nodded in Bajkusa's direction. "*Javelin* did well, Captain," he said. "I appreciate your effort, and I'd like you to tell your entire ship's company that, as well."

"Thank you, Sir," Bajkusa replied. Then he decided to see if he couldn't interject a small note of caution of his own into the discussion. Indirectly, of course. "It was a closer thing than the raw log chips might indicate, though, Sir. Their EW was very good. We'd closed to just a little over two light-minutes, and I didn't even have a clue that they were a warship until they cleared their wedge. I was holding my overtake down mainly because I didn't want to attract anyone else's attention, but it never even occurred to me that the 'merchie' I was closing in on was a damned cruiser!"

"I can certainly understand why that would have been a shock," Dunecki agreed wryly.

"Especially in a system the damned Manties are hanging on to so tightly," Amami put in, and Bajkusa nodded sharply.

"That was my own thought," he said. "It's not like the Manties to invite a Confed cruiser in to keep an eye on their interests. It's usually the other way around," he added, watching the commodore carefully out of the corner of one eye. Dunecki frowned, and for just a moment the commander hoped that his superior was considering the thing that worried him, but then Dunecki shrugged.

"No, it's not," he acknowledged. "But your sensor

readings make it fairly clear that it was either an awfully big light cruiser or decidedly on the small size for a heavy. God knows the Confeds have such a collection of odds and sods that they could have sent just about anything in to watch Melchor, but the Manties don't have any light cruisers that come close to the tonnage range your tac people suggest, and they've been retiring their older heavy cruisers steadily since they started their buildup. They can't have very many this small left in their inventory. Besides, no Manty would be as clumsy—or as stupid—as this fellow was! Clearing his wedge at barely two light-minutes after all the trouble they'd gone to convince you that they were a freighter in the first place?" The commodore shook his head. "I've encountered a lot of Manty officers, Commander, and none of them was dumb enough to do that against something as small and fast as a frigate."

Bajkusa wanted to continue the debate, if that was really what it was, but he had to admit that Dunecki had a point. A rather sizable one, in fact. Much as he loved *Javelin*, Bajkusa was perfectly well aware why no major naval power was still building frigates and why those navies which had them were retiring them steadily. They were the smallest class of hyper-capable warship, with a tonnage which fell about midway between a dispatch boat and a destroyer, and that gave them precious little room to pack in weapons. Indeed, *Javelin* was only a very little more heavily armed than a light attack craft, although her missiles had somewhat more range and she did have *some* magazine capacity, and she and her ilk no longer had any true viable purpose except to serve as remote reconnaissance platforms. Even that was being taken away from them by improvements in the remote sensor drones most navies regularly employed, and Bajkusa strongly suspected that the frigates' last stand would be as cheap, very light escorts to run down even lighter pirates . . . or as commerce raiders (or pirates) in their own right.

So, yes, Commodore Dunecki had a point. What Manticoran cruiser captain in his right mind would have let *anything* get that close without detection. And if he had detected *Javelin* on her way in, then why in Heaven's name clear his wedge before he had her into engagement range? It certainly couldn't have been because he was afraid of the outcome!

"No," Dunecki said with another shake of his head. "Whoever this joker is, he's no Manty, and we know for a fact that no Andermani ships would be in Melchor under present conditions, so that really only leaves one thing he could be, doesn't it? Which means that he's in exactly the right place for our purposes. And as small as he is, there's no way he can match *Annika*'s weight of metal."

"Absolutely, Sir!" Amami enthused.

"But he may not be there for long," Dunecki mused aloud, "and I'd hate to let him get away—or, even worse—find out that Wegener is worried enough about keeping an eye on his investment that he doubles up on his picket there and comes up with something that could give us a real fight. That means we have to move quickly, but we also need to be sure we coordinate properly, Commander Bajkusa. So I think that while I take *Annika* to Melchor to check on the situation, I'm going to send you and *Javelin* off to Lutrell. If my brother's kept to the schedule he sent me in his last dispatch, you should find *Astrid* there. He'll probably send you on to Prism with his own dispatches, but emphasize to him that by the time he hears from you our good friend the Governor is about to find himself short one cruiser."

He smiled thinly, and Bajkusa smiled back, because on that point at least, he had complete and total faith in Dunecki's judgment.

Honor dragged herself wearily through the hatch and collapsed facedown on her bunk with a heartfelt groan. Nimitz leapt from her shoulder at the last moment and landed on the pillow where he turned to regard her with a reproving flirt of his tail. She paid him no attention at all, and he bleeked a quiet laugh and curled down beside her to rest his nose gently in the short-cropped, silky fuzz of her hair.

"Keeping us out late, I see, Ma'am," a voice observed brightly, and Honor turned her head without ever lifting it completely off the pillow. She lay with it under her right cheek and turned a slightly bloodshot and profoundly disapproving eye upon Audrey Bradlaugh.

"I'm pleased to see that *someone* finds the situation amusing," she observed, and Audrey chuckled.

"Oh, no, Honor! It's not that someone finds it amusing—it's that the entire ship's *company* does! And it's such an appropriate . . . resolution, too. I mean, after all, it was you and Del Conte between you who got rid of that asshole Santino in the first place, so it's only appropriate that the two of you should wind up on the same watch doing his job. Much better than he did, I might add. Of course, it is kind of entertaining to watch the Captain and Commander Layson—not to mention Commander Hirake—kicking your poor, innocent butt in the simulator every day. Not, of course, that I would for one moment allow the fact that you systematically annihilated Nassios and me in that sim last week—or me and Basanta last Tuesday, now that I think about it—to affect my judgment in any way."

"You are a vile and disgusting person," Honor informed her, "and God will punish you for abusing me in this fashion when I am too weak and exhausted to properly defend myself."

"Sure He will," Audrey replied. "As soon as He stops laughing, anyway!"

Honor made a rude sound and then closed her eyes and buried her face in the pillow once more. She was relieved that Audrey and the other middies had decided to take her acting promotion without jealousy, but there was an unfortunate edge of accuracy to Audrey's teasing. More than one edge, in fact.

Honor had been more than a little appalled when Commander Layson called her into his day cabin to inform her that the Captain had decided to elevate her to the position of acting assistant tactical officer. However good a tactician she might consider herself as a midshipwoman, and however exciting the notion of such a promotion might be, there was no way in the universe that she could consider herself ready to assume the duties of such a position. Nor had the Exec's blunt explanation of the situation which had impelled Captain Bachfisch to elevate her to such heights done much for her ego. It wasn't so much that Commander Layson had said anything at all unreasonable, as it was that his analysis had made it perfectly plain that the Captain had had no one else at all to put into the slot. If they *had* had anyone else, the Exec had made clear enough, then that someone else would undoubtedly have been chosen. But since Ms. Midshipwoman Harrington was all they had, she would have to do.

And just to see to it that she did, Commander
Layson had informed her with an air of bland gen-
erosity, he, Commander Hirake, and the Captain himself would be only too happy to help her master her
new duties.

She'd thanked him, of course. There was very little
else that she could have done, whatever she'd sensed
waiting in her future. Nor had her trepidation proved
ill founded. None of them was quite as naturally
fiendish as Captain Courvoisier, but Captain
Courvoisier had been the head of the entire Saganami
Island Tactical Department. He hadn't begun to have
the amount of time that Honor's trio of new instructors had, and he'd certainly never been able to devote
his entire attention to a single unfortunate victim at
a time.

As Audrey had just suggested, Honor wasn't used
to losing in tactical exercises. In fact, she admitted to
herself, she had become somewhat smugly accustomed
to beating the stuffing out of other people, and the
string of salutary drubbings the tactical trinity of HMS
War Maiden had administered to her had been a chas-
tening experience. Just as they had been intended to
be. Nor had her lordly new elevation altered the fact
that this remained her snotty cruise. When she took
her tac watch on the bridge (although, thank God, no
one was prepared to even suggest that she be given
the *bridge* watch itself!) she was indeed the ship's duty
tactical officer. But when she was off watch, she was
still Ms. Midshipwoman Harrington, and no one had
seen fit to excuse her from all of the other "learning
experiences" which had been the lot of RMN snotties
since time out of mind.

All of which meant that she was running even
harder now than she had during her final form at

Saganami Island. Which seemed dreadfully unfair, given how much smaller a campus *War Maiden* was!

"You really are bushed, aren't you?" Audrey asked after a moment, and the amusement in her voice had eased back a notch.

"No," Honor said judiciously. " 'Bushed' is far too pale and anemic a word for what I am."

She was only half-joking, and it showed.

"Well, in that case, why don't you just kick off your boots and stay where you are for a while?"

"No way," Honor said, opening her eyes once more. "We've got quarters inspection in less than four hours!"

"So we do," Audrey agreed. "But you and Nassios covered my posterior with Lieutenant Saunders on that charting problem yesterday, so I guess the three of us could let you get a few hours of shut-eye while we tidy up. It's not like your locker's a disaster area, you know."

"But—" Honor began.

"Shut up and take your nap," Audrey told her firmly, and Nimitz bleeked in soft but equally firm agreement from beside her head. Honor considered protesting further, but not for very long. She'd already argued long enough to satisfy the requirements of honor, and she was too darned exhausted to be any more noble than she absolutely had to.

"Thanks," she said sleepily, and she was already asleep before Audrey could reply.

"There she is, Sir," Commander Amami said. "Just as you expected."

"There we *think* she is," Anders Dunecki corrected meticulously. Whatever Bajkusa might have thought, the commodore was far from blind to Amami's tendency to accept his own theories uncritically, and he made a conscious effort to keep that in mind at times like this. "She could still be a legitimate merchantman," he added, and Amami rubbed gently at his lower lip in thought.

"She is on the right course for one of the Dillingham supply ships, Sir," he conceded after a moment. "But according to our intelligence packet, there shouldn't be another Dillingham ship in here for at least another month, and there really isn't a lot of other shipping to the system these days."

"True," Dunecki agreed. "But the flip side of that argument is that if there isn't much other shipping in the first place, then the odds are greater that any additional merchies that come calling are going to slip through without our intelligence people warning us they're on their way."

"Point taken, Sir," Amami acknowledged. "So how do you want to handle this?"

"Exactly as we planned from the beginning," Dunecki said. "I pointed out that this *could* be a merchantman, not that I really believed that it was one. And it doesn't matter if it is, after all. If we treat it as a Confed cruiser from the outset, then all we'll really do if it turns out to be a merchie is to waste a little caution on it. But if it turns out to be a cruiser and we assume otherwise, the surprise would be on the other foot. So we'll just close in on the contact all fat and happy—and dumb. We won't suspect a thing until it's got us exactly where it wants us."

He looked up from his plot to meet Amami's eyes, and their thin, shark-like smiles were in perfect agreement.

❖   ❖   ❖

"The contact is still closing, Sir," Lieutenant Commander Hirake reported from the com screen at Captain Bachfisch's elbow.

War Maiden's senior tactical officer was once again in Auxiliary Control with Commander Layson, but Honor was on the command deck. She would have liked to think that she was there while the lieutenant commander was in AuxCon because the Captain had so much faith in her abilities. Unfortunately, she knew it was exactly the other way around. He wanted her under his own eye, and if something happened to the bridge, he wanted to be sure that Layson would have the more experienced tactical officer to back him up.

"I noticed that myself," Bachfisch replied to Hirake with a small smile. "May I assume that your latest report is a tactful effort to draw to my attention the fact that the contact seems to be an awfully large and powerful 'pirate'?"

"Something of the sort, Sir," Hirake said with an answering smile, but there was a hint of genuine concern in her expression. "According to CIC, she outmasses us by at least sixty thousand tons."

"So she does," Bachfisch agreed. "But she obviously doesn't know that we aren't just another freighter waiting for her to snap us up. Besides, if she were a Peep or an Andy, I'd be worried by her tonnage advantage. But no regular man-of-war would be closing in on a merchie this way, so that means whoever we have out there is a raider. That makes her either a straight pirate or a privateer, and neither of them is likely to have a crew that can match our people. Don't worry, Janice. I won't get cocky or take anything for granted, but I'm not scared of anything short of an Andy that size—certainly not of anything armed with the kind of crap available from the tech base here in the Confederacy! Anyway, pirates and privateers are what we're out here to deal with, so let's be about it."

"As you say, Sir," Hirake replied, and Honor hid a smile as she gazed down at her own plot. The lieutenant commander had done her job by reminding her captain (however tactfully) of the enemy's size and potential firepower, but the confidence in her voice matched that of the Captain perfectly. And rightly so, Honor concluded. The contact closing so confidently upon them obviously didn't have a clue of what it was actually pursuing, or it would have come in far more cautiously.

"Captain, I have a hail from the contact," Lieutenant Sauchuk reported suddenly.

"Oh?" Bachfisch arched one eyebrow. "Put it on the main screen and let's hear what he has to say, Yuri."

"Aye, aye, Sir."

All eyes on *War Maiden*'s bridge flipped to the main com screen as a man in the uniform of the Silesian Confederacy's navy appeared on it.

"*Sylvan Grove*," he said, addressing them by the name of the Hauptman Cartel freighter whose transponder ID codes they had borrowed for their deception, "this is Captain Denby of the Confederate Navy. Please maintain your present course and attitude while my ship makes rendezvous with you."

"Oh, of *course* you are," Honor heard Senior Chief Del Conte murmur all but inaudibly behind her.

"I think we owe the good captain a reply, Yuri," Bachfisch said after a moment. "Double-check your filters, and then give me a live pickup."

"Aye, aye, Sir," Sauchuk replied. He checked the settings on his panel carefully, then nodded. "You're live, Skipper," he said.

"Captain Denby, I'm Captain Bullard," Bachfisch said, and Honor knew that *War Maiden*'s computers were altering his image to put him into a merchant officer's uniform, rather than the black and gold of the RMN, just as the raider's computers had put *him* into Confed naval uniform. "I hope you won't take this the wrong way," Bachfisch went on, "but this isn't exactly the safest neighborhood around. It's not that I don't believe you're who you say you are, but could I ask just why it is that you want to rendezvous with us?"

"Of course, Captain Bullard," the face on his com screen replied in the slightly stiff tone of an officer who didn't particularly like to be reminded by a mere merchant skipper of how pathetic his navy's record for maintaining order within its own borders was. "I have aboard seventeen of your nationals, the survivors from the crews of two Manticoran freighters. We took out the 'privateer' who captured their ships last week, and it seemed to me that the fastest way to repatriate them would be to turn them over to the Dillingham manager here in Melchor."

"I see," Bachfisch replied in a much warmer and less wary voice. He felt a brief flicker of something almost like admiration for "Captain Denby's" smoothness, for the other man had come up with what was actually a plausible reason for a merchantman here in Silesia to allow a warship to close with it. And "Denby" had delivered his lines perfectly, with just the right note of offended dignity coupled with a "see there" sort of flourish. "In that case, Captain," he went on, "of course we'll maintain heading and deceleration for rendezvous."

"Thank you, Captain Bullard," the man on his com screen said. "Denby out."

❖   ❖   ❖

"Considerate of them to let us maintain course," Janice Hirake observed to Abner Layson.

"He doesn't have much choice if he's going to keep us dumb and happy," Layson pointed out, and Hirake nodded. Warships could pull far higher accelerations than any huge whale of a merchantman, and it was traditional for them to be the ones who maneuvered to match heading and velocity in the case of a deep space rendezvous.

"Still, it's handy that he came in so far above the plane of the ecliptic. Keeps him well above us and on the wrong side of our wedge."

"Somehow I doubt that they arranged things that way just to oblige us," Layson said dryly. "On the other hand, sneaking up on somebody *can* sometimes put you in a less than optimal position yourself, can't it?"

"Indeed it can," Hirake said with a small, wicked smile.

"I wish we had a little better sensor angle on them, Sir," Lieutenant Quinn muttered from one side of his mouth, and Lieutenant Commander Acedo glanced at him. Acedo was *Annika*'s tactical officer, and Quinn was the most junior commissioned member of his department. But the younger man had a nose for trouble which Acedo had learned to trust, or at least listen very carefully to.

"I'd like to have a better look at them myself," the lieutenant commander replied. "But thanks to *Javelin*, we've already got a pretty good notion of what we're up against. At this point, I have to agree with the Commodore—it's more important to keep him guessing about us by avoiding the deeper parts of his sensor well. Besides, the fact that he's got his wedge between him and *our* sensors should help keep him confident that we don't know that he's a warship, too."

"I can't argue with that, Sir," Quinn acknowledged. "I guess I just want the best of both worlds, and sometimes you just can't have that."

"No, you can't," Acedo agreed. "But sometimes you can come pretty close, and the way the Old Man's set this one up qualifies for that."

Two cruisers slid inexorably together, each convinced that she knew precisely what the other one was and that the other one didn't know what *she* was . . . and both of them wrong. The distance between them fell steadily, and *Annika's* deceleration reduced the velocity differential with matching steadiness.

"Zero-zero interception in five minutes, Sir," Honor announced. Her soprano sounded much calmer in her own ears than it felt from behind her eyes, and she raised her head to look across the bridge at the Captain. "Current range is two-one-six k-klicks and present overtake is one-three-three-one KPS squared. Deceleration is holding steady at four-five-zero gravities."

"Thank you, Tactical," Bachfisch replied, and his calm, composed tone did more than she would have believed possible to still the excitement jittering down her nerves. The fact that their sensors still had not had a single clear look at the contact made her nervous, but she took herself firmly to task. This, too, she thought was a part of the art of command. For all of his calm, the Captain actually *knew* no more about the contact than Honor herself, but it was his job to exude the sort of confidence his people needed from him at this moment. Captain Courvoisier had stressed more than once that even if she was wrong—or perhaps *especially* if she was wrong—a commanding officer must never forget her "command face." Nothing could destroy a crew's cohesion faster than panic, and nothing produced panic better than the suggestion that the CO had lost her own confidence. But it had to be harder than usual, this time. The raider was well within effective energy range already, and just as *War Maiden's* own crew, her people must be ready to open fire in a heartbeat. At such short range, an energy weapon duel would be deadly, which would be good . . . for whoever fired first.

Of course, the raider was expecting only an unarmed merchantship. However prepared they thought they were, the sheer surprise of finding themselves suddenly broadside-to-broadside with a King's ship was bound to shock and confuse them at least momentarily. And it was entirely possible that they wouldn't even have closed up all of their weapons crews simply to deal with a "merchantman."

"Stand ready, Mr. Saunders," the Captain said calmly. "Prepare to alter course zero-nine-zero degrees to starboard and roll port at one hundred ten thousand kilometers."

"Aye, aye, Sir," Lieutenant Saunders acknowledged. "Standing by to alter course zero-nine-zero degrees to starboard and roll port at range of one hundred ten thousand kilometers."

"Stand by to fire on my command, Ms. Harrington," Bachfisch added.

"Aye, aye, Sir. Standing by to fire on your command."

"Get ready, Commander Acedo," Anders Dunecki said quietly. "At this range he won't risk challenging us or screwing around demanding we surrender, so neither will we. The instant he rolls ship to clear his wedge, blow his ass out of space."

"Yes, Sir!" Acedo agreed with a ferocious grin, and he felt just as confident as he looked. The other ship would have the advantage of knowing when she intended to alter course, but *Annika* had an even greater advantage. The commander of the enemy cruiser had to be completely confident that he had *Annika* fooled, or he would never have allowed her to come this close, and the only thing more devastating than the surprise of an ambush was the surprise of an ambusher when his intended victim turned out not to have been surprised at all.

"Coming up on one hundred ten thousand kilometers, Sir!"

"Execute your helm order, Mr. Saunders!" Thomas Bachfisch snapped.

"Aye, aye, Sir!"

War Maiden responded instantly to her helm, pivoting sharply to her right and rolling up on her left side to swing her starboard broadside up towards the raider, and Honor leaned forward, pulse hammering, mouth dry, as the icons on her plot flashed before her. It almost seemed as if it were the raider who had suddenly altered course and position as the strobing amber circle of target acquisition reached out to engulf its blood-red bead.

"Stand by, Ms. Harrington!"

"Standing by, aye, Sir."

The amber circle reached the glowing bead of the contact and flashed over to sudden crimson, and Honor's hand hovered above the firing key.

"*Fire!*"

❖   ❖   ❖

Both ships fired in the same instant across barely a third of a light-second.

At such a short range, their grasers and lasers blasted straight through any sidewall any cruiser could have generated, and alarms screamed as deadly, focused energy ripped huge, shattered wounds through battle steel and alloy. Surprise was effectively total on both sides. Commodore Dunecki had completely deceived Captain Bachfisch into expecting *Annika* to be fatally unprepared, but despite his discussion with Commander Bajkusa, Dunecki had never seriously considered for a moment that *War Maiden* might be anything except a Silesian warship. He was totally unprepared to find himself suddenly face to face with a *Manticoran* heavy cruiser. *War Maiden*'s tautly trained crew were head and shoulders above any SN ship's company in training and efficiency. They got off their first broadside two full seconds before Dunecki had anticipated that they could. Worse, Silesian ships tended to be missile-heavy, optimized for long-range combat and with only relatively light energy batteries, and the sheer weight of fire smashing into his ship was a stunning surprise.

But even though Dunecki was unprepared for *War Maiden*'s furious fire, the Manticoran ship was still smaller and more lightly armed than his own. Worse, Captain Bachfisch had assumed that *Annika* was a typical pirate and anticipated at least a moment or two in which to act while "Captain Denby" adjusted to the fact that the "freighter" he was stalking had suddenly transformed itself from a house tabby to a hexapuma, and he didn't get it. It was the equivalent of a duel with submachine guns at ten paces, and both ships staggered as the deadly tide of energy sleeted into them.

✦   ✦   ✦

Honor Harrington's universe went mad.

She'd felt herself tightening internally during the long approach phase, felt the dryness of her mouth and the way her nerves seemed to quiver individually, dancing within her flesh as if they were naked harp strings plucked by an icy wind. She had been more afraid than she had ever been in her life, and not just for herself. She had won friendships aboard *War Maiden* during the long weeks of their deployment, and those friends were at risk as much as she was. And then there was Nimitz, alone in his life-support module down in Snotty Row. Her mind had shied away from the thought of what would happen to him if his module suffered battle damage . . . or if she herself died. 'Cats who had adopted humans almost invariably suicided if their humans died. She'd known that before she ever applied for Saganami Island, and it had almost made her abandon her dream of Navy service, for if she put herself in harm's way, she put *him* there, as well, and only Nimitz's fierce, obvious insistence that she pursue her dream had carried her to the Academy. Now the reality of what had been only an intellectual awareness was upon them both, and a dark and terrible fear—not of death or wounds, but of loss—was a cold iron lump at the core of her.

Those fears had flowed through her on the crest of a sudden visceral awareness that she was not immortal. That the bloody carnage of combat could claim her just as easily as any other member of *War Maiden*'s company. Despite all of her training, all of her studies, all of her lifelong interest in naval and military history, that awareness had never truly been hers until this instant. Now it was, and she had spent the slow, dragging hours as the contact gradually closed with *War Maiden* trying to prepare herself and wondering how she would respond when she knew it was no longer a simulation. That there were real human beings on the other side of that icon on her plot. People who would be doing their very best to kill her ship—and her—with real weapons . . . and whom she would be trying to kill in turn. She'd made herself face and accept that, despite her fear, and she had thought—hoped—that she was ready for whatever might happen.

She'd been wrong.

HMS *War Maiden* lurched like a galleon in a gale as the transfer energy of PSN *Annika's* fire bled into her. The big privateer carried fewer missiles and far heavier energy weapons than her counterparts in the Silesian navy, and her grasers smashed through *War Maiden's* sidewall like brimstone sledgehammers come straight from Hell. The sidewall generators did their best to bend and divert that hurricane of energy from its intended target, but four of the heavy beams struck home with demonic fury. Graser Two, Missiles Two and Four, Gravitic Two, Radar Two and Lidar Three, Missile Eight and Magazine Four, Boat Bay One and Life Support Two . . . Entire clusters of compartments and weapons bays turned venomous, bloody crimson on the damage control panel as enemy fire ripped and clawed its way towards *War Maiden's* heart. Frantic damage control reports crashed over Honor like a Sphinxian tidal bore while the ship jerked and shuddered. Damage alarms wailed and screamed, adding their voices to the cacophony raging through the heavy cruiser's compartments, and clouds of air and water vapor erupted from the gaping wounds torn suddenly through her armored skin.

"Heavy casualties in Missile Two!" Senior Chief

Del Conte barked while secondary explosions still rolled through the hull. "Graser Six reports loss of central control, and Magazine Four is open to space! We—"

He never finished his report, and Honor's entire body recoiled as a savage explosion tore through the bridge bulkhead. It reached out to the senior chief, snatching him up as casually as some cruel child would have, and tore him to pieces before her eyes. Blood and pieces of what had been a human being seemed to be *everywhere*, and a small, calm corner of her brain realized that that was because they *were* everywhere. The explosion killed at least five people outright, through blast or with deadly splinters from ruptured bulkheads, and Honor rocked back in her padded, armored chair as the wall of devastation marched through *War Maiden*'s bridge . . . and directly over the captain's chair at its center.

Captain Bachfisch just had time to bend forward and raise an arm in an instinctive effort to protect his face when the blast front struck. It hit from slightly behind into his right, and that was all that saved his life, because even as his arm rose, he whipped the chair to his left and took the main force across the armored shell of its back. But not even that was enough to fully protect him, and the force of the explosion snatched him up and hurled him against the opposite bulkhead. He bounced back with the limp, total bonelessness of unconsciousness and hit the decksole without ever having made a sound.

He was far from the only injured person on the bridge. The same explosion which blew him out of his chair threw a meter-long splinter of battle steel across the com section. It decapitated Lieutenant Sauchuk as neatly as an executioner, then hurtled onward and drove itself through Lieutenant Saunders' chest like an ax, and Honor's mind tried to retreat into some safe, sane cave as the chaos and confusion and terror for which no simulation, no lecture, could possibly have prepared her enveloped her. She heard the whistling rush of air racing for the rents in the bulkhead even through the screams and moans of the wounded, and instinct cried out for her to race across the bridge to help the hurt and unconscious helmet up in time. Yet she didn't. The trained responses her instructors at Saganami Island had hammered mercilessly into her for four long T-years overrode even her horror and the compulsion to help. She slammed her own helmet into place, but her eyes never left the panel before her, for she dared not leave her station even to help the Captain before she knew that AuxCon and Lieutenant Commander Hirake had taken over from the mangled bridge.

War Maiden's energy mounts lashed out again, with a second broadside, even as the raider fired again, as well. More death and destruction punched their way through the hull, rending and tearing, and the heavy cruiser shuddered as one hit blew straight through her after impeller ring. Half the beta nodes and two of the alphas went down instantly, and fresh alarms shrilled as a fifth of *War Maiden*'s personnel became casualties. Lieutenant Commander LaVacher was one of them, and a simultaneous hit smashed home on Damage Control Central, killing a dozen ratings and petty officers and critically wounding Lieutenant Tergesen.

War Maiden's grasers continued to hammer at her larger, more powerful—and far younger—foe, but Honor felt a fresh and even more paralyzing spike of terror as she realized that they were still firing under the preliminary fire plan which *she* had locked in under Captain Bachfisch's orders. AuxCon should have overridden and assumed command virtually instantly . . . and it hadn't.

She turned her head, peering at what had been Senior Chief Del Conte's station through the banners of smoke riding the howling gale through the shattered bulkhead, and her heart froze as her eyes picked out AuxCon on the schematic displayed there. The compartment itself appeared to be intact, but it was circled by the jagged red and white band which indicated total loss of communications. AuxCon was cut off, not only from the bridge, but from access to the ship's computers, as well.

In the time it had taken to breathe three times, *War Maiden* had been savagely maimed, and tactical command had devolved onto a twenty-year-old midshipwoman on her snotty cruise.

The bridge about her was like the vestibule of Hell. Half the command stations had been wrecked or at least blown off-line, a quarter of the bridge crew was dead or wounded, and at least three men and women who should have been at their stations were crawling frantically through the wreckage slapping helmets and skinsuit seals on unconscious crewmates. She felt the ship's wounds as if they had been inflicted upon her own body, and all in the world she wanted in that moment was to hear someone—*anyone*—tell her what to do.

But there was no one else. She was all *War Maiden* had, and she jerked her eyes back to her own plot and drew a deep breath.

"Helm, roll ninety degrees port!"

No one on that wounded, half-broken bridge, and Honor least of all, perhaps, recognized the cool, sharp soprano which cut cleanly through the chaos, but the helmsman clinging to his own sanity with his fingernails recognized the incisive bite of command.

"Rolling ninety degrees port, aye!" he barked, and HMS *War Maiden* rolled frantically, snatching her shattered starboard broadside away from the ferocity of her enemy's fire.

Something happened inside Honor Harrington in the moment that her ship rolled. The panic vanished. The fear remained, but it was suddenly a distant, unimportant thing—something which could no longer touch her, would no longer be permitted to affect her. She looked full into the face of Death, not just for her but for her entire ship and everyone aboard it, and there was no doubt in her mind that he had come for them all. Yet her fear had transmuted into something else entirely. A cold, focused purpose that sang in her blood and bone. Her almond eyes stared into Death's empty sockets, and her soul bared its teeth and snarled defiance.

"Port broadside stand by for Fire Plan Delta Seven," that soprano rapier commanded, and confirmations raced back from *War Maiden's* undamaged broadside even as *Annika's* fire continued to hammer harmlessly at the impenetrable belly of her wedge.

Honor's mind raced with cold, icy precision. Her first instinct was to break off, for she knew only too well how brutally wounded her ship was. Worse, she already knew that their opponent was far more powerful—and better crewed—than anyone aboard *War Maiden* had believed she could be. Yet those very factors were what made flight impossible. The velocity differential between the two ships was less than six hundred kilometers per second, and with half her after impeller ring down, *War Maiden* could never hope to pull away from her unlamed foe. Even had her drive been unimpaired, the effort to break off would undoubtedly have proved suicidal as it exposed the after aspect of her impeller wedge to the enemy's raking fire.

No, she thought coldly. Flight was not an option, and her gloved fingers raced across the tactical panel, locking in new commands as she reached out for her ship's—*her* ship's—only hope of survival.

"Helm, stand by to alter course one-three-five degrees to starboard, forty degree nose-down skew, and roll starboard on my command!"

"Aye, aye, Ma'am!"

"All weapons crews," that voice she could not quite recognize even now went on, carrying a calm and a confidence that stilled incipient panic like a magic wand, "stand by to engage as programmed. Transmitting manual firing commands now."

She punched a button, and the targeting parameters she had locked into the main computers spilled into the secondary on-mount computers of her waiting weapons crews. If fresh damage cut her command links to them, at least they would know what she intended for them to do.

Then it was done, and she sat back in her command chair, watching the enemy's icon as it continued to angle sharply in to intercept *War Maiden*'s base track. The range was down to fifty-two thousand kilometers, falling at five hundred and six kilometers per second, and she waited tautly while the blood-red icon of her enemy closed upon her ship.

Commodore Anders Dunecki cursed vilely as the other cruiser snapped up on its side. He'd hurt that ship—hurt it badly—and he knew it. But it had also hurt him far more badly than he had ever allowed for. He'd gotten slack, a cold thought told him in his own viciously calm voice. He'd been fighting the Confeds too long, let his guard down and become accustomed to being able to take liberties with them. But his present opponent was no Silesian naval unit, and he cursed again, even more vilely, as he realized what that other ship truly was.

A Manty. He'd attacked a *Manty* warship, committed the one unforgivable blunder no pirate or privateer was ever allowed to commit more than once. That was why the other cruiser had managed to get off even a single shot of her own, because she was a Manty and she'd been just as ready, just as prepared to fire as he was.

And it was also why his entire strategy to win Andermani support for the Council for an Independent Prism had suddenly come crashing down in ruins. However badly the People's Republic might have distracted the Manticoran government, the RMN's response to what had happened here was as certain as the energy death of the universe.

But only if they know who did it, his racing brain told him coldly. *Only if they know which system government to send the battle squadrons after. But that ship has got to have detailed sensor records of Annika's energy signatures. If they compare those records with the Confed database, they're bound to ID us. Even if they don't get a clean hit, Wegener will know who it must have been and send them right after us. But even he won't be able to talk the Manties into hitting us without at least some supporting evidence, and the only evidence there is in the computers of that ship.*

There was only one way to prevent that data from getting out.

He turned his head to look at Commander Amami.
The exec was still listening to damage reports, but
Dunecki didn't really need them. A glance at the
master schematic showed that *Annika*'s entire port
broadside must be a mass of tangled ruin. Less than
a third of her energy mounts and missile tubes
remained intact, and her sidewall generators were at
barely forty percent efficiency. But the Manty had to
be hurt at least as badly, and she was smaller, less
able to absorb damage. Better yet, he had the overtake advantage and her impeller strength had dropped
drastically. He was bigger, newer, better armed, and
more maneuverable, and that meant the engagement
could have only one outcome.

"Roll one-eight-zero degrees to starboard and maintain heading," he told his helmsmen harshly. "Starboard broadside, stand by to fire as you bear!"

Honor watched the other ship roll. Like *War
Maiden*, the bigger ship was rotating her crippled
broadside away from her opponent's fire. But she
wasn't stopping there, and Honor let herself feel a
tiny spark of hope as the raider continued to roll, and
then the weapons of her undamaged broadside lashed
out afresh and poured a hurricane of fire upon *War
Maiden*. The belly of the Manticoran ship's impeller
wedge absorbed that fire harmlessly, but that wasn't
the point, and Honor knew it. The enemy was
sequencing her fire carefully, so that *something*
pounded the wedge continuously. If *War Maiden*
rolled back for a broadside duel, that constant pound-
ing was almost certain to catch her as she rolled,
inflicting damage and destroying at least some of her
remaining weapons before they ever got a chance to
bear upon their foe. It was a smart, merciless tactic,

one which eschewed finesse in favor of brutal prac-
ticality.

But unlike whoever was in command over there,
Honor could not afford a weapon-to-weapon battering match. Not against someone that big who had
already demonstrated her capabilities so convincingly.
And so she had no choice but to oppose overwhelming firepower with cunning.

Every fiber of her being was concentrated on the
imagery of her plot, and her lips drew back in a feral
snarl as the other ship maintained her acceleration.
Seconds ticked slowly and agonizingly past. Sixty of
them. Then seventy. Ninety.

"Helm! On my mark, give me maximum emergency
power—redline everything—and execute my previous
order!" She heard the helmsman's response, but her
eyes never flickered from her plot, and her nostrils
flared.

"Now!"

Anders Dunecki had a handful of fleeting seconds
to realize that he had made one more error. The
Manty had held her course, hiding behind the shield
of her wedge, and he'd thought that it hadn't mattered whether that arose out of panic or out of a
rational realization that she couldn't have gone toe-
to-toe with *Annika* even if she hadn't been so badly
damaged.

Yet it did matter. The other captain hadn't panicked, but he *had* realized he couldn't fight *Annika*
in a broadside duel . . . and he had no intention of
doing so.

Perhaps it wasn't really Dunecki's fault. The range
was insanely short for modern warships, dropping
towards one which could be measured in hundreds

of kilometers and not thousands, and no sane naval officer would even have contemplated engaging at such close quarters. Nor had either Dunecki or Bachfisch planned on doing any such thing, for each had expected to begin and end the battle with a single broadside which would take his enemy completely by surprise. But whatever they'd planned, their ships were here now, and no one in any navy trained its officers for combat maneuvers in such close proximity to an enemy warship. And because of that, Anders Dunecki, for all of his experience, was completely unprepared for what *War Maiden* actually did.

Strident alarms jangled as HMS *War Maiden*'s inertial compensator protested its savage abuse. More alarms howled as the load on the heavy cruiser's impeller nodes peaked forty percent beyond their "Never Exceed" levels. Despite her mangled after impeller ring, *War Maiden* slammed suddenly forward at almost five hundred and fifty gravities. Her bow swung sharply towards *Annika*, but it also dipped sharply "below" the other ship, denying the big privateer the deadly down-the-throat shot which would have spelled *War Maiden*'s inevitable doom.

Annika began a desperate turn of her own, but she had been taken too much by surprise. There wasn't enough time for her to answer her helm before *War Maiden*'s wounded charge carried her across her enemy's wake.

It wasn't the perfect up-the-kilt stern rake that was every tactical officer's dream. No neat ninety-degree crossing with every weapon firing in perfect sequence. Instead, it was a desperate, scrambling lunge—the ugly do-or-die grapple of a wounded hexapuma facing a peak bear. Honor's weapons couldn't begin to fire down the long axis of the enemy ship in a "proper" rake . . . but what they could do was enough.

Six grasers scored direct hits on the aftermost quarter of PSN *Annika*. They came in through the open after aspect of her wedge, with no sidewall to interdict or degrade them. They smashed into her armored after hammerhead, and armor shattered at their ferocious touch. They blew deep into the bigger ship's hull, maiming and smashing, crippling her after chase armament, and the entire after third of her sidewall flickered and died.

Annika fought to answer her helm, clawing around in a desperate attempt to reacquire *War Maiden* for her broadside weapons, but Honor Harrington had just discovered that she could be just as merciless a killer as Anders Dunecki. Her flying fingers stabbed a minor correction into her tactical panel, and *War Maiden* fired once more. Every graser in her surviving broadside poured a deadly torrent of energy into the gap in *Annika*'s sidewall, and the big privateer vanished in a hell-bright boil of fury.

Nimitz sat very straight and still on Honor Harrington's shoulder as she came to a halt before the Marine sentry outside the Captain's day cabin. The private gazed at her for a long, steady moment, then reached back to key the admittance signal.

"Yes?" The voice belonged to Abner Layson, not Thomas Bachfisch.

"Ms. Harrington to see the Captain, Sir!" the Marine replied crisply.

"Enter," another voice said, and the Marine stepped aside as the hatch opened. Honor nodded her thanks as she stepped past him, and for just a moment he allowed his professional nonexpression to vanish into a wink of encouragement before the hatch closed behind her once more.

Honor crossed the cabin and came to attention. Commander Layson sat behind the captain's desk, but Captain Bachfisch was also present. *War Maiden*'s CO was propped as comfortably as possible on an out-sized couch along the cabin's longest bulkhead. He looked awful, battered and bruised and with his left arm and right leg both immobilized. Under almost any other circumstances, he would still have been locked up in sickbay while Lieutenant Chiem stood over him with a pulser to keep him there if necessary. But there was no room in sickbay for anyone with non-life-threatening injuries. Basanta Lakhia was in sickbay. Nassios Makira wasn't; he'd been in After Engineering when the hit came in, and the damage control parties hadn't even found his body.

Honor stood there, facing the executive officer and her captain, and the eighteen percent of *War Maiden*'s company who had died stood silently at her shoulder, waiting.

"Stand easy, Ms. Harrington," the captain said quietly, and she let her spine relax ever so slightly. Bachfisch gazed at her for a long, quiet moment, and she returned his gaze as calmly as she could.

"I've reviewed the bridge tapes of the engagement," Bachfisch said at last, and nodded sideways at Layson. "So have the Exec and Commander Hirake. Is there anything you'd like to add to them, Ms. Harrington?"

"No, Sir," she said, and in that moment she looked more absurdly youthful even than usual as a faint flush of embarrassment stained her cheekbones, and the treecat on her shoulder cocked his head as he studied her two superiors intently.

"Nothing at all?" Bachfisch cocked his head in a

gesture that was almost a mirror image of Nimitz's, then shrugged. "Well, I don't suppose anything else is really needed. The tapes caught it all, I believe."

He fell silent for another moment, then gestured at Commander Layson with his good hand.

"Commander Layson and I asked you to come see us because of what's on those tapes, Ms. Harrington," the captain said quietly. "Obviously, *War Maiden* has no choice but to cut her deployment short and return to the Star Kingdom for repairs. Normally, that would require you to transfer to another ship for the completion of your middy cruise, which would unfortunately put you at least six T-months or even a T-year behind your classmates for seniority purposes. In this instance, however, Commander Layson and I have decided to endorse your Form S-One-Sixty to indicate successful completion of your cruise. The same endorsement will appear in the records of Midshipwoman Bradlaugh and Midshipman Lakhia. We will also so endorse Midshipman Makira's file and recommend his posthumous promotion to lieutenant (junior-grade)."

He paused once more, and Honor cleared her throat.

"Thank you, Sir. Especially for Nassios. I think I can speak for all of us in that."

"I'm sure you can," Bachfisch said. He rubbed his nose for just a moment, then surprised her with a crooked grin.

"I have no idea what's going to happen to my own career when we return to Manticore," he told her. "A lot will no doubt depend on the findings of the Board of Inquiry, but I think we can safely assume that at least a few critics are bound to emerge. And not without some justification."

It was all Honor could do not to blink in surprise at the unexpected frankness of that admission, but he went on calmly.

"I got too confident, Ms. Harrington," he said. "Too sure that what I was looking at was a typical Silesian pirate. Oh," he waved his good hand in a small, brushing-away gesture, "it's fair enough to say that we very seldom run into anyone out here, pirate or privateer, with that much firepower and that well-trained a crew. But it's a captain's job to expect the unexpected, and I didn't. I trust that you will remember that lesson when you someday command a King's ship yourself."

He paused once more, his expression clearly inviting a response, and Honor managed not to clear her throat again.

"I'll certainly try to remember, Sir," she said.

"I'm sure you will. And from your performance here in Melchor, I have every confidence that you'll succeed," Bachfisch said quietly. Then he gave himself a small shake.

"In the meantime, however, we have some practical housekeeping details to take care of. As you know, our casualties were heavy. Lieutenant Livanos will take over in Engineering, and Ensign Masters will take over Communications. We're fortunate that everyone in Auxiliary Control survived, but we're going to be very short of watch-standing qualified officers for the return to Manticore. In light of our situation, I have decided to confirm you as Assistant Tac Officer, with the acting rank of lieutenant (junior-grade) and the promotion on my own authority to the permanent rank of ensign." Honor's eyes widened, and he smiled more naturally. "Under the circumstances, I believe I can safely predict that regardless of the outcome of my own Board, this is one promotion which BuPers will definitely confirm."

"Sir, I—I don't know what to say, except, thank you," she said after a moment, and he chuckled.

"It's the very least I can do to thank you for saving my ship—and my people—Ms. Harrington. I wish I had the authority to promote you all the way to J. G., but I doubt that BuPers would sign off on that even under these circumstances. So all you'll really get is a five or six-month seniority advantage over your classmates."

"And," Commander Layson put in quietly, "I feel sure that the Service will take note of how and why you were promoted. No one who doesn't know you could have expected you to perform as you did, Ms. Harrington. Those of us who have come to know you, however, would have expected no less."

Honor's face blazed like a forest fire, and she sensed Nimitz's approval of the emotions of her superiors in the treecat's body language and the proprietary way his true hand rested on her beret.

"I expect that we've embarrassed you enough for one afternoon, Ms. Harrington." Bachfisch's voice mingled amusement, approval, and sympathy, and Honor felt her eyes snap back to him. "I will expect you and Commander Hirake to join me for dinner tonight, however, so that we can discuss the reorganization of your department. I trust that will be convenient?"

"Of course, Sir!" Honor blurted.

"Good. And I'll have Chief Stennis be sure we have a fresh supply of celery on hand."

Nimitz bleeked in amused enthusiasm from her shoulder, and she felt her own mouth curve in her first genuine smile since *Annika*'s explosion. Bachfisch saw it, and nodded in approval.

"Much better, Ensign Harrington! But now, short-handed as we are, I'm sure that there's something you ought to be doing, isn't there?"

"Yes, Sir. I'm sure there is."

"In that case, I think you should go attend to it. Let's be about it, Ensign."

"Aye, aye, Sir!" Ensign Honor Harrington replied, then snapped back to attention, turned sharply, and marched out of the captain's day cabin to face the future.

Changer of Worlds

David Weber

Branch Leaper paused midway down the long picketwood limb, and his ears went up in surprise as he tasted the first hint of the approaching mind glow.

Mind *glows*, he corrected himself as he realized two People made their unannounced way along the broad highway of branches towards him. There was something very familiar about one of the mind glows, yet Branch Leaper could not quite decide what it was. He ought to be able to, and he knew it, and yet . . .

He sat bolt upright on his rearmost pair of limbs, fluffy tail curled about his toes, and peered in the direction of the oncoming mind glows. They were very powerful, he noted respectfully, and he tasted the overlaid harmonies of a mated pair. The female glow was the stronger of the two, of course. It almost always was, and yet it had to be *very* powerful to be stronger in this case. That was what baffled him about the elusively familiar taste of the male mind glow. He ought to recognize so strong a mind glow if he had ever encountered it even briefly, yet it was as if its very strength was what made it *un*familiar. Besides, he knew all mated pairs of Bright Water Clan, and the unseen travelers were not from among them.

His whiskers twitched in perplexity. It was not unheard of for a mated pair to travel through a strange clan's territory, but good manners usually required that they warn that clan of their presence. Not that the People took such journeys amiss—except, perhaps, he admitted, during times of great famine at the very end of the cold days of a turning, when even a single pair of additional hunters might make the difference between life or death for the clan's kittens. But that was rare, and usually it was simply a matter of courtesy.

He sat a moment longer, then moved to the nearest picketwood bole and flowed smoothly up it. He found a comfortable spot in the fork of a branch and settled down to wait. The strangers were approaching quickly, and his wait should not be long.

Nor was it. The People were less concerned about measuring things like the passage of time than were the two-legged humans with whom they shared their world, but Branch Leaper judged that no more than two or three hands of the human's "minutes" could have elapsed before the pair upon whom he waited came into sight. They were moving rapidly, the male leading with the air of one completely familiar with the territory about him, and Branch Leaper's tail kinked straight up behind him as his eyes combined

with the taste of the newcomer's mind glow to bring
true recognition at last.

<*Laughs Brightly!*> he mind-called. <*We did not
know you had returned! Nor*—> his mind voice chuckled wryly, despite a genuine sense of shock <—*that
you had found a mate!*>

The male paused, as did his mate, and looked
about alertly. His eyes found Branch Leaper almost
instantly, and the Bright Water scout tasted the
matching recognition in his mind glow.

<*I know you did not know, Branch Leaper,*> he
replied, his answering mind voice laced with ironic
amusement. He made no reference to Branch
Leaper's shock, but the scout knew the other tasted
the embarrassment he had felt at revealing his astonishment. But Laughs Brightly had bonded to a human
over two hands of turnings ago, and those who had
bonded to humans almost never mated. They might
well partner temporarily when they were able to
return to their home clans' ranges, but the adoption
bond itself almost always precluded the very possibility of a true mating. True, there were very occasional exceptions to that rule, yet Branch Leaper knew
that Laughs Brightly's human was only rarely here on
the world of the People, which ought to have made
it impossible for Laughs Brightly even to *meet* a
female of the People, far less mate with one! No
wonder Branch Leaper had not recognized his mind
glow, for the possibility that Laughs Brightly might
have taken a mate since last they met had never so
much as crossed the Bright Water scout's mind.

But perhaps the fact that he had done so explained
the tremendous, unexpected power of his mind glow,
Branch Leaper mused. As Laughs Brightly and his
new mate came still closer, Branch Leaper was forced

to reduce his own sensitivity, much as if he were squinting mental eyes against a blinding light. It was almost painful, at least until he could become accustomed to it, and he felt his surprise at discovering Laughs Brightly had mated fading into sheer awe as the power of those fused mind glows washed over him. Those who bonded to the humans normally found their mind voices strengthened at least as greatly as those who found mates among the People, but Branch Leaper had never come within mind voice range of any of the People who had established *both* bondings!

Or not, at least, until today.

<*Forgive me, older brother,*> Branch Leaper said contritely after a moment. <*I did not mean to seem so surprised. It was simply that I thought you off-world with Dances on Clouds. It did not occur to me that you might meet another of the People.*>

<*Or that one who has bonded to a human would take a mate, either, younger brother,*> Laughs Brightly replied wryly. <*Well, I suppose I should not blame you for that. I certainly never thought that I would mate, and even if the thought had come to me, I would have assumed I would find a female who could stand me only here upon our own world. But—*> He flipped his ears ironically, and Branch Leaper felt himself bleeking a soft laugh at the rich humor of that powerful mind voice.

<*But I have forgotten the courtesy Swift Darter pounded into me as a kitten,*> the scout said after a moment, his mind glow contrite as he turned to Laughs Brightly's new mate. <*Welcome to Bright Water's range,*> he told his new sister. <*May you hunt well and often among us, sister-of-choice.*>

<*Thanks to you who greets me, younger brother,*>

she replied with exquisite formality, and, despite himself, Branch Leaper felt his ears and tail alike go up as the crystal purity of her mind voice rolled through him. No! It could not be! No clan would have allowed—

<*I am called Golden Voice among the People of Sun Leaf Clan,*> she told him, and he managed to flick his ears in acknowledgment despite his disbelief. He gazed at her for long moments, tasting the half-amused, half-resigned tolerance in her mind glow as he tried to grapple with who and what she was. Clearly she had anticipated such a reaction . . . and so must Laughs Brightly, Branch Leaper recognized. He did not know the older treecat as well as he might have, for Laughs Brightly was home too infrequently, but he *did* know the older scout well enough to realize how he would have responded to such emotions about his mate if he had *not* prepared himself for them ahead of time.

A fresh ripple of embarrassment flickered through Branch Leaper, but this time he did not apologize. There was no true need, since Golden Voice and Laughs Brightly obviously both knew exactly what had sparked it. Besides, he rather doubted he could find a way to apologize without making things still worse, for nothing he had ever been taught by Swift Darter or any of the older clan elders suggested how to go about responding properly to such an unheard of situation.

So instead of apologizing, he merely gave himself a quick shake, knowing they tasted the unvoiced apology in his mind glow anyway, and returned his attention to Laughs Brightly.

<*You are bound to meet with the elders?*> The question was superfluous, since that was obviously

Laughs Brightly's and Golden Voice's intention, but it was a way to get past the potential insult of his disbelief.

<*We are,*> Laughs Brightly confirmed. <*Would you accompany us?*>

<*Gladly,*> Branch Leaper replied sincerely, and turned to lead the way down the highway of the picketwood to the central nesting place of Bright Water Clan.

Branch Leaper had come to grips with his astonishment by the time they reached their destination. He remained uncertain what he thought of the unprecedented choices Golden Voice clearly had made in her life, but the humming vibrancy of the bond between her and Laughs Brightly burned in the back of his brain like bright fire. As he became accustomed to it, its almost painful intensity shifted and changed, transmuting into something just as powerful yet less fierce, a welcoming beacon and not the blinding light it had first appeared. And as he adjusted to it, he also tasted more of its subtle nuances. He was only a scout, no mind teacher or memory singer, yet even he could taste the strange, unending strain of sorrow which hovered always in their shared mind glows. It came from Golden Voice, he realized. A sense of bereavement, of unendurable sadness and wrenching loss. It was not at the surface of her mind glow, and he rather doubted that she was even fully aware of it, for it had the flavor of an old wound—one which might never fully heal, but which one had no choice but to live with.

It seemed wrong to taste such a thing in such a brilliant mind glow, and yet, as he tasted it, Branch Leaper slowly realized that in an odd way he doubted

he would ever be able to define even for himself, that
sorrow was part of what made this pair glow so
brightly. It was as if the sorrow, the sense of loss, had
somehow tempered the steel of the joy they took in
one another, as if the knowledge of what Golden
Voice had lost made them even more aware of all that
they now had.

And whatever Branch Leaper or anyone else might
think of the propriety of Golden Voice's having mated
with anyone, he knew no one who ever tasted their
bond could ever doubt its depth and power. Surely
anything which produced such brilliance and joy in
those who shared it could not be wrong, whatever
he might think of the decisions which had led her
into a position in which it might be forged. And even
if that had not been so, the People's most ancient
traditions made the bonding of mates an intensely
private thing. No one could avoid tasting their mind
glows, but the choice to mate, and who to mate with,
was one no other of the People—not even a clan's
elders—had the right to challenge or question. Which
was as it ought to be, of course. It was merely that
all the *rest* of the People's customs insisted that
Golden Voice should never have—

He shook that thought off once more, with less
difficulty this time—no doubt a sign that he had
grown more accustomed to it—and led the way
towards the tallest tree at the heart of Bright Water's
central nesting place. More adult members of the clan
appeared as he, Laughs Brightly, and Golden Voice
crossed the interlacing picketwood branches towards
their destination, and he tasted their surprise, mir-
roring his own as they saw Laughs Brightly and
realized it was *his* mind glow they had tasted.

Branch Leaper's ears cocked wryly at some of the

emotions he tasted. Laughs Brightly was enough older than he, and had adopted Dances on Clouds long enough ago, that Branch Leaper had never seen first-hand the pranks and jokes which had earned Laughs Brightly his name among the People, but he had heard sufficient tales of them to understand the naming. Now he tasted a certain resignation among some of his older clan mates as they absorbed the newfound strength of Laughs Brightly's mind glow and contemplated what he might be able to accomplish now. It was, perhaps, as well that he and Dances on Clouds were so seldom on the People's world!

They reached the tall tree, and, as always, Branch Leaper felt his pace slow, his manner become more sober and dignified. This tree had been the center of the Bright Water range for over ten hands of hands of turnings, longer even than the entire time the humans had been on the surface of the People's world. Fewer than two hands of clans could claim to have maintained the same range for so many turn-ings, and *this* tree had been the nesting place of some of the greatest mind singers of all the people, includ-ing Sings Truly herself. It was not the way of the People to feel awe of one another, for a race which could taste the mind glows and emotions—even the very thoughts—of its clan leaders and memory singers knew one another too well for that. Usually. Yet Branch Leaper always felt a deep, almost reverent awe whenever he ascended this tree and realized that his claws touched the same bark, the same wood, as those of the legendary Sings Truly and all of her successors.

Now he reached the high branch he sought and paused. The large nest of Bright Water Clan's cur-rent senior memory singer stood before him, and it would not be necessary for him to use the attention chime to announce his arrival. Wind of Memory sat before her nest's entrance, flanked by Songstress and Echo of Time, and almost two-thirds of the clan's elders had assembled with them. Clearly someone else had sent word of their coming ahead, for this was every one of the elders who had been present in the central nesting place, and their mind glows were gravely formal.

<Greetings, Branch Leaper,> Wind of Memory's musical mind voice was like the crystal sound of the "wind chimes" the humans had given the delighted People, and Branch Leaper flicked his ears in profoundly respectful acknowledgment. Yet even as he did so, he remembered the power and beauty of Golden Voice's mind voice.

<Greetings, Senior Singer. Elders,> he replied, including the assembled clan leaders in his response. *<I was bound for the wide water below the tree hopper's dam when I met Laughs Brightly and his new mate.>* He tasted the stir of the elders' interest as he confirmed what they must surely already have known. <When we met, of course, I returned hither to accompany our new sister-of-choice.>

<That was well done, younger brother,> Wind of Memory acknowledged gravely.

It had not been necessary, of course, but it *had* been only courteous. Under normal circumstances, Laughs Brightly would have become a member of Sun Leaf Clan, for it was customary for the male to become a member of his mate's clan on those rare occasions when People mated with anyone other than members of their own birth clans. But the fact that he and Golden Voice had journeyed to Bright Water Clan clearly suggested that they did not intend to follow custom in this matter—*either*, Branch Leaper thought dryly—and it did make a sort of sense. Laughs Brightly was bonded to Dances on Clouds, one of Death Fang's Bane's descendants, and Death Fang's Bane Clan's range bordered on Bright Water's. Of course, human clans did not consider their "ranges" (or their clans, for that matter) exactly as the People did, but the parallels were close enough. If Golden Voice was not bonded to a human herself, it would be reasonable for her to join the clan of her mate, if it was closer to her mate's human's clan, and Sun Leaf Clan was distant, indeed. But if she had chosen to come among a clan strange to her, it would have been discourteous in the extreme for Branch Leaper not to accompany her here to meet her new brothers and sisters. And elders. *Especially* elders. And especially in this case.

<*I greet you, sister-of-choice,*> Wind of Memory went on, turning to Laughs Brightly's new mate. <*I had not expected Laughs Brightly to find a mate among the People, particularly given the strength of his bond to Dances on Clouds. Yet I taste the strength of the bond you share with him, and his mind glow has grown still stronger since last he was among us. It is a powerful bonding you share, and I wish you joy of it.*>

<*I thank you, Senior Singer,*> Golden Voice replied, and Branch Leaper felt a shudder of shock ripple through the assembled elders and all the other members of Bright Water Clan who had followed them to Wind of Memory's nest as that incredible mind voice poured through them. Wind of Memory twitched bolt upright, her ears standing fully erect, and Songstress actually hissed beside her. Not in challenge, but in disbelief, for Golden Voice's mind voice sang in their minds with the pure, sweet power

of one of the humans' great bells. It was easily more powerful than Wind of Memory's, yet Wind of Memory held her position as Bright Water's senior singer precisely because her own mind voice was so strong.

<*You are the one they call Golden Voice!*> Echo of Time blurted, startled into the exclamation. Golden Voice turned bright green eyes to her, cocking her head to one side, and Echo of Time's gaze fell, her mind glow burning with consternation. The disapproval of her mind voice could not have been greater if she had made it so on purpose, and her humiliation at her own bad manners was blazingly apparent. Yet so was the fact that she was not at all convinced that her disapproval was unmerited, and Branch Leaper tasted echoes of the same emotions from other members of the clan.

<*I am, Memory Singer,*> Golden Voice replied after a long moment. Her own mind voice showed no trace of anger or resentment, only calm self-assurance and possibly just a flicker of resigned amusement, as if she were well accustomed to such reactions. Which, Branch Leaper reflected, she undoubtedly was.

<*Forgive my surprise, sister-of-choice.*> Echo of Time's apology was sincere, but it was for her own bad manners in failing to control her reaction and not an admission that her disapproval was wrong.

<*Why?*> Golden Voice asked simply. <*Were our positions reversed, I might well feel as you do, Memory Singer. Certainly—*> she allowed herself a dry mental chuckle <*—my own sire and dam were . . . perplexed by my choices. And as for my own clan's memory singers—!*>

She flicked the tip of her tail as a human might have rolled her eyes, and Wind of Memory surprised them all—including herself, Branch Leaper suspected—with a bleek of laughter. All eyes turned to her, and she flicked her ears.

<*I have no doubt they found you "perplexing," sister-of-choice,*> the senior memory singer agreed wryly. <*Indeed, I have received their memory song of your decision, and I have always been amazed that they did not argue more strenuously with you.*>

<*I suppose I should be also,*> Golden Voice admitted. <*I found them quite strenuous enough, Senior Singer, yet I was only a kitten at the time, and it is the way of the young both to be certain of their own course and to feel much abused when their elders do not share their certainty.*>

<*Indeed. Though I see you have grown quite elderly since that time,*> Wind of Memory observed in a dust-dry mind voice, and it was Golden Voice's turn to bleek in laughter, for she was very young. Less than half Laughs Brightly's age, Branch Leaper estimated, though it was hard to be certain. Like all females, she was much smaller than the average male, and her dappled brown and gray pelt did not boast the tail rings which indicated a male's age. Both of those things made estimating her age difficult, and the fact that she was so . . . different from any other female he had ever met only complicated matters still further.

<*I am not yet ancient, Senior Singer,*> Golden Voice admitted, <*yet I do not regret my choices. And Sun Leaf Clan had a full two hands of well-trained memory singers. It was not as though they truly needed yet another, and the hunger for the human mind glow was upon me.*> She gave another ear flick, meeting Wind of Memory's gaze squarely. <*We do not deny the need to taste the human mind glow to our hunters, or our scouts, or to any other male. And other*

females have bonded with the humans, if not a great
many. It would have been wrong and unjust of my
elders to deny me the right to bond simply because
I had the potential of a memory singer.>

<*You did not have "the potential," sister-of-choice,*>
Songstress said, speaking up for the first time. <*You*
are a memory singer, whether you have claimed or
accepted the duties of one or not, and this is some-
thing you know as well as I. If it would have been
wrong or unjust of Sun Leaf Clan's elders and memory
singers to deny you the right to bond with a human,
was it not also wrong of you to refuse the responsi-
bility to your clan which comes with the mind voice
and the depth of memory you own?>

A mental hush hovered at the memory singer's
forthright demand. Among humans, Branch Leaper
had been told, such a query would have been considered an insult, or at least insufferably rude, but
that was something he had never truly understood.
Among the People, there was no real point in not
asking it, or in trying to conceal the emotions which
went with it, for there was no way one of the People
could *not* know that another harbored that question
or those feelings. There were questions the People
simply did not ask of one another, but they were few
and fell into areas which had been considered deeply
private in even the oldest of memory songs. Personally, Branch Leaper had always assumed that that was
because the People's ancestors had learned the hard
way that those areas—like the reasons a couple chose
to mate—were the most likely to provoke conflict. A
people who heard one another's thoughts and tasted
one another's mind glows could not possibly have put
all potential areas of conflict off limits, however, and
outside those which had been sanctified by iron

custom, the People addressed one another with a frankness which would have been devastating in any mind-blind society.

Yet for all that, the challenge and disapproval of Bright Water's second ranking memory singer hung before Golden Voice like a set of bared fangs. The younger female turned her calm regard on Songstress for several long breaths, then flicked the tip of her tail in acknowledgment.

<*I am what—and who—I am, Memory Singer,*> she said then. <*I did not choose the strength of voice or mind glow or memory I possess, just as I did not choose the need to taste the human mind glow. And I have paid for my choices with sorrow as well as joy.*>

A stab of grief ripped through her mind glow, the subtle sorrow Branch Leaper had tasted from the first exploding to the surface. It was only for an instant, yet all who tasted it flinched before it. It was a memory singer's grief, with all the vibrant power of a memory singer's mind behind it, and in that searing instant all within the reach of her mind voice were one with her, sharing the agony of loss and bereavement as her adopted human died and the bitter knife of death slashed the delicate binding and interweaving which had made Golden Voice and her human both individuals and one being. It was as if the very sun above them had exploded, destroying all the world— not in fire, but in freezing cold and utter desolation, and Branch Leaper cowered down on all six limbs, pressing his belly to the branch beneath him as the perfect reproduction of that moment of loss and torment took him by the throat. He tasted Golden Voice's need to follow her person into darkness, the need to cling to his mind glow's glory wherever it went . . . and the desperate need to escape the dreadful emptiness his death had left in her soul and mind.

Yet there was more than simple despair in that shared moment. There was another mind glow, one which clung to her even more desperately than she had hungered for the peace of nonbeing. It had gripped her fiercely, refusing to release her and blazing against the darkness. It was not like her human's mind glow had been. For all its power, it was weaker, almost muted—a subtler beauty, in more delicately blended colors, without the unbridled strength of the human mind glows. Yet also unlike the human mind glows, it engaged hers on all levels, merging with it, anchoring itself within her even as she had anchored herself within it.

It had been Laughs Brightly, Branch Leaper realized, and turned his awed gaze upon the older male. Weaker than a human mind glow though it might have been, still the sheer, raw power of his demand for Golden Voice to live had dwarfed anything a male should have been able to produce. Yet even as that sense of awe touched him, Branch Leaper wondered why he felt it. So far as he knew, never in all the history of People and humans had both halves of a mated pair also adopted humans . . . and never before had a female with the mind voice and mind glow of a memory singer bonded with *any* human. Laughs Brightly and Golden Voice had passed into territory none of the People had ever explored. No doubt it was only natural for them to discover things there which the People had never expected.

<*Yes, you have paid,*> Songstress agreed after a moment, but if her mind voice was a bit more subdued, there was no less disapproval in it. <*Yet had*

*you remained with Sun Leaf Clan as you ought to
have, that price would never have been demanded of
you.>*

*<No doubt that is true, Memory Singer. Yet the only
way to avoid the price would have been to deny the
joy from whence it sprang, and it is the decisions I
have made—and the prices I have paid—which make
me what I am today. You say that I am a memory
singer, and perhaps there is truth in that. Yet I have
also bonded with a human and tasted the beauty and
power of his mind glow . . . and the anguish of its loss.
And I have mated with Laughs Brightly and known
the joy and the glory of becoming one with another
who can taste and be tasted in return. And I have
borne our kittens and tasted the soft magic of their
mind glows in my womb and welcomed them into the
world as they opened their eyes upon its sunlight for
the very first time. I have known and done these
things, Memory Singer. Not simply in the memory
songs I have tasted and made my own and sung for
others.>*

*<And those of us who have not done those things,
who can know them "simply" in the songs we taste
and sing, are somehow less than you who have done
them?>* Songstress demanded.

<I did not say that, Memory Singer,> Golden Voice
replied calmly, *<nor do I think it.>* Songstress glared
at her for a moment, but then her tail flicked in
acknowledgment. Golden Voice's mind glow was clear
and bright, and Songstress tasted her sincerity as
clearly as any other person present.

*<I say only that I have known and done them
myself,>* Golden Voice continued. *<It was by my own
choice and will, yet I ask you this, Memory Singer.
You have sung the songs of all of those who have*

bonded with humans, beginning with your own clan's Climbs Quickly and Death Fang's Bane. More of Bright Water Clan's scouts and hunters have bonded with humans than any other clan's, and you know the mind taste of Death Fang's Bane Clan, the bright light and power that beckons to People from all over this world. Had you been born with that same need, that same hunger to embrace the human mind glow, would you have refused it?>

<I would have thought of my responsibility to my clan,> Songstress retorted, but her gaze fell once more as she tasted Golden Voice's gentle rebuke. Songstress was hands of turnings older than Golden Voice, yet in that moment Golden Voice had somehow become by far the elder, and her mind voice was chiding.

<I, too, thought of my responsibilities, Memory Singer,> she said almost kindly. *<Did you think I could not have done so? Yet that was not my question. I asked you if you would have refused the hunger for the human mind glow if it had come upon you.>*

<I—> Songstress began, then hesitated. The moment of hesitation stretched out, and then it became something else. The memory singer met Golden Voice's eyes once more, her very silence an admission of the younger female's point, for she *had* tasted that hunger and need in the memory songs of others. As no one but a memory singer could, she had shared it and become one with it, and as such, she knew—as no one but a memory singer could— how impossible it was not to answer.

<I do not think I envy you, sister-of-choice,> Wind of Memory said into the silence. *<Any memory singer knows the need to embrace the mind songs of the People, to hear and feel and taste all those who have*

come before us as they live again through us. And
because we have sung the songs of those who bonded
with humans, even in the days when the human life
span was so short that to do so was to embrace death
as well, any memory singer knows that hunger and
need, as well. To choose between them . . ."

She shook her head slowly, in a gesture the People
had borrowed from their human friends, but Golden
Voice looked at her serenely.

<*Life is choice, Memory Singer. The fact that no*
one of the People has ever made the choices I have
made, or lived the life I have lived, cannot change
that, and if there have been times of pain and loss,
there has also been joy and love.> Her prehensile tail
reached out, wrapping itself gently but tightly about
Laughs Brightly. <*I have Laughs Brightly, and our*
kittens—yes, and his human, as well, for Dances on
Clouds has love enough for a hand of hands of People,
and just as Laughs Brightly, she and the humans who
follow her have become as much my clan as ever Sun
Leaf Clan was. Perhaps that is the reason one who
might have been a memory singer bonded with a
human yet also mated.>

<*What do you mean?*> Wind of Memory asked
intently, and Golden Voice regarded her levelly for
several long breaths. Branch Leaper tensed and felt
the same reactions from the other members of his
clan—especially Songstress and Echo of Time—as
they tasted her mind glow. There was deep serenity
in it, despite her youth, but also an inflexible determination, unyielding as the duralloy of the metal
knives and axes the humans had given the People.
It was not challenge. It went beyond that, like some
irresistible natural force—like the wind that toppled
even the mightiest picketwood or crown oak. He had

no idea what lay behind it, yet at that moment, he felt almost sorry for the elders and memory singers of Sun Leaf Clan who must have encountered something just like it when they tried to force her to become a memory singer herself.

<I mean that the time to end our great deception has come, Memory Singer,> Golden Voice said very quietly. <It is time and past time for us to reveal our full cleverness to the humans.>

<No!> It was not one of the memory singers, but rather Bark Master, second of Bright Water's elders, whose mind voice shouted the instant denial. All eyes turned to him, but he did not retreat. <Sings Truly herself told us we must conceal our full cleverness, and she was right,> he said stubbornly. <It was the path of wisdom to hide it until we had learned more of the humans, and it is the path of wisdom now. We are protected by the human rangers. They aid us in the hard times of the cold turnings, their healers have conquered many of the illnesses which once came among us and killed, we have learned much from them yet remained always ourselves. We may no longer distrust them, yet we do not truly know how they will respond when they discover that we have deceived them for so long. And even if that were not true, it would be foolish to unsettle and change everything between our two peoples when we already have all that we might desire!>

<With all respect, Elder, you are wrong,> Golden Voice said, and in that moment her mind voice held the regal assurance which echoed still in the mind songs of Sings Truly herself. She was perhaps a quarter of Bark Master's age and the newest member of his clan, to boot, yet she faced his vehemence with neither trepidation nor personal challenge, and Branch

Leaper felt a deep respect for her—and an even deeper envy of Laughs Brightly.

<*Why so, sister-of-choice?*> Wind of Memory asked. She alone tasted almost as calm as Golden Voice, yet she watched the younger female unblinkingly, her concentrated gaze a pale reflection of the intensity with which she tasted the other's mind glow and mind voice.

<*Because it is no longer necessary . . . and because we are no longer kittens, Senior Singer,*> Golden Voice told her. <*There is no need to learn still more of the humans. Surely you, who have sung the songs of every human who has ever been adopted, of every one of the People who has ever returned to tell of all he and his person have seen and done, must see that. You know the name of every human—their human names, as well as those the People have given—who has ever been adopted. You know the full songs of their lives, of how they have protected and kept our secrets . . . and of how the other humans with whom we share this world have also learned to protect and accept us. We might hide our full cleverness forever, but if we do so only to insure the safety of the People while we learn more of the humans, then we have hidden it long enough. If we are never to reveal the truth, then we must find a better reason than fear of the humans' reaction, Senior Singer.*>

Wind of Memory considered that, then flicked her ears in agreement.

<*More than that, though,*> Golden Voice continued, <*great changes are about to befall our humans— and through them, us—on all sides. They are at war—*> she used the human word, for the mind voices of the People had no matching reference, yet all who heard it knew of what she spoke <*—with an*

enemy with far more nests, far more people, than our humans. Laughs Brightly and I have met some of those enemies.> The tail wrapped about her mate tightened again, and his tail slipped comfortingly about her, as well. *<I lost my human to them, and Laughs Brightly has lost those he cared for deeply, and who Dances on Clouds loved, to them, as well, and some of them are truly evil, in a way few of the People could ever fully understand. Most are not, of course. Indeed, the mind glows of many of those we have met might equally well have been the mind glows of our own humans. Yet Laughs Brightly and I have also seen the weapons they use and tasted the fear of many of the humans—of the enemy humans, as well as our own—of where this war may lead. It may come even here, for our humans are dreadfully outnumbered. They are brave and determined, and I believe they fight much better than their enemies, yet not the bravest heart may hold back the ice days or forbid the mud days' floods. Their weapons can kill even worlds, Senior Singer—accidentally, as well as deliberately. I know our humans would die before they willingly permitted such weapons to be used here, for this is their world, as well, and they would protect us as fiercely as they do their own younglings. Yet still it may happen, and what would become of Bright Water Clan, or the memory songs of its People, if such a weapon should strike here, in this central nesting place?>*

A cold mental silence answered her, and Branch Leaper felt that same icy chill at his own heart. He had never even considered such a possibility, yet he knew now that he should have. He, too, had heard the memory songs, tasted the very mind glows, of Laughs Brightly and his human as they faced the terrible weapons Golden Voice had just described. And in those songs, Laughs Brightly had always known that such terrible human tools might be unleashed even here on the world of the People. Yet somehow the connection had never made itself for Branch Leaper, for such devices were too utterly beyond his own ken. And as he tasted the stunned silence about him, he knew he was not alone in that. That perhaps even the memory singers themselves had not recognized—or admitted to themselves that they did—the implications of all Laughs Brightly and others like him from other clans had reported to their memory singers.

<There is nothing the People can do to prevent such disaster,> Golden Voice went on with that same terrible, unflinching honesty and awareness, <and as I have said, our own humans would face death willingly to prevent it for us. Yet that does not mean that we should be blind to the chance that it might befall us despite all they can do.>

<Yet you yourself have just pointed out that there is nothing we can do to avert it,> Bark Master pointed out. His mind voice was no longer stubborn. It was half-stunned and frightened, yet his response was not one of simple panic. He spoke as a clan elder, one whose responsibility it was to recognize the dangers which beset Bright Water and to avert them . . . and who knew now that there was a danger he could not avert, however hard he might seek to do so.

<No, but we may take steps to allow for the consequences,> Golden Voice told him. <That is one reason I say that it is time to end our deception. The People live on only one world; our humans claim three as their own nest places, with many others as the nest places of their allies and friends. I believe it is time that the People also spread their nest places wider,

sought ranges on other worlds, as well as this one of our own.>

<Other worlds?!> Bark Master stared at her in disbelief, and she flicked her ears with just a hint of impatience.

<Clan Elder, it is past time for such a decision,> she said firmly, with all the authority of the memory singer she had never become. *<We have known for hands of hands of turnings that those worlds are there. Laughs Brightly and I have visited many of them, tasted their air and their water, smelled their soil, climbed their trees. Not all would make good homes for the People, and even many of those which would would not allow us to live there as we have always lived here. We would be forced to learn new ways and new things, to adjust our customs, perhaps even change many of them completely. Yet to live is to make decisions and to grow; to refuse decisions or to grow is to die inside, even if the body lives on. The People have always been slow to change, yet we have always known that change cannot be avoided . . . and that change is not always evil or wrong simply because it is change. More than that, we have our humans to help us. Do you think, after all that we have learned of them, all the rules they have made among their own kind to protect us, that they would not help us in this?>*

<But they could not help us as they always have in the past,> Wind of Memory pointed out, raising a true-hand to gesture at the dense green leaves and broad picketwood branches about them. *<If we must change our ways and our customs on those other worlds, we could no longer live as the People have always lived, or apart from our humans.>*

<We could not,> Golden Voice agreed. *<That is*

one of the great reasons I say it is time to drop our deception. If we would live on the other worlds of our humans—or even on still more distant worlds—then we must weave new patterns with all humans. We must allow them to realize how clever we truly are, and even those of the People who do not bond to humans must learn to live among them. Not simply as we do now, when any of the People may visit any human nesting place for a time and then return to our own ranges, but permanently, and that may be hard. And in time, I suspect, we must also find ways to do things that they need, so that they will learn to treat us as our bonded humans do—as partners whose skills and work are valued, and not simply as kittens to be protected, as so many other humans now see us. We have permitted ourselves to be seen so for too long, Memory Singer. Indeed, there are times when I wonder if we have not come to see ourselves so.>

Wind of Memory began to reply hotly, then stopped, and Branch Leaper tasted her sense of surprise as she made herself consider Golden Voice's words and found a bitter strain of truth behind them.

<Yet there is still another reason why I believe this is the time to consider such a move,> Golden Voice went on into the silence. *<You of Bright Water know even better than I how for many generations the People have sought out the humans of Death Fang's Bane Clan and bonded to them . . . and why. Many have been chosen from other human clans, especially that of their High Clan, yet again and again the people have chosen from Death Fang's Bane and its daughter clans. And why was that, Memory Singer?>*

<Because they are so much less mind-blind than most humans,> Wind of Memory replied.

<Exactly,> Golden Voice said. *<Oh, there are other reasons, as well. They are a good clan, one whose people have always cared deeply for the world we share and for the People. There have been those with whom no person would bond, of course, for they are no more perfect than the People are, but for the most part, those of Death Fang's Bane Clan have been humans any person might be proud to bond to. Yet the true reason we have chosen so many of them has been the brilliance of their mind glows and the strength of the bonds we have made with them. I bonded to one not of that clan—>* again that burst of curiously serene, bottomless sorrow flowed from her, but this time without the jagged, knifelike edges *<—and I will never regret it. Yet I tell you that Laughs Brightly's bond with Dances on Clouds is as much stronger than was mine with Hunter of Stars as a memory singer's voice is stronger than that of a hunter or a scout. I do not think Dances on Clouds realizes even now how much like one of the People she is, for she tastes Laughs Brightly's mind glow almost as one of the People would. You who have sung their songs know this, but you know only what Laughs Brightly has been able to tell you of it, while I have seen it as another looking in through my own bond to him, and I tell you that Dances on Clouds can actually hear his thoughts.>*

<That is impossible,> one of the other elders said flatly. *<Humans are mind-blind. Even Darkness Foe could hear the thoughts of a memory singer only because hands of hunters and scouts aided her!>*

<I do not think Darkness Foe truly heard her thoughts even then,> Golden voice said calmly. *<I have listened to that song many times, and I believe that he tasted her song without truly hearing it. But*

Dances on Clouds does *hear Laughs Brightly. Not as one of the People would, and certainly not as clearly. I do not even think she hears with the same senses the People use. It is almost as if . . . as if her ability to taste his mind glow is so strong that his mind voice flows to her through the same link.>* She turned and looked up at her mate, and he flicked his ears.

<Golden Voice is correct, I think,> he said. *<Dances on Clouds—>* the tenderness and love in his mind voice flowed through them all like a gentle wind as he named his human *<—does not hear me as the People would, does not hear my thoughts as thoughts. I do not know precisely how she does hear them, for it had not occurred to me until the last few hands of turnings that she might do so at all.>*

Mental ear flicks of assent flowed through his audience, for this was Bright Water Clan, and all of its people had heard the memory songs of how Laughs Brightly had made Dances on Clouds taste the mind glow of the evil-doers from whom she and he had saved the elders of Dances on Cloud's other world from murder.

<Since that time, she has learned to taste the mind glows of other humans more and more clearly,> Laughs Brightly went on. *<She does not yet realize it, but she no longer truly needs her bond to me even for that. I believe our bond makes it easier, yet she has reached out several times with her own mind, without even realizing that she has done it.>* He cocked his head, and the other People tasted his pride and wonder at what his human had achieved. *<At the same time, she and I have come closer than any others of our kind—closer even than Swift Striker and Darkness Foe, I believe—to truly speaking mind-to-mind. It is difficult to describe, for human minds are*

so different from those of the People. As Golden Voice says, she does not hear as we hear one another. Rather it is almost as it is with a very young kitten, when thought and feeling have not truly separated one from another. I am still exploring this new ability, still seeking ways to strengthen it, and since mating with Golden Voice, my bond with Dances on Clouds seems to have grown still stronger and deeper.> He sent a wave of love and tenderness to his mate, but his eyes met those of his clan's elders. *<We have come far, and thanks to the humans' "Prolong," we will have many hands of turnings yet to come still further. I do not know that other humans and people will find the same ability, but if even a single bonding can make the final step and truly hear one another, communicate as clearly as People with People or human with human . . .>*

His mind voice trailed off, and Golden Voice took up the discussion once more.

<There are other reasons to act now, of course, just as I am certain many among us can find reasons why we should not change our ways. Yet I ask you all to consider this. Not only do Dances on Clouds and Laughs Brightly share a deeper, clearer bond than any other of the People has ever forged with a human, but she has become a great elder among humans. Not as great as Soul of Steel, perhaps, for she does not head our humans' High Clan, but a great elder upon her other world nonetheless. She is the branch by which the People might cross into that other world, for she has the authority to make us welcome, and her love for Laughs Brightly—and for me and for our kittens—burns like a crown fire at her heart. She will help and aid us if we ask, and she and those who follow her will protect us even as Death Fang's Bane

Clan has always guarded and protected the People here.>

She fell silent, and a great stillness seemed to hover in the central nesting place of Bright Water Clan. It lingered endlessly, and then Wind of Memory shook herself like a kitten caught in the rain. She turned and gazed about her at the assembled elders and all the other adults who listened and watched, then looked back to Golden Voice.

<*You have wasted no time setting a hunter among the tree hoppers of your new clan, sister-of-choice!*> she observed in a mind voice made of mingled worry, resignation, hope, and deep amusement. <*And you have done it before we even offered you and Laughs Brightly a nest to share while you are among us! Perhaps Sun Leaf Clan is more fortunate than it knows to have avoided so, ah,* energetic *a memory singer!*>

<*I have often thought my elders were more fortunate than they realized . . . in many ways, Senior Singer,*> Golden Voice replied so demurely that even many of those she had shocked most deeply bleeked with laughter.

<*Perhaps they are, and perhaps they are not,*> Wind of Memory said much more seriously. <*Yet I do not jest when I say that what you have proposed to us this day may be even more important—or dangerous—to the People than anything Sings Truly herself ever proposed. It is certainly the most important thing anyone has suggested* since *Sings Truly, and I suppose I am pleased and proud that you have brought it to the clan from whence she and Climbs Quickly sprang.*>

<*Even if Golden Voice is correct,*> Crooked Tail, another of the elders, put in, <*it need not mean that*

we overset all the old ways in a single day, Senior
Singer. If we follow her suggestion, surely we would
send only a small number of people to Dances on
Cloud's other world to begin with. No more than a
hand or two, at most.>

<Do not deceive yourself, Crooked Tail,> Wind of
Memory replied. <Yes, we would start with only a very
few People. At least one memory singer must go,
since—> she darted a humorous glance at Golden
Voice <—I have no intention of attempting to convince
a mated female, with kittens of her own, who has also
bonded to a human, to do what all of Sun Leaf Clan's
elders could not convince an untried kitten to do so
many turnings ago! And there must be hunters and
scouts . . . three hands, at least, I would say. But it is
not the numbers that matter in this—not truly. What
matters is the change. I would not think it would come
immediately, for I would still advise moving with caution, yet such a move would require the People to show
our true cleverness to the humans. And that will change
the entire relationship between all humans and all
People, everywhere, forever.>

<You speak truly, Senior Singer,> Golden Voice
agreed. <Yet I will add this. For all that Sings Truly
counseled caution, she always knew the day must come
when the People took this step. I think she might still
agree with you that we must not move with reckless
haste . . . but I also think she would be astonished that
it has taken us this long to come this far.>

<So what, precisely, do you recommend, sister-of-
choice?> Wind of Memory asked in a mind voice from
which all hostility had faded.

<It is customary for a mother of the People who
has bonded to a human to foster her kittens with her
clan,> Golden Voice replied. <I would not do that.

*Rather, Laughs Brightly and I will take them to
Dances on Clouds' other world with us. And when
we do, as Wind of Memory has suggested, we will take
others with us to help teach and raise them . . . and
to open a new door to the humans.>*

<It is a bold plan . . . and a risky one,> Bark Master
said slowly. <It will not be decided here and now,
sister-of-choice, and it does not concern only our clan.
We must consult with the other clans and their
elders.>

<I understand. But I also understand that, as they
have so often, the other clans will follow the lead of
Bright Water. It was this clan which opened the first
door; if it chooses to open the next, it will not be alone
in that decision long.>

<Perhaps not,> Bark Master conceded, <yet it
would be discourteous, as well as dangerous, to move
in this without so much as seeking their opinions. It
will take some days, at least two or three hands of
them.>

<Which will be amply soon,> Golden Voice told
him. <Dances on Clouds will not leave for considerably longer than that. There will be time for much
discussion.>

<Indeed,> Laughs Brightly put in, his pride in his
mate burning bright in his mind glow as he tucked
an arm about her. <But whatever the decision, Golden
Voice and I, and our kittens, will leave with Dances
on Clouds.> There was not as much shock or surprise
at hearing such an announcement from a scout as
there might have been in other clans. This was Bright
Water Clan, after all . . . and its elders knew Laughs
Brightly of old.

<We understand that, Laughs Brightly,> Wind of
Memory told him now, her mind voice and mind glow

rich with resigned laughter, *<but at least allow us the illusion that the vote of all the rest of the People in the world matters just a bit!>*

<Oh, of course, Senior Singer!> Laughs Brightly assured her with a bleek of amusement. *<It would never do for us to be impolite, after all, now would it?>*

Honor Harrington looked up from her book viewer as the oldest 'cat door on Sphinx opened. Her great-great-great-etc.-grandmother Stephanie and Lionheart had first used that door hundreds of T-years before, and she smiled as the two latest treecats to use it flowed through it.

"Hi, Stinker!" she said, setting down her mug of cocoa. "Have a nice visit with the folks?"

"Bleek!" Nimitz agreed, flowing across the floor to her with an air of almost unbearable complacency. He looked like someone who had just discovered he owned an entire celery patch of his own, Honor thought, and shook her head with a grin.

"He really can be sort of full of himself, can't he?" she asked the smaller, dappled treecat who had accompanied him, and Samantha bleeked an agreement of her own. She crossed to the couch and hopped lightly up on it to peer down into the basket at Honor's side. Four adorable balls of fluffy fur slept deeply in it—one of them snoring faintly—and Samantha bleeked again, softer and more gently, and reached out a wiry, true-hand to stroke one of her children tenderly.

"I promised to keep an eye on them," Honor told her, reaching out to caress Samantha's ears in turn, and Nimitz's mate turned to gaze up at her with brilliant green eyes. For a moment they looked so serious and thoughtful Honor blinked in surprise, but then Samantha seemed to shake herself. She turned away from her sleeping children and flowed into Honor's lap, curling herself into a neat circle, and Nimitz leapt up beside his mate and his person.

Samantha buried her nose against Honor and gave a huge sigh, then closed her eyes and began to buzz a slow, deep purr as Honor's long fingers stroked her fluffy coat. Within less than five minutes, the purr had faded into slow, deep breathing, and Honor gazed down at the utterly relaxed, silken warmth so trustingly asleep in her lap. Then she looked at Nimitz, curled neatly beside her on the couch, and shook her head.

"Look at her!" she said softly, and chuckled. "Sleepy as she is, you'd think she'd been out changing the world or something!"

"Bleek!" Nimitz agreed, and then rested his own chin on his person's thigh beside Samantha's, and the soft buzz of his purr rose over his mate's slow breathing as Honor chuckled again and laid her hand on his head.

From the Highlands

Eric Flint

THE FIRST DAY

Helen

Helen used the effort of digging at the wall to control her terror. She thought of it as a variation of Master Tye's training: *turn weakness into strength*. Fear drove her, but she shaped it to steady her aching arms instead of letting it loosen her bowels.

Scrape, scrape. She didn't have the strength to make big gouges in the wall with a pitiful shard of broken rubble. The wall was not particularly hard, since it was not much more than rubble itself. But her slender arms and little hands, for all their well-honed training under Master Tye's regimen, were still those of a girl just turned fourteen.

So what? She couldn't afford to make much noise, anyway. Now and then, she could hear the low sound of her captors' voices, just beyond the heavy door which they had placed across the entrance to her "cell."

Scrape, scrape. Weakness into strength. *The root breaks the rock. Wind and water triumph over stone.*

So she had been trained. By her father, as much as by Master Tye. *Decide what you want, and set to it like running water. Soft, slight, steady. Unstoppable.*

Scrape, scrape. She had no idea how thick the wall was, or even whether it was a wall at all. For all she knew, Helen might simply be digging an endless little tunnel through the soil of Terra.

Her abductors had removed the hood after they got her into this strange and frightening place. She was still somewhere in the Solarian League's capital city of Chicago, that much she knew. But she had no idea where, except that she thought it was in the Old Quarter. Chicago was a gigantic city, and the Old Quarter was like an ancient Mesopotamian *tel*. Layer upon layer of half-rubbled ruins. They had descended deep underground, using twisted and convoluted passageways that she had not been able to store in her memory.

Scrape, scrape. *Just do it. Running water conquers all.*

Eventually.

While she scraped, she thought sometimes of her father, and sometimes of Master Tye. But, more often, she thought of her mother. She could not really remember her mother's face, of course, except from holocubes. Her mother had died when Helen was only four years old. But she had the memory—still as vivid as ever—of the day her mother died. Helen had been sitting on her father's lap, terrified, while her mother led a hopeless defense of a convoy against an overwhelming force of Havenite warships. But her mother had saved her, that day, along with her father.

Scrape, scrape. The work was numbing to the mind, as well as the body. Mostly, Helen didn't think of anything. She just kept one image before her: that of her mother's posthumously-awarded Parliamentary Medal of Honor, which, in all the many places they had lived since, her father always hung in the most prominent place in their home.

Scrape, scrape. Helen would get no medals for what she was doing, true. But she didn't care, anymore than her mother had cared.

Scrape, scrape. *Running water.*

Victor

When he spotted the figure he was looking for, Victor Cachat was swept by another wave of doubt and hesitation.

And fear.

This is crazy. The best way I can think of to guarantee myself the place of honor—in front of a firing squad.

The uncertainty was powerful enough to hold him rooted in one spot for well over a minute. Fortunately, the grubby tavern was so crowded and dimly lit that his immobility went unnoticed by anyone.

It was certainly unnoticed by the man he was staring at. It took Victor no more than seconds to decide that his quarry was already half-drunk. True, the man sitting at the bar was neither swaying nor slurring the few words he spoke to the bartender. In this, as in everything, Kevin Usher kept himself under tight control. But Victor had seen Usher sober—occasionally—and he thought he could detect the subtle signs.

In the end, it was that which finally overcame Victor's fears.

If he denounces me, I can always claim he was too drunk to know what he's talking about. It's not as if Durkheim won't believe me—he makes enough wisecracks himself about Usher's drinking habits, doesn't he?

At the moment when he came to that conclusion, Victor saw the man sitting next to Usher slide off his bar stool. An instant later, Victor had taken his place.

Again, he hesitated. Usher wasn't looking at him. The Marine citizen colonel was hunched over, staring at nothing beyond the amber liquid in his glass. Victor could still, if he chose, leave without committing himself.

Or so he thought. Victor had forgotten Usher's reputation.

"This is a gross violation of procedure," said the man sitting next to him, without moving his eyes from the glass. "Not to mention the fact that you're breaking every rule of tradecraft. Durkheim would skin you alive." Usher took a sip of his drink. "Well, maybe not. Durkheim's a bureaucrat. What he knows about field work wouldn't tax the brains of a pigeon."

Usher's soft voice gave no indication of drunkenness, beyond the slow pacing of the words. Neither did his eyes, when he finally lifted them toward Victor.

"But what's more important—*way more*—is that I'm off duty and you're disturbing my concentration."

Victor's angry response came too quickly to control. "Fuck you, Usher," he hissed. "As much practice as you get, you could drink in the middle of a hurricane without spilling a drop."

A thin smile came to Usher's face. "Well, well," he drawled. "Whaddaya know? Durkheim's little wonderboy can actually use cuss words."

"I learned to swear before I learned to talk. That's why I don't do it."

The thin smile grew thinner. "Oh, what a thrill. Another Dolee about to spin his tale of poverty and deprivation. I can't wait."

Victor reined in his temper. He was a little shocked at the effort, and realized that it was his own fear which was bubbling up. Victor had learned to control himself by the time he was six years old. That was how he had survived the projects, and clawed his way out.

Out—and up. But he wasn't sure he liked the vista.

"Never mind," he muttered. "I know I'm breaking tradecraft. But I need to talk to you privately, Usher. And I couldn't think of another way to do it."

The smile left Usher's face completely. His eyes went back to the glass. "I've got nothing to say to State Security outside of an interrogation room." The smile came back—*very* thin. "And if you want to get me into an interrogation room, you'd damned well better get some help. I don't think you're up to it, wonderboy."

For just an instant, the large hand holding the shot glass tightened. Glancing at it, Victor had no doubt at all that it would take a full squad of State Sec troops to bring Usher into an interrogation room. And half of them would die in the trying. Lush or not, Usher's reputation was still towering.

"Why?" Victor mused. "You could have been an SS

citizen general by now—citizen *lieutenant* general—
instead of a Marine citizen colonel buried here."

Usher's lips, for just an instant, twisted into a grimace. A half-formed sneer, maybe. "I don't much care
for Saint-Just," was the answer. "Never did, even
before the Revolution."

Victor held his breath for a moment, before
exhaling it sharply. He glanced quickly around the
room. No one was listening, so far as he could tell.
"Well," he drawled, "you don't seem too concerned
with your health, that's for sure."

Usher's lips quirked again. "Are you referring to
my drinking habits?"

Victor snorted. "You'll be lucky if you die of cir-
rhosis of the liver, you go around making wisecracks
about the head of State Security."

"I wasn't making a wisecrack. I was stating a simple
fact. I despise Oscar Saint-Just and I've never made
a secret of it. I've told him so to his face. Twice. Once
before the Revolution, and once after." Usher
shrugged. "He didn't much seem to care, one way
or the other. You can say that much for Saint-Just—
he doesn't kill people out of personal spite. And I'll
grant you that he isn't personally a sadist—unlike most
of the people working for him."

Victor flushed at the implied insult. But he made
no retort, for the simple reason that he couldn't. In
the short time since his graduation from the SS Academy, Victor had learned that Usher's sneer was all too
close to the truth. Which, of course, was why he was
sitting in this tavern in the first place, as dangerous
as it was.

Usher lifted the glass and took a sip. From the
color of the liquid and what he had read in Usher's
file—very *big* file, even if Victor suspected half of it

was missing—he was sure it was Terran whiskey. Sour mash, technically, from some small province called Tennessee.

Usher rolled the glass in his hand, inspecting the amber contents. "But I decided it would be best if I made myself scarce. So, after a time, I took the commission they offered me in the Marines and volunteered to head up the security detachment at the embassy on Terra. Six months' travel, it is, from here to the People's Republic. The arrangement suits me fine. Saint-Just too, apparently."

Usher downed his drink in one gulp and set the shot glass on the table. The motion was swift and sure. The shot glass didn't even make so much as a clink when it hit the table top.

"Now get to the point, wonderboy. Why are you here? If you're trying to set me up, don't bother. My attitude toward SS is just as well known to Rob Pierre as it is to Saint-Just." For a moment, a wicked little gleam came to Usher's eyes. "But Pierre's a bit fond of me, don't you know? I did him a favor, once."

Usher's eyes came to Victor, and the gleam got a lot more wicked. "So go look for a promotion somewhere else."

Victor started to speak, but cut his response short. The bartender had finally arrived. "What'll you have?" he asked, as he refilled Usher's shot glass without being prompted. The Marine citizen colonel was a regular in the place.

Victor ordered a beer and waited until it was served before speaking. "I'm not trying to set you up for anything, Usher. I need your advice."

Usher was back to staring at his drink. The only sign he had heard Victor was a slight cock in his eyebrow. Victor hesitated, trying to think of the best way to say what he had to say. Then, shrugging, went straight to it.

"Durkheim's been dealing with the Mesans. And their cult sidekicks here on Terra. That stinking outfit called the Sacred Band."

Silence. Usher stared at his drink for a few seconds. Then, in another swift motion, drank half of it in one toss. "Why does that not surprise me?" he murmured.

The man's apparent indifference caused a resurgence of Victor's anger.

"Don't you even care?" he demanded, hissing. "For the sake of—"

"Ah! Stop!" Usher flashed him that wicked smile. "Don't tell me wonderboy was about to call on the deity? Rank superstition, that is—*citizen.*"

Victor tightened his jaws. "I was about to say: 'for the sake of the Revolution,' " he finished lamely.

"Sure you were. Sure you were." The Marine citizen colonel leaned over, emphasizing his next words.

"Poor, poor wonderboy. You just discovered that the Revolution has a few blots on its stainless escutcheon, did you?" He turned away, hunching his shoulders, and brought the glass back to his lips. "Why *shouldn't* Durkheim get cozy with the scum of the universe? He's done everything else. State Sec's so filthy already a little more slime won't even show."

Again, Victor flushed at the insult; and, again, made no retort.

Usher started to down the drink, but paused. The pause was very brief. When he set the empty glass down on the table, he spoke very softly: "Did you know you were being followed?"

Victor was startled, but he had enough self-control to keep from turning his head. "*Shit,*" he hissed,

momentarily losing his determination to avoid
profanity.

The thin smile came back to Usher's face. "I will
be damned. I do believe you are the genuine article,
wonderboy. Didn't know there were any left. How
well can you take a punch?"

The *non sequitur* left Victor's mind scrambling to
catch up. "Huh?"

"Never mind," murmured Usher. "If you don't
know, you're about to find out."

The next half minute was a complete blur. Victor
only had fragmented images:

Usher roaring with rage, almost every word an
obscenity. Customers in the bar scrambling away. Himself sailing through the air, landing on his back. Up
again—somehow—sailing onto a table. Usher's face,
contorted with fury, still roaring obscenities.

Most of all:

Pain, and Usher's hands. Big hands. *God, that
bastard's strong!* Victor's attempts to fend them off
were as futile as a kitten's attempts to pry open a
mastiff's jaws.

But he never quite lost consciousness. And some
part of Victor's brain, somewhere in the chaos, understood that Usher wasn't actually trying to kill him. Or
even really hurt him that badly.

Which was a good thing, since after the first few
seconds Victor had no doubt at all that Usher could
have destroyed him utterly. That much of the man's
reputation was no figment of the Revolution's mythology, after all. Despite the terror of the moment, some
part of Victor was singing hosannas.

The admiral and the ambassador

Edwin Young was a tall man, with a lanky physique. The uniform of a rear admiral in the Royal Manticoran Navy—stretched to the very limits of official regulations with little sartorial touches and curlicues—fit him to perfection. The man's fine-boned features and long, slender fingers completed the image of an aristocratic officer quite nicely. So did the relaxed and languid manner in which he sat in his chair behind the large desk in his office.

Even at a glance, anyone familiar with the subtleties of Manticoran society would have assumed the admiral was a member of the nobility—and high-ranked nobility, at that. The intelligence captain who sat across the desk from him thought that the small, tastefully-subdued pin announcing Young's membership in the Conservative Association was really quite unnecessary.

The pin was also against Navy regulations, but the admiral clearly wasn't concerned about being called on the carpet for wearing it while in uniform. The only Manticoran official who outranked him on Terra was Ambassador Hendricks. As it happened, the Manticoran Ambassador to the Solarian League was in the same room with the admiral and the captain, standing by the window. And, as it happened, the ambassador was wearing the identical pin on his own lapel.

The intelligence captain's eyes, however, were not really focused on the admiral's pin. They were focused on the admiral's neck. It was a long neck, slender and supple. Entirely in keeping with Admiral Young's elite birth and breeding.

The captain was quite certain he could break it easily.

Not that he would bother, except as a side-effect. The captain had already considered, and discarded, several different ways in which he could snap the admiral's neck. But they were all too quick. What the captain primarily wanted was the pleasure of crushing the admiral's windpipe, slowly and methodically.

Eventually, of course, the vertebra would be crushed. The pulverized fragments would sever the spinal cord and complete the job. Probably too quickly, since the captain was an immensely powerful man and he could not recall ever having been as enraged as he was at the moment. But—

The captain restrained his fury. The effort involved was difficult enough that he only caught the last few words of the admiral's concluding summary.

"—as I'm sure you will agree, Captain Zilwicki. Once you've had a chance to think it through in a calmer and more rational state of mind."

Through ears still rushing with the sound of his own blood, the captain heard the ambassador's voice chiming in:

"Yes. There is simply no reason they would harm your daughter, Captain. As you have pointed out yourself, that would be quite out of character even for the Peeps. As it is, this brutal and desperate deed goes far beyond normal boundaries of intelligence work."

The captain's blocky form remained still and unmoving in his chair, his thick hands clutching the arm rests. Only his eyes swiveled, to bring the pudgy figure of Ambassador Hendricks under his gaze.

The captain spared only a moment's glance at Hendrick's jowls. He had already concluded that the fat girdling the Ambassador's neck would present no obstacle whatever to strangling him also. But he still favored two or three maneuvers which were quite illegal in tournament wrestling. And for good reason, since all of them would result in ruptured internal organs. The captain thought Hendricks' obese appearance would be much improved, with blood hemorrhaging from every orifice in his body.

He forced his mind away from those thoughts, and brought his attention back to the ambassador's words.

"—can't believe SS is so arrogantly insane to pull something like this. On the eve of Parnell's arrival here on Terra!"

Admiral Young nodded. "They're going to be suffering the worst public relations disaster they've ever had here in the Solarian League. The last thing they'd do is compound it by murdering a fourteen-year-old girl."

Even to himself, the captain's voice sounded thick and hoarse.

"I keep telling you," he snarled, no longer even bothering with military formalities, "that this is *not* a Peep operation. Or, if it is, it's a rogue operation being conducted outside of the loop. There's no way of telling what the people who took Helen might do. I have *got* to have leeway to start investigating—"

"Enough, Captain Zilwicki!" snapped the ambassador. "The decision is made. Of course, I understand your concern. But, at least for the moment, all of our attention must be focused on the opportunities presented to us by Parnell's arrival here on Terra. As a professional intelligence officer, rather than a worried father, I'm sure you agree. We can play along with this Peep diversionary maneuver easily enough. What we *musn't* do is allow it to actually divert us."

"And mind your manners," growled Young. The admiral leaned back even further in his chair, almost slumping in it. "I've made allowances for your behavior so far because of the personal nature of the situation. But you *are* a naval officer, Captain. So you'll do as you're told—*and* stay within the boundaries of military protocol while you're at it."

For a moment, the captain almost hurled himself across the desk. But a lifetime of discipline and self-control stayed with him. And, after a few seconds, reasserted itself.

What kept him steady even more than training and habit was a simple reality: getting himself arrested, or even confined to quarters due to indiscipline, was the surest way he could think of to make his daughter's already slim chance of survival nonexistent.

That realization brought his own final decision. *I'll get Helen out of this, no matter what the cost. Damn everything else.*

The thought brought the first real calmness back to Anton Zilwicki since his daughter had been abducted. It drenched his fury like a bucket of icewater and restored his normally methodical way of thinking.

First things first, he told himself firmly. *Get the hell out of here before they put any actual restrictions on your movements.*

He rose abruptly to his feet and saluted. "As you wish, Admiral. I'll send the communication to the kidnappers from my own home. With your permission. I think that would be better."

"Yes," agreed the ambassador firmly. "If you send it from here, or your own office, they might get suspicious." His tone of voice actually managed a bit of warmth. "Good thinking there, Captain. I'm quite certain, along with the Admiral, that this is a long-term gambit on the part of the Peeps to create a conduit for disinformation. They'll be reassured if their contact with you seems completely private."

The words were spoken in the manner of an old intelligence hand, congratulating a novice on having figured out a simple task. Given the circumstances, Captain Zilwicki almost burst into laughter. The captain *was* an "old intelligence hand." What Hendricks knew about the craft was simply the maneuvers he'd learned as an ambitious nobleman in Manticore's political arena. That arena was complex and tortuous, true, but it was a far less savage place than Zilwicki had inhabited for many years now.

But he let none of his contempt show. He simply nodded politely, bowed, and left the room.

Anton

Sometime later, when he entered his apartment, Zilwicki found Robert Tye still sitting in the lotus position in the center of the living room. To all appearances, the martial arts master had not moved a muscle since the captain left that morning. Tye had his own way of controlling rage.

The martial artist raised an eyebrow. Zilwicki shook his head.

"About what I expected, Robert. The imbeciles are taking this at face value. And they're so obsessed with the propaganda coup provided by Parnell's coming testimony on the Peep regime that they don't want to deal with anything else. So I've been ordered to follow the kidnappers' instructions."

For a moment, Tye studied the captain. Then, a

slight smile came to his face. "And clearly you have no intention of complying."

Zilwicki's only response was a faint snort. He returned the martial artist's scrutiny with one of his own.

Robert Tye had been the first person Anton contacted after he discovered Helen's abduction when he returned to his apartment the previous evening. The captain was still not quite certain why he had done so. He had acted out of impulse, and Anton was not by nature and habit an impulsive man.

Slowly, Anton took a seat on a nearby couch, thinking all the while. He and Helen had been on Terra for slightly over four years. Because of his duties in the Navy, Anton had lived a rather peripatetic life and he was sometimes concerned over the toll that took on Helen. Having to change schools and sets of friends frequently was difficult for a child.

But his daughter, to his surprise, had greeted the announced move to Chicago with enthusiasm. Helen, following in her mother's footsteps, had begun studying the martial arts at the age of six. As was his daughter's habit—her father's child, in this—Helen had studied the lore of the art as well as the art itself. To her, Chicago meant only one thing: the opportunity to study under one of the galaxy's most legendary martial artists.

Anton had been worried that Tye would not accept a young girl for a student. But the martial artist had done so readily. At his age, Tye had once told Anton, he found the presence of children a comfort. And, in the years which followed, Helen's *sensei* had become a part of their little family. More like a grandfather, in many ways, than anything else.

"Are you sure you want to be part of this, Robert?"

he asked abruptly. "I'm not sure it was right for me to get you involved. Whatever I wind up doing, it's bound to be—"

"Dangerous?" suggested Tye, smiling.

Anton chuckled. "I was going to say: *illegal*. Highly illegal."

The martial artist's shoulders moved in a slight shrug. "That does not concern me. But are you so certain your superiors are in error?"

Zilwicki's jaws tightened. His already square face now looked like a solid cube of iron.

"Trust me, Robert. Something like this is completely out of character for Peep intelligence. And they've got nothing to gain."

His expression changed. Not softening so much as simply becoming more thoughtful. "By the nature of my position in Manticoran intelligence, I don't know anything of real use to the Peeps anyway. Not enough, that's for sure, to warrant such a risky gambit." He moved a hand across his knee, as if brushing off a fly. "The Admiral thinks the Peeps are engaging in a long-run maneuver, designed to turn me into an ongoing conduit for disinformation. Which is probably the single most asinine thing that asinine man has ever said in his life."

The martial artist cocked his head a bit. The gesture was a subtle suggestion that the captain's own subtlety had escaped Tye's understanding.

"Robert, the reason the Admiral's theory is nonsense is because it's in the nature of things that a long-run campaign of disinformation has to be reasonably stable. Disinformation campaigns take time— lots of time. You can't suddenly have your turned agent start flooding his own intelligence service with 'information' which seems odd and contrary to other information. It has to be done in a careful and subtle manner. Slowly adding one little bit of information at a time, until—over a period of months, more often years—a warped perception of reality becomes accepted without anyone really knowing when and how it happened."

"All right, I can understand that."

Zilwicki ran fingers through his short-cropped, coarse black hair. "Kidnapping a man's daughter and using her as a threat is about as far removed from 'stable' as I can imagine. Even if the father involved submitted completely, the situation would be impossible. If nothing else, in his anxiety the father would push the campaign too quickly and screw it up. Not to mention the difficulty of keeping a captive for a long period, on foreign soil where you can't simply toss her into a prison. And you'd have to do so, because under those circumstances the father would insist on regular proof that his child was still alive and well."

For all the captain's tightly controlled speech, his anxiety drove him to his feet. "Say whatever else you want about the Peeps, Robert, but they're not stupid. This is completely out of character for them in a hundred different ways."

"So now what shall we do?"

"I'll start with my contacts in the Chicago police," growled Zilwicki. He stalked over to the side table and stared down at the piece of paper resting on it. A cold, almost cruel smile came to his face.

"Can you believe this? An actual *ransom note?*" The barked little laugh which followed was harsh. "Professional intelligence! God in Heaven, what Hendricks knows about that subject could be inscribed on the head of a pin. Or his own head."

The savage smile widened. "Apparently, these so-called 'pros' have never heard of modern forensics. Which is not the least of the reasons I don't think this was done by the Peeps."

Zilwicki's eyes moved to the door of the apartment. The same door which, the day before, someone had managed to open without leaving any sign of a forced entry. "Everything about this operation smacks of amateurs who are too clever for their own good. Oil mixed with water. The ransom note is archaic. Yet the door's modern security devices were bypassed effortlessly.

"Idiots," he said softly. "They'd have done better to burn it open. Would have taken a bit of time, with a modern door. But as it is, they might as well have left another note announcing in bold letters: *inside job*. Whoever they were, they had to have the complicity of someone in the complex's maintenance staff. Within twenty-four hours, if they move fast—and they will—the Chicago cops can get me profiles of everyone who works in this complex along with the forensics results. I don't think it'll be that hard to narrow the suspects down to a very small list."

"Will the police cooperate to that extent?"

"I think so. They owe me some favors, for one thing. For another, they have their own attitude toward kidnapping, which usually makes them willing to bend the rules a little."

His eyes came back to the ransom note sitting on the side table. An actual note, written by an actual person, on actual paper. Again the captain barked a laugh. "Professional intelligence!"

THE SECOND DAY

Helen

At first, Helen had planned to just leave the digging shards out in the open, lying with the rest of the rubble which half-filled the cell. But soon enough she realized that if her captors took a close look at the interior of the cell, they would surely notice the signs of recent use on the shards.

Not that such an inspection was very likely. From what she could tell, her captors were so arrogant that they apparently never even considered the possibility that a fourteen-year-old girl might try to thwart them.

Helen had never gotten a good look at her captors, after the first few moments when they had jimmied their way into the apartment and abducted her. They had fitted a hood over her head right away and somehow smuggled her out of the huge complex without being spotted. How they managed that feat was a mystery to Helen, since the complex had a population density which was astonishing to anyone from Manticore. She had realized from the first terrifying hour that they must have planned her abduction carefully, and had the assistance of someone within the apartment complex's maintenance staff.

Once they got her underground, they had eventually removed the hood. Helen didn't think they had planned on doing that, but it had quickly proven necessary—unless they wanted to carry her. The footing in the subterranean labyrinth was so treacherous that Helen had continually tripped while wearing the hood. She had been snarled at and cuffed several times before the abductors finally bowed to the inevitable and took off the hood.

Her captors' angry exasperation with her was just another sign of the carelessness which lay beneath the arrogant surface. For all the meticulous planning that had clearly gone into her abduction, her captors had apparently never thought of such minor obstacles. From Helen's careful study of military history—she firmly intended to follow her parents' footsteps and have a career in the Navy—she recognized the classic signs of opponents who were too full of themselves and never bothered to consider what the enemy might do. Or to simply understand what the ancient Clausewitz had called the inevitable "friction of war."

But, even though the hood had been removed, they had cuffed her immediately whenever her eyes veered in their direction. And since they had shoved her into this cell they still demanded that she face the wall whenever they entered with her food. According to the novels she had read, that was a good sign. Captors who didn't want to be recognized were not planning to kill you.

That was the theory, at least. Helen didn't place too much credence in it, however. She still had no idea who her captors were, or why they had kidnapped her. But of one thing she had no doubt at all: they would no more hesitate to kill her than they would an insect. Granted, at the age of fourteen she could hardly claim to be an expert on human villainy. But it was obvious enough, just from the way her captors *walked*, that they considered themselves a breed apart. She had seen little of their faces, but she had not missed the little strut with which all of them moved. Like leopards, preening before sheep.

There were four of them: two males, and two females. From the few glances she'd gotten, they'd looked enough alike that Helen thought they might be part of the same family. But now that she had a chance to think about it calmly, she was beginning to think otherwise. Her captors had made no attempt to remain silent in her presence, for the good and simple reason that they spoke their own language. Helen didn't know the tongue, but she thought she recognized the language group. Many of the phrases resonated with the Old Byelorussian that was still spoken in some of the more rural areas of the Gryphon highlands. She was almost certain her captors were speaking a derivative of one of the Slavic languages.

And, if so, there was an ugly possibility. Her father had mentioned to her, once, that the genetic "super-soldiers" who had been at the heart of Earth's terrible Final War had originally been bred in Ukrainian laboratories. The "super-soldiers" had been supposedly annihilated in those wars. But her father had told her that some of them survived. And still lurked, somewhere in the great human ocean which was humanity's home planet.

By all accounts, those genetic "super-soldiers" had looked upon other people as nothing more than beasts of burden. Or toys for their amusement.

Or insects . . .

That last image brought a peculiar kind of comfort. Helen realized she was pursuing the ancient strategy of one of Terra's most successful species. Like a cockroach, she would find safety in the walls.

Her lips quirked in a smile, she went back to digging.

Victor

Durkheim came to visit Victor in the hospital. As always, the head of State Security's detachment at the Havenite embassy on Terra was curt and abrupt.

"Nothing really serious," he muttered. "Spectacular set of cuts and bruises, but nothing worse. You're lucky."

Durkheim was thin to the point of emaciation. His bony, sunken-cheeked face was perched on the end of a long and scrawny neck. Standing at the foot of the quick-heal tank and staring down at him, the SS citizen general reminded Victor of nothing so much as holographs he had seen of a Terran vulture perched on a tree limb.

"So what happened?" he demanded.

Victor's answer came without hesitation. "I was just trying to get Usher to cut down on the drinking. Looks bad for our image here. I never imagined—"

Durkheim snorted. "Talk about foolish apprentices!" There was no heat in his voice, however. "Leave Usher alone, youngster. Frankly, the best thing for everybody would be if he'd just drink himself to death."

He placed a clawlike hand on the rim of the tank and leaned over. Now, he *really* looked like a carrion-eater.

"Usher's still alive for the sole reason that he's a Hero of the Revolution—never mind the details—and Rob Pierre is sometimes prone to sentimentalism. *That's it*." Hissing: "You understand?"

Victor swallowed. "Yes, sir."

"Good." Durkheim straightened up. "Fortunately,

Usher keeps his mouth shut, so there's no reason to do anything about the situation. I don't expect he'll live more than another year or so—not the way he guzzles whiskey. So just stay away from him, henceforth. That's an order."

"Yes, sir." But Durkheim was already through the door. As always, watching him, Victor was a bit amazed. For all Durkheim's cadaverous appearance and the angular awkwardness of his stride, the SS official managed to move very quickly.

Victor almost laughed. The way Durkheim jogged out his elbows as he walked resembled a vulture flapping his wings. But Victor managed to keep the humor under control. He was not *that* naive.

Like any predator, Durkheim would eat carrion. But he was still a predator, and a very dangerous one. Of that, Victor had no doubt at all.

He was released from the hospital three hours later. It was too late in the day for Victor to go to the embassy, so he decided he might as well return to his apartment. His apartment was buried in the enormous, towering complex in which the People's Republic of Haven leased a number of apartments for its embassy staff. Unfortunately, the complex was located in the city's easternmost district, on the landfill which, over the centuries, had slowly extended kilometers into Lake Michigan. A prestigious address, to be sure, but it meant a long trip on Chicago's labyrinthine public transport system. The hospital was located on the edge of the Old Quarter, not far from the tavern which was Usher's favorite watering hole.

Victor sighed. And *that* meant—

It was not that Victor had any prejudice against the hordes of poor immigrants who thronged in the Old

Quarter and mobbed public transport in its vicinity. In truth, he felt more comfortable in their midst than he did among the Solarian elite that he hobnobbed with in the embassy's frequent social functions. The Old Quarter's residents reminded him of the people he had grown up with, in the Dolist projects of Nouveau Paris.

But there was a reason, after all, that Victor had fought so hard to get out of those projects. So it was with no great enthusiasm that he resigned himself to spending an hour crammed into the transport network. The Solarian League's capital city liked to boast of its public transportation system. Yet Victor had noticed that none of Chicago's elite ever used it.

So what else is new? He consoled himself with thoughts of the inevitable coming revolution in the Solarian League. He had been on Terra long enough to see the rot beneath the glittering surface.

Not more than five minutes after he forced himself into the mob packing one of the transport capsules—a good name for the things, he thought ruefully—he felt someone pressing against him.

Like everyone else, Victor was standing. He had been told once that the capsules had originally been built with seats, but those had long since been removed from the capsules used in the Old Quarter due to the pressure of overcapacity. Victor had the relatively short stature common to Havenites raised on a Dolist diet, but he was still taller than most of the immigrants in the Old Quarter.

He glanced down. The person pressed so closely against him—too closely, even by capsule standards—was a young woman. From her dusky skin tone and facial features, she shared the south Asian genetic background which was common to a large number of

Chicago's immigrant population. Even if it hadn't been for the lascivious smile on her face, beaming up at him, he would have known from her costume that she was a prostitute. Somewhere back in the mists of time, her outfit traced its lineage to a sari. But this version of the garment was designed to emphasize the woman's supple limbs and sensuous belly.

Nothing unusual, in the Old Quarter. Victor had lost track of the number of times he had been propositioned since he arrived on Terra, less than a year ago. As always, he shook his head and murmured a refusal. As a matter of class solidarity, if nothing else, Victor was never rude to prostitutes. So the refusal was polite. But it was still firm, for all that.

He was surprised, therefore, when she persisted. The woman was now practically embracing him. She extended her tongue, wagging it in his face. When he saw the tongue's upper surface, Victor stiffened.

Speak of the devil. Mesa's genetic engineers always marked their slaves in that manner. The markings served the same purpose as the brands or tattoos used by slavers in the past, but these were completely ineradicable, short of removing the tongue entirely. The marks were actually part of the flesh itself, grown there as the genengineered embryo developed. For technical reasons which Victor did not understand, taste buds lent themselves easily to that purpose.

The stiffness in his posture was partly due to revulsion, but mostly to sheer anger. If there was any foulness in the universe as great as Mesa and Manpower Inc., Victor did not know what it was. But this woman, he reminded himself, was herself a victim of that monstrosity. So Victor used his anger to drive the revulsion under. He repeated the refusal—even more firmly—but this time with a very friendly smile.

No use. Now the woman had her mouth against the side of his head, as if kissing him.

"Shut up, wonderboy," she whispered. "He'll talk to you. Get off at the Jackson transfer and follow me."

Victor was stiff as a board. "My, my," she whispered. "He was right. You *are* a babe in the woods."

Anton

The Chicago police lieutenant's frown was worthy of Jove. "I'm warning you, Anton—if we start finding dead bodies lying around in this complex, I'll arrest you in a heartbeat."

Zilwicki's eyes never lifted from the packet the lieutenant had handed him. "Don't worry about it, Muhammad. I'm just looking for information, that's all."

Lieutenant Muhammad Hobbs studied the shorter man for a moment. Then, the small figure of Robert Tye sitting on the floor of Zilwicki's apartment. Then, the cybernetics console tucked into a corner. Even at a glance, it was obvious that the capabilities of that console went far beyond anything that would normally be found in a private residence.

For a moment, Hobbs' dark face darkened still further. Then, sighing softly, he murmured: "Just remember. We're really going out on a limb for you with this one, Anton. At least half a dozen of us, starting with me, will be lucky if we just lose our pensions."

The Manticoran officer finally lifted his eyes from the forensics packet and nodded. "I understand, Muhammad. No dead bodies. Nothing, in fact, that would be awkward for the police."

"Such as a rush of people into hospitals with broken bones," growled the policeman. Again, his eyes moved to Tye. "Or worse."

Tye smiled gently. "I believe you misinterpret the nature of my art, Lieutenant Hobbs."

Muhammad snorted. "Save it for the tourists. I've seen you in tournaments, *sensei*. Even playing by the rules, you were scary enough."

He pointed a finger at Zilwicki. "And this one? I can't recall ever seeing him in a lotus, contemplating the whichness of what. But I use the same gym he does, and I *have* seen him bench-press more pounds than I want to think about."

The policeman straightened and arched his shoulders, as if relieving himself of a small burden. "All right, enough," he growled. He turned away and headed for the door. "Just remember: no dead bodies; no hospital reports."

Before the door had even closed, Zilwicki was sitting in front of the console. Within a few seconds, he had loaded the data from the police forensics report and was completely absorbed by the material appearing on the screen.

Victor

Victor had never been *into* the Old Quarter before. He'd skirted the edges of it often enough, and gone through it in public transport capsules. But this was the first time he'd actually walked through the streets.

If the word "streets" could be used at all. Urban planners, following the jargonistic tendencies of all social sciences, often preferred the term "arteries" to

refer to public thoroughfares. The euphemism, applied
to the Old Quarter, was no euphemism at all. Except
for being square in cross-section rather than round,
and the fact that human beings passed through them
instead of blood corpuscles, the "streets" were as complex, convoluted, tortuous and three-dimensional as
a body's circulatory system. More so, really, since the
clear distinction between arteries and veins was absent
here.

Victor was hopelessly lost within minutes. In that
short space of time, the woman leading him had
managed to take him through more streets than he
could remember—including four elevator transits,
three occasions when they passed through huge underground "plazas" filled with vendors' booths and shops,
and even one instance in which she strode blithely
through some kind of lecture or public meeting and
exited by a door in the back next to the toilets. The
only logic to her route that Victor could follow was
that the "streets" always got narrower, the ceiling
lower, and the artificial lighting dimmer.

At least I won't have to worry about being followed.

As if the thought had been spoken aloud, the
women ahead of him cocked her head and said: "See?
This is how you do it." She chuckled throatily. "Anybody asks, you just went to get laid. Who's going to
prove otherwise?"

Suddenly, she stopped and turned around. The
motion was so abrupt that Victor almost ran into her.
He managed to stop, but they were now standing
practically nose to nose. Well—nose to forehead. Like
most Mesan genetic slaves except the heavy labor and
combat breeds, the woman was very small.

She grinned up at him. The grin had a generic
similarity to the professional leer she had bestowed

upon him in the transport capsule, but there was more actual emotion in it. Humor, mainly.

Like all solemn and dedicated young men who don't suffer from extreme egotism, Victor suspected that the humor was at his expense. The woman immediately proved him right.

"You don't even have to fake it," she announced cheerfully. "If you want it kinky, of course, I charge extra. Unless it's too kinky, in which case I won't do it at all."

Victor liked her grin. It was almost friendly, in a rakish sort of way. But he still stammered out another refusal.

"Too bad. You would have enjoyed it and I could have used the money." She eyed him speculatively. "You sure?" The grin grew more rakish still. "Maybe a little bondage? Not—"

Here came the throaty chuckle. "—that you don't look like you're tied up in knots already."

Fortunately, Victor didn't have to think up a suitable rejoinder to that remark. The woman just shrugged, turned, and got under way again.

They spent another few minutes following the same kind of twisted route. Two minutes into it, Victor remarked that he was quite certain they had shaken whoever might have been tailing him from the hospital.

The woman's reply came with a snort: "Who's trying to? This is how you get to where I live, wonderboy." Again, that throaty chuckle. "I'm not in the business of shaking tails *that* way."

The chuckle became an outright laugh. For the next minute or so, leading him through the crowded "public arteries," the woman ahead of him put on a dazzling display of shaking her tail. Long before she was done, Victor was beginning to deeply regret his refusal.

Duty first! Discipline!

But he kept the thought to himself. He could well imagine her response, and the rakish grin and chuckle which would accompany it.

Victor spent the remaining minutes of their trek simply studying his surroundings. Chicago's Old Quarter—or "the Loop," as it was sometimes called, for no reason that anyone understood—was famous from one end of the Solarian League to the other.

Notorious, rather, in the way that such largely-immigrant neighborhoods have been throughout history. Dens of vice and iniquity, of course. *You can buy anything in the Loop.* But there was also a glamorous aura surrounding the place. Artists, writers and musicians abounded, filling the Old Quarter's multitude of taverns and coffeehouses. (*Real* coffee—the true Terran strain. Victor had tried some once, but found he didn't like it. In this, as in many things, the earnest young revolutionary from the slums of Nouveau Paris was more conservative than any decadent elitist.) The artists were invariably "avant-garde" and had the poverty to prove it. The writers were mostly poets and enjoyed a similar income. The musicians, on the other hand, often did quite well. Except for opera, the Loop was the center of Chicago's musical night life.

Rich or poor, the culturally inclined habitués of the megametropolis' Old Quarter rubbed elbows with their more dangerous brethren. Over the centuries, the Loop had become the center of the Solarian League's criminal elite as well as every brand of political radical.

Chicago drew all of them like a magnet, from everywhere in the huge and sprawling Solarian League. But since respectable Solarian society generally refused to acknowledge the existence of such things as widespread poverty and crime, the bureaucrats who were the real political power in the League saw to it that the unwelcome riffraff was kept out of sight and, and much as possible, out of mind. As long as the immigrants stayed in the Loop, except for those who worked as servants, they were generally left alone by the authorities. Within limits, the Loop was almost a nation unto itself. Chicago's police only patrolled the main thoroughfares and those sectors which served as entertainment centers for the League's "proper" citizens. For the rest—*let them rot*.

In some ways—poverty, danger, congestion—the Loop reminded Victor of the squalid Dolist slums which had grown like a cancer during the long reign of Haven's Legislaturalist regime. But only up to a point. The Dolist slums in which Victor had been born and spent his entire life until he volunteered to join State Security were grim, gray and sullen places. That was beginning to change, as popular fervor for the Revolution and the war against the Manticoran elitists swelled and Victor's class of people began to accept the necessity for discipline. Still, the Dolist quarters of the People's Republic of Haven were *slums*.

Victor suspected that the Loop was even more dangerous than the slums of Haven. Yet, there was a key difference. The Loop was a *ghetto*, not simply a collection of tenements. And, like many ghettoes throughout history, there was a real vibrancy to its life. Beneath the grime and the poverty and the sneers of respectable society, the Loop possessed a certain genuine verve and élan.

Alas, that dashing *joie de vivre* extended to pick-pockets as well. By the time Victor reached their destination, he had lost his wallet. He did manage to hang onto his watch, but it was a close thing.

When the woman reached her apartment, she began punching in the codes to unlock the door. It was a time-consuming process, given the number of locks. She even had a key for one of them—a real, genuine, antique metal *key*. As he waited, Victor suddenly realized that he didn't know her name. He was deeply embarrassed by his lapse into elitism.

"I'm sorry," he muttered. "My name's Victor. I forgot to ask—"

Triumphantly, the woman turned the key and the door finally opened. Just as triumphantly, she bestowed her grin on Victor.

"Sorry, wonderboy. I only give out my name to paying customers."

She swept through the door like a grande dame making an entrance into a palace. Sheepishly, Victor followed.

The door led directly into a small living room. Usher was there, sprawled comfortably on a couch.

"He's all yours, Kevin," announced the woman. "But I'll give you fair warning. He ain't no fun at all."

She moved toward a door on the right, shaking her tail with verve and élan and *joie de vivre*. "I'll be in the bedroom. Probably masturbating, even if the pay is scandalous."

She closed the door behind her. Also with verve and élan and *joie de vivre*.

Victor took a deep breath and let it out in a rush. "She's quite something," he pronounced.

Usher smiled. The same thin, wicked smile that

Victor remembered. "Yeah, I know. That's why I married her."

Seeing Victor's wide eyes, Usher's smile became very thin, and very wicked. "There's no mention of her in my file, is there? That's lesson number one, junior. The map is not the territory. The man is not the file."

Helen

Helen was working much faster now. From experience, she had grown confident that her captors would only enter her cell to feed her. They seemed completely oblivious to the possibility that she might try to escape.

The heavy door which they used to lock her in the cell had clearly been brought there from somewhere else. An impressive door, in many ways—solid and heavy. It looked like a new door, in fact. Helen suspected they had purchased it for that very purpose. And then, must have spent many hours fitting the door frame into the ragged entrance and sealing it shut.

She found it hard not to laugh, imagining her father's sarcasm. *Amateurs!* A splendid door, sure enough—except it had no peephole. If her captors wanted to check on Helen, the only way they could do so was to open the door itself. Which, needless to say, they had equipped with several locks—even, judging by the sounds, with a heavy chain to secure the entire frame to the exterior wall. As if a fourteen-year-old girl was likely to smash through it by main force!

The end result was that Helen would always have

advance warning if her captors entered her cell. Enough time, hopefully, to cover her work—although that would become less feasible as her tunnel deepened.

She broke off from her labor for a moment. She had now managed to get two feet into the wall, almost too deep for her to reach the face any longer. The hole she was digging was just big enough for her to squeeze into once it became necessary to continue the work inside. And it was still small enough to keep covered with an old panel which she had found lying among the pieces of rubble in the cell.

Thinking the situation through, Helen realized that she would have to figure out some kind of timing device before she went much further. Unfortunately, her captors had taken her chrono before they thrust her into the cell. Once she was actually working inside the tunnel, the loud warnings which her captors inadvertently made when they opened the door might not penetrate. And, even if they did, might not leave her enough time to come out and cover her tracks before they entered the cell.

But she didn't spend much time pondering that problem. Helen had always enjoyed working with her hands, especially after her father introduced her to the pleasures of model-building. She was adept at jury-rigging little gadgets, and was quite sure she could manage to design and build some sort of simple time-keeper.

Instead, she concentrated on a cruder and more fundamental problem. Digging itself, fortunately, was not proving difficult. Helen had discovered, once she broke through the first few inches, that the rubble beyond was not much more than loose fill. She was quite certain, by now, that she was somewhere deep beneath the Old Quarter, in the endless layers of rubble and ruins which marked the ancient center of the city. Chicago was well over two thousand years old. Especially during the war centuries, no one had bothered to remove old and crumbled buildings and structures. Just—leveled them, and built over the wreckage.

The real problem was the classic quandary of all tunnel escapes: *where do you put the dirt?*

Regretfully, because it would be so time-consuming, she came to the conclusion that she would have to mix the fresh fill with the old dirt and dust covering the cell. Carefully blending them, so that the color contrast would not be too noticeable. Over time, of course, the color would start to change and the level of the floor would slowly rise. But she hoped that the process would be too imperceptible for her captors to notice.

All that, of course, presupposed that she had weeks ahead of her. She had no idea if that presumption was accurate. It probably wasn't. For all Helen knew, her captors intended to kill her in the next hour. But she had no other option, other than to sit and wait. Like a sheep.

Damn that! The memory of her mother kept her strong; Master Tye's training kept her steady. And she knew that her father would be coming for her. Not soon, perhaps, but surely. Her father was like that. If he had none of the romance which surrounded her mother's memory, he was as certain as the sunrise and the tides.

She went back to work. Scrape, scrape.

Anton

After he finished studying the police forensics report, Anton rose from the console and moved over to the window overlooking the city. He was oblivious to the view, however. Which was probably just as well, since the "picture window" in his relatively inexpensive apartment simply had a view of another enormous residential complex across the boulevard. If he craned his neck, he might catch a glimpse of the busy street far below.

But his eyes were not focused on the sight. His mind was turned completely inward.

"Jesus Christ," he murmured. "I knew this wasn't a Peep operation, but I wasn't expecting *this*."

From behind, he heard Robert Tye's voice. "You know the identity of the culprits?"

Zilwicki nodded. "The Sacred Band," he growled. "The 'Scrags,' as they're sometimes called. The genetic markers are unmistakable." He turned away from the window and stared down at the martial artist. "You've heard of them?"

"They're supposed to be a fable, you know," replied Tye. "An urban legend. All the experts say so."

Zilwicki said nothing. After a moment, Tye chuckled dryly. "As it happens, however, I once had one of them as a student. Briefly. It didn't take me long to figure out who he was—or what he was, I should say—since the fellow couldn't resist demonstrating his natural physical prowess."

"That would be typical," murmured Zilwicki. "Arrogant to the last. What happened then?"

Tye shrugged. "Nothing. Once his identity became

clear, I told him his company was no longer desired. I was rather emphatic. Fortunately, he was not *quite* arrogant enough to argue with me. So he went on his way and I never saw him again."

"One of them works in this building," said Zilwicki abruptly. "His profile leaps right out from the rest of the employee files. The bastard didn't even bother with plastic surgery. The bone structure's obvious, once you know what to look for, even leaving aside the results of his medical exams. 'In perfect health,' his doctors say, which I'm sure he is. The man's name is Kennesaw and he's the maintenance supervisor. Which explains, of course, how he was able to circumvent the apartment's security."

His eyes moved back to the window, and again grew unfocused. "And it also explains why the Scrags selected Helen as their victim. Opportunity, pure and simple. Almost a random choice, given that they must have wanted someone connected to the Manticoran embassy."

"And why that?" asked Tye. "What does the Sacred Band want with your people?"

Zilwicki shrugged. "That's still a mystery. But if I had to guess, I'd say that they're working for Manpower Inc."

Tye's eyes widened a bit. "The Mesan slave-breeders? I didn't realize there was a connection."

"It's not something Manpower advertises," chuckled Anton harshly. "As much effort as those scum put into their respectable appearance, you can understand why they wouldn't want to be associated in the public mind with monsters out of Terran history. Half-legendary creatures with a reputation as bad as werewolves or vampires."

"Worse," grunted Tye. "Nobody really believes

werewolves or vampires *ever* existed. The Final War was all too real."

Zilwicki nodded. "As for the Sacred Band itself, the attachment to Manpower is natural enough. For all that they make a cult of their own superhuman nature, the Scrags are nothing more today than a tiny group. Manticoran intelligence has never bothered to investigate them very thoroughly. But we're pretty sure they don't number more than a few dozen, here in Chicago—and fewer still, anywhere else. They're vicious bastards, of course, and dangerous enough to anyone who crosses them in the slums of the city. But powerless in any meaningful sense of the term."

He shrugged. "So, like many other defeated groups in history, they transferred their allegiance to a new master and a new cause. Close enough to their old one to maintain ideological continuity, but with real influence in the modern universe. Which the Mesans certainly have. And, although Manpower Inc. claims to be a pure and simple business, you don't have to be a genius to figure out the implicit political logic of their enterprise. What the old Terrans would have called 'fascism.' If some people can be bred for slavery, after all, others can be bred for mastery."

"But—" Tye squeezed his eyes shut for a moment. "Oh, for the simple problems of the dojo," he muttered. Then: "I still don't understand. Why is Manpower doing this? Do they have some personal animus against you?"

"Not that I can think of. Not really. It's true that Helen—my wife—belonged to the Anti-Slavery League. But she was never actually active in the organization. And although not many officers go so far as to join the ASL, anti-Mesan attitudes are so widespread in the Navy that she didn't really stand out in any way. Besides, that was years ago."

Slowly, his mind ranging, Anton shook his head. "No, Robert. This isn't personal. The truth is, I don't even think Manpower is at the bottom of it. I wasn't kidding when I said they bend over backward to appear as respectable as possible. There's no way the Mesans would have gotten involved in something like this unless someone offered them a very powerful inducement. Either in the nature of a threat or a reward."

He clasped both hands behind his neck and spread his elbows. The gesture, which was simply a means of inducing relaxation, also highlighted the captain's immensely thick and muscular form.

After a moment, realizing what he was doing, Zilwicki smiled slightly and lowered his arms. The smile bore a trace of sadness underneath. His dead wife, Helen, had often teased him about the mannerism. "The Zilwicki maneuver," she'd called it, claiming it was a subconscious attempt at intimidation.

Yet, if he relinquished that form of projecting power, the cold grin which came to Anton's face probably served the purpose even better. "But now that the Scrags and Manpower have entered the picture, I think I've found the angle I need to get around Young and Hendricks. And, if I'm right, it'll be pure poetic justice."

Once again, Zilwicki sat down before the console. "This will probably take a couple of days, Robert. Unless those two are even dumber than I think they are, their security codes are going to take some effort to crack."

"Can you do it at all?" asked Tye.

Zilwicki chuckled humorlessly, as his thick fingers

manipulated the keyboard with ease. "One of the advantages to looking the way I do, Robert—especially when people know I used to be a 'yard dog'—is that they always assume I must be some kind of mechanical engineer. As it happens, my specialty is software. Especially security systems."

Tye's face crinkled. "I myself shared that assumption. I've always had this splendid image of you, covered with grease and wielding a gigantic wrench. How distressing to discover it was all an illusion."

Anton smiled, but said nothing in reply. Already, he was deeply engrossed in his work.

By late afternoon, he leaned back in his chair and sighed. "That's as much as I can do for the moment. The next stage is pure numbers-crunching, which will take at least twenty-four hours. Probably longer. So we've got some time to pay a visit on Kennesaw. But first—"

The look which now came over Zilwicki's face made Tye think of someone who'd just seen a ghost. The intelligence captain's expression was almost haggard, and he seemed a little pale.

"What's wrong?"

Anton shook his head. "Just something I can't postpone any longer. I've been able to block it out of my mind so far, but now—"

Again, his fingers began working at the keyboard. Tye rose to his feet and padded over. Some sort of schematic diagram was filling the screen. None of it meant anything to the martial artist.

"What are you doing?"

Zilwicki's face was as gaunt as a square face could get, but his fingers never faltered in their work. "One of the standard techniques in kidnapping, Robert, is to simply kill the victim immediately. That eliminates the trouble of guarding the person, and it removes any witnesses."

He grunted. "But it's something which is done either by pure amateurs or complete professionals. The amateurs because they don't realize just how hard it is to dispose of a body quickly without leaving any evidence, and the pros because they know how to do it. What I'm hoping is that the people who took Helen know enough, but not too much."

As he had been speaking, several different diagrams and schematics had flashed across the screen. Now, as a new one came up, Zilwicki concentrated on it for some time. Then he grunted again. This time, however, the sound carried an undertone of satisfaction.

"Good. There are plenty of traces of organic disposal, of course, but not what a human body would show. If there had been, the alarms would have gone off. And the alarms themselves haven't been tampered with. Unless it was done by a software maestro, which I'm willing to bet Kennesaw isn't. Or any other member of the Sacred Band. Not, at least, when it comes to this kind of specialized stuff."

The haggard look vanished. Zilwicki's fingers began working again. "But I *am* a software maestro, if I say so myself, and while this is tricky it's not impossible. *If* you know what you're doing."

Robert Tye cleared his throat. "Do you enjoy speaking gobbledygook, Anton?"

Zilwicki smiled crookedly. "Sorry. Occupational hazard for a cyberneticist. Modern technology makes disposing of a human body quite easy, Robert. Any garbage processing unit in a large apartment complex such as this one can manage it without even burping.

In the Star Kingdom, we just live with that reality and the police do their best. But you Solarians are addicted to rules and regulations. So, without any big public fanfare having been made about it, almost all publicly available mechanisms which utilize enough energy to destroy a human body also have detectors built into them. If you don't know about them, or don't know how to get around the alarms, simply shoving a corpse into the disposal unit will have the police breathing down your neck in minutes."

He tapped a final key and leaned back, exuding a certain cold satisfaction. "They may have killed Helen, but they didn't do what I most feared—killed her right away and shoved her into the building's disintegrator."

There was silence for a moment. Then, speaking very softly, Tye said: "I take it you *have*—just now—circumvented the alarms."

"Yeah, I did. For the next twenty-fours, nothing disintegrated in this building is going to alert the police. And after the alarms come back on, it will be far too late to reconstruct anything at all—even if you know what you're looking for."

The captain rose to his feet, glanced at his watch, and headed for the door. "Come on, Robert. Kennesaw works the day shift. He should be coming back to his apartment in about half an hour."

Victor

"He did *what?*" demanded Usher. The Marine citizen colonel lost his air of casual relaxation and sat upright on the couch. The tendons on the back of his large hand, gripping the armrest, stood out like cables.

Knowing—all too well—what those hands were capable of, Victor almost flinched. He did shrink back slightly in his own chair. "I'm not *positive* about that, Kevin. Not that last bit, anyway, about the Zilwicki girl. I'm sure he sent the order to the Mesans he's been talking to, but I may not have interpreted it correctly. It was—"

Usher wiped his face wearily. "You were right, Victor. We'll have to make sure, of course. But I'll bet on it."

It was the first time Usher had called him by his name instead of one or another appellation. Oddly enough, Victor found that he was delighted. But perhaps it was not so odd. In the short time that he had spent in Usher's secret apartment, Victor had decided that Usher was what he had always *thought* he would encounter in the field during his time at the SS Academy. Not simply an older, more experienced comrade serving as his mentor—but the spirit of comradeship itself.

Usher rose slowly to his feet and paced into the kitchen. When he came back, he was holding two bottles of that ancient Terran beverage called *cola*. Wordlessly, he handed one of them to Victor. Then, seeing the slight frown in the young SS officer's face, Usher chuckled drily.

"Lesson number—what is it, now?—eight, I think. A *reputation* for being a drunk can keep you out of as much trouble as being one gets you into." He padded to his couch and sunk into it. "I've got a high capacity for alcohol, but I don't drink anywhere near as much as people think."

Usher took a swig from his bottle. "No, this is exactly the kind of scheme Durkheim would dream up. Typical desk pilot idea—and Durkheim's a good one. It's a brilliantly conceived maneuver, sure enough. In one stroke, he gets both Parnell and Bergren assassinated, manages to keep the obvious culprits—*us*—from getting blamed, shifts the blame— or, at least, muddies the waters—by getting a Manty intelligence officer tied to the thing, and even, maybe, gets us a little bit of the first good media coverage since the Harrington news broke. Reminds the public that on the question of genetic slavery we're still the best guys in town."

Usher was silent for a moment, as he resumed his seat on the couch. Then: "Parnell, you may remember, was the admiral who cleaned out that Manpower nest on Esterheim when the Legislaturist regime was using extirpation of the slave trade as their excuse for territorial expansion. Bergren, as the Secretary of Foreign Affairs, gave the official approval for it. So killing them could seem like Mesa's overdue revenge." He took another swig from the bottle and snorted savagely. "The idiot! Talk about your castles in the air."

Seeing Victor's gape, Usher chuckled. His quick sketch of Durkheim's purpose had left young Cachat behind in a cloud of dust. *Way* behind. Victor's account of Durkheim's actions had included no mention of the purpose of those actions, for the good and simple reason that Victor was as mystified by Durkheim's doings as he was outraged.

Usher leaned forward. "Think it through, Victor. Why else would the head of SS on Terra be having black liaisons with Manpower and their stooges? And why else would he do something as insane as have the daughter of a Manty officer kidnapped?"

Victor shook his head. The gesture was not one of negation, simply that of a man trying to clear his head of confusion. "I don't get it. Parnell, sure—I can see why he'd want to have him killed, the moment he sets foot on Terra. But we had a discussion of that already—the entire officer staff—and it didn't take us more than twenty minutes to decide unanimously—Durkheim too!—that we'd automatically get the blame for *anything* that happened to Parnell. Even if he tripped on the sidewalk or came down with a virus." Victor winced. "Which would only make the propaganda damage that much worse."

The wince turned into a lasting grimace. "Is it really true, Kevin?" he asked softly. "I mean—what they say Parnell's going to say?" He was holding his breath without realizing it.

"Victor," Kevin replied, in a voice equally soft, "I made my decision to accept a commission in the Marines the day I heard Saint-Just had appointed Tresca as the new commander of the prison planet. That wasn't handwriting on the wall, that was blazing comets in the sky. Every old timer in the underground knew Tresca, and knew what that appointment meant. It was Saint-Just's way of telling us that the good old days of the comradeship were *over.*" He sighed, groping blindly for the bottle of cola sitting on the stand next to the couch. "Yeah," he said, "it's true. I don't doubt it for a minute."

Victor expelled his breath in a rush. The sorrow that came over his face in that moment belonged to a much older man.

Shakily, Victor tried to regain his composure. "Okay. But I still don't see how that changes anything. We knew—Durkheim told us—that whether the charges were true or not—and he swore they were all lies from an old Legislaturalist elitist admiral—that almost everyone in the Solarian League was going to *believe*

them. Just because Parnell and Harrington were still
alive after all, and we *had* been nailed with our pants
down on that score. Since we'd lied about that, sure
enough, who'd believe us when we insisted that the
tales they brought back from their supposed graves
were all fabrications?"

For the first time, the young officer took a sip of
his own drink. "So I *still* don't see how anything's
changed." His brow creased. "And you said Bergren
too. Why him?"

Usher snorted. "The truth is, Victor, Bergren is the
main target. I doubt if even Durkheim thinks the odds
are better than fifty-fifty that we won't get blamed for
Parnell, even if he is killed by Scrags and even if there
is a Manty officer tied into it. But he's cut from the same
cloth as Saint-Just. Durkheim cares a lot more about
real power than anybody's perception of it. Bergren's
the last remaining holdover from the Legislaturalist
regime. The only reason he's remained here as our
ambassador, since the Revolution, is because he had the
good luck—or the good sense—to bring his whole family with him. So Saint-Just didn't have any real way of
blackmailing him into returning, where he could be
conveniently found guilty of something and shot. Or
simply 'disappeared.' So they decided to just leave him
here in place. If nothing else, Bergren's existence was
a way of showing that the new regime's extermination
of the Legislaturalists was because of their actual crimes
rather than their simple status. 'See? Didn't we leave
one of them—the only honest man in the den of
thieves—as the head of our embassy on Terra?'"

Usher drained half the bottle before continuing.
"But now—" He finished the bottle in one long
guzzle. Watching him, and despite his anguish at
seeing so much of what he believed turn to ashes,

Victor had to fight down a laugh. Usher could claim that he didn't drink as much as everybody said—which Victor was willing enough to believe—but that easy, practiced chugalug proved that "not as much" was still a long way from abstention.

"But now everything's changed." Usher rose. Again, he began pacing about in the small living room. "Harrington's escape from the dead—not to mention the several hundred thousand people she brought out of Hell with her—is going to rock the regime down to its foundations. Durkheim knows damn well that Saint-Just's only concern now is going to be holding on to power. Screw public relations. There isn't any doubt in his mind—mine either—that once Parnell arrives Bergren will officially defect." His lips twisted into a sneer. "Oh, yeah—Bergren will do his very best 'more in sorrow than in anger' routine. And he's good at it, believe me, the stinking hypocrite."

For a moment, Usher's thoughts seem to veer elsewhere. "Have you ever dug into any of that ancient Terran art form, Victor, since you got here? The one they call 'films'?"

Victor shook his head. For a brief instant, he almost uttered a protest. Interest in archaic art forms—everybody knew it!—was a classic hallmark of elitist decadence. But he suppressed the remark. All of his old certainties were crumbling around him, after all, so why should he make a fuss about something as minor as that?

Usher may have sensed the unspoken rebuke, however, for he gave Victor that wicked, half-jeering smile. "Too bad for you, youngster. I have, and lots of them are excellent." He rubbed his hands gently. Then, speaking in a peculiar accent: "I am shocked! Shocked! To discover gambling in Rick's casino!"

The phrases were meaningless to Victor, but Usher seemed to find them quite amusing. "Oh, yeah. That's what Bergren'll say. Bet on it, lad." He paced about a little more, thinking. "Durkheim is certainly betting on it. So he'll move quick and see to it that Bergren's killed before he has a chance to defect. And he'll just hope that using Manpower and their local Scrag cult to do the wet work will distract suspicion from us. We Havenites *do*, after all, have our hands cleaner than anybody else on that score. *That* much is not a lie."

Victor felt a little warmth coming back into his heart. "Or, at least, we did until Durkheim started mucking Playing games with that scum," snarled Usher.

For a minute, the citizen colonel looked like he might spit on the floor. But, he didn't. For all the modest size and furnishings of the apartment, it was spotlessly clean and well kept. Whatever Victor thought of Usher's wife's occupation—and Usher's relationship to her, for that matter, which still shocked his puritanical soul—slatternliness obviously didn't extend into their own home.

But Victor didn't dwell on that. He'd lost enough heroes for one day, and firmly decided that he wasn't going to pass any judgments on Usher or his wife until he was certain that he was capable of judging anything correctly. Which, going by the evidence, he most certainly wasn't yet.

So, struggling, he tried to keep his mind focused narrowly. "What you're saying, in other words, is that by going completely outside the loop and using Manpower and the Scrags to do the dirty work—and tangling a Manty agent up with them—Durkheim can get rid of Parnell and Bergren both. And maybe even keep Haven from taking the blame."

Usher nodded. It was Victor's turn to shake his

head. "All right. That much I can follow. But there are still two things I don't understand. First, why would Manpower agree? They hate our guts!"

The answer came to Victor before he even finished the question. The cold and pitiless look on Usher's face may have helped. "Oh, shit," Victor groaned, lapsing for a moment into profanity.

"Yeah, you got it, lad. Of course, whether or not Durkheim will be able to come through with his promise is another thing—Saint-Just will have to sign onto it—but don't doubt for a minute what the promise was. *You do this for us and we'll look the other way, from now on, whenever Manpower starts extending the slave trade into our space.*"

Victor was mute. Perhaps out of kindness, Usher prompted him off the subject. "What was the other question?"

Victor swallowed, trying to focus his mind on top of heartbreak. "Yeah. You seem to have figured it all out—and you even said it was brilliant—but then you also said Durkheim was an idiot. So I'm confused about what you really—"

Usher snorted. "Oh, hell—Victor, for Christ's sake! Grow up! Hanging onto illusions is one thing. I'll forgive you for that, easily enough." For a moment, he looked uncomfortable. Then, shrugged. "Truth is, if I hadn't realized you *had* those illusions I wouldn't be talking to you in the first place."

The soft moment passed. The cold and pitiless look was back. "But there's no excuse for plain *stupidity*. You're supposed to be a field agent, dammit! Durkheim's complicated scheme is right out of the book. You know, the one titled: *'Harebrained Schemes Hatched by Desk Pilots Who Don't Know a Dead Drop From a Hole in the Ground.'*"

Victor couldn't help laughing. In that moment, Usher reminded him of one of his instructors. A sarcastic and experienced field man, who had peppered his lectures with anecdotes. Half of which, at least, had been on the subject of desk pilots and their harebrained schemes.

Usher sat back down on the couch and shook his head wearily. "Every single damned thing in Durkheim's plot is going to go wrong, Victor. Trust me. The man forgets he's dealing with real people instead of ideological abstractions. And real people have this nasty habit of not quite fitting properly into their assigned pigeonholes."

Usher leaned forward, sticking up his right thumb. "The *first* thing that's going to go wrong already has, and don't think for a moment even Durkheim isn't nervous about it. I'll bet you any amount of money you choose that he expected Manpower would use some of their own professionals to do the dirty work with the kid. Instead, no doubt because they want to keep their distance in case the thing goes sour— no idiots *there*—they turned it over to the Scrags they keep on their leash. They'll save their pros for the attacks on Parnell and Bergren."

He squinted at Victor. "Do you really know anything about the Scrags?"

Victor started to give a vigorous, even belligerent, affirmative response, but hesitated. Other than a lot of abstract ideological notions about fascistic believers in a master race—

"No," he said firmly.

"Good for you, lad," chuckled Usher. "Okay, Victor. Forget everything you may have heard. The fundamental thing you've got to understand about the Scrags is that they're a bunch of clowns." He waved a hand. "Oh, yeah, sure. Murderous clowns. Perfect physical specimens, bred and trained to be supreme warriors. Eat nails, can walk through walls, blah blah blah. The problem is, the morons believe it too. Which means they're as careless as five year olds, and never think to plan for the inevitable screw-ups. Which there always are, in any plan—much less one as elaborate as this scheme of Durkheim's. So they're going to foul up, somewhere along the line, and Durkheim's going to be scrambling to patch the holes. The problem is, since he organized this entire thing outside of SS channels, he doesn't have a back-up team in place and ready to go. He'll have to jury-rig one. Which is something you *never* want to do in a situation as"—another dry chuckle—"as 'fraught with danger,' as they say, as this one."

He held up the thumb of his left hand. "And the *other* thing that's going to go wrong—this one is guaranteed, and it's a real lulu—is that the Manty officer he selected to be the official patsy in the scheme is going to tear him a new asshole." Usher pressed the palms of his hands to his temples. The gesture combined utter exasperation with fury. "In the name of God! Bad enough Durkheim screws around with a Manty's kid. But *Zilwicki's?*" He drove up onto his feet. "What a cretin!"

Victor stared at him. He was acquainted with Anton Zilwicki, in the very casual way that two intelligence officers belonging to nations at war encounter each other at social functions in the capital of a neutral state, but the 'acquaintance' was extremely distant. Thinking about it, Victor could only summon up two impressions of the man. Physically, Zilwicki had a rather peculiar physique. Almost as wide, he seemed, as he was tall. And, from his accent, he came from the highlands of Gryphon.

Victor frowned. "I don't quite understand, Kevin. Zilwicki's not a field agent. He's an analyst. Specializes in technical stuff. Software, as a matter of fact. The guy's basically a computer geek. He's the one who tries to find out how much tech transfer we're getting from the Sollies."

Usher snorted. "Yeah, I'm sure that's what Durkheim was thinking. But you're forgetting three other things about him. First of all, the kid's mother was *Helen* Zilwicki, who was posthumously awarded Manticore's Parliamentary Medal of Honor for hammering one of our task forces half-bloody with a vastly inferior force of her own."

Victor was still frowning. Usher sighed. "Victor, do you really think a woman like that married a *wimp*?"

"Oh."

"Yeah. *Oh.* Second, he's from the Gryphon highlands. And while I think those highlanders are possibly the galaxy's all time political morons—they hate the aristocracy so they put their faith in Aristocrat Number One—you won't find anywhere a more maniacal set of feudists. Talk about stupid! Snatching one of their kids, in the scale of intelligence, ranks right up there with snatching a tiger's cub."

He slapped his hands together and rubbed them, in that mock-gleeful way of saying: *oh, yes—here comes the best part!* "And—just to put the icing on the cake—Anton Zilwicki may not be a field agent but he's hardly your typical desk pilot either."

He cocked an eyebrow at the young SS officer. "You've met him?" Victor nodded. Usher put his hand at shoulder level. "Short fellow, 'bout yay tall." He spread his arms wide, cupping the hands. "And about yay wide."

He dropped his arms. "The reason for that build

is because he's a weightlifter. Good enough that he could probably compete in his weight class in the Terran Olympics, which are still the top athletic contest in the settled portion of the universe."

Usher frowned. "The truth is, though, he probably ought to give it up. Since his wife died, he's become a bit of a monomaniac about the weightlifting. I imagine it's his way of trying to control his grief. But by now he's probably starting to get muscle-bound, which is too bad because—"

The wicked smile was back. "—there ain't no question at all that he could compete in the Olympics in his *old* sport, seeing as how he won the gold medal three times running in the Manticoran Games in the wrestling event. Graeco-Roman, if I remember right."

Usher was grinning, now. "Oh yeah, young man. That's your genius boss Raphael Durkheim. And to think I accused the Scrags of being sloppy and careless! Durkheim's trying to make a patsy out of somebody like *that*."

Victor cleared his throat. "I don't think he knew all that." Which, of course, he realized was no excuse. Durkheim was *supposed* to know about such things. And that, finally, brought Victor to a new awareness.

"How is it that *you* know this stuff about Zilwicki?"

Usher stared at him for a moment in silence. Then, after taking a deep breath, said:

"Okay, young Victor Cachat. We have now arrived at what they call the moment of truth."

Usher hesitated. He was obviously trying to select the right way of saying something. But, in a sudden rush of understanding, Victor grasped the essence of it. The elaborate nature of Usher's disguise, combined with his uncanny knowledge of things no simple Marine citizen colonel—much less a drunkard—could possibly have known, all confirmed the shadowy hints Victor had occasionally encountered elsewhere. That there existed, somewhere buried deep, an *opposition*.

"I'm in," he stated firmly. "Whatever it is."

Usher scrutinized him carefully. "This is the part I always hate," he mused. "No matter how shrewd you are, no matter how experienced, there always comes that moment when you've got to decide whether you trust someone or not."

Victor waited; and, as he waited, felt calmness come over him. His ideological beliefs had taken a battering, but there was still enough of them there to leave him intact. For the first time—ever—he understood men like Kevin Usher. It was like looking in a mirror. A cracked mirror, but a mirror sure and true.

Usher apparently reached the same conclusion. "It's *my* Revolution, Victor, not Saint-Just's. Sure as hell not Durkheim and Tresca's. It belongs to me and mine—we fought for it, we bled for it—and we will damn well have it *back*."

"So what do we do?" asked Victor.

Usher shrugged. "Well, for the moment why don't we concentrate on this little problem in front of us." Cheerfully, he sprawled back on the couch. "For one thing, let's figure out a way to turn Durkheim's mousetrap into a rat trap. And, for another, let's see if there isn't some way we can keep a fourteen-year-old girl from becoming another stain on our banner. Whaddaya say?"

The Scrag

Kennesaw sensed his assailants' approach as he was opening the door to his apartment. Like all of the

Select, his hearing was incredibly acute, as was the quickness with which his mind processed sensory data. Before the attack even began, therefore, he had already started his pre-emptive counterassault.

Given the areas of Chicago that Kennesaw frequented, he was quite familiar with muggers. It was one of the things he liked about the city, in fact. The high level of street crime kept his fighting reflexes well-tuned. He had killed three muggers over the past several years, and crippled as many more.

The fact that there were two of them did not faze him in the least. Especially once he saw, as he spun around launching his first disabling kick, that both of the men were much shorter than he was.

It took a few seconds for his assumptions to be dispelled. How many, exactly, he never knew. Everything was much too confusing. And painful.

His target was the older and more slightly built of the two men. Kennesaw almost laughed when he saw how elderly the man was. One blow would be enough to disable him, allowing Kennesaw to concentrate on destroying the thick-set subhuman.

But the kick never landed. Somehow, Kennesaw's ankle was seized, twisted—off balance now—

—his vision blurred—an elbow strike to the temple, he thought, but he was too dazed to be certain—

—agonizing pain lanced through his other leg—

—his knees buckled—

And then a monster had him, immobilizing him from behind with a maneuver Kennesaw barely recognized because it was so antique—even preposterous. But his chin was crushed to his chest, his arms dangling and paralyzed, and then he was heaved back onto his feet and propelled through the half-open door of his apartment.

On their way through, the monster smashed his face against the door jamb. The creature's sheer power was astonishing. Kennesaw's nose and jaw were both broken. He dribbled blood and teeth across the floor as he was manhandled into the center of his living room.

By now, he was only half-conscious. Anyone not of the Select would probably have been completely witless. But Kennesaw took no comfort in the fact. He could sense the raging animal fury that held him immobile and had so casually shattered his face along the way.

His legs were again kicked out from under him. A skilled and experienced hand-to-hand fighter, Kennesaw had expected that. What he *hadn't* expected was that the monster, instead of hurling him to the floor and pouncing on him, would do the exact opposite. Kennesaw was dragged down on top of the creature, who still held him from behind in that suffocating clasp.

He landed on a body that felt as unyielding as stone. An instant later, two legs curled over his thighs and clamped his own legs in a scissor lock. The legs were much shorter than his own, but thick and muscular. Kennesaw was vaguely surprised to see that they apparently belonged to a human being. He wouldn't have been shocked to see them clad in animal fur. Like a grizzly bear.

Some time passed. How much, Kennesaw never knew. But eventually he was able to focus on the face which was staring down at him. The genes which had created that face clearly had most of their origins in eastern Asia. The face belonged to the old man, the one he had tried to disable with a kick.

The man spoke. His voice was soft and low. "I used

to be a biologist, Kennesaw, before I decided to concentrate on my art. What you're seeing here is an illustration of the fallacy of Platonic thinking applied to evolutionary principles."

The words were pure gibberish. Something of Kennesaw's confusion must have shown, because the face emitted a slight chuckle.

"It's sometimes called 'population thinking,' Kennesaw. A pity you never learned to apply those methods. Instead, you made the classic mistake of categorizing people into abstract types instead of recognizing their concrete variations."

Gibberish. Another chuckle.

"You're only a 'superman,' Kennesaw, if you compare the average of the Sacred Band to the average of the rest of humanity. Unfortunately, you're now in the hands of two men who, in different ways, vary quite widely from the norm. Partly because of our own genetic background, and partly due to training and habit."

The almond-shaped eyes moved slightly, looking past Kennesaw's own head. "I'm not sure how well this is going to work. I'm sure he's got an absolutely phenomenal pain threshold."

Finally, Kennesaw heard the monster speak. "Don't care," came a hoarse grunt. "I'm sure he was one of the men who took her, which means there'll be traces of where they went somewhere in the apartment."

The Oriental face frowned. "Then why—"

Even as dazed as he was, the brief exchange made clear to Kennesaw the identity of his assailants. He managed some grunting words of his own. "You crazy, Z'wicki? Anyt'in' happen t'me, 'ey'll kill 'er."

The clasp tightened, and Kennesaw couldn't prevent a low groan.

"I don't think so. As sloppy as you people are, they'll just assume you're goofing off somewhere. How would I know you were involved?"

Despite the crushing pain, some part of Kennesaw's brain was still functioning objectively. So he understood the incredible strength which lay behind those words. Precious few, if any, of the Select themselves would have been able to so completely immobilize Kennesaw. Much less, at the same time, manage to speak in what was almost a normal tone of voice!

"And you've already told me the only thing I really needed to know from you," continued the hoarse voice from behind. "I'm not cold-blooded enough to kill a man I'm not sure is guilty."

It took a moment for the meaning to register on Kennesaw. He tried to grunt another warning, but the hoarse voice overrode his words.

"This is called a full nelson, Scrag. It's an illegal maneuver in tournament wrestling. Here's why."

In the brief time that followed, Kennesaw understood some of what the little Oriental had been trying to explain to him. Variation. He never would have believed that any subhuman would have been strong enough to—

But the thought was fleeting. The pressure on his neck, crushing his broken chin into his chestbone, drove everything but pain and terror away. And then his vertebra ruptured and Kennesaw thought no more at all.

Victor

Victor spent the evening in the company of Usher's wife, being given a guided tour of the upper levels of the Loop. He had intended, burning with desire to undo Durkheim—somehow—to return to work immediately. But Kevin had driven that notion down with his usual sarcasm.

"And just what do you intend to do, youngster?" he demanded. "Stay out of trouble, dammit! I'll get the ball rolling at my end. You don't do anything—*nothing*, you understand—until you either hear from me or Durkheim approaches you, whichever comes first."

Victor frowned. Kevin chuckled. "He will, he will— I'll bet on it. Didn't I tell you this scheme of his is going to start unraveling? And that, when it does, he's going to have to slap together a jury-rigged back-up team to clean up the mess?"

Usher didn't wait for a response. Clearly enough, he had once again left Victor behind in a cloud of mental dust. "So who do you think he's going to approach? Not one of his experienced field agents, I'll tell you that. No, he'll go to the same wet-behind-the-ears, naive, trusting, dumb-as-a-brick, do-as-he-says young zealot that he used to pass messages to the Mesans in the first place. You."

"*Me?*" Victor scratched his cheek. "Why? He never told me what those messages were, or who I was passing them to. I figured it out on my own. As far as he knows, I don't know anything about the situation."

Victor hesitated, youthful pride warring with his innate honesty. Honesty won.

"The truth is, Kevin, I really am kind of"—sigh— "wet behind the ears." He scowled. "It hasn't helped any that Durkheim hasn't given me any really important assignments since I got here, fresh out of the Academy. All he's used me for is routine clerical stuff and as an occasional courier. My knowledge of fieldcraft is really pretty much book-learning. If *I* was putting together a back-up team to clean up a mess like this, I'd want an experienced field agent in charge of it."

"You don't think like Durkheim does," replied Kevin. "You're still thinking in terms of making the assignment *work*. For that, sure, you'd want a real pro." He shook his head. "But don't ever forget that Durkheim is a bureaucrat, first and foremost. His central concern—now and always—is going to be his position within the power structure, not the needs of the struggle. When a job goes sour, his first thought is going to be: *cover my ass*. And for *that*, ain't nothing better than a dumb young greenhorn—especially one who has a reputation for zealotry."

Victor flushed a bit. "What's a 'greenhorn'?" he growled.

"It's a Terran term. Refers to a variant they have here of cattle. A young bull, essentially, who's got a lot more testosterone than he does good sense."

Victor's flush deepened. "You're saying he'll expect me to *fail*?"

Kevin grinned. "Go down in flames and smoke, as a matter of fact. With enough pyrotechnics that he can wash his hands clean and claim afterward the whole thing was your idea and he didn't know anything about it until the *boom* happened."

Kevin looked away for a moment, thinking. "What I imagine he'll do is give you a squad of experienced SS troops, with a citizen sergeant in charge that he trusts. Someone with some familiarity with the Old Quarter—the upper levels, at least. You'll be told that the Scrags have run wild—went ahead and *kidnapped* a Manty officer's daughter, the maniacs. He'll probably claim they were simply supposed to search his apartment and panicked when they found the girl there."

Usher waved his hand. "Yeah, of course the story's ridiculous. Why didn't they just kill her on the spot? But he won't be expecting you to scrutinize his story for logical fallacies."

By now, Victor had caught up with Usher's thought train. "So I take this squad into the Loop with orders to find the girl and get her back." His face tightened. "No. Not get her back. Just—"

"He won't give *you* that instruction, Victor. No matter how zealous or naive he thinks you are, Durkheim's not dumb enough to think he can tell a youngster to murder a girl in cold blood without creating possible problems. No, he'll tell *you* the job is to rescue her. And kill the Scrags while you're at it. But the citizen sergeant will see to it that the girl doesn't survive."

"Or me either." The statement was flat, direct.

Usher nodded. "Or you either. When the dust clears, what do we have? A young and inexperienced Havenite SS officer, discovering some kind of Mesan/Scrag skullduggery underway, went charging off half-cocked—entirely on his own initiative and without getting authorization—and made a mess out of everything. Both he and the girl die in the crossfire. Who's to say otherwise?"

"The whole story's preposterous!" protested Victor. "The Manties'll never believe it. Neither will the Sollies, for that matter."

Kevin laughed harshly. "Of course they won't. But they won't be able to prove any different, and Durkheim doesn't care what they think anyway. After Harrington's escape—sure as hell after Parnell arrives here and starts shooting his mouth off—nobody on

Terra will believe what Haven says about anything. So what's another little goofy story? All Durkheim cares about is covering his ass with Saint-Just."

Usher laughed again, and just as harshly. "Who won't believe the story either, mind you. But he'll be satisfied that Durkheim had enough sense to cut his losses. And Saint-Just has enough problems to deal with now that he's not going to run the risk of penalizing Durkheim."

Silence followed, for perhaps half a minute, while Victor digested this—indigestible—meal. He felt nauseated. As a young and eager SS officer, Victor had prepared himself for ruthlessness in the struggle against elitism. But *this*—

"All right," he said. "So what do we do?"

"You leave that to me, Victor." Usher's face was bleak. "I'll do my best to see to it that both you and the girl survive. But I can't make any promises. The truth is, I'm going to be using you for bait. And bait has a way of getting eaten."

Victor nodded. He'd already deduced that much. But Victor had understood the risks of being an SS intelligence officer when he applied to the Academy. Danger, he could accept. Foulness—for no more purpose than a bureaucrat's self-aggrandizement—he could not.

"Good enough. Concentrate on the girl's survival." Stiffly, with all the pride of a greenhorn: "I can take care of myself."

Usher grinned. "The girl might surprise you, lad. Don't forget whose kid she is. She even has her mother's name. Oh, and I might mention something *else* that I'm sure Durkheim doesn't know—she's the youngest person who ever got a brown belt from Robert Tye."

Victor sighed. Again, he was in a cloud of dust. "What's a brown belt? And who's Robert Tye?"

I'm getting a little tired of that damn grin, he thought sourly, seeing its reappearance. The words which followed didn't help a bit.

"Not a devotee of the martial arts, are you? Well, I'd figured as much from our little fracas in the tavern." Grin.

So, Victor had wound up idling away the day with Usher's wife in the Loop. Her name—or so she claimed, in defiance of all logic—was Virginia. Victor had his doubts, especially in view of her scandalous clothing and the way she continually tormented him.

But he was obscurely relieved when she explained that she wasn't really a prostitute.

"Not any more, anyway," Ginny explained—although, at the moment she spoke the words, she was doing her best to prove to the world otherwise, the way she was pressed against him as they ambled through one of the bazaars in the Old Quarter. Under Victor's prodding, as they made their way through the crowded streets and open-spaced bazaars, Virginia gave him some of her life's history.

Before too long, he was sorry he had asked. Not because Virginia prattled—to the contrary, her narrative was terse and brief. But simply because it is one thing to understand, in ideological terms, that a social institution is unjust. It is another thing entirely to hear that injustice graphically described by one of its victims. The first causes abstract anger; the second, nausea and helpless fury.

Virginia had been born—bred—on Mesa. C-17a/ 65-4/5 was the name on her tongue. The label, it might be better to say. The "C" line was one of Manpower Inc.'s most popular breeds, always in demand on the market. Sex slaves, in essence. "17" referred to the somatic type; the "a" to the female variant. Her genotype had been selected and shaped for physical attractiveness, and for as much in the way of libidinal energy and submissiveness as Mesa's gengineers could pinpoint in the genetic code. Which, of course, was not much—especially since the two desired psychological traits tended to be genetically cross-linked with a multitude of opposing character-istics. One of which, unfortunately, was a type of intelligence popularly characterized as "cleverness." As a result, a high percentage of C-lines had a ten-dency to escape captivity once they left the extreme security environment of Mesa itself.

To combat that tendency, and in an attempt to "phe-notypically induce" the desired submissiveness, the developing C-lines were subjected to a rigorous train-ing regimen. Manpower's engineers, of course, had an antiseptic and multisyllabic jargon phrase to describe it: "Phenotype developmental process." But what it amounted to, in layman's terms, was that C-lines were systematically and continually raped from the age of nine.

"The worst of it," Virginia mused, "is that there wasn't even any real lust involved. No emotion at all. The rapists—sorry, the phenotype technicians—have to be chemically induced to even get an erection." She actually managed a giggle. "Sometimes, looking back, I almost feel sorry for them. Almost. I don't think there exists anybody in the galaxy as bored with sex as those people."

"Nine?" Victor asked shakily.

She shrugged. "Yeah. It hurts. A lot, in the

beginning. And it's even worse for the b-variants. Those are the boys."

Victor felt like he was wading in a cesspool. But he finally understood the sheer savagery of the Audubon Ballroom. He had never approved of the kind of terrorist tactics which their militants often applied to individual targets. Counterproductive, ideologically. But—

She laughed harshly. "Almost! Ha! That one time Jeremy X and his comrades caught a phenotype technician here on Terra—stupid bastard went on vacation, can you believe it?—I raced down to see the body like everybody else."

At one time, Victor would have winced. Now, he simply growled his own satisfaction. He knew the incident she was referring to. It had been one of the most famous exploits of the Ballroom, and one which had produced a gale of official outrage. The Solarian League's Executive Council met in an elaborate palace. As part of the palace's decor, there was a statue in the center of the antechamber. The statue was a human-sized replica of a gigantic and long-destroyed ancient monument called the Statue of Liberty. The Council members had not been amused to arrive one day and find the naked body of a "phenotype engineer" impaled on the statue's torch, with a sign hanging around his neck which read: *Hoist on his own petard, wouldn't you say?*

He took a deep breath. "I *still* think the tactics are counterproductive."

Virginia smiled slyly. "That's what Kevin says, too." The smile faded. "I don't know. I suppose you're right. But—"

She took her own deep breath. "You don't know what it's like, Victor," she said softly. There was a hint of moisture in her dark eyes. "All your life you're told you're inferior—*genetically*. Not really human. You wonder about it yourself. Sometimes I think the way I put on such a slutty act is just because—" No hint, now; the tears were welling. She wiped them away half-angrily. "So maybe you and Kevin are right. All I know is that after I saw that body I felt a lot better about myself."

The moment passed, and Virginia went back to her customary badinage. "Anyway, after I escaped I made my living as a whore. The pay's good and what else do I know how to do?" Sourly: "Kevin insisted that I give it up, when he proposed."

Victor had learned enough to resist his natural impulse: *But surely you were glad to abandon that life of degradation!* Virginia, he was quite certain, had been happy enough to quit the trade. But she enjoyed goosing the greenhorn.

Ginny goosed him again. "And he was so mean to my pimp, too." Sigh. "Poor Angus. He was so refined, and Kevin is *such* a ruffian."

When she realized he wasn't going to rise to the bait, Ginny grinned. The grin, of course, was lascivious. Whatever the reality of their relationship and repartee, Victor realized that Ginny was a far more experienced field agent than he was. Except for that one brief teary-eyed moment, she had never once broken cover. Any of Durkheim's men who was following them would be quite certain by now that Victor Cachat had finally abandoned his stiff and proper ways. Another puritanical revolutionary undone by the fleshpots of Terra. *Join the club.*

And so, just as Usher had planned, it would never occur to them that the same Victor Cachat was getting a better introduction to the Loop and its secrets than they'd ever gotten.

"Smart man," mused Victor.

"Isn't he?" agreed Ginny happily.

THE THIRD DAY

Helen

Helen had no way of keeping track of time, beyond the meals which her captors gave her. After four meals, she decided that they were feeding her twice a day. Which, if she was right, meant that she had now been imprisoned for three days.

The food was plentiful, but consisted of nothing more than some kind of standard rations. For troops, possibly, although Helen suspected darkly that the rations were designed for convict laborers. Nasty stuff. *She* certainly wouldn't feed crap like that to armed soldiers. They'd mutiny within a week.

The stuff didn't do wonders for her digestion, either. Fortunately, her captors had provided her with a modern portable toilet instead of the crude bed pan which was always provided in the adventure novels she loved to read. She got plenty of use for the thing. More than her captors had intended, in fact, because she had quickly learned that the slot behind the heatflash disposal mechanism was perfect for concealing her digging shards.

That was about the only good thing about the disposal mechanism. It was so old and poorly maintained that it barely served for its official function. And not well enough to cover the stench which slowly, as the hours and days went by, began to fill the cell.

But that too, Helen decided, was all to the good.

She noticed that after the second day, her captors came in and out of her cell as quickly as possible. Holding their breath all the while.

So she continued her dogged tunneling in a cheerful enough mood. She even had to restrain herself, once, from humming.

Victor

The next day seemed endless to Victor. The only assignment Usher had given him was to do nothing, beyond his normal tasks as an SS officer in the embassy. Which, in Victor's case, amounted to glorified clerical work.

He even found himself looking forward to the evening. He was supposed to meet with Virginia again, in a tavern deep in the Loop, and then spend the rest of the night with her at a nearby cheap hotel. The cover was the obvious one of a man having an assignation with a prostitute.

Despite his certainty that Ginny would tease him mercilessly—especially once they were in the hotel room—Victor was looking forward to it. Partly because she might have news, and partly because it would at least give him the feeling he was doing *something*. Mostly, he just wanted to see her again.

In the solemnly self-critical manner which was Victor's way, he spent some time examining that desire. Eventually, he was satisfied that there wasn't any foul concupiscence lurking beneath. It was just—

He *liked* Ginny, he realized. There was something clean at the center of the woman, which came like fresh water after the murky filth he had been plunged into. And, although he wasn't sure, he thought she liked him also. Victor had had few friends in his life, and none at all since he left the Academy. For all his stern devotion to duty, he realized, he had been suffering from simple loneliness for a long time.

By the time lunch break came around, Victor was actually feeling quite relaxed. Then, on his way to the cafeteria, he spotted Usher marching down another hallway toward the barracks and felt himself tighten up all over again.

If the Marine citizen colonel noticed him as well, he gave no sign of it. A moment later Kevin was gone, passing through the door into the section of the big building set aside for the Marine detachment which guarded the embassy.

Victor's stride, upon seeing Usher, had turned into an almost-stumbling shuffle. Then, frantically trying to recover his poise, he *did* stumble. He only kept himself from falling by an awkward half-leap which drew the eyes of all the other people in the corridor at the time. There were three of them—two clerks and a Marine citizen sergeant.

Flushing with embarrassment, Victor avoided their gaze and resumed his march toward the cafeteria. At first, he was almost petrified with fear. *Had he given away his connection to Usher by his own carelessness and tyro stupidity?*

But by the time he reached the entrance to the cafeteria, he came to the realization that his mishap was nothing to fear. In fact, much as he hated to admit it, even if the stumble was reported to Durkheim it would probably do some good. There was, after all, another perfectly logical explanation for why he might be taken aback by meeting Kevin Usher again.

A voice coming from behind him, speaking in a

whisper which was still loud enough to be heard by anyone within twenty feet, confirmed the supposition.

"Try not to piss your pants, will you? The Citizen Colonel doesn't usually slap around punks more than once."

An instant later, almost roughly, Victor was shouldered aside by the citizen sergeant he had noticed in the corridor. Standing stock still, he stared at the Marine marching past him into the cafeteria. Then, realizing he was blocking the way of the two clerks, he stepped back. He saw one of the clerks glance at him as he went by, his lips twisted into a slight smirk.

By now, Victor realized, the story of his encounter with Kevin Usher in the tavern would have gone through the entire embassy staff. Causing no chagrin to anyone, not even other SS officers, and much amusement to many.

But it was not embarrassment which kept him standing in the doorway for another few seconds. It was simple surprise. Somehow—he hadn't noticed at the time—the citizen sergeant had managed to slip a note into his hand while he was manhandling Victor out of the way.

Victor recognized the fieldcraft, of course. From training if not from actual practice. But he was more than a little astonished to see it performed so precisely and perfectly by a man whom he would have assumed did nothing more precise than blow people apart in a combat assault.

Fortunately, Victor didn't forget his own fieldcraft. So he didn't make any of the tyro's mistakes, such as trying to read the note immediately. He just slipped it into his pocket and went to the line to get his food.

Nor did he try to read the note surreptitiously while he was eating. He was too well trained, for one thing.

For another, he was far too preoccupied studying the Marines in the cafeteria.

And that, too, was a well-trained sort of study. Victor never gave the Marines sitting at their own table more than an occasional glance. He didn't really need to, after all, since he had observed Marines at lunch many times in the past.

Or, it might be better to say, had *seen* them. But he realized now that the Marines, as visible as they always were in the embassy, remained almost like ghosts in his actual knowledge. What *really* went on in the barracks? What did those combat troops *think* about anything?

He didn't know, he realized—and neither did almost any SS officer. As an institution, of course, State Security was always deeply concerned about the attitudes and political reliability of the military. But that assignment was so important that it was kept carefully shielded from the view of most SS men. As a rule, for a small detachment like the one guarding the embassy on Terra, only one officer would really know anything about the Marines.

That officer, in this case, was a certain Paul Gironde. About whom, Victor realized, he also knew almost nothing. Even by SS standards, Gironde was a close-mouthed sort of fellow. The few times Victor had found himself in a conversation with Gironde, the conversation had been brief. From boredom on Victor's part, if nothing else.

But of one thing Victor was almost certain, from certain subtleties in the way he had seen Durkheim and Gironde interact in the past. Gironde, while he was a respected SS officer, was not one of Durkheim's cronies.

Then came the hardest moment of the day, as Victor

fought down a smile. He knew only one of the classical allusions which Kevin Usher was so fond of spouting. And he couldn't, even then, remember the actual Latin words. But he knew what they meant.

Who will guard the guardians?

Victor didn't finally read the note until he was in the jam-packed capsule heading into the Loop. There, carefully cupping the note in his palm while he was surrounded by a motley horde, he could be sure of reading it unobserved. By anyone, at least, connected in any way with State Security.

That his assignation with Virginia was in the Old Quarter, some time in the evening, he already knew. The note would tell him exactly when and where.

And so it did, in feminine handwriting, and then some:

Gary's Place. 8. Wear something pink. I love pink. It reminds me—

What it reminded Ginny of turned Victor's own face pink as well. But, this time, he made no effort to restrain his laugh. Why should he? In the crowded transportation capsules carrying the city's menials back into the Old Quarter after a day's work, there was a lot of laughter.

He found the time, before entering the tavern, to hunt down a clothing store and buy a scarf. A pink scarf. Bright pink, in fact. Victor felt silly wearing the thing. And it was probably a lapse into decadent habits on his part. Putting on a useless piece of garment just to please a lady!

But—

She wasn't *his* lady, true. A lady she was, nonetheless, and some part of Victor took pleasure in the fact itself. In a way he couldn't explain, it seemed like another victory, of which there had been precious few in his life. A small one, perhaps, but a victory sure and certain.

Anton

"And there it is," said Anton softly. He leaned back from the console and arched his back against the chair. He was stiff from the long hours he had spent there. All day, in fact, since early in the morning. And it was now almost ten o'clock at night.

Robert Tye, who had been standing at the window staring at the brightly lit city, turned his head and cocked an eyebrow. Catching a glimpse of the little movement, Anton chuckled.

"Bingo, as you Terrans would put it. And where does that silly expression come from, anyway?"

Tye shrugged. "What did you find?"

Anton pointed a finger at the screen. "I had plenty already, just from the embassy's general files and the ambassador's. But the real gold mine is here in Admiral Young's personal records." He shook his head, half with anger and half with bemusement. "What a jackass."

Tye came over and stared at the figures. As always with the material which Anton had brought up on the screen over the past two days, none of it meant anything to him.

"Surely he wasn't stupid enough . . ."

Anton barked a little laugh. "Oh, no—he was quite clever. Which was his undoing, in the end. When amateurs try to cover up stuff like this, they almost always make it too complicated. Keep your laundry simple, that's the trick."

The martial artist's face was creased with a frown. "Why would Young launder money? From what you've told me, the man's so rich he doesn't need to supplement his wealth."

"Money," hissed Anton. "Money's not this bastard's vice, Robert. He wasn't trying to cover up his income. He was covering his *expenses*."

"Oh." Tye's nostrils grew a little pinched, as if he were in the presence of a bad smell.

"So were most of the people on this list," continued Anton. "And, I'm pretty sure, most of the people on that list of Hendricks' I turned up earlier. Although that'll take some time to determine, since the ambassador was quite a bit less careless than Young was."

Anton pushed back the chair and rose to his feet. He needed to stretch a little. As he paced around, swinging his arms in a little arc to ease the tension in his back, he kept staring at the screen. His expression was intense, as he considered a new possibility.

After a moment, Tye's eyes grew almost round. Apparently, the same possibility had just occurred to the martial artist. "You don't think *they* were involved . . . ?"

Hearing the question put so directly, Anton's answer crystallized.

"No," he said, shaking his head firmly. "I was wondering myself, once I saw how closely they've been connected to the Mesans. But there's no earthly reason for them to do it. Helen means nothing to them, and if they wanted to strike at me—and for what purpose?—they both have far quicker and simpler ways to do it. I *am* their subordinate, after all."

He left off his arm-swinging and began a little set of isometric exercises, one palm against another. "But if you look at it another way, everything begins to make sense. Those same ties to Manpower would make Young and Hendricks the perfect patsies."

Now he slapped the palms together. "And *that*—that, Robert—is what explains Helen. She's the daughter of a Manticoran intelligence agent. Another prybar, that's all. Another angle. Whoever's behind this isn't trying to get information of any kind, much less start a disinformation campaign." He barked another laugh. "Or, at least, not a subtle one. There's all hell brewing here, Robert, and when the explosion comes Manticore is being set up to take the blame."

"The blame for what?"

Anton smiled thinly. "Give me a break. I can't figure out everything in a few days." He studied the screen a little longer. "And, in truth, I'm beginning to suspect that the culprit—or culprits, if there's more than one—is being too clever himself."

"Peeps, you think? They're the obvious ones who'd want to damage the Star Kingdom's standing on Terra. Especially now. Parnell should be arriving in three days, according to the newscasts."

"Maybe." Anton shrugged. "But it still doesn't feel right."

He pointed a thick finger at the screen. "Too *clever*, Robert. Too clever by half. Whatever this scheme is, it's got way too many threads waiting to come loose."

"A Rube Goldberg machine, you're saying."

The Manticoran officer scowled. "And there's *another* stupid Sollie expression. I've asked six of you people since I got here, and nobody can tell me who this 'Rube Goldberg' fellow was supposed to have been."

Tye chuckled. But Anton noted, a bit sourly, that he gave no answer himself.

"Too many threads . . ." he mused. "I'd almost

laugh, except the minute the thing starts coming apart the first casualty will be Helen."

Anton turned his head and stared at the data packet lying next to the console. Lieutenant Hobbs had brought it over just before noon. It hadn't taken the police lab long at all to analyze the material which Anton had given them the night before.

Muhammad's visit had been brief. He hadn't even come into Anton's apartment. He had just handed him the packet, scowling, and said nothing more than: "I am *not* going to ask where you got five pairs of shoes, Anton. Not unless I find the feet that used to fit them." Then he left.

Anton had read the data immediately, of course. That had taken no time at all, practically. The data was crystal clear: the owner of the shoes had—recently, and probably frequently—been in the lower depths of the Loop. Below the densely populated warrens, in the labyrinth of tunnels and passageways which marked the most ancient ruins of the city.

The intensity with which Anton now studied that packet was no less than that which he had earlier bestowed on the screen. Again, he was considering a possibility.

And, again, came to a decision. Quickly enough, if not as quickly as before. The decision, this time, was affirmative. And it was one which he came to only with reluctance.

"No way around it," he muttered. Then, snorting: "God, to think it would come to this! Talk about supping with Satan with a long spoon."

Tye was startled. "You're planning to talk to *Manpower*?"

Anton laughed. No curt bark, either, but a genuine laugh. "Sorry," he choked. "I misspoke. Calling that woman 'Satan' is quite unfair, actually. Hecate would be more accurate. Or Circe, or maybe Morgana."

Tye scowled. "What woman? And are you trying to get even with me by using meaningless Manticoran expressions? Who the hell are Hecate and the others? I'm not a student of the Star Kingdom's mythology, you know."

He scowled even further, hearing Anton's ensuing laughter. The more so, no doubt, since Anton didn't bother to explain the source of the humor.

When Anton was done laughing, Tye gestured at the door. "Are we leaving now? To see whomever this mysterious woman might be."

Anton shook his head. "It's much too late. I'll put in a call right away, of course, but I doubt if we'll get an audience with her until tomorrow morning sometime."

"An 'audience'? What is she, some kind of royalty?"

"Close enough," said Anton softly. He was studying the screen again, where Edwin Young's vile nature was displayed in antiseptic columns of figures. "The admiral would call her 'the Lady from the Infernal Regions,' I imagine. As much as I probably despise the woman, I suppose that's as good a character reference as you could ask for."

"What's 'the Infernal Regions'?" demanded Tye. "A province of the Star Kingdom? And what do you mean: you *probably* despise her?"

Anton didn't bother to answer the first question. As for the other, he shrugged.

"I've never actually met her. But her reputation, as they say, precedes her."

Tye cocked his head. "Nice expression, that. 'Her reputation precedes her.' Another old Manticoran saying?"

THE FOURTH DAY

Helen

When she broke through the wall, Helen was astonished. She had long since stopped actually thinking about escape. She had kept digging simply to keep herself occupied and control the terror.

She held her breath. There hadn't been much noise when her digging shard punctured the surface. But, for all she knew, she had simply penetrated into a space within sight of her abductors. Even if they heard nothing, they might spot the little trickle of dirt spilling on the opposite side.

So she waited, holding absolutely still and breathing as little as possible. She started a little count—*one, one thousand; two, one thousand, three*—until she reached three hundred.

Five minutes. And—nothing.

She tried to look through the small little crack the shard had made in the wall, but quickly gave up the effort. The hole where she had been digging was almost eighteen inches deep and not much wider than her arm. She couldn't get her eye close enough to see anything. Nor was there any light coming through the crack. She had known she broke through by feel alone.

She waited another five minutes before she started digging again. Then, moving very slowly and carefully so as to make as little noise as possible, she began to widen the hole.

The Lady Catherine Montaigne, Countess of the Tor

"Anton Zilwicki, Captain in Her Majesty's Royal Manticoran Navy," announced Lady Catherine's butler, as he came through the door to her study. "And Mr. Robert Tye." Isaac stepped aside and politely held the door for the visitors coming through behind him.

Isaac finished the introduction: "Lady Catherine Montaigne, Countess of the Tor."

Cathy rose from her reading chair. For a moment, before she focused her attention on her visitors, she allowed herself an amused glance at Isaac.

My, he does that well! Her butler—Isaac insisted on the title, though it was absurd—seemed every inch the perfect servant. He rattled off the aristocratic titles without a trace in his voice of Isaac's utter hatred of any and all forms of caste society. He even managed to wear the traditional menial's costume as if he had been born in it.

Which, of course, he hadn't. As was the custom of escaped Mesan slaves, except those who joined the Audubon Ballroom, Isaac had taken a surname shortly after obtaining his freedom. Isaac Douglass was now his official name, Isaac having chosen the most popular surname for such people, in memory of Frederick Douglass. But he had been born V-44e-684-3/5, and the name was still marked on his tongue.

Cathy's amusement was fleeting, however. Almost immediately, she realized that Isaac was tense. The symptoms were extremely subtle, a slight matter of his stance and poise, but she could read them. Isaac's feet were spread apart a bit farther than normal, his knees were slightly bent, and his hands were clasped in front of his groin. Cathy was no devotee of *coup de vitesse* herself, but she had no difficulty recognizing the "standing horse."

Why?

Her eyes went to her visitors, trying to find an answer. The man in front, the naval officer, seemed to pose no threat. Zilwicki was on the short side, and extremely stocky. His shoulders were so wide he almost seemed deformed. Put him in the right costume, grow a thick beard instead of a neat mustache, and he'd be the spitting image of a dwarf warlord out of fantasy novels. But his stance was relaxed, and Cathy could read no expression on his square face.

Then, noticing the intensity lurking in the man's dark brown eyes, she began to wonder. Her eyes moved to Zilwicki's companion. Robert Tye, wasn't it?

Tye solved the mystery for her. The little man's head was turned, examining Isaac. Suddenly, Tye's round face broke into a very cheery smile. Because of his pronounced epicanthic fold, the expression almost turned Tye's eyes into pure slits.

"With your permission, Lady Catherine, I will assume the lotus. I believe your—ah, *butler*—would find that more relaxing."

Tye didn't wait for Cathy's response. An instant later, folding himself down with astonishing ease and grace, Tye was sitting cross-legged on the lush carpeting. His legs were tightly coiled, each heel resting on the upper thigh of the opposite leg. His hands were placed on his knees, the fingers widespread.

Isaac seemed to straighten a bit. And his hands were now clasped behind his back instead of in front of his groin.

"Do you know this man, Isaac?" she blurted out.

Isaac's headshake was so slight it was not much

more than a tremor. "No, ma'am. But I know *of* him. He is quite famous among martial artists."

Cathy stared at Tye. "*Coup de vitesse*?"

Tye's cheerful smile returned. "Please, Lady Catherine! Do I look like a barbarian?"

Zilwicki interrupted. "Master Tye is here at my request, Lady Catherine." His tight mouth twitched in one corner. "It might be better to say, at his insistence."

Cathy was struck by the man's voice. His accent, partly—Zilwicki still bore the imprint of his obvious Gryphon highlander upbringing. But, mostly, it was that Zilwicki's voice was so deep it was almost a rumble.

Her natural impulsiveness broke through the moment's tension.

"Have you ever considered a singing career, Captain? I'm sure you would make a marvelous Boris Gudonov."

Again, Zilwicki's mouth made that little twitch. But his eyes seemed to darken still further.

"My wife used to say that to me," he murmured. "But I think she was mostly just tired of coming to church choirs, dressed in suitably conservative clothing. She'd have rather swept into the opera house in one of the glamorous gowns I bought for her. Which, sad to say, almost never got worn."

For all the affectionate humor in the remark, Cathy did not miss the sorrow lurking behind it. That, and the name, finally registered.

"*Helen* Zilwicki?"

The captain nodded.

"My condolences, Captain."

"It's been many years, Lady Catherine," was Zilwicki's reply. His deep-set eyes seemed almost black, now. Perhaps that was simply a shading, due to the relatively dim lighting in the study. His mass of black hair—cut short, in the military style, but very thick—added to the impression, of course. But Cathy did not doubt for a moment that, despite the disclaimer, the man before her had never stopped grieving his loss.

"I'm surprised you made the connection so quickly," he added. "Zilwicki is a common name on Gryphon." The captain paused; then: "And I wouldn't have expected someone on your end of the political spectrum to remember such things."

Cathy shook her head. The gesture was not so much one of irritation as simple impatience. "Oh, please! Captain, I warn you right now that I *detest* being pigeonholed."

"So I deduced, studying your file. But I'm still surprised." Zilwicki spread his hands in a little economical gesture. "My apologies."

She stared at him. "You studied *my* file? Whatever for?" Her jaws tightened. "And let me say, Captain, that I also detest being spied upon!"

Zilwicki took a deep breath. "I had no choice, Lady Catherine. Because of the situation, I am forced to operate completely outside of the command chain, and I need your help."

"*My* help? With regard to *what* situation?"

"Before I explain, Lady Catherine, I must tell you that I was not exaggerating when I said I was operating *completely* outside the command chain. In fact—"

He took another deep breath. "When this is all over, however it ends, I expect to face a court-martial. I won't be surprised if the charges include treason as well insubordination and gross dereliction of duty."

His eyes seemed like ebony balls. But it was fury

rather than sorrow which filled his voice. "Ambassador Hendricks and Admiral Young were quite explicit in their instructions to me. And I propose to shove those instructions as far up their ass—pardon my language—as possible. With or without lubricant, I don't much care."

Cathy hated her own laughter. She had heard it, on recordings, and it sounded just as much like a horse's bray as she'd always suspected. But she couldn't suppress the impulse. She wasn't good at controlling her impulses, and laughter came easily to her.

"Oh, splendid!" she cried. Then, choking: "No lubricant, Captain—not for those two! In fact—" Choke; wheeze. "Let's see if we can't splinter those instructions good and proper beforehand. Leave the bastards bloody."

Captain Zilwicki's mouth began to twitch again. But the twitch turned into an actual smile, and, for the first time, the humor which filled his voice seemed to creep into his eyes.

He was quite an attractive man, Cathy decided, once you got past that forbidding exterior. "And just how can I help you in this magnificent project, Captain? Whatever it is."

Helen

Helen was so engrossed in her work that she completely forgot to gauge its duration. For the first time, escape was actually a tangible reality instead of an abstract possibility. It was only when the digging shard set loose a small pile of sand—a pocket of dust, rather, encysted within the crumbled stones and fill—that she remembered.

Helen was immediately swept by panic. She began hastily backing out of the small tunnel into her cell. As soon as she emerged, she scrambled over—still on her hands and knees—to her makeshift "hourglass."

Empty.

Now the panic was almost overwhelming. Helen had made the timing device out of an old container she had found in a corner of the cell. A paint can, she thought, although the thing was so ancient that it was hard to tell. Fortunately, the can had been made of some kind of synthetic substance. Metal would have long since corroded away.

Helen had punched a small hole in the bottom with a sharp stone. Then, as soon as her captors provided her with the next meal, she began experimenting by filling the can with the dry and powdery dust which covered the cell's "floor." After three meal cycles, she had been satisfied that the can would run empty long before her captors returned with another meal. But she had always been careful to emerge from the tunnel and cover her traces while there was still dust in the container.

Empty. *But for how long?* For all she knew, Helen's captors were about to enter the cell.

For a moment, she almost pressed her ear against the door to see if she could hear them. But there was no point to that. The impulse was pure panic, nothing else. Helen forced herself to remember her training.

Breathing first. Master Tye always says that. Breathing first.

She took a slow, deep breath, letting the air fill her mind with calmness at the same time as it filled her lungs with oxygen. Another. Then another.

Under control. Now moving quickly but surely,

Helen began to cover her tracks. First, she fitted the panel over the tunnel entrance. Then, as always, she piled debris against it, making sure that the various pieces were in the same arrangement.

After that, she began mixing the fresh fill with the old dirt and dust covering the floor. That was slow work, because Helen had to be careful to stay as clean as possible. Her captors provided her with enough water to wash her hands and face, but nothing more. Of course, after days spent in the cell—which was really nothing more than a grotto in the ruins—she was dirtier than she'd ever been in her life. But she couldn't make it too obvious that the grime covering her was more than could be expected from the surroundings.

Finally, she put on the rest of her clothing. Whenever she went into the tunnel, Helen wore nothing but underwear. She had no way to wash her outer garments. If she'd worn them while she was digging, her clothes would have become utterly filthy. Even her captors, who seemed as indifferent toward her as they would to a lab rat, would have noticed soon enough.

She finished just in time. She heard voices on the other side of the door. By the time her captors started the process of unbolting the door, Helen had assumed the position they demanded of her when they brought food and fresh water. Squatting in a corner, staring at the wall. Docile and obedient.

She heard the door open, and her captors coming into the cell. Two of them—a woman and a man, judging from the sound of the footsteps.

The woman made a comment in that unknown language. Helen didn't understand the words, but she grasped the emotional content. Contemptuous and

derisive humor; alloyed, she thought, with more than
a trace of lasciviousness. True, Helen wasn't certain
about that last. She had just reached the stage in her
life when her body began to take a new shape, and
Solarian mores were very similar to Manticoran ones
when it came to sexual disrespect. But she thought
she could recognize a leer when she heard one.

The man responded with his own laughing remark,
and Helen had no doubt at all about *his*. She couldn't
see his face, but the words alone practically drooled.

She heard the sounds of the food and water being
placed on the floor next to the pallet which served
her as a bed. Again, the man said something and
laughed, and the woman joined him. Listening, Helen
thought she had never heard such a coarse and foul
sound in her life.

But that was the end of it. They did not come over
to her, nor did they do one of their occasional and
very cursory inspections of the cell.

Swine. Helen willed herself into a pose of utter
subservience. A mouse huddling in the presence of
cats. She concentrated on her breathing.

They left. Helen waited until she heard the chain
being put into place before she moved a muscle.
Then, scurrying like a mouse, she began to refill the
hourglass.

Running water.

Cathy

After Zilwicki finished, Cathy felt as confused as
she'd ever been in her life. *Nothing* of what he'd said
made any sense.

"But surely the police—"

Zilwicki shook his head firmly. "No, Lady Catherine. On *that* subject Ambassador Hendricks and Admiral Young are perfectly correct. My daughter wasn't kidnapped by common criminals. This was a political act, of some kind. The Solarian police simply aren't equipped to deal with that, and I don't want to get the Solarian League's intelligence services anywhere near it." His square, blocky face tightened. "I trust those people not much more than I do the Peeps."

Cathy rose from her chair and moved over to the window. The act was not done from any desire to admire the view, but simply because she always found it necessary to be on her feet when she was trying to puzzle out a problem. It was one of her characteristic traits, which her friends were fond of teasing her about. Lady Prancer, they sometimes called her. Cathy thought the nickname was a bit grotesque, but she admitted the logic of it. Her nervous way of moving constantly, combined with her braying laugh and her tall and gangly figure, often reminded *her* of a skittish filly.

Once she was at the window, of course, she found it impossible not to admire the view. She was certainly paying enough for it, after all. Her apartment was located near the very top of one of the Solarian capital's most expensive apartment complexes. Cathy was looking down on the city from well over a mile above street level. Insofar as the term "street level" could be applied to Chicago, that is. Whatever other changes had come over the city in the millennia of its existence, Chicago still retained its fondness for underground passages and covered walkways. Which was logical, since the climate—and the wind—had *not* changed.

Cathy stared down at the teeming metropolis. It was like looking into a gigantic canyon. On the surface streets far below, and on the multitude of conduits which connected the various buildings on every level, she could see the crowds scurrying like ants. Most of them seemed in a great hurry. Which, in fact, they were. It was lunch hour, for the millions who worked in Chicago's center. And that, too, had not changed over the centuries. Lunch hour was never long enough.

She shook her head abruptly and turned back to face her visitors. The quick and jerky motions, though she had no way of realizing it, reminded the captain of a gawky young horse. Once again, silently, someone bestowed the old nickname on her.

"All right, I can understand that. I guess. But why are you so certain that the ambassador and the admiral are wrong in their approach?" She held up her hand and fluttered the long and slender fingers. "Yes, yes, Captain! I know they're both assholes, but that doesn't mean they're incompetent."

She flashed her visitor a jittery grin. "You'll have to pardon my language. I know I curse too much. Can't help it. Comes from being forced through snooty private schools when I was a youngster. Maybe that's why I'm such a rebellious creature." She pranced back to her chair and flung herself into it. "That's what my parents' psychologists said, anyway. Personally, I think they're full of shit."

Anton

Watching and listening to her, Anton was struck by how closely Lady Catherine's speech resembled her movements. Quick and explosive, with scant respect for grammatical elbow room. Her wide mouth and expressive blue eyes added to the effect, as did the great mane of curly blond hair. The only part of the woman's face which seemed subdued was her snub nose, as if it were the deaf mute in a lively village. And despite the title, and the Tor fortune which lay behind it, Lady Catherine's face *was* that of a villager, not a countess. She even had some sunburned skin peeling off of her nose. With her extremely fair complexion, of course, that was not surprising. But most Manticoran noblewomen would have been too mortified by the prospect to have taken the risk of getting a sunburn in the first place. Lady Catherine, Anton suspected, suffered that small indignity with great frequency and a complete lack of concern.

Oddly enough, the naval officer found the ensemble thoroughly charming. He had come here reluctantly, driven by nothing more than sheer and pressing need, and with the full expectation that he would dislike the countess. Like all Gryphon highlanders, Anton Zilwicki detested the aristocracy in general—and the left wing members of it with a particular passion. No one in the Manticoran aristocracy was further to the left than Lady Catherine Montaigne. Even hardcore Progressives like Lady Descroix considered her "utopian and irresponsible." Countess New Kiev, the ultra-doctrinaire leader of the Liberal party, had once denounced her on the floor of the House of Lords as a "dangerous demagogue."

Perhaps, he mused whimsically, that was because his own personality was attracted to opposites, when it came to women. His dead wife had not resembled Lady Catherine in the least, physically. Helen had been short, dark-complected, and on the buxom side.

True, there was a closer ideological correlation. Helen, somewhat unusually for a naval officer, had generally followed the Progressives—but only up to a point, and always on the very right edge. And when it came to naval affairs, she was as pure a Centrist as you could ask for. She had *certainly* never been accused—as Lady Catherine had, innumerable times—of consorting with dangerous and violent radicals. But, like Lady Catherine, Helen had exuded rambunctious energy. And, though she had rarely lapsed into profanity, Helen had had the same way of expressing her opinions directly and forcefully.

Quite unlike Anton himself, who always tried—and almost always succeeded—in maintaining a tight and focused control over his thoughts and actions. Old Stone Face was the nickname his wife had bestowed upon him. Even his daughter, who was the one person to whom Anton unbent, teased him about it. Daddy Dour, she sometimes called him. Or just Popsicle.

On the rare occasions when he thought much on the subject, Anton ascribed his personality to the stark upbringing of the Gryphon highlands. The Navy's psychologists, in their periodic evaluations, had an infinitely more complex way of explaining the matter. Anton could never follow their reasoning, partly because it was always presented in that fearsome jargon so beloved by psychologists, but mostly—

Because I think they're full of shit.

But he didn't speak the words. He simply gave Lady Catherine a friendly smile. "I don't mind, ma'am. Curse all you want."

He planted his hands on his knees. His hands, like his face and body, were square and blunt. "But I'm telling you, the ambassador and the admiral—and

Admiral Young's whole little flock of armchair intelligence advisers—"

He couldn't resist: "—are full of shit."

All traces of humor vanished. "My daughter was *not* kidnapped by the Peeps. Or, if she was, it's some kind of black operation being done completely outside the Havenite command chain. By amateurs, to boot."

Lady Catherine frowned. "How can you be so certain of that? The demands they are making upon you, in exchange for keeping your daughter unharmed—"

Anton flicked the fingers of his hands, without removing the hands themselves from his knees. In its own way, the gesture was also explosive.

"Doesn't make sense. For at least three reasons. First of all, the demands were left in my apartment. *Written*, if you can believe it, on a sheet of paper."

Seeing the frown on the Countess' face, Anton realized that he had to elaborate.

"Ma'am, no field agent in his right mind would leave that kind of physical evidence on the scene of a crime. They would have communicated with me electronically, in some form or other. Leaving aside the fact that a physical note is legal evidence, it's almost impossible to keep some traces of yourself off of it. Modern forensic equipment—and the stuff the Solarians have is every bit as good as what the Manticoran police use— is damned near magical, the way it can squeeze information out of any kind of physical object a person has been in touch with."

He reached into a pocket and pulled out a small, flat package. "As it happens, although the Chicago police are not officially involved, I do have some personal contacts. One of them saw to it that the ransom note was given the full treatment. As well as

the evidence which I, ah, uncovered elsewhere. The
results are on this disk."

He tapped the package against his knee. "But I'll
get to that in a moment. First, let me finish my train
of thought."

With his left hand, he held up a finger. "So that's
point number one. The people who abducted my
daughter were not professional Havenite agents, nor
were they following orders from one. Or, if he was
one, he was a desk pilot rather than a field man."

He flicked up his middle finger to join the first.
"Point two. The action itself—*kidnapping*, for God's
sake—is completely out of whack with the supposed
result. I'm an officer in naval intelligence, true, but
my specialty is technical evaluation. My background's
in naval construction. I was a yard dog before my wife
was killed. After that—"

He paused for a moment, forcing his emotions
under. "After that, I transferred into the Office of
Naval Intelligence." Another pause. "I guess I wanted
to do something that would strike the Peeps directly.
Unlike Helen, however, I was never good enough at
naval tactics to have much hope of climbing to a command position in the fleet. So intelligence seemed like
the best bet."

Lady Catherine cocked her head. There was something faintly inquisitive about the gesture. Anton
thought he understood it, and, if so, was a bit astonished at her perspicacity.

He smiled ruefully, running his fingers through his
coarse mat of hair. "Yeah, I know. 'And how many barrels of oil will thy vengeance fetch thee in Nantucket
market, Captain Ahab?' "

She returned the smile with a great, gleaming one
of her own. Her eyes crinkled with pleasure. "Good

for you!" she exclaimed. "A rock-hard Gryphon highlander who can quote the ancient classics. I'll bet you
learned to do it just so you could show up the
Manticore nobility."

For all the gravity of his purpose, and his own
tightly controlled terror for his daughter, Anton found
it impossible not to laugh. Chuckle, at least. "Only
at first, Lady Catherine! After a while, I started
enjoying them in their own right."

But the humor faded. Here, too, there was old
heartbreak. It had been his wife Helen—a Manticoran
herself, and from "good stock" if not the nobility—
who had first introduced Anton to *Moby Dick*. Not,
in truth, because Helen had been a devotee of classic
literature, but simply because she had shared the
passion for any kind of naval fiction which was common to many officers in the Manticoran navy. Among
whose ranks was firmly held the opinion that Joseph
Conrad was the greatest author of all time, except
for a vocal minority which held forth for Patrick
O'Brian.

He brought his focus back to the moment. "The
point, Lady Catherine, is that I simply don't *know*
enough of any real value to the Peeps to make it
worth their while to commit such a crime."

"They *are* brutal bastards," stated the countess.
"Especially those sadists in State Security. I wouldn't
put anything past those thugs."

Again, Anton was surprised by the countess. Most
Liberals and Progressives he'd met, especially aristocrats, were prone to downplay or even semi-excuse
the viciousness of the Havenite regime with a lot of
left-wing jargon. As if tyranny stopped being tyranny
when you added more syllables to the term.

He shook his head. "That's irrelevant. They might

well be brutal enough—SS is *certainly* brutal enough—but—"

He couldn't resist another chuckle. Talk about role reversals! "Lady Catherine, I am hardly an apologist for the Peeps but I'm also not a cretin. However foul that regime may be, they're not storybook ogres out of a child's fairy tale. There's simply no *purpose* to this. Not enough, anyway." He leaned forward, elaborating. "I was sent here to keep track of technology transfers from the Solarian League to the People's Republic of Haven. Because of my technical background, I can make sense out of information than most intelligence specialists—" He hesitated. "Oh, hell, let's call ourselves 'spies,' why don't we?"

The countess smiled; Anton continued: "Which most spies can't. But it's in the nature of my work that I am trying to ferret out the enemy's secrets, rather than keeping our own. So why would the Peeps go to the extreme of kidnapping my daughter in order to force information out of me that they already have? It's not as if they need me to tell *them* what technology they're getting from the League."

"What about—"

"That idiot theory of the admiral's? That the Peeps are playing a long-term game, figuring they can use me to pass along disinformation?"

The countess nodded. Anton turned his head and stared at the giant windows along the wall. Even sitting where he was, a good twenty feet away, the view was breathtaking. But he was completely oblivious to it.

"That brings me to the third reason this doesn't make sense. It just isn't *done*, Lady Catherine." He sighed heavily. "I don't know if I'll have any more success trying to convince you of that than I did with the ambassador and the admiral."

Anton hesitated, gauging the personality of the woman sitting across from him. The *noble*-woman. Then, moved by a sudden feeling that he understood her nature—some of it, at least—decided for straight-forwardness.

"Lady Catherine, I will say this bluntly. Almost every aristocrat I know—sure as hell Ambassador Hendricks and Admiral Young—screws up when they try to understand the Peeps. They always look on them from the top down, instead of the bottom up. If they're right-wing, with a sneer; if left-wing, with condescension. Either way, the view is skewed. The Havenites are *people*, not categories. I'm *telling* you, this kind of personal attack on a man's family is so utterly beyond the pale that I can't imagine any professional Peep intelligence officer authorizing it. Not a field man, at least. It just—" He paused, setting his jaws stubbornly. "It just isn't done, that's all. Not by us, not by them."

Lady Catherine cocked her head again. "Are you trying to tell me that spies follow a 'code of ethics'? Including Haven's *State Security?*"

Anton's gaze remained steady. "Yes." He spread his hands slightly. "Well . . . I wouldn't call it code of ethics, exactly. It's more like a code of honor—or, better yet, the code duello. Even the Ellington Protocol doesn't allow you to just up and shoot somebody whenever you feel like it."

"That's true. But there's an official sanction standing behind—"

"And there is here too, ma'am," said Anton forcefully. "Any code of conduct has a practical basis to it, no matter how buried it might be under the formal trappings. Spies don't go around attacking each other's families, if for no other reason, because once you open *that* can of worms there'd be no end to it." He grimaced. "Well, I'm putting the thing too sharply. Certain kinds of attacks are permissible—long hallowed, in fact. Seducing a spy's spouse, for instance. But kidnapping a child and threatening to kill her—" Again, he set his jaws stubbornly. "It just isn't *done*, Lady Catherine. I can't think of a single instance, for all the savageness of this war between us and the Peeps, when anything like that has happened."

He took a deep breath before continuing. "As for State Security . . ." Another pause; then: "The thing is much more complicated, Lady Catherine, than people realize. The image most Manticorans have of State Security is that they're simply an organization of goons, thugs and murderers. Which"—he snorted—"they certainly have plenty of, God knows. Some of the foulest people who ever lived are wearing SS uniforms, especially the ones who volunteer for duty in concentration camps."

Seeing the countess' little start, Anton nodded. "Oh, yes. You didn't realize that, did you? The fact is, ma'am, that State Security allows its people a lot more latitude in choosing their assignments than the Peep navy does. Or the Manticoran navy, for that matter. It's quite a democratic outfit, in some ways, as hard as that might be to imagine."

He eyed her shrewdly. "But it makes sense, if you think about it. Whatever else Oscar Saint-Just is, he is most definitely not stupid. He knows full well that his precious State Security is a—a—" When he found the metaphor he was looking for, Anton barked a laugh. "A manticore, by God! A bizarre creature made up of the parts of completely different animals."

Again, Anton started ticking off his fingers. "A goodly chunk—undoubtedly the majority, by now—are people who joined after the Revolution looking for power and status. They've got as much ideological conviction as a pig in a trough. A fair number of those are former officers in the Legislaturalist regime's secret police. That's where you find your pure goons and thugs."

Another finger. "Then, there are a lot of young people who join up. Almost all of them are Dolists, from the lowest ranks of Havenite society. Some, of course, are just sadists looking for a legitimate cover or angry people looking to inflict revenge on the so-called 'elites.'" He shook his head. "But not most of them, ma'am. Most of them are genuine idealists, who believe in the Revolution and can see the gains it's starting to bring their own class—"

Lady Catherine started to interject a denial but Anton drove over it.

"Sorry, ma'am—*it has*. Don't ever think otherwise. A lot of people in Manticoran intelligence thought the Havenite empire would collapse, after the Revolution." He snorted. "Especially in the diplomatic service. Bunch of upper class snobs who think poor people are nothing but walking stomachs. Sure, Rob Pierre's war has brought Haven's Dolists a lot of bloody grief—not to mention that he's even frozen their stipend. But don't think for a moment that those Dolists are nothing but mindless cannon fodder. For *them*, the Revolution also meant lifting the Legislaturalists' hereditary yoke."

For a moment, Anton's eyes seem to smolder. Gryphon highlanders had chosen a different political course than Peep's Dolists—like Anton himself, they were fierce Crown Loyalists down to the newborn babes—but no highlander had any difficulty understanding the fury of the underdog. Over the centuries, highlanders had had their own bitter experience with Manticore's aristocracy. Anton himself hated the People's Republic of Haven—for killing his beloved wife, if for no other reason—but he had never shed any tears over the Legislaturalists executed by Rob Pierre and his cohorts after the Revolution. In Anton's opinion, a fair number of the *Manticoran* aristocracy would look pretty good, hanging by the neck. Half the members of the Conservative Association, for a certainty—with Ambassador Hendricks and Admiral Young right at the front of the line.

His innate sense of humor overrode the moment's anger. Indeed, for a moment, he felt a certain embarrassment. The friendly-faced woman sitting across from him—whom he had approached for help, after all, not the other way around—was also a member of that same aristocracy. Very prominently, as a matter of fact. If the countess was ranked only middling-high in the Manticoran nobility's stiff hereditary terms— all the stiffer for the fact that they had been artificially created when the planet was settled—the Tor fortune was greater than that of most dukes and duchesses.

Something in his thoughts must have shown, for Lady Catherine was suddenly beaming from ear to ear.

"Hey, sailor!" she chortled. "Go easy on me, willya? I can't help it—I was born there."

In that moment, Anton was stunned by how beautiful she looked. It was bizarre, in a way—a matter of pure personality radiating through the barrier of flesh. The countess' face was not pretty in the least, beyond a certain open freshness. And while her figure was definitely feminine, its lanky—almost bony—lines were quite a ways outside the parameters of what was normally considered, by males at least, "sexy." Yet Anton knew, without having to ask, that Lady Catherine had never even considered the body-sculpting which was so popular among Manticore's upper crust. Even though for her, unlike most people, cost was no obstacle. As expensive as body-sculpting was, Lady Catherine could have paid for it out of the equivalent of pocket change.

It was just—the way she was. *Here I am. This is how I look. You don't like it? Then go—*

Anton couldn't help it. He was grinning himself. He could just imagine the coarse profanities which would follow.

The moment lasted, and lasted. Two people, strangers until that day, grinning at each other. And as it lasted, began to undergo what Anton, from his reading of the classics, understood as a *sea change.*

And so, his shock deepened. He had come here, carrying years' worth of a widower's grief and the newfound rage of a father whose child was in danger, looking for nothing more than help. And found— damned if it wasn't true!—the first woman since that horrible day when Helen died who genuinely *interested* him.

He tried to pull his eyes away, but couldn't. And as the grin faded from the countess' face, he understood that he was not imagining anything. She, too, was feeling that tremendous pull.

The image of his daughter broke the spell. Helen, as a four-year-old girl, had been sitting on his lap at the very moment her mother died. Helen the mother had saved Helen the child. The father's responsibility remained.

Lady Catherine cleared her throat. Anton knew that she was trying to leave him the emotional space he needed, and was deeply thankful. Yet, of course, the same uncanny intuitiveness just deepened the attraction.

"As you were saying, Captain . . ." Her voice was a bit husky.

Anton finally managed to look away from her. He ran a blunt-fingered hand through his stiff and bristly black hair.

"The thing is, ma'am—"

"Call me Cathy, why don't you? Anton."

He took the hand away. "Cathy, trust me on this. There are fissure lines running all through Havenite society. State Security is no exception. Oscar Saint-Just knows that as well—hell, *better than*—anyone in the universe. Except maybe Rob Pierre himself."

He leaned forward, extending his hands. "So he's careful to keep the sheep separated from the goats. More precisely—since no one has still been able to nail down telepathy—he lets the goats and the sheep separate themselves. The thugs volunteer for the concentration camps, and the young idealistic firebrands head for the front lines. Which, for spies, means places like Chicago."

He nodded toward the window. "And that's mostly the kind of State Security out there. In the lower ranks, at least. Tough, yes—even ruthless. But I *know* they weren't the ones who took my daughter."

Cathy leaned forward herself, also extending her hands. But where Anton's movements had been tight and controlled, hers were jerky and expressive. "Anton, I can't honestly say that I share your assessment. I don't have your expertise in intelligence, of course, but my own work has brought me into contact with any number of young—ah, 'firebrands.' Some of them, I hate to say it, wouldn't shrink from *any* blow directed at their enemy."

Anton shook his head. "No, they wouldn't. But they *would* shrink from using the wrong weapon."

He held up the package in his hands. "This is the forensic report. You're welcome to look at it if you want, but I can summarize the gist. The people who broke into our apartment and took my daughter— probably male and female both, judging from the chemical traces—left a clear genetic track. Crystal clear, in fact—the idiots were even careless enough not to eradicate skin oils from the note."

"And they weren't Peeps."

"No. The genetic evidence carried not a trace of the normal Peep pattern. And it hardly matters, anyway, because the pattern they did carry is unmistakable. They were members of the Sacred Band— or, at least, people who came from that very distinct genetic stock."

Cathy didn't quite gasp, but her hand flew to her throat. "Are you *serious*?"

Anton was not surprised to see that Lady Catherine—*Cathy*—had not only heard of the Sacred Band but obviously didn't doubt their existence. Most people wouldn't have understood the term, and most of the ones who did would have immediately insisted that it was a fairy tale—a legend, like vampires. His suspicion was confirmed, and that knowledge brought him great satisfaction. There was only one way that the countess could have found out about the Sacred Band—she had been told by the very people Anton was searching for. The same people he had come here to find.

The countess was now staring blindly at the

window. "But that makes no sense at all!" Her lips tightened. "Although I can now understand why you're so insistent that this wasn't a Peep operation."

She gave Anton a shrewd glance. There was hostility in her eyes, but it wasn't directed at him. "And— *of course*—I can understand why the ambassador and the admiral wouldn't believe you."

She sprang to her feet. "Fucking assholes!" The countess began pacing back and forth, waving her hands. "Fucking assholes," she repeated. "Charter members of the Conservative Association, the both of them, God rot their souls. Since their only guiding political principle is *gimme*—"

Anton smiled grimly.

"—they can't possibly understand people who take ideology seriously." For an instant, like a prancing filly, she veered at him. "You're a Crown Loyalist, I imagine."

"Rock hard."

Cathy brayed laughter. "Gryphon highlanders! Just as thick-skulled as their reputation." But she veered even closer. "S'okay. I forgive you." She ran slim fingers through his bristly hair before prancing away. Coming from anyone else except his daughter, that act of casual intimacy would have infuriated Anton. Coming from Cathy, it sent a spike down his spine which paralyzed him for an instant.

She was moving back and forth in front of the window, now. Her movements were jerky—almost awkward and ungainly—but they also expressed a fierce energy.

Anton was dazzled by the sight. The bright sunshine penetrated her skirt—a modest enough garment, in its own right, but not made of a heavy fabric— and showed her long legs almost as if they were bare.

Very slender, they were, though the muscles were obviously well-toned. Anton felt a sudden rush of sheer passion, imagining them—

He *forced* that thought away. And, with his capacity for concentration, succeeded within seconds. But he retained a small glow in his heart. He hadn't felt that kind of rush since his wife died. There was something pure about it, like an emotional cleanser.

Cathy came to an abrupt halt, spun around to face him, and planted her hands on her hips. Extremely slim, those hips. Anton suspected that they had been a lifelong despair for her. "Snake hips," she'd probably muttered, staring at herself in a mirror. *He* thought, on the other hand—

Down!

"Shit!" exclaimed the countess. "No Peep I know would come within a mile of either a Mesan or a Scrag"—*yes! She knew the pejorative nickname*— "unless it was to blow their fucking head off. As much as they hate us Manticoran 'elitists,' we're just Beelzebub in their demonology. The Great Satan himself is called Manpower Inc. and Hell is on a planet named Mesa."

"Exactly," said Anton. "However dictatorial and brutal they are, the Peeps are also ferocious egalitarians. You can get executed in Haven for arguing too hard in favor of individual merit promotion." Again, he quoted from the classics: " 'All animals are equal even if some animals are more equal than others.' There's no room in there for hereditary castes—especially slave castes!—or for genetic self-proclaimed supermen."

He sighed heavily. "And, in all honesty, I have to say that in this, if nothing else, the Peeps have a pretty good track record." Another sigh, even heavier. "Oh, hell, let's be honest. They have an excellent track record. Manpower doesn't go anywhere near Havenite territory. That was true even before the Revolution. Unlike—"

"Unlike Manticoran space!" interjected the countess angrily. "Where they don't hesitate for a minute. *Damn the laws.* The stinking scum know just where to find Manticoran customers."

Anton scowled. "Cathy, that's not fair either. The Navy—"

She waved her arms. "Don't say it, Anton! I know the Navy officially suppresses the slave trade. Even does so in real life, now and again. Though not once since the war started. They're too preoccupied, they say."

Anton scowled even more deeply. Cathy waved her arms again. "All right, all right," she growled, "they *are* preoccupied with fighting the Peeps. But even before the war started, the only instance where the Navy ever hit the Mesan slave trade with a real hammer is when—"

Both of them broke into wide grins, now. The news of the incredible mass escape from the Peep prison planet of Hell was still fresh in everyone's mind.

"—when Harrington smashed up the depot on Casimir," she concluded. The countess snorted. "What was she, then? A measly lieutenant commander? God, I love impetuous youth!"

Anton nodded. "Yeah. Almost derailed her career before it even got started. Probably *would* have, if Courvoisier hadn't twisted some Conservative admirals' arms out of their sockets. And if—"

He gazed at her steadily. "—a certain young and impetuous left-wing countess hadn't given a blistering speech on the floor of the House of Lords, demanding to know why the first time a naval officer fully enforced the laws against the slave trade she wasn't getting a medal for it instead of carping criticism."

Cathy smiled. "It was a good speech, if I say so myself. Almost as good as the one that got me pitched out of the House of Lords entirely."

Anton snorted. Although membership in the Manticoran House of Lords was hereditary, not elective, the Lords did have the right under law to officially exclude one of its own members. But given the natural tendency of aristocrats to give full weight to lineage, it was very rarely done. To the best of Anton's knowledge, at the present moment there were no more than three nobles who had had their membership in the Lords revoked. One of them, the Earl of Seaview, had been expelled only after he was convicted in a court of law of gross personal crimes—which all the members of the Lords had long known were his vices, but had chosen to look the other way over. The other two were Honor Harrington and Catherine Montaigne, for having, each in her own way, deeply offended the precious sensibilities of Manticore's aristocracy.

Anton cleared his throat. "Actually, Cathy, that speech is why I'm here."

She paused in her jerky pacing and cocked her head. "Since when does a Crown Loyalist study the old speeches of someone who even aggravates Liberals and Progressives?"

He smiled. "Believe it or not, Cathy, that speech made quite a hit in the highlands. As it happens, one of our Gryphon yeomen was on trial at the time. Shot the local baron—eight times—for molesting his daughter. The prosecutor argued that a murderer is a murderer. The defense countered by quoting your speech."

"The part about 'one person's terrorist being another's freedom fighter,' I should imagine."

Anton nodded. But there was no humor at all in the face. Finally, Cathy understood his purpose in coming to see her. Her hand flew to her throat again, and this time she did gasp.

"Oh, my God!"

Anton's eyes were like coal, beginning to burn. "Yeah, that's it. I didn't come here to discuss the ins and outs of the political complexities which might or might not be involved with my daughter's kidnapping. Frankly, Cathy, I don't give a good God-damn. The ambassador and the admiral can order me to treat this like a political maneuver, but they're—"

He clenched his jaws. "Never mind what they are. What *I* am is a man of Gryphon's highlands. I was that long before"—he plucked the sleeve of his uniform—"I became an officer in Her Majesty's Navy."

The eyes were burning hot, now. "I can't use my normal channels, because the ambassador and the admiral would shut me down in a heartbeat. So I've got to find an alternative." He glanced at the little man still squatting on the floor. "Master Tye agreed to help—insisted, in fact—but I need more than that."

Once again, he lifted the little package which contained the forensic data. "The Scrags who kidnapped my daughter live—or operate—somewhere in Chicago's Old Quarter. You know what that maze is like. Only someone who knows it like the back of his hand could have a chance of finding Helen in there."

Cathy made an attempt to head him off. "I know several people who live in the Loop. Lots of them, in fact. I'm sure one of them—"

Anton shot to his feet. *"From the highlands, woman!"* His Gryphon accent was now so thick you could cut it with a knife. And the black rage of the Star Kingdom's most notorious feudists had shattered the outer shell of control.

"You are—have been for years—one of the central leaders of the Anti-Slavery League. And *by far* the most radical. That's why you've been here for years, in what amounts to exile." Anton's words, for all the Gryphon slurring, came out like plates from a stamping mill. "So don't tell me you don't know *him*."

"Never been proved!" she exclaimed. But the protest was more in the nature of a squeak.

Anton grinned. Like a wolf, admiring the grace of a fox. "True, true. Consorting with a known member of the Audubon Ballroom—any member, much less *him*—is a felonious offense. In the Star Kingdom as well as anywhere in Solarian territory. You've been charged with it on four occasions. Each time, the charges were dropped for lack of evidence."

A very angry wolf, and a rather frightened fox. "Cut the crap, Cathy! You know him and I know you do and so does the whole damn universe. This isn't a court of law. I need his help, and I intend to get it. But I don't know how to contact him. You do."

"Oh God, Anton," she whispered.

He shook his head. "What did they think, Cathy? That I would *obey* them?" The next words came through clenched teeth. "*From the highlands.* When they gave me that command, they broke faith with me. Damn them and damn all aristocracy! I'll do as I must, and answer only to the Queen. If she—*she*, not they!—chooses to call that treason, so be it. I'll have my daughter back, and I'll piss on the ashes of those who took her from me."

He reached into another pocket and drew out another package. Identical, to all appearances.

"You can tell him I'll give him this, in exchange for his help. I've spent the past two days hacking into the embassy's intelligence files to get it."

Anton's grin was now purely feral. There was no more humor in it than a shark's gape. "When I broke into the personal records of Young and Hendricks I hit the gold mine. I didn't expect either one of them to be stupid enough to have direct financial dealings with Manpower, and they don't. Technically, under Manticoran anti-slavery laws, that would lay them open to the death penalty."

Cathy's left hand was still clutching her throat. With her other hand, she made a waving gesture. "That's not the form it takes, in the Star Kingdom. Slavery's an inefficient form of labor, even with Manpower's genetic razzle-dazzle. No rich Manticoran really has much incentive to dabble in slave labor unless they're grotesquely avaricious. *And* willing to take the risks of investing in the Silesian Confederacy or the Sollie protectorates. Our own society's got too high a tech base for slavery to be very attractive."

"You might be surprised, Cathy—you *will* be surprised—at how many Manticorans *are* that stupid. Don't forget that the profit margin in Silesian mines and plantations can be as high as the risk." Anton shrugged. "But you're basically right. Most of the Star Kingdom's citizens who deal with Manpower do so from personal vice, not from greed."

Cathy's face was stiff, angry. " 'Personal vice!' That's a delicate way of putting what happens on those so-called pleasure resorts." She stared at the package in Anton's hands. Her next words were almost whispered. "Are you telling me—"

Anton's shark grin seemed fixed in place. "Oh, yeah. I was pretty sure I'd find it. That whole Young clan is notorious for their personal habits, and I'd seen enough of the admiral to know he was no exception." He held up the package. "Both he and the ambassador have availed themselves of Manpower's so-called 'personal services.' Both of them have invested in those 'pleasure resorts,' too, using Solarian conduits. Along with lots of others, for whom they acted as brokers."

"They kept *records*?" she gasped. "Are they that *stupid*?"

Anton nodded. "That arrogant, anyway." He looked down at the package in his hand. "So there it is, Cathy. I thought of using this information to blackmail them into rescinding my orders, but that would take too long. I've got to find my daughter *quickly*, before this whole crazy scheme—whatever it is—starts coming unglued. Which it will, as sure as the sunrise. And when it does, the first thing that'll happen is that Helen will be murdered."

Her hand was still clutching her throat. "My God, Anton! Don't you understand what he'll do if—"

"What do I care, Cathy?" No shark's grin ever held such sheer fury. "You'll find no Gryphon highlanders on this list, I can tell you that. Nobles aplenty, o' course"—the word *nobles* practically dripped vitriol—"but not a one of *my* folk."

Finally, the fury began to ebb. "I'm sorry, Cathy. But this is the way it must be. My daughter"—he waved the package—"weighed against *these*?"

Cathy

Cathy lowered her hand and sighed. Then, shrugged. It was not as if she disagreed with his moral

assessment, after all. Though she still found it difficult to match the man's ruthlessness with what she
sensed of the man himself. But then, Cathy had no
children of her own. So, for a moment, she tried to
imagine the rage that must be filling Anton. Raising
a daughter from the age of four as a widower, and
coming from that unyielding highland clansmen
background—

She glimpsed, for an instant, that seething void—
like the event horizon of a black hole—and her mind
skittered away.

"I'm sorry," Anton repeated, very softly. "I must
do what I must." He managed a harsh chuckle. "In
this area, you know, tradition rules. There's a term
for what I need. Goes back centuries—millennia. It's
called *wet work*."

Cathy grimaced. "How crude!" Again, a sigh. "But
appropriate, I suppose. I'm sure Jeremy would agree."

She sighed again. "All right, I'll serve as your conduit to him. But I warn you in advance, Anton, he's
got a peculiar sense of humor."

Anton held up the package anew. "Then I imagine this will tickle his fancy."

Cathy stared at the object in Anton's hand.
Innocuous-looking thing, really. But she knew full well
what would happen once Jeremy got his hands on it.
Jeremy had come into the universe in one of Manpower Inc.'s breeding chambers on Mesa.
K-86b/273-1/5, they had called him. The "K" referred
to the basic genetic type—in Jeremy's case, someone
bred to be a personal servant, just as Isaac's "V"
denoted one of the technical combat breeds. The
"-86b" referred to one of the multitude of slight vari-
ants within the general archetype. In Jeremy's case,
the variant designed to provide clients with acrobatic

entertainment—jugglers and the like. Court clowns, in essence. The number 273 referred to the "batch," and the 1/5 meant that Jeremy was the first of the quintuplets in that batch to be extracted from the breeding chamber.

Cathy ran her hand down her face, as if wiping away filth. In truth, she knew, Manpower's "scientific" terminology covered a genetic method which was almost as fraudulent as it was evil. It was the modern equivalent of the grotesque medical experiments which the ancient Nazis of fable were said to have practiced. Cathy was not a professional biologist, but in the course of her long struggle against genetic slavery she had come to be a lay expert on the subject. Genes were vastly more fluid things than most people understood. The specific way in which a genotype developed was as much a result of the environmental input at any given stage of development as it was on the inherent genetic "instructions." Genes reacted differently depending on the external cue.

Manpower's genetic engineers, of course, knew that perfectly well—despite the claims of their advertising that their "indentured servants" could be counted on to behave exactly as they were programmed. So they tried to provide the "proper environment" for the developing genotypes. On the rare occasions when a biologically-sophisticated prospective client pressed them on the subject, Manpower provided them with a learned and jargon-ridden explanation of what they called the "phenotype developmental process."

Strip away the pseudoscientific claptrap and what it amounted to was: *We breed the embryos in artificial wombs, making the best guess we can based on their DNA; and then we spend years torturing the*

*children into proper alignment. Making the best guess
we can.*

And, within limits, it worked—usually. But not
always, by any means. Certainly not in Jeremy's case.
Within less than a week after his sale, he had made
his escape. Eventually, he arrived on Terra, through
one of the routes maintained by the Anti-Slavery
League. Within a day of his arrival, he had joined the
Audubon Ballroom, probably the most radical and
certainly the most violence-prone group within the
general umbrella of the anti-slavery movement. Then,
following the custom of that underground movement—
whose membership was exclusively restricted to
ex-slaves—had renamed himself Jeremy X. Within a
short time, he had risen to leadership in the Ballroom.
Today, he was considered one of the most dangerous
terrorists in the galaxy. Or, to many—herself included,
when all was said and done, despite her disapproval
of his tactics—one of its greatest freedom fighters.

But if anyone could get Captain Anton Zilwicki's
daughter back alive, it would be Jeremy X. Certainly
if she were held captive in the Loop. And if, in the
months and years which followed, a number of
Manticore's most prominent families found themselves
attending an unusually large number of funerals, Cathy
could not honestly say the prospect caused her any
anguish. Rich people who trafficked in slavery for the
sole purpose of indulging their personal vices would
get little in the way of mercy from her.

And they would get none at all from a man whose
birth name was still marked on his tongue. *Wet work,
indeed.*

As she ushered the captain and his companion to
the door, Cathy remembered something.

"Oh, yes. Satisfy my curiosity, Anton. Earlier, you said there were three types of people in State Security. But you never got around to explaining the third sort. So who are they?"

"It's obvious, isn't it? What happens to a young idealist, as the years go by and he discovers his beloved Revolution is covered with warts?"

Cathy frowned. "They adapt, I imagine. Get with the program. Either that or turn against it and defect."

Anton shook his head. "Many do adapt, yes. The majority of them, probably. And when they do they are often the most vicious—just to prove to their superiors, if nothing else, that they can be counted on. But almost none ever defect and there are a lot of them who just fade into the woodwork, trying to find a corner where they can still live. Don't forget that, from their point of view, the alternative isn't all that attractive."

His lips twitched. "Even a Gryphon traditionalist like me isn't all that fond of some aspects of Manticoran society. Try to imagine, Cathy, how a man from the Legislaturalist regime's Dolist ranks is going to feel, at the prospect that he'd have to bow and scrape before the likes of Pavel Young, Earl of North Hollow."

Cathy was startled. "Surely they don't know—"

"Of course they do!" Anton's mouth started to twitch again, but the twitch turned into a genuine smile. "The Peeps tend to be a little schizophrenic on the subject of Honor Harrington, you know. On the one hand, she's their arch-nemesis. On the other, she's often been their favorite example of the injustices of Manticoran elitist rule.

"Not any more, of course," he chuckled. "From the news coverage, I'd say the Salamander's days in exile and disgrace are *finished*. Doubt there's more than three Conservative Lords who'll still argue she's unfit for their company."

Cathy brayed her agreement. "If that many!"

"But don't think the Peep propagandists didn't make hay while the sun was shining, Cathy. At least until Cordelia Ransom decided that there was more propaganda value in having Harrington 'executed.' " Anton scowled. "That whole stinking Pavel Young affair was plastered all over every media outlet in the Havenite empire, for weeks on end. Hell, they didn't even have to make anything up! The truth was stinking bad enough. A vile and cowardly aristocrat used his wealth and position to ruin an excellent officer's career. Even paying for the murder of her lover— and getting away with it until Harrington finally cornered him into a personal duel. And *then*, when she shot him in self-defense after he violated the dueling code, the Lords blamed *her?* Because she shot him *too many times?*"

The highlander's soul was back in charge, never mind the uniform. "A pox on all aristocracy," he hissed. "Inbred filth and corruption."

Belatedly, he remembered. "Uh, sorry. Nothing personal. Uh, Lady Catherine."

"S'okay, Anton. I forget I'm a countess myself, as often as not." She rubbed her sunburned nose.

"I—I'm really sorry we met this way, Cathy. I would have liked—I don't know—"

Cathy placed her hand on his arm and gave it a little squeeze. She was a bit startled by the thick muscle under the uniform. "Don't say anything, Anton. Let's get your daughter back, shall we? The rest can take care of itself."

He flashed her a thankful smile. They were now

at the door, which Isaac was holding open in his best butler's manner. Robert Tye had already stepped through and was waiting for Anton in the corridor beyond.

Anton and Cathy stared at each other for a moment. Now that they were standing side by side, she realized how much taller she was than the stocky captain. But, also, that the width of his shoulders was not an illusion created by his short stature. He really *was* almost misshapen. Like a dwarf warrior from the hills, disguised in a uniform.

Anton gave her a quick little bow, and hastened through the door. Then, stopped abruptly.

"Good Lord—I forgot to ask. How long will it take you—" He broke off, glancing quickly into the corridor.

Cathy understood. "I should be in contact with the individual quite shortly, I think. I'll get in touch with you, Captain Zilwicki."

"Thank you." He was gone.

Helen

By the time Helen finished widening the tunnel enough to squeeze herself through, two-thirds of the dust in her makeshift hourglass had fallen through the hole. She had to wage a fierce battle to keep herself from leaving immediately.

That natural impulse was almost overwhelming. But it would be stupid. It wasn't enough to simply get out of the cell. She also had to make her *escape*. And that was not going to be easy.

Again, Helen's success had caught her off guard. She had never really thought about what she would do if she ever got out of the cell. But now she realized that she needed to think about it before she plunged into the darkness.

The darkness was literal, not figurative. Helen had stuck her head through the hole as soon as she widened it enough. And seen—

Nothing. Pitch black. Her own head, filling the hole, had cut off the feeble illumination provided by the cell's light fixture. Helen had never experienced such a complete darkness. She remembered her father telling her, once, of the time he and her mother had visited Gryphon's famous Ulster Caverns on their honeymoon. As part of the tour, the guide had extinquished all the lighting in their section of the caverns, for a full five minutes. Helen's father had described the experience, with some relish—not so much because he was fascinated by utter darkness as because he'd had the chance to fondle his new bride in flagrant disregard for proper public conduct.

Remembering that conversation, Helen had to control herself again. She was swept by a fierce urge to see her father as soon as possible. If Helen's long-dead mother was a constant source of inspiration for her, it was her father who sat in the center of her heart. Helen was old enough to recognize the emptiness which lurked just beneath her father's outward cheer and soft humor. But he had always been careful not to inflict that grief on his daughter.

Oh, Daddy!

For a moment, she almost thrust herself into the hole. But among her father's many gifts to her had been Master Tye's training, and Helen seized that regimen to keep her steady.

Breathe in, breathe out. Find the calm at the center.

Two minutes later, she backed out of the hole and went through the now-familiar process of disguising her work. Since she had plenty of time, she took more care than usual placing the coverings over the hole and blending in the fresh fill. But her own ablutions were as skimpy as she could make them. Just enough to remove the obvious streaks of dirt.

Helen had no idea how long it would take her to find water in that darkness beyond—if there was any water to be found at all. So she planned to drink the remaining water as soon as she heard her captors approaching. That way she could save the new water bottle her captors would bring her. She might have to live on that water for days.

Or, possibly, forever. Helen knew full well that she might simply die in the darkness. Even if she could elude her captors—even if she found water and food—she had no idea what other dangers might lurk there.

She stretched herself out on the pallet and began Master Tye's relaxation exercises. She also needed as much rest as possible before setting forth.

Breathe in, breathe out. As always, the exercises brought calmness. But, after a time, she stopped thinking about them. Master Tye faded from her mind, and so did her father.

There was only her mother left. Helen had been named after her mother. Her father, born and bred in the highlands, had insisted upon that old Gryphonite custom, even though Helen's mother herself—a sophisticate from the Manticoran capital of Landing—had thought it was grotesque.

Helen was glad for it. More now than ever. She drifted into sleep like a castaway, staying afloat on the image of the Parliamentary Medal of Honor.

Cathy

As soon as Isaac closed the door on the departing figure of Captain Zilwicki, a huge grin spread across his face. "I should be in contact with the individual quite shortly, I think," he mimicked. "Talk about understatements!"

Cathy snorted and stalked back into the living room. Once there, she planted her hands on her hips and glared at the bookcase against the far wall. It was a magnificent thing, antique both in age and function. Cathy was one of that stubborn breed who were the only reason that the book industry (*real* books, dammit!) was still in business. But she insisted on having real books, wherever she lived—and lots of them, prominently displayed in a proper bookcase.

That was so partly because, in her own way, the Lady Catherine Montaigne, Countess of the Tor, was also a traditionalist. But mostly it was because Cathy herself found them immensely useful.

"You can come out now," she growled.

Immediately, the bookcase swung open. Between the piece of furniture's own huge size and the shallow recess in the wall, there was just enough room for a man.

Not much room, of course. But the reputation of Jeremy X was far larger than his actual size. The vicious terrorist and/or valiant freedom fighter (take your pick) was even shorter than Captain Zilwicki, and had nothing like his breadth of shoulder.

Wearing his own cheerful grin, Jeremy practically bounded into the room. He even did a little somersault coming out of the recess. Then turned, planted his own hands on hips, and exclaimed admiringly: "Tradition!"

Turning back around and rubbing his hands in an utterly theatrical manner, he said: "Never met a Gryphon highlander before. What a splendid folk!"

He gave Cathy a squint that was every bit as theatrical as the hand-rubbing. "You've been holding out on me, girl. I know you have—don't deny it!"

Cathy shook her head ruefully. "Just what the universe *didn't* need. Slavering terrorist fiend meets to-the-bloody-death Gryphon feudist. Love at first sight."

Still grinning, Jeremy hopped into one of the plush armchairs scattered about the large room. "Don't give me that either, lass. I was watching. Through that marvelous traditional peephole. You were quite taken by the Captain. Don't deny it—I can tell these things, you know. I think it must be one of the experiments those Mesan charmers tucked into my chromosomes. Trying for clairvoyance or something."

Cathy studied him. For all Jeremy's puckish nature, she never allowed herself to forget just how utterly ruthless he could be. The Audubon Ballroom's feud against Manpower Inc. made the worst Gryphon clan quarrels of legend seem like food fights.

Still, in her own way—dry, so to speak, rather than "wet"—Cathy was just as unyielding. "Dammit, Jeremy, I'll say it again. If you—"

To her astonishment, Jeremy clapped his hands once and said: "Enough! I agree! You have just won our long-standing argument!"

Cathy's jaw sagged. Glaring, Jeremy sprang to his feet. "What? Did you really think I took any pleasure in killing all the people I have? *Did you now?*"

He didn't wait for a response. "Of course I did!

Enjoyed it immensely, in fact. Especially the ones I could show my tongue to before I blew 'em apart. To hell with that business about revenge being a dish best served cold. It's absolute nonsense, Cathy—take my word for it. *I know.* Vengeance is hot and sweet and tasty. Don't ever think it isn't."

He grinned up at her impishly. "Ask the good Captain, why don't you? He's obviously a man of parts. Wonderful fellow!" Jeremy lowered his voice, trying to imitate Zilwicki's basso rumble: " '—*and I'll piss on the ashes of those who took her from me.*' "

He cackled. "T'wasn't a metaphor, y'know? I dare say he'll do it." Jeremy cocked his head at Isaac. "What do you think, comrade?"

Unlike Jeremy, Isaac preferred restraint in his mannerisms and speech. But, for all its modesty, his own smile was no less savage. "Isaac Douglass" was his legal name, but Isaac himself considered it a pseudonym. Isaac X, he was, like Jeremy a member of the Ballroom.

"I'll bring the combustibles," he pronounced. "The Captain's so preoccupied with his daughter's plight that he'll probably forget. And wouldn't that be a terrible thing? To fail of revenge at the very end, just because you forgot to bring the makings for a good fire?"

Isaac's soft laughter joined Jeremy's cackle. Staring from one of them to the other, Cathy felt—as she had often before—like a fish stranded out of water. For all the years she had devoted to the struggle against genetic slavery, and for all the closeness of her attachment to the Mesan ex-slaves themselves, she knew she could never see the universe the way they did. There was no condemnation of them in that knowledge. Just a simple recognition that no one born into the lap of privilege and luxury, as she had been, could ever really feel what they felt.

But neither was there any condemnation of herself. Decades earlier, as a young woman newly entered into the Anti-Slavery League, Cathy had been a typical guilt-ridden liberal. Like many such women, she had tried to assuage her guilt by entering a number of torrid affairs with ex-slaves—who, of course, had generally been quite happy to accept the offer.

Jeremy had broken her of that habit. That, and the guilt which lay beneath it. He was already quite famous when she met him, a romantic figure in the lore of the underground. Cathy had practically hurled herself upon him. She had been utterly shocked by his blunt and cold refusal. *I am no one's toy, damn you. Deal with your guilt, don't inflict it on me. Stupid girl! Of what crimes could you possibly be guilty, at your age?*

It was Jeremy who had taught her to think clearly; to separate politics from people; and, most of all, not to confuse justice with revenge or guilt with responsibility. And if Jeremy's conclusion had been that he would have his justice and enjoy his revenge too— *why not? As long as you know the difference*—he had enabled her to do otherwise. Unlike most youthful idealists, Cathy had never "grown wiser" with age. She had simply become more patient. Close friends and comrades, she and Jeremy had become over the years, for all their long-standing and often rancorous quarrel over tactics.

Now—

"Stop joking!" she snarled at him. Then, at Isaac: "And you! Quit playing at your stupid butler act!"

Jeremy left off his cackling and plopped himself back in the armchair. Moving more sedately, Isaac did the same.

"I am *not* joking, Cathy," Jeremy insisted. "Not in the least."

Seeing the suspicion and skepticism in her eyes, Jeremy scowled. "Didn't I teach you *anything*? Revenge is one thing; justice is another." He nodded toward the door. "That marvelous officer of yours is about to hand me the instrument for my justice. In the Star Kingdom, at least. D'you think for a minute that I'm such a fool that I'd forgo it for simple revenge?"

She matched his scowl with no difficulty at all. "*Yes*. Damn you, Jeremy! What else have we been arguing about for the past how many years?"

He shook his head. "You're mixing apples and oranges. Or, to put it better, retail with wholesale." He held out his left hand, palm up, and tapped it with his right forefinger. "As long as my comrades and I only had the names of the occasional Manticoran miscreant, now and then, justice was impossible. Even if we'd gotten the bastards hauled into court for violating Manticore's anti-slavery laws, so what? You know as well as I do what the official stance of the Star Kingdom's government would be."

Now, he did a sing-song imitation of a typical Manticoran aristocrat's nasal drawl: " 'Every barrel has a few bad apples.' "

Cathy thought the imitation was a lot better than his earlier mimicry of Zilwicki's Gryphon basso. Which was only to be expected, of course—he'd been in Cathy's company often enough, and she herself spoke in that selfsame accent. She'd tried to shed it, in her earlier days, but found the effort quite impossible.

Jeremy shrugged. "There was no way to prove otherwise." His eyes gleamed pure fury for a moment. "So better to just kill the bastards. If nothing else, it made us feel better—and there was always the chance that another upcoming piglet would decide the risk wasn't worth the reward. But *now*—"

He studied her intently. "Tell me what you think, Lady Catherine Montaigne, Countess of the Tor. Tell me true. How many names of Manticore's highest and most respectable society d'you think are on that list of Zilwicki's?"

She shuddered slightly. "I don't even want to think about it, Jeremy. *Too damned many*, that's for sure." Her wide lips pressed together, holding back an old pain. "I won't be entirely surprised if I even see some of my childhood and college friends. God knows how far the rot has spread. Especially since the war started."

She waved feebly at the door. "I was being unfair to the Captain's precious Navy. Of all Manticore's major institutions, the Navy's probably been the best when it comes to fighting the slave trade. Since they've had their hands full with the Haven war, the swine have been able to feed at the trough unhindered. In the dark; out of sight, out of mind."

"The best *by far*," agreed Jeremy forcefully. "And now—" He clapped his hands and resumed his gleeful, grotesquely melodramatic hand-rubbing. If he'd had mustachios, Cathy had no doubt at all that he'd be twirling them.

But Jeremy X had no mustachios, nor any facial hair at all. That was because K-86b/273-1/5 had been genetically designed for a life as a house servant, and Manpower Inc.'s social psychologists and market experts had unanimously decreed that facial hair was unsuitable for such creatures. Jeremy had once told Cathy that he considered *that* Mesa's final and unforgivable crime. And the worst of it was—she hadn't been sure he was joking. Jeremy X joked about every-thing, after all; which didn't stop him from being as murderous as an avalanche.

"Everything will come together perfectly," Jeremy chortled, still rubbing his hands. "With Zilwicki's list in our hands, we'll be able to kick over the whole barrel and show just how deep the slave-trade infec-tion really is." He spread his hands, almost apologeti-cally. "Even in the Star Kingdom, which everybody admits—even me—is better than anywhere else. Except Haven, of course, but those idiots are busily saddling themselves with another kind of servitude. So you can imagine how bad it is in the Solarian League, not to mention that pustule which calls itself the Silesian Confederacy."

Cathy frowned. "Nobody will believe—"

"Me? The Audubon Ballroom? Of course not! What a ridiculous notion. We're just a lot of genetically deformed maniacs and murderers. Can't trust anything we say, official lists be damned. No, no, the list will have to be made public by—"

Cathy understood where he was going. "*Absolutely not!*" she shrieked. "That idea's even crazier!" She began stalking back and forth, her long legs moving as gracelessly as a bird on land. "And it's fucking impossible, anyway! I'm a disreputable outcast myself! The only living member of the nobility cast out from the House of Lords except that fucking pedophile Seaview and—"

Her screech slammed to a halt. So did her legs. She stumbled, and almost fell flat on her face.

A very pale face—paler than usual—stared at Jer-emy with eyes so wide the bright blue irises were almost lost.

Jeremy left off his cackling and hand-rubbing. But

he made up for it by beginning a grotesque little ditty, sung to the tune of a popular nursery rhyme, and waving his fingers in time with the rhythm.

> *"Oh! Oh! The witch is back!*
> *The witch is back! The witch is back!*
> *Oh, woe! The witch is back!*
> *The wickedest witch*
> *In the wo-orld!"*

The ditty ended, replaced by—for Jeremy—an unusually gentle smile. "Oh, yes, Lady Catherine. Tell me again, why don't you—*now*—just how likely d'you think it is that some holier-than-thou Duke or Duchess is going to get up in the House of Lords and huff and puff about just who belongs and who doesn't. *Today*? After their most notorious outcast just shoved their own crap down their precious blue-veined throats?"

He rose to his feet with the lithe grace and speed—so *quickly* he could move—that made Jeremy X such a deadly, deadly man beneath the puckery and the theatrics. *"Harrington's back from the grave*, Cathy. Don't you understand—*yet*—how much that changes the political equation?"

Cathy stood ramrod straight. She was unable to move a muscle, or even speak. She realized now that she *hadn't* thought about it. Had shied away from the thought, in fact, because it threatened her with her worst nightmare. Having to return to the Star Kingdom, after the years of exile, and re-enter the political arena that she detested more than anything else in the universe.

Except—slavery.

"Please, Cathy," pleaded Jeremy. For a rare

moment, there was not a trace of banter in his voice. "Now is the time. *Now.*" He turned his head and stared out the window, as if by sheer force of will his eyes could see the Star Kingdom across all the light years of intervening space. "Everything works in our favor. The best elements in the Navy will be roaring. So will almost the whole of the House of Commons, party affiliation be damned. The Conservative Lords will be huddling in their mansions like so many sheep when the wolves are out running with the moon. And as for your precious Liberals and Progressives—"

Cathy finally found her voice. "They're not *my* Progressives, damn you! Sure as hell not my *Liberals.* I despise Descroix and New Kiev and they return the sentiment—and you know it perfectly well! So—"

"From the highlands, woman!" This time, Jeremy made no attempt to imitate Zilwicki's voice. Which only made his roaring fury all the more evident. Cathy was shocked into silence.

"From the highlands," he repeated, hissing the words. He pointed a stiff finger at the richly-carpeted floor. "Not half an hour ago, as fine a man as you could ask for stood in this room and explained to you that he was quite prepared to cast over everything—*everything*, woman—career and respect and custom and propriety—life itself if need be, should the Queen choose to place his neck in a hangman's noose—and for what? A daughter? Yes, that—*and his own responsibility.*"

He breathed deeply; once, twice. Then: "Years ago, I explained to a girl that she bore no guilt for what her class or nation might have done. But I'll tell the woman now—*again*—that she does bear responsibility for herself."

He glanced at the door. "You know I've never cared much for doctrine, Cathy, one way or the other. I'm a concrete sort of fellow. So even though I think 'Crown Loyalty' is about as stupid an ideology as I could imagine, I've got no problem with *that* man."

His eyes were fixed on her, hard as diamonds. "So don't tell me that they're not *your* Liberals or *your* Progressives. That's ancient history, and damn it all. *Make* them yours—Lady Catherine Montaigne, Countess of the Tor. Whether you asked for that title or not, it is yours. The responsibility comes with it."

She avoided his gaze, hanging her head. Not with shame, simply with reluctance. Jeremy's eyes softened, and his humor returned. "Listen to me, Lady Prancer," he said softly. "It's time the filly finally re-entered the race. And no filly, now, but a true grande dame. You'll dazzle 'em, girl. I can hear the roar of the crowd already."

"Cut it out," she muttered. "New Kiev has a death lock on the Liberals."

"Not after Zilwicki's list gets made public!" cried Jeremy gleefully.

Cathy's eyes widened, and her head came up. Her mouth formed a perfect round O of surprise.

Jeremy laughed. "Are you *still* such a naif? Do you really think the only traffickers in human misery sit in the Conservative Association?"

O.

"You *are*! Ha!" Jeremy was back to cackling and hand-rubbing—the whole tiresome lot. "Oh, sure—New Kiev herself will be clean as a whistle. Descroix, too, most likely. But I'll bet you right now, Cathy— don't take the wager, I'll strip you of your entire fortune—that plenty of their closest associates will be standing hip deep in the muck. Won't be surprised if that whole stinking Houseman clan's in up to their necks—with each and every one of the self-righteous swine oinking sophisticated gobbledygook to explain why slavery isn't really slavery and everything's relative anyway."

O.

Cackle, cackle. "Bet on it! If anything, Zilwicki's list will hit the Liberals and the Progressives harder than the Conservatives. There won't be as many of them on the list, of course, but nobody expects anything more than piggishness from High Ridge and his crowd. But I do believe, once the rock's turned over, that we'll find the Liberals and Progressives have taken their holier-than-thou draft to the bank one too many times." Cackle, cackle. "Their ranks will be shaken to the core—in the Lords as much as the Commons. Bet on it!" His hand rubbing went into high gear. "Just the right time for *another* disgraced outcast to make her return. And demand her rightful place in the sun."

Cathy hissed. "I *hate* those people."

Jeremy shrugged. "Well, yes. Who in their right mind wouldn't? But look at it this way, Cathy—"

He spread his arms wide, theatrically. Christ on the Cross. "*I'm* giving up the pleasure of shooting each and every one of the slaving bastards. Justice before vengeance, alas. If I shoot even one of them they'll make *me* the issue. So you can console yourself, as you sit through endless hours of rancorous debate in the House of Lords, with the knowledge that you finally won me over to the tactics of nonviolence."

From his armchair, Isaac hissed. Still standing in crucifix position, Jeremy wiggled his fingers. "Only in the Star Kingdom, comrade. That still leaves us the Solarians and the Silesians for a hunting ground."

Cathy glared at him. "Aren't you forgetting something, you great political strategist?"

Jeremy dropped his arms. "Finding Zilwicki's daughter? *In the Loop?*"

He cocked his head at Isaac. Simultaneously, both men stuck out their tongues, showing the mark.

Like two cobras, spreading their hoods.

THE FIFTH DAY

Helen

The first few hours of her escape were a nightmare. The world Helen had entered was lightless chaos, as if the primordial ylem were made of stone and dirt and refuse. She realized soon enough that she had entered some kind of interconnected pockets of open space, accidentally formed and molded over the centuries, branching off from each other with neither rhyme nor reason beyond the working of gravity on rubble and debris.

Branching off in *all* directions, to make it dangerous as well as confusing. Twice, within the first few minutes, she almost fell into suddenly yawning holes or crevasses. She wasn't sure which. Thereafter, she was careful to feel her way thoroughly before inching forward on her hands and knees.

Soon enough, those knees and hands were beginning to get bruised and scraped. The pain was not Helen's principal concern. Although Master Tye's syncretic regimen emphasized its philosophical and emotional aspects, it was still, when all was said and done, a school of the martial arts. So, like any such school which is not simply oriented to the tournament world,

Master Tye had trained Helen in the various manners in which to handle pain.

Pain, thus, she could ignore. At least up to a point, but even for a fourteen-year-old girl that point was far beyond a matter of mere scrapes and bruises. What she *couldn't* ignore, however, was the fact that she would begin to leave a trail of blood. Not much of a trail, true, but a trail nonetheless. Soon enough her captors would discover her absence and begin a pursuit. Unlike her, they would undoubtedly have portable lamps to guide them in their path. They would be able to move much faster than she.

Seeing no option, she tore off the sleeves of her blouse and wrapped them around her hands. For a moment, she considered removing the blouse completely and using the rest of the material to protect her knees. But she decided, after a gingerly tactile inspection of her knees, that the tough material of her trousers would hold up for quite a bit longer.

That done, she resumed her slow progress, feeling her way in the dark.

She had no idea how long she spent in that horrid place before she finally saw a glimmer of light. Early on, she tried to count off the seconds, but she soon discovered that she needed all of her concentration to avoid injuries.

At first, she thought the light was nothing more than an optical illusion, her mind playing tricks on her. But, since there was no real reason to go in any other direction, she decided to crawl toward it. After a time, she realized that she was actually seeing something.

A powerful surge of relief swept over her. Of course, she had no idea if that source of light was a refuge. For all she knew, she had been crawling in circles and was headed back toward the tunnel she had made in her own cell. But by that point, she was desperate simply to be able to *see* something. *Anything*.

It proved to be the light cast through some kind of ancient aperture. A drain grille, she thought. But it was impossible to be sure. The metal which had once spanned that hole had long since rusted away. The reason she thought it had been a grille was because the area she was looking into, standing on tiptoe and peering over the bottom lip, seemed to be some kind of ancient aqueduct or storm drain. Or—

Yuck. A sewer.

But the distaste passed almost as soon as it arrived. Whatever that broad low channel was, lined with still-solid masonry on all sides, it was an escape route. Besides, even if it had once been a sewer, it hadn't been used as such in many centuries. Other than a small, sluggish little rill running down the center of the age-darkened channel, the aqueduct/storm drain/sewer was as dry as a bone.

Helen placed her water bottle and little packet of food on the ledge. Then, using her arm strength alone, she hauled herself into the opening. Most girls her age wouldn't have been able to manage that feat of sheer muscle power, but Helen was very strong. Once her head, shoulders and upper torso were onto the ledge, it was a quick matter to scramble—wriggle, rather—through the opening and slide down the sloping ceramacrete ramp beyond.

Except it wasn't ceramacrete, Helen realized as soon as she felt the roughness of the surface scratching at her. She wasn't sure what the masonry was, but she suspected it might be that ancient and primitive stuff called *concrete*. She felt like she was entering a pharaoh's tomb.

Once she got her feet under her, she reached back and hauled down the water bottle and the food packet. Then, wobbling a bit on unsteady legs, she began walking as quickly as she could along the narrow ledge which bordered the former water channel. Since she had no idea which direction to take, she simply decided to follow the lamps which periodically lined the passageway. The lamps were some kind of jury-rigged devices and were very infrequent in their placement. She would have thought the lighting was absolutely terrible if she hadn't spent hours in total darkness. But they seemed to be a little less sparse to her left, so that was the direction she took.

She was so relieved to finally be able to see where she was going that it wasn't until she had traveled perhaps three hundred yards, moving as quickly as she could while using a pace she could maintain for hours, that the obvious question sprang into her mind.

Jury-rigged lamps, in a long-unused passageway. So jury-rigged by whom?

The answer came almost simultaneously with the question. She had been approaching a bend in the passageway when she recognized the puzzling nature of the lamps. She came to a complete halt, peering into the dimness beyond. Helen was aware, vaguely, that the Loop's long-forgotten subterranean passageways were reputed to be filled with all manner of dangers. She had simply not worried about it, since her captors had been a far more tangible menace. But now—

The lurkers apparently decided she had spotted

them, for within two seconds they were scrambling around the bend and racing toward her.

Shambling toward her, rather. After an instant's spike of fear, Helen saw that the three men approaching bore no resemblance whatsoever to her captors. *They* had strutted like leopards; *these* scurried like rats. Her abductors' clothing had been simple jumpsuits, but clean and well made. The creatures lurching toward her wore a pastiche of rags and filthy garments that were almost impossible to describe. And where her male captors had been clean-shaven and short-haired, these *things* looked more like shaggy apes than people.

Short, stooped apes, however. One of them was shouting something in a language she didn't recognize at all. The other two were simply leering. At least, Helen *thought* they were leering. It was hard to tell because of the beards.

Whatever. One thing was certain—they were not advancing with any friendly intent. And if tunnel rats are not leopards, they can still be dangerous.

Helen didn't even consider the narrow ledge. In that cramped space, the advantage would all be against her. For a moment, she thought of fleeing. She was pretty sure that she could outrun the three men, even burdened with a water bottle and a package of food. They were about as far removed from physically fit specimens of humanity as could be imagined.

But she discarded that idea almost instantly. For one thing, she didn't want to retrace her steps back in the direction of her captors. For another—

Even fourteen-year-old girls, pushed hard enough, can become enraged. She was *tired* of this crap!

Rage, of course, was the ultimate sin in Master

Tye's universe. So, as she sprang off the ledge and half-ran, half-slid down the concrete slope to the flat and wide expanse of the channel—fighting room— she summoned his memory to her aid. *Breathing first.*

By the time Helen trotted down to the largest dry space within reasonable range, carefully set the water bottle and the food packet to one side, and assumed the standing horse, the rage was harnessed and shackled to her purpose.

Calmly, she waited, breathing steadily. Her three assailants—there was no doubt about *that* any longer, not with one of them brandishing a club and another holding a short length of rope—spread out and advanced upon her.

Scuttled, say better. Helen's eyes remained fixed on a blank space in her mind, but she absorbed the way they moved, their balance—everything. By the time the men began their charge, she had already decided upon her course of action. Master Tye would not have approved—*keep it simple, child*—but for all Helen's control over her rage it was still there, burning at the center.

So the man facing her went down in a tangle, his legs twisted and swept away by the Falling Leaf, tripping his club-wielding companion. The one still standing—the rope-holder—fell to the Sword and Hammer, clutching his groin and bleating pain and shock through a broken face. The bleating ended the moment his buttocks hit the cement, as Helen's heel completed the Scythe. A sturdier man would have been stunned; his scrawny neck snapped like a twig.

The club-holder was starting to rise when the Owl By Night crushed him from existence. Master Tye would have scolded Helen for using that Owl—*keep it simple, child!*—but he could not have chided her for the execution. Beak and talons had all found their mark, and in just the proper sequence.

The man still alive joined his fellows in death three seconds later. Again, the Scythe; and again, the Scythe.

When it was over, Helen fought for breath. Not because she was winded, but simply because her mind was reeling from the destruction. She had practiced those maneuvers a thousand times—for years, now, against padded and armored opponents—but had never really quite believed—

Nausea came, was driven down. Rage and terror also. She fought and fought for her center.

Breathing first. Breathing first.

Kevin

When Usher let himself into the hotel room in the Loop which Victor had rented for that night, the young SS officer was asleep. Seeing Cachat's fully-clothed form lying on the room's only bed next to Ginny, Usher grinned. The first night Victor had rented a hotel room for his new "debauched habits," he had insisted on sleeping on the floor.

Usher glanced at the table in the room. Clearly enough, Victor and Ginny had spent the previous evening playing cards. If Kevin knew his wife—and he did—Ginny would have teased Victor by suggesting a game of strip poker. Seeing the lay of the final hands, Kevin's face twisted into a moment's derision.

Gin rummy, for God's sake.

But there was no real sarcasm in it. And, as his eyes moved back to the sleeping form of the young officer, Kevin Usher's expression took on something which might almost be called paternalism. In truth, in the past few days, he had become quite fond of Victor Cachat. He even had hopes of awakening the wit which he was certain lay buried somewhere inside that solemn young soul.

But first, he's got to learn not to sleep so soundly.

Kevin's method for teaching that lesson was abrupt and effective. After Victor lurched upright, gasping and wiping the glassful of cold water off his face, he stared bleary-eyed at the culprit. Next to him, Ginny murmured something and rolled over, her own eyes opening more slowly.

"Up, young Cachat!" commanded Usher. "The game is afoot!"

As usual, the classical allusion went right over Victor's head. Kevin snorted again.

"You're hopeless," he growled. Kevin pointed an accusing finger at his wife. Ginny, like Victor, had been sleeping in her clothes.

"I'm not a cuckold *yet*? What is *wrong* with you, Cachat?"

Victor scowled. "That wasn't funny yesterday either, Kevin." Then, seeing the grin on the citizen colonel's face, Victor's eyes widened.

"Something's happened. What?"

Kevin shook his head. "Not sure exactly. But Gironde just called and told me Manpower's headquarters suddenly came alive last night. Busy as ants in the middle of the night they are, over there. I'll bet damn near anything Durkheim's scheme just fell apart at the seams."

Confused, Victor shook his head. "Citizen Major Gironde? He's in the SS. Why is he calling you? And what's he doing watching the Mesans anyway? Durkheim assigned him to—"

He clamped his jaws shut, almost with a snap. Kevin smiled, and sat down at the card table. "Good, lad," he murmured. "Remember: the map is not the territory. The file is not the man."

Victor replied with a murmur himself, quoting one of Kevin's own maxims: " 'And there's nobody easier to outmaneuver than a maneuverer.' "

"Exactly," said Kevin. His eyes went to the only window in the room. It was a small window; grimy as only a cheap Loop hotel window ever gets. The view beyond was completely obscured, which was not the least of the reasons Kevin had insisted on a hotel in the Loop. Windows which can't be seen out of can't be seen into either. Not, at least, without specialized equipment.

Of course, the SS detachment on Terra *had* such equipment—and plenty of it. But the equipment was under the control of an SS officer and couldn't be checked out without his permission. A certain Citizen Major Gironde, as it happened.

"Dollars to donuts," Kevin mused, "the girl escaped. I can't think of anything else right now that would stir up Manpower's headquarters. Not in the middle of the night, anyway."

Victor was confused again. "What are 'dollars'? And 'donuts'?"

"Never mind, lad," replied Kevin, shaking his head. "Are you ready?"

Classical allusions might have been above Victor's head, but the last question wasn't. Instantly, his face was set in stone, hard and firm as unyielding granite.

By now, Ginny was lying half-erect on her elbow, her cheek nestled in the palm of her hand. She gazed up at Victor's face admiringly. "Anybody ever mention you'd make a great poster boy for an SS recruitment drive?"

Ginny's repartee usually left Victor confused and embarrassed. But not this time.

Hard; firm—unyielding as granite.

Durkheim

Durkheim was awakened by the insistent ring of the communicator. Silently, he cursed the Mesan idiots who were careless enough to call him at his own residence. Granted, the communicator was a special one, carefully scrambled. Still—

He only spent a few seconds on that curse, however. Soon enough, he had other things to curse the Mesans for—and not silently.

What did you expect—you morons!—using Scrags? I can't believe anyone would be stupid enough to think—

But he didn't indulge himself for very long in that pointless exercise. For one thing, the Mesan on the other end was indifferent to his outrage. For another, Durkheim himself had always understood that his plan was too intricate to be sure of success. So, from the very beginning, he had designed a fallback.

After breaking off his contact with the Mesan, Durkheim spent an hour or so staring at the ceiling of his bedroom. He didn't bother to turn on a light. He found the darkness helpful in concentrating his attention, as he carefully went over every step of his next maneuver.

Then, satisfied that it would work, he even managed to get some sleep. Not much, unfortunately. The problem wasn't that Durkheim couldn't get to sleep— he'd never had any trouble doing that—but simply that he had to reset the alarm to a much earlier hour.

He would have to be at work by the crack of dawn, in order to have everything in place.

Helen

It didn't take Helen long to find the lair of her three would-be assailants, even moving as carefully as she was. The place was less than a hundred yards distant, just around the bend in the channel.

She spent five minutes studying it, before she crept forward. The "lair" was just that—a habitation fit more for animals than men. The lean-to propped against the sloping wall of the channel reminded her of a bird's nest. Made by a very large and very careless bird. The shack—even that term was too grandiose— had been assembled from various pieces of wreck- age and debris, lashed together with an assortment of wire and cordage. At its highest, it was not tall enough for even a short adult to stand up. From one end to the other, it measured not more than fifteen feet. There was no opening at her end, so Helen supposed that whatever entrance existed was on the opposite side.

She hesitated, but not for long. Her water was getting low and so, soon enough, would her food. There might well be something in that lean-to, how- ever unpalatable. Besides, she had no choice but to go past it—unless she wanted to retrace her steps back toward her captors—and so she might as well investigate it along the way.

The decision made, she moved quickly, racing toward the lean-to on quick and almost silent feet. If there were more men lurking within, she saw no reason to give them any more warning than necessary.

One or two, she was certain she could handle. More than that, she could outrun them.

But there were no men in the lair to pose any danger to her. Instead there was something infinitely more dangerous—a moral dilemma.

The boy, she thought, was probably not more than twelve years old. Hard to tell, due to his bruises and emaciation under the rags. The girl was perhaps Helen's own age. But that was even harder to determine, despite the fact that she wore no clothing at all. The girl didn't have bruises so much as she seemed a single giant bruise.

Helen removed the filthy blanket and gave the girl a quick examination. The examination, for all its brevity, was both thorough and fairly expert. Her father had also seen to it that Helen received first aid instruction.

When she was done, and despite her recognition that an immense complication had just entered her life, Helen felt relieved. Immensely relieved, in truth. Less than half an hour earlier, for the first time in her life, she had killed people. Despite her concentration on her own predicament, some part of Helen's soul had been shrieking ever since. Now, it was silent. Silent and calm. If ever men had deserved killing, those men had.

Since she entered the lean-to, the boy had huddled silently against one side, staring at her with eyes as wide as saucers. Finally, he spoke.

"You won't hurt my sister, will you?" he whispered. His pale eyes moved to the battered figure lying on the pallet. The girl, for her part, was conscious. But she was just staring at Helen through slitted eyes, as if she were blinded by the light. "I don't think Berry can take much more hurting."

He started to cry. "I don't know how long we've been here. It seems like forever since they caught us. We were just looking for food. We weren't going to steal any from them, honest. I tried to tell them."

Helen heard the girl whisper something. She leaned over.

"Go away," were the words. "They'll come back soon."

Helen shook her head. "They're dead. I killed them."

The girl's eyes popped open. "That's a lie," she whispered. "Why are you lying?"

Helen looked at the boy. "What's your name?"

"Larens. People call me Lars."

Helen jerked her head. "Go down the channel, Lars." She pointed the direction. "That way. Just around the bend."

He didn't hesitate for more than a few seconds. Then, scurrying like a mouse, he scrambled out of the lean-to. While she waited for him to return, Helen did what she could to help Berry. Which wasn't much, beyond digging out some food and wiping off the grime with the cleanest rag she could find. Fortunately, while Helen didn't find much food there were enough water bottles that she was able to use some of it to wet the rag.

Throughout, other than an occasional hiss when Helen rubbed over a particularly sore spot, Berry kept silent. The girl was obviously weak, but Helen's principal fear—that the girl's wits were gone—soon proved false. As best as she could, given her condition, Berry tried to help by moving her limbs and torso to accept the rag.

Still, it was obvious that the girl was in no condition to walk. Helen wondered what was taking Lars so long to return. But while she waited she started assembling the makings of a stretcher. Or, at least, a travois—she wasn't sure Lars would be strong enough to hold up his end of the thing.

"What are you doing?" whispered Berry, watching Helen dismantle part of the lean-to. Helen had found two rods which she thought would make a suitable frame. She had no idea what they had been originally, nor even what they were made of. Some kind of artificial substance she didn't recognize. But, for all that they were a bit more flexible than she would have liked, they were about the right length and, she thought—hoped—strong enough.

"We've got to get out of here," Helen explained. "There are some people chasing after me. Just as bad as those three. Worse, probably."

That news caused Berry to sit erect. Try to, at least. The effort was too much for her. But, again, she gave evidence that her mind was still intact.

"If you—you and Lars—can get us maybe two hundred yards, there's a crossover to another channel. And after that—not far—there's another. That one leads up, and then down. That'll be hard. I'll try to walk, but you'll probably have to carry me. But if we can get down there it's the perfect place to hide."

For a moment, something like pride seem to come into the battered face. "That's my secret place. Mine and Lars'." Softly: "It's a special place."

Helen had already decided that she would have to take the two children with her. In truth, the "decision" had come automatically—even though she understood that she was almost certainly ruining her chances of escape. Now, for the first time, she realized that Lars and Berry would be an asset as well as a liability. She was quite certain that they were two of the small horde of vagrant children who were reputed to dwell in the lower reaches of the Loop. Castoffs of castoffs. They would know the area—their part of it, at least—as well as mice know their cubbyholes and hideaways. Helen would be moving slower, but at least she would no longer be moving blind.

She heard Lars re-entering the lean-to.

"What took so—"

She closed her mouth, seeing the object Lars was gripping. She recognized the knife. It had belonged to one of her assailants. Lars had apparently wiped it off, but the blade was still streaked with drying blood.

Lars' eyes were bright and eager. On his hands and knees, he scurried over to his sister and showed her the knife.

"Look, Berry—it's true! They can't ever hurt you again." He gave Helen an apologetic glance. "I think they were already dead. But I made good and sure."

Berry managed to lift her head and stare at the knife. Then, smiling for the first time since Helen had met her, she laid her head back down. "Thank you, brother," she whispered. "But now we have to help Helen go away to our special place. There are more men coming to hurt her."

Less than ten minutes later, they were on their way. Lars, somewhat to Helen's surprise, proved strong enough—or determined enough—to carry his end of the stretcher. He had trouble at first because he refused to relinquish the knife. But, soon enough, he discovered the obvious place to carry it.

As they stumbled as quickly as they could down the channel, Helen found it hard not to laugh. She'd read about it, of course, in her beloved adventure books. But she'd never actually thought to *meet* one—

especially twelve years old! A pirate, by God, with the blade clenched between his teeth to prove it.

Suddenly, she felt better than she had since she was first abducted. She actually had to restrain herself from whooping with glee.

Durkheim

Victor Cachat reported to work as early as ever the next morning, Durkheim noted. The young officer's new found vice hadn't affected him that much, apparently. Quite the little whore-chaser the boy had turned into, according to the reports.

But Durkheim didn't let any of his amusement show when he summoned Cachat into his office, immediately upon his arrival.

"We've got a problem," the SS commander snapped. "And I need you to fix it."

In the time that followed, as Durkheim spun his tale and elaborated his instructions, Victor Cachat leaned forward in his chair and listened attentively. Durkheim, though not generally given to humor, almost found himself laughing. Cachat could have made an ideal poster boy for an SS recruitment drive. *Young and earnest officer of the Revolution, eager and willing to do his duty.*

And though Durkheim noticed the hard, dark gleam in the eyes of the officer across the desk from him, he thought nothing of it. Simply the natural ruthlessness of a young zealot. Ready, at an instant's notice, to strike down the enemies of the Revolution with neither pity nor remorse.

Anton

By the time Anton reached the rendezvous, he was utterly lost. Not in the sense that he had any trouble following the directions given to him by Lady Catherine's messenger. Anton had years of experience finding his way through the three-dimensional maze of giant warships under construction, guided by nothing more than blueprints or verbal instructions. But when he walked through the door of the small coffeehouse at the end of an alley in the Old Quarter, he couldn't for the life of him have told anyone if he was headed north, east, south or west. He *thought* he still knew up from down, but he was beginning to wonder about that.

He wasn't entirely pleased, then, to see Robert Tye bestowing upon him that particularly obnoxious grin by which the expert greets the tyro. Tye had taken a different route than he. But, though they had left at the same time, it was obvious the old martial artist had been comfortably ensconced on his seat at the table for quite some time.

But Anton didn't give Tye much more than a sour glance as he strode up to the table. His attention was riveted on the other two people sitting there. In the case of one, because he was fascinated. In the case of the other, because he was flabbergasted—even outraged.

"What are you doing here?" he demanded. "Lady Catherine," he added, a bit lamely.

Cathy started to bridle, but Jeremy cut her off.

"Didn't I say it?" he remarked cheerfully. "The good Captain's sweet on you, girl."

That remark caused both Anton and Cathy to choke off whatever words they had been about to speak and glare at Jeremy. The ex-slave bore up under the burden with no apparent effort.

"Those who speak the truth are always despised," he added, turning to Robert. "Isn't that so?"

Tye said nothing, but the smile on his face as he reached for his coffee indicated his full agreement. Anton and Cathy looked back at each other. Cathy seemed to flush a bit. Anton didn't—his complexion was quite a bit darker than her ivory pale skin—but he did straighten stiffly and clear his throat.

"I am simply concerned for the Countess' safety," he pronounced.

"Isn't that what I just said?" asked Jeremy. "Why else would a proper Gryphon highlander give a damn about the well-being of an idle parasite?" He cocked an eye at Cathy. "Well . . . parasite, at least. You can hardly accuse the lady of being idle."

Anton restrained his temper. Partly, by reminding himself of his daughter. Partly—

Damn the imp, anyway! But there was a trace of humor lurking under the irritation. Anton could not deny that the impudent little man—like a sprite, he was, both in size and demeanor—had cut rather close to the truth.

Bull's-eye, actually, admitted Anton, as his eyes moved back to the countess. This morning, Cathy was not wearing an expensive gown made of thin material. She was dressed in much heavier garments— pants and a long-sleeved shirt—suitable for outdoor hiking. The outfit was obviously well-used and fitted her comfortably.

Cathy, Anton knew, was in her fifties. But she was a third-generation prolong, with the youthful appearance that such people carried for decades. Although most people would have said her outfit did nothing for her tall, slim figure, Anton thought it made her perhaps even more appealing than the gown she had been wearing the previous evening. The practical clothing fit her plain, open face to perfection. Young, healthy, vigorous—a woman who enjoyed life to the fullest.

He found himself swallowing, and groping for words.

"I *am* concerned, Cathy," he muttered. "This is likely to be dangerous."

"Not for the two of you," announced Jeremy. "And her presence here is essential anyway." He gestured politely to the remaining chair at the table. "Sit, Captain Zilwicki. There is news—and a change in plans."

That announcement drove all other thoughts out of Anton's mind. He slid into the chair and leaned over the table, planting his hands on the edge. "What news?" His enormous shoulders, hunched with apprehension, made his square and blocky head look like a boulder perched atop a small mountain.

Finally, Jeremy's grin went away, replaced by a much kindlier smile. "Good news, Captain. For now, at least. Your daughter has escaped her captors."

Anton had been holding his breath. Now, he let it out in a rush.

"*Where is she?*" he demanded, half-rising. He had to restrain himself from reaching across the table and shaking the answer from Jeremy. Fortunately, years of habit as an intelligence officer did not completely desert him. His was the one trade which, along with philosophers, always understood the precedence of epistemology.

So, after a moment, Anton lowered himself slowly

back into the chair. "How do you know?" he demanded.

Still smiling, Jeremy shook his head. "I'll not give you an answer to that question, Captain. Not that I don't trust you, of course." The impish grin made its reappearance. "Heavens, no! But after this is all over, I'm afraid you might remember that you are an officer in Her Majesty's Royal Manticoran Navy and feel compelled to strike a blow on your Queen's behalf."

Jeremy was not the first person who had underestimated the intelligence hidden beneath the Gryphon highlander's thick-headed appearance. It did not take Anton more than five seconds to make the connections.

"I was right," he stated flatly. He glanced at Cathy. "You told him our conversation?"

She nodded. Now it was Anton's turn to bestow a grin on Jeremy. And if his grin could hardly be called impish, it had something of the same devilish humor in it.

"It *was* a rogue Peep operation. And you've been in touch with the Peeps. The ones who aren't pleased with the rogue."

Jeremy started. Something in the expression on his face led Anton immediately to a further conclusion.

"No," he rumbled. "I've got it backwards. The operation was outside of normal channels, but it was no rogue who ordered it." His grin was now utterly humorless. A murderous grin, in truth. "It was Durkheim, wasn't it? That stinking pig. And the ones you have contact with are the real rogues."

There was no expression at all on Jeremy's face. His pale gray eyes, staring at Anton, were as flat as iron plates. Slowly, he swiveled his head and looked at Cathy.

"Tell me again," he rasped.

"You're too fucking smart for your own good," she snickered. She beamed upon Anton. "He's such a clever little man. But he always has to poke the wild animals, and sometimes he forgets to use a long enough stick." Her smile was very approving. Very warm, in fact. "Congratulations, Anton. It's nice to see him get bitten for a change."

"The reminder was good enough," rasped Jeremy. "I don't need the whole song and dance."

"Yes, you do," retorted Cathy forcefully.

Jeremy ignored her. He was back to staring at Anton with those flat, flat eyes. Suddenly, Anton was reminded that Jeremy X, whatever impish exterior he chose to project, was also one of the galaxy's deadliest men.

For a moment, he began to utter some sort of reassurance. But then, moved by his innate stubbornness and his own cold fury, he bit back the words and simply returned the stare with one of his own. Which, if it was not exactly ruthless, also indicated that he was not a man who intimidated easily, if at all.

Anton heard Cathy suck in a breath. In his peripheral vision, he saw Robert Tye's sudden stillness. But his eyes never left Jeremy's.

And then, after perhaps three seconds, the moment passed. Depth seemed to return to Jeremy's gaze, and the little man leaned back in his chair.

"Ah, but you wouldn't, Captain. Would you, now? It's that highland sense of honor moves you. You'd keep the knowledge that there was an opposition amongst the Peeps to yourself, and not pass it on to your superiors."

Anton snorted. "We've known for years that there was disaffection among the Havenites."

Jeremy's gaze didn't waver. After a moment, Anton looked away. "But, yeah, this is the first time there's ever been any concrete indication that it extends into SS. And the first time—given the relatively small size of the Peep contingent here—that we could probably pinpoint the individuals."

He drew in a deep breath, swelling his chest and squaring his shoulders. Then: "From the highlands, as you say."

"A life for a life, Captain," said Jeremy softly.

Anton understood the obscure reference at once. For some reason, that made him feel oddly warmhearted toward the man across the table from him. A *concrete* sort of fellow. Much like himself, whatever other differences separated them.

"Yes," he murmured. "The daughter for the mother, and I'll take the knowledge to the grave."

Jeremy nodded solemnly. "Good enough." And now he was back to being the imp. "And good it is, boyo! Because it'll be those selfsame wretched rotten Peeps who'll get your daughter. Not you or me."

Anton goggled him.

Imp. "Oh, yes—for a certainty. We've other fish to fry."

Goggled him.

Damned imp. "But it's as plain as the nose on your face, man! They can get close to her, through the manhunt. Girlhunt, I should say. We can't."

Anton was clenching his fists. "Then *what*—"

Jeremy shook his head. "And to think he was so shrewd not a moment ago. Think it through, Captain. The rotten wretched Peeps—*Peep*, I should say—can *get* the girl. But that's not to say he can get her *out*."

Again, it didn't take Anton more than a few seconds

to make all the connections. He turned his head and gazed at Cathy.

"And that's why you're here. To distract them, while"—a stubby forefinger shot out from his fist, pointing at Jeremy—"he settles his accounts."

"Long overdue accounts," murmured Jeremy. The flat, flat eyes were back.

Anton leaned back in his chair, pressing himself against the table with the heels of his hands. Slowly, the fists opened.

"That'll work," he announced. "If the Peep's good enough, at least."

Jeremy shrugged. "Don't imagine he's really all that *good*. But he doesn't have to be, now does he, Captain? Just *determined* enough."

Helen

Not for the first time, Helen bitterly regretted the loss of her watch. She had no idea how long it took her and her two companions to finally make their way into Berry's "special place." Hours, for a certainty—many hours. Just as Berry had feared, making the upward climb—and, even more so, the later descent—had been extremely difficult. Berry, for all that she had tried heroically, had simply been too injured and feeble to make it on her own. And her brother, for all his own valiant efforts, too small and weak to be of much assistance. So, for all practical purposes, Helen had been forced to make what would have been an arduous enough trip for herself burdened by the weight of another strapped to her back.

By the time they finally got to their destination, she was more exhausted than she had ever been in

her life. If it hadn't been for the years she had spent
in Master Tye's rigorous training, she knew she would
never have made it at all.

Vaguely, with fatigue-induced lightheadedness, she
tried to examine her surroundings. But it was almost
impossible to see anything. The two small lanterns
they had taken with them from the vagabonds' lean-to
were too feeble to provide much illumination.

They were resting on a large pallet under a lean-to.
Both the pallet and the lean-to, Lars told her, had
been built by him and his sister after their mother
disappeared (some unspecified time since—months
ago, Helen judged) and they had found this place.
The lean-to nestled against some sort of ancient stone
staircase. It was the buttress of the staircase, actually. They had come down very wide stairs to a platform, where the stairs branched at right angles to
either side. At Berry's command, Helen had taken the
left branch and then, at the bottom, curled back to
the right. There, thankfully, she had found the lean-to
and finally been able to rest.

Now, lying exhausted on the pallet, Berry nestled
against her right side. A moment later, dragging a
tattered and filthy blanket out of the semi-darkness,
Lars spread it over them. A moment later, he was
nestled against Helen's left.

Helen whispered her thanks. She didn't really need
the blanket for warmth. In the depths of the Loop,
the temperature never seemed to vary beyond a
narrow range, which was quite comfortable. But there
was something primordially comforting about being
under that sheltering cover, even as filthy as it was.

No filthier than me! she thought, half-humorously.
What I wouldn't give for a shower!

But that thought drew her perilously close to

thoughts of her father and their warm apartment. Always warm, that apartment had been. Not so much in terms of physical temperature—in truth, her father preferred to keep the climate settings rather low—but in terms of the heart.

Oh, Daddy!

Summoning what strength remained, Helen drove the thought away. She could not afford that weakening. Not now. But, as it fled, some residue of the thought remained. And Helen realized, as she lay there in the darkness cuddling two new-found children of her own, that she finally understood her father. Understood, for the first time, how courageously he had struggled, all those years, not to let his own loss mangle his daughter. And how much love there must have been in his marriage, to have given him that strength. Where another man, a weaker man, might have felt himself weakened further by his wife's self-sacrifice, her father had simply drawn more strength from it.

People had misunderstood him, she now realized—she as much as any. They had ascribed his stoicism to simple stolidity. The resistance of a Gryphon mountain to the flails of nature, bearing up under wind and rain and lightning with the endurance of rock. They had forgotten that mountains are not passive things. Mountains are *shaped*, forged, in the fiery furnace. They do not simply "bear up"—they *rise* up, driven by the mightiest forces of a planet. The stone face had been shaped by a beating heart.

Oh, Daddy . . . She drifted off to sleep, as if she were lying on a continent rather than a pallet. Secure and safe, not in her situation, but in the certainty of stone itself. Her father would find her, soon enough. Of that she had no doubt at all.

Stone *moves*.

THE SIXTH DAY

Victor

When they found the bodies, Victor had to restrain himself from grinning. Whoever had cut the three men had done so with as much enthusiasm as lack of skill. So far as Victor knew, there was no antonym for the word "surgical." But if there was such a term, the half-severed heads of the wretched vagabonds lying sprawled in the middle of the dry channel exemplified it perfectly.

The small mob of Scrags accompanying Victor and his squad of SS troopers were convinced that the girl had done it. And *that* was the source of Victor's humor. He wasn't sure what amused him the most: their fury, their bewilderment, or—the most likely source—their obvious relief. As in: *There but for the grace of God . . .*

There was more ferocity than genuine humor in Victor's suppressed grin. The Scrags were notorious, among other things—the females as much as the males—for their predatory sexual habits. Victor had no doubt at all that they had planned to rape the Zilwicki girl when her immediate purpose was served. Before killing her.

Now, looking at the corpses, the thoughts of the Scrags were not hard to read. *Easier said than done . . .*

Victor leaned over the sergeant's shoulder. "And?" he asked.

Citizen Sergeant Kurt Fallon shook his head. "I don't think it was the girl cut 'em, sir." He pointed to the small pools of blood which had spread out from the wounds. The blood was dry and covered with insects, as were the corpses themselves. "They didn't bleed much, as you can see. Not for those kinds of wounds. She couldn't have cut 'em any time soon after she killed 'em. And why would she wait?"

"*Did* she kill them?" asked Victor.

Fallon nodded, pointing to the small tracking device in his left hand. Victor was unable to interpret the readings on the screen. The chemo-hormone sensor was a highly specialized piece of equipment. As rare as it was expensive. That was the reason, Durkheim had told Victor, that he was assigning Fallon to the squad. The citizen sergeant was an expert with the device.

"Her traces are all over them," said Fallon. "Adrenaline reading's practically off the scale. That means either fear or fury—or both—and as you can see . . ." He shrugged. "She didn't have much to fear. Besides—"

He pointed to the head of one of the corpses. The filthy, bearded thing was unnaturally twisted. "Broke neck." He pointed to another. "Same." Then, at the third, whose throat had clearly been crushed as well as slit. "And again."

Fallon rose. "Didn't know the girl had training, but that's what you're seeing." He studied the sensor screen. "But there's someone else's readings here, too. Besides her and the croaks. Male readings. Prepubescent, I'm pretty sure."

Victor glanced around. The Scrags had now collected in a body around them, staring at the tracker in the sergeant's hand. For all their strutting swagger, and their pretensions at superhuman status, the Scrags were really nothing much more than Loop vagabonds themselves. They were clearly intimidated by the technical capacity of the SS device. During the hours in which they had organized a search for the girl after discovering her escape, before they finally admitted their screw-up to their Mesan overlords, the Scrags had accomplished absolutely nothing. After they found the bodies and the lean-to, the girl's trail seemed to have vanished.

"Can we follow her?" Victor asked. "Or *them*?"

Fallon nodded. "Oh, sure. Nothing to it. Won't be quick, of course. But—" He cast a sour glance at the nearby Scrags. "Since they at least had the sense to come to us before too much time had gone by, the traces are still good. Another couple of days, and it would have been a different story."

"Let's to it, then."

They set off, following the traces picked up by the sensor. Victor and Citizen Sergeant Fallon led the way, flanked by the other three SS soldiers in Fallon's squad. Victor and Fallon didn't bother carrying their weapons to hand. The other SS soldiers did, but they held the pulse rifles in a loose and easy grip. The Scrags trailed behind, with their own haphazard weaponry. For all the bravado with which they brandished the guns, they reminded Victor of nothing so much as a flock of buzzards following a pack of wolves.

He glanced sideways at Fallon. The citizen sergeant was too preoccupied with reading the tracker to notice the scrutiny. There was no expression on his lean-jawed, hatchet face beyond intense concentration.

Like a hawk on the prowl. Which, Victor knew, was an apt comparison. Fallon *was* a raptor—and he was hunting bigger prey than a fourteen-year-old girl.

And that, of course, was the other reason Durkheim had assigned Fallon and his squad to

Victor. The hatchet-faced man was a hatchetman in truth. And Victor's neck was the target of his blade.

Anton

As he watched the rally, Anton was struck by the irony of his situation. He really didn't approve of this kind of gathering. For all the stiff-necked belligerence of Gryphon's yeomanry toward nobility, the highlanders were very far from being political radicals. They were a conservative lot, when all was said and done. That was especially true of the large percentage—perhaps a third of the population—which belonged to the Second Reformation Roman Catholic Church, a sect which retained its ancient attitude of reverence for monarchy and obedience to authority in general.

Anton himself had been raised in that creed. And if his continued membership as an adult was more a cultural than a religious habit—his basso was much sought after by church choirs, and he enjoyed singing himself—his career as a naval officer had done nothing to weaken his traditional political attitudes. *A strong monarchy resting on a stout yeomanry*—that was Moses and the prophets, for Gryphon highlanders. Their quarrel with the nobility was, in a sense, the opposite of radicalism. It was Gryphon's *nobles*, after all—not the commoners—who were continually seeking to subvert the established order.

So, watching the huge crowd of poor immigrants who were packed into the amphitheater, applauding the firebrand speakers and chanting distinctly anti-establishment slogans, Anton felt a bit like a church deacon trapped in a sinners' convention. That was all the more so since the rally's hidden purpose was directly bound up with the scheme to rescue his daughter. In a certain sense, *he* was responsible for this disreputable and unseemly affair.

Something of his discomfort must have shown in his posture. Sitting on one of the benches next to him, far up in the galleries, Robert Tye leaned over and whispered: "I'm told this sort of thing is contagious. Spreads like an aerosol, I believe."

Anton gave him an acerbic glance. Tye responded with a sly smile. "But perhaps not, in your case," he murmured, straightening back up. " 'My strength is as the strength of ten, because my heart is royalist.' "

Anton ignored the jibe. On the podium far below, he could see that Cathy was next in line for the speaker's dais. He thought so, at least, from the way she was fidgeting in her chair and hurriedly scanning through her handwritten notes.

Anton had to force *himself* not to fidget. In his case, the problem was not nervousness so much as the fact that he was torn by conflicting impulses. On the one hand, Anton was fascinated by the prospect of finally hearing Cathy speak in public. Even as a young woman in the Manticoran House of Lords, the Countess of the Tor had been a famous orator. Notorious, it might be better to say. From what he had learned since he arrived on Terra, her reputation had not declined in exile. Rather the contrary.

On the other hand—

Anton took a deep breath and let it out slowly. His lips quirked in a wry smile of self-deprecation.

Leave it to a thick-skulled highlander to get infatuated with a damned wild-eyed radical! What the hell is wrong with me?

Trying to distract himself, Anton let his gaze roam the amphitheater. "Soldier Field," it was called, a name whose original meaning was long-forgotten, buried under the rubble of Chicago's fabled millennia. The structure was so ancient that here and there Anton could even see a few patches of that incredibly primitive construction material called *cement*.

Over the centuries, of course, the original shell of the amphitheater had been rebuilt and rehabilitated time after time. In a way, there was something almost mystical about the place. There was nothing much left of the original gathering area except the space itself. The material components which encapsulated that large and empty cyst buried deep below the modern city's surface had changed time and again, as the millennia crept forward. But the emptiness always remained, as if the spirits of the people who filled it—forgotten ghosts, most of them—kept the city's encroachment at bay.

Here, over the centuries, Chicago's outcasts had come, time and again, to voice their grievances and air their complaints. And mostly, Anton suspected, just to be able to look around the one place in the Old Quarter which was *not* cramped and crooked. The one place where the masses who swarmed in the city's ghetto could actually *see* themselves, and see their number.

An incredible number, in truth. Given that the rally had been literally organized on a moment's notice, he was astonished by the size of the crowd. Anton had no idea how many people were packed into the amphitheater, but he was certain that the figure was in the tens of thousands.

All of whom, at that moment, roared their approval of the speaker's concluding slogan. Anton winced, as much from the sheer aural impact as the content of the slogan itself.

Self-determination! Ha! He enjoyed sour thoughts, for a few seconds, of how that principle might be applied by the notoriously cantankerous and particularistic highlanders of his youth. *Every hill a kingdom, every hollow a realm!*

Sheer nonsense. *The crown welds the nation, and that's that. Otherwise—chaos.*

But he left off the rumination. Cathy had risen from her chair and was advancing toward the podium in her characteristically jerky and high-stepping gait. She reminded Anton of a young racing horse approaching the starting gate.

He braced himself. *Oh, well,* he thought, *it'll all be for the best, once I hear her prattling nonsense. Let this idiot infatuation be dispelled.*

His military training recognized the subtle but ferocious security which protected the Countess of the Tor. Anton spotted Isaac immediately, standing at the foot of the speaker's platform. Cathy's "butler"—who was actually her chief bodyguard—had his back turned toward her. His attention was entirely given to the crowd packed near the podium. Within seconds, Anton spotted several other people maintaining a similar stance. He recognized none of them, but he knew that they were all either members of the Audubon Ballroom or other organizations of Mesan ex-slaves in alliance with the Ballroom.

The sight made him relax a bit. The genetic slaves who escaped from Manpower's grip and made their way to the Loop were the lowest of the low, by the standards of Solarian society. For all the League's official egalitarianism, there was a taint which was attached to those genetically manipulated people. *Subhumans,* they were often called in private.

The Old Quarter's other immigrants—who

constituted, of course, a vastly larger body of people than the ex-Mesans—were by no means immune to that bigotry. Indeed, some of them would express it more openly and crudely than any member of the genteel upper crust. But if those immigrants shared the general attitude that the ex-slaves were the lowest of the low, they also understood—from close and sometimes bitter experience—that there was a corollary.

The hardest of the hard. Not all of the blows which Jeremy X and his comrades struck fell on the rich and powerful. A time had been, once, and not so many years ago, when a Mesan ex-slave had to fear pogroms and lynchings in the Old Quarter. The Audubon Ballroom had put a stop to that, as savagely as they felt it necessary.

Cathy reached the podium and began to speak. Her words, amplified by the electronic devices built within the speaker's stand, brought instant silence to the entire amphitheater.

Anton was impressed. The immigrants who lived in the Loop were drawn from dozens of the Solarian League's so-called "protectorate worlds." Most of them subscribed to a general principle of solidarity among the downtrodden, but that unity was riven—fractured, often enough—by a multitude of political differences and cultural animosities. No one had tried to shout down the previous speakers, representing one or another of the various groups which had agreed to sponsor this rally. But neither had they felt constrained to listen quietly. Cathy was the first speaker who was getting the huge crowd's undivided attention.

In truth, Anton was not simply impressed—he was a bit shocked. He had known, abstractly, that Cathy had the authority to call for such a rally on a moment's notice. Or so, at least, Jeremy X had claimed when he laid out his plans for Helen's rescue in the coffeehouse. But seeing that authority manifested in the concrete was an altogether different experience.

How does she do it? he wondered. *She's not even from the League, much less one of its protectorates. For God's sake, the woman's a foreign aristocrat!*

Cathy began to speak, and Anton began to understand. Slowly and grudgingly, of course—except for that part of him which realized, with deepening shock, that his ridiculous infatuation was not about to go away.

Part of it, he decided, was precisely *because* she was a Manticoran aristocrat. If the Star Kingdom had a certain reputation for arrogance and snobbery among the huge population of the Solarian League, it also had a reputation for—to a degree, at least—living up to its own standards. Quite unlike, in that respect, the officially egalitarian standards of the League itself. The Sollie upper crust and the comfortable middle classes on the Core Worlds could prattle all they wanted about democracy and equality, and sneer at the "reactionary semi-feudalism" of the Star Kingdom. The immigrants packed into that amphitheater knew the truth.

In the far-off and distant protectorate worlds from which they had come—fled, rather—the iron fist within the Sollie velvet glove was bare and naked. The protectorate worlds were ruled by the League's massive bureaucracy, whose institutional indifference was married to the avarice of the League's giant commercial interests. If none of those protectorate worlds was precisely a hell-hole, a modern equivalent of the King Leopold's Congo of ancient legend, they *did* bear a close resemblance to what had once been called "banana republics" and "company towns." *Neocolonialism*, many of the previous speakers had called it, and even Anton did not disagree with that characterization.

There was nothing of that nature within the Star Kingdom. Anton himself, as a Gryphon highlander, could attest to that. The conflict between Gryphon's yeomanry and its aristocracy was the closest the Star Kingdom had ever come to that kind of open class war. And that conflict paled in comparison to anything which these immigrants had experienced.

But most of it, he realized as Cathy's speech unfolded, was due to the woman herself. Anton had been expecting another histrionic speech, like the ones which had preceded Cathy's, wherein the speakers bellowed hackneyed slogans and shrieked phrases which, for all their incendiary terminology, were as platitudinous and devoid of content as any politician's. What he heard instead was a calm, thoughtful presentation of the logic of genetic slavery and the manner in which it undermined any and all possibility for human freedom. Speaking in her husky, penetrating contralto—without, he noted with some amusement, any of the profanity which peppered her casual conversations—Cathy took up the arguments advanced by the Mesans and their apologists and began carefully dissecting them.

For all that her own motivation was clearly one of simple morality, Cathy did not appeal to that. Rather, as cold-bloodedly as any Machiavellian politician devoted to *Realpolitik*, she examined the *logic* of slavery—especially slavery which was connected to genetic differentiation. Her speech was filled with a multitude of examples drawn from human history, many of them dating back to the ancient era when the

planet on which she now stood was the sole habitat
of the human species. Time and again, she cited the
words of such fabled sages as Douglass and Lincoln,
showing how the logic of genetic slavery was nothing
new in the universe.

Two things, in particular, struck Anton most about
her speech. The first was that the woman had
obviously, like many exiles before her, taken full
advantage of her long years of isolation to devote
herself to serious and exhaustive study. Anton had
been aware, vaguely, that even professional scholars
considered the Countess of the Tor one of the galaxy's
authorities on the subject of "genetic indentured
servitude." Now he saw the proof of that before his
own eyes, and reacted to it with the traditional respect
which Gryphon highlanders gave to any genuine
expert. The Liberal and Progressive Manticoran aristocrats whom Anton had encountered in the past had
repelled him, as much as anything, by their light-
minded and casual knowledge of the subjects they so
freely pontificated about. *Lazy dabblers*, was his
opinion of them. His former wife Helen's opinion had
been even harsher, for all that she considered herself a Progressive of sorts. There was nothing of that
dilettantism in the woman standing at the podium.

The second thing was the *target* of her speech.
Although Cathy was focusing on the plight of the
Mesan slaves, her words were not addressed to them
but to the big majority of the audience in the
amphitheater—who were not Mesans. The point of her
remarks—the pivot of them, in fact—was her attempt
to demonstrate that any waffling on the issue of genetic
slavery by *any* political movement which demanded
justice for its own constituents would surely undermine
its own cause.

Before she was more than ten minutes into the speech, Anton found himself leaning forward and listening attentively. A part of his mind, of course, paid no attention to her words. In one sense, the entire rally and Cathy's speech itself was a gigantic diversion designed to cover the effort to rescue his daughter. But that part was quiescent, for the moment, simply waiting with the stoic patience of Gryphon's great mountains. The rest of his mind, almost despite his own volition, found himself enjoying the quick humor and slowly unfolding logic of the woman he was listening to.

So it was almost—not quite—with regret, that he broke away when he felt the nudge on his elbow.

He turned his head. One of Jeremy's comrades was leaning over his shoulder. He recognized the young woman, although he did not know her name.

"It's time," she said.

Anton and Robert Tye immediately rose and began following her out of the amphitheater. Dressed as they were in the typical clothing worn by many immigrants in the Old Quarter, nobody took note of their departure.

"How far?" asked Anton, the moment they had exited from the amphitheater itself and could no longer be overheard.

The woman smiled, almost ruefully. "Would you believe it? Not more than a mile. They're somewhere in the Artinstute."

Tye's eyes widened. "I thought that was a fable," he protested.

"Nope. It exists, sure enough. But talk about your buried—!" She broke off, shaking her head. "Never been there myself. Don't know anyone who has, actually."

Anton frowned. "But you're sure Helen's there?"

They were moving quickly now, almost running down a long and sloping ramp. Over her head, the woman said: "Guess so. Jeremy didn't seem the least unsure about it."

Anton was not entirely mollified. From what he had seen of Jeremy X, he suspected the man was never "unsure about it" with regard to anything. He could only hope the assurance was justified.

And now they *were* running, and Anton drove everything out of his mind except his own implacable purpose.

Helen

When Helen awoke, the first thing she saw was a blue glint. It came from somewhere high on the wall opposite the pallet where she was resting. The "wall" was more in the nature of collapsed rubble, which seemed to have forced its way into some kind of opening. As if one wall—she could still see remnants of what must be an ancient structure—had been filled by the centuries-long disintegration of walls which came after. The glint seemed to come from a piece of that most ancient wall, a jagged and broken shard. *Blue*. As if it were shining by its own light. Helen stared at it, puzzled.

When she finally realized the truth, she sat upright, almost bolting. *That was sunlight! Shining through something!*

Next to her, Berry stirred. The girl had apparently already been awake. Seeing the direction of Helen's stare, Berry followed her eyes. Then, smiled.

"It's so special, this place," she whispered. "There's light down here—all the way down here!—coming from someplace above. Must be little crevices or something, all the way up to the surface."

The two girls stared at the blue glint. "It's the Windows," Berry whispered. "I *know* it is. The Shkawl Windows everybody always talks about but nobody knows where they are. I found it—me and Lars."

Helen had never heard of the "Shkawl Windows." She was about to ask Berry what they were, when another thought occurred to her. She looked around. Then, seeing that the cavernous area she was in was too poorly lit by the feeble light to see more than a few feet, listened.

"How long have I been asleep?" she asked, her voice tinged by worry. "And where's Lars?"

"You've been sleeping forever, seems like. You must have been real tired."

Berry nestled closer. "Lars said he was going back to make sure we didn't leave any tracks. He took a lantern with him." She frowned and raised her head. "But he's been gone a long time, now that I think about it. I wonder—"

Helen rummaged under the blanket, searching for the other lantern. When she found it, she rose and headed for the stairs. "Stay here," she commanded. "I'll find him."

But Lars found her, instead. And brought the terror back.

"People are coming," he hissed. "With guns."

Startled, Helen lifted her eyes. She had been looking at the floor, picking her way through the debris which filled what seemed to have once been a wide hallway. From a corner twenty feet ahead and to her left, Lars flicked his lantern on and off, showing her where he was hidden.

She extinguished her own lantern and moved toward him, as quickly as she could in the darkness.

"Who are they?" she whispered.

"Most of 'em are Scrags," came the answer. "Must be a dozen of 'em. Maybe more. But there's some other people leading them. I don't know who *they* are, but they're real scary-looking. One of them has some kind of gadget."

Helen was at his side, her hand resting on the boy's shoulder. She could feel the tremor shaking those slender bones.

"I think they're tracking us with it, Helen," he added. His voice was full of fear. "Our smell, maybe. Something."

Helen felt a shiver of fear herself. She knew that there were such devices, because her father had mentioned them to her. But the devices were very expensive.

Which meant—

Helen didn't want to think about what it meant. Whatever it was, it was bad news.

"How close are they?" she whispered.

"Not too far any more. I spotted 'em a while ago. After that I stayed ahead of them, hoping they were going somewhere else. It was easy 'cause they've got a lot of lanterns and they're not afraid to use them."

The fear in his voice was stronger. For a waif like Lars, anyone who would move through the dark caverns of the lower Loop without worrying who might spot them was an automatic danger. The arrogance of power.

"Stay here," she whispered. A moment later, after adjusting the lantern to its lowest power setting, Helen began moving ahead into the darkness. The soft glow emitted by the lantern was enough to illuminate her immediate footsteps, no more. She was searching for the oncoming enemy—and that they *were* her enemies, she didn't doubt at all—using her ears and her nose.

She found them two minutes later. And felt the worst despair of her life. There would be no escaping *these*.

The Scrags, maybe. But not the five people in front.

From her vantage point, peeking around another corner in the endless hallways which seemed to make up this place, Helen studied the oncoming searchers. She gave no more than a momentary scrutiny to the Scrags bringing up the rear, strutting and swaggering exactly the way she remembered them. It was the five people in front that she spent her time examining.

They were dressed in civilian clothing, but Helen knew at once that they were trained professionals. She had spent her whole life as a military brat. Everything about those four men and one woman shrieked: *soldiers.* It was obvious in the way they maintained their positions, the way they held their weapons, everything—

Peeps! The thought flooded her, unbidden. It made no sense that a Peep military detachment would be down here, but Helen never questioned the logic. Peeps were her enemies. Peeps had killed her mother. Who else—what other *soldiers?*—would be looking for her? She was much too politically unsophisticated to understand the illogicality of an alliance between Scrags and Peeps. Enemies were enemies, and there's an end to it. Such is the root of highland political logic, as it has been throughout human existence.

Helen had been born in a military hospital in the great orbiting shipyard called *Hephaestus*, and had only occasionally visited Gryphon. No matter. She was her father's girl. From the highlands.

She focused her eyes on the two Peeps in the very forefront. The leaders, obviously. The one on the left had all the earmarks of a veteran. He was studying a device held in his hand, his hatchet face bent forward and tight with concentration.

Her eyes moved to the man standing next to him. The officer in charge, she realized. She wasn't certain—it was hard to be, with prolong—but she thought he was as young in actual fact as his face would indicate.

She took no comfort in that youthfulness. She saw the veteran's head nod, like a hatchet striking wood, and his lips move. The young officer's face came up and he was staring directly at her, from a distance of not more than twenty yards.

He could not see Helen in the darkness, but she could see him clearly. There was nothing soft and childlike in that lean face; nothing boyish in the wiry body. She saw his jaw tighten, and the dark gleam which seemed to come into his eyes. That was the face of a young fanatic, she knew, who had just come to an irrevocable decision. Pitiless and merciless in the way that only youth can be. Helen realized, in that instant, his true purpose.

That was the face of a killer, not a captor.

And so, in the end, Helen belonged to her mother also. Helen Zilwicki came back to life, reborn in the daughter named after her. As she continued her examination, Helen gave no thought at all to her own certain death. That her enemies would catch Helen herself, and kill her, she did not doubt for an instant. But perhaps, if she did her job and led them astray before they trapped her, the monsters would be satisfied with her alone. And not seek further in the darkness, for her own new-found children.

Victor

"Almost there," said Citizen Sergeant Fallon. "She can't be more than a hundred yards away. And whoever's with her. Youngsters, I think, the way these readings keep coming up. One boy and one girl, would be my guess. Her age or younger."

Victor raised his head and stared at the wide opening which loomed before them. The room they were in, for all its size, was like a half-collapsed ancient vault. It was well-illuminated by their lanterns, but the ancient corridor ahead was still buried in darkness.

He hesitated for not more than a second or two. His jaws tightened with decision.

Here. Now.

Victor hefted the flechette gun in his hands. Except for one of the Scrags, Victor had the only flechette gun in the party. Everyone else was armed with pulse rifles. As casually as he could manage, he looked over his shoulder and studied the soldiers and the Scrags following him. Quickly, easily—an officer doing a last inspection of his troops before he led them into combat. He spotted the Scrag holding the other flechette gun and fixed her location in his mind.

"Citizen Sergeant Fallon and I will take the point," he said. His voice sounded very harsh, ringing in his own ears. The other three soldiers in the SS detachment, hearing the announcement, seemed to relax a bit. Or so, at least, Victor hoped.

Fallon cleared his throat. "If you'll pardon me saying so, sir, I think—"

Whatever he thought went with him. Victor leveled the flechette gun and fired. He had already set the weapon at maximum aperture. At that point-blank range—the muzzle was almost touching Fallon when Victor pulled the trigger—the volley of 3mm darts literally cut him in half. The citizen sergeant's legs, still connected by the pelvis and lower abdomen, flopped to the ground. Fallon's upper body did a grotesque reverse flip, spraying blood all over. The Scrags standing near him were spewed with gobbets of shredded intestine.

The butt of the gun came up to Victor's shoulder quickly and easily. He took out Citizen Corporal Garches next. Other than Fallon, she was the only combat veteran in the Peep detachment. The other two were simply typical SS guards.

A burst of flechettes shredded Garches. Victor's aim moved on, quickly. The Scrag holding the other flechette gun came under his sights. The woman was standing paralyzed. She seemed completely in shock. One of her hands, in fact, had left the gun and was wiping pieces of Fallon from her face. An instant later, her face was disintegrated, along with the rest of her body above the sternum.

SS next. *Quick!* He swung the flechette gun back and took out the two remaining members of Fallon's squad with a single shot. They never did more than gape before Victor erased them from existence.

Victor had never been in combat, but he had always taken his training seriously. He had never stinted on the officially mandated hours spent on the firing range and the sim combat tanks. Indeed, he had routinely exceeded them—much to the amusement of other SS officers.

Dimly, he heard the Scrags shouting. He ignored the sounds. Some part of his mind recognized that the genetic "supermen" were beginning to react, beginning to raise their own weapons, beginning—

No matter. Victor stepped into their very midst, firing again and again. In close quarters, a flechette gun was the most murderous weapon imaginable. The weapon didn't kill people so much as it ripped them apart. In seconds, the underground cavern was transformed into a scene from Hell. Confusion and chaos, blood and brains and flesh spattering everywhere, the beams from wildly swinging hand lanterns illuminating the area like strobe lights.

Abstractly, Victor understood his advantage—had planned for it. Despite his lack of actual combat experience, he had *trained* for this. Had spent hours, in fact, thinking through this very exercise and quietly practicing it in the sim tanks over the past two days. He *expected* what was happening, where the Scrags were still half-paralyzed with shock.

Or, even where they weren't paralyzed, they had so much adrenaline unexpectedly pumping into them that their motions were too jerky, too violent. When they managed to get off shots, they missed their target—or hit one of their own. Shrieks and shouts turned the nightmare scene into pure bedlam. The noise, added to the bizarrely flickering light beams, added to the gruesome splatter of wet human tissue flying everywhere, was enough to overwhelm any mind that wasn't braced for it.

Victor ignored it all. Like a methodical maniac, he just kept stepping into them. Almost in their faces, surrounded by their jerky bodies. Twice knocking rifle barrels aside to get a clear shot himself. He expected to die, in the instant, but he ignored that certainty also.

He ignored everything, except the need to slay his enemies. Ignored, even, the plan which he and Kevin Usher had agreed upon. Victor Cachat was supposed to spray the Scrags with a single burst of automatic fire. Just enough to scatter them and confuse them, so that the Ballroom would have easy pickings while Victor made his escape.

It was insane to do otherwise. If the Scrags were not trained soldiers, still and all they were genetically conditioned warriors with superb reflexes and the arrogance to match their DNA. *Suicide to stand your ground, lad,* Kevin had told him. *Just scatter them and race off. See to the girl. The Ballroom will take care of the rest.*

But Victor Cachat was the armed fist of the Revolution, not a torturer. A champion of the downtrodden, not an assassin lurking in ambush. So he thought of himself, and so he was.

The boy inside the man rebelled, the man demanded the uniform he had thought to wear. Say what they would, think what they would.

Officer of the Revolution. Sneer and be damned.

Victor waded into the mob of Scrags, firing relentlessly, using the modern flechette gun in close quarters like a rampaging Norseman might have used an ax. Again and again and again, just as he had trained for in the years since he marched out of the slums to fight for his own. He made no attempt to take cover, no attempt to evade counterfire. Never realizing, even, that the sheer fury of his charge was his greatest protection.

But Victor was no longer thinking of tactics. Like a berserk, he would meet his enemies naked. The Red Terror against the White Terror, standing on the open field of battle. As he had been *promised*.

He would *make* it so. Sneer and be damned!

The shots went true and true and true and true. The boy from the mongrel warrens hammered supermen into pulp; the young man betrayed wreaked a war god's terrible vengeance; and the officer of the Revolution found its truth in his own betrayal.

Sneer and be damned!

Jeremy

"Crazy kid!" hissed Jeremy. He and the others had been following Victor and his would-be executioners. They were now hidden in the shadows toward the rear of the chamber. Jeremy sensed his Ballroom comrades raising their own pulse rifles. They were aiming at the mob of shrieking Scrags swirling in the center of the vault. But there was no way to fire without hitting Victor himself. He was right in the midst of the Scrags.

What was left of them, anyway. Half the Scrags were down already, ripped to shreds by Cachat's murderous madness.

Murderous, yes, and mad besides. But Jeremy X had been accused of the same, often enough. And there were times, the truth be told, when he thought the accusation was dead on the money.

Such a time was now.

"Hold your fire!" he shouted to his comrades.

With the agility of the acrobat he had been brought into the world to be, Jeremy sprang over the rubble and landed lightly on his feet. Then, bounding forward like an imp, he hefted the handguns which were his favored weapons. One in each hand, as befitted his version of the court jester, gleefully calling out the battlecry of the Ballroom.

"Shall we dance?"

The Scrags who had managed to survive Cachat's fire just had time to spot the capering fool, before they were cut down. Court jester or no, Jeremy X was also, in all likelihood, the deadliest pistoleer alive. The shots came like a master pianist's fingers, racing through the finale of a concerto with a touch as light and unerring as it was thunderous. The sound was all darts flying and striking. There were no screams, no groans, no hisses of pain. Each shot was instantly fatal, and the shots lasted not more than seconds.

Not one of the Scrags managed so much as a single shot at Jeremy. The only moment of real danger for him came at the very end, as the last Scrag fell to the ground. His body one way, his head another. Jeremy's shot had severed the neck completely.

Jeremy found himself looking down the barrel of Cachat's flechette gun. Jeremy was the last thing still standing in the chamber, and the young SS officer had naturally brought the deadly weapon to bear on him.

A tense moment, that. Cachat's young face looked like the face of a ghost. Pale, taut, emotionless. Even his eyes seemed empty.

But the moment passed, the gun barrel swung aside, and Jeremy gave silent thanks to *training*.

By the time Jeremy's comrades made their way into the chamber, it was all over. Stillness and silence. Slowly, Victor Cachat lowered the flechette gun. More slowly yet, as if in a daze, he began to examine his own body. Astonished, it seemed, to find himself alive.

"And well you should be," muttered Jeremy. The lanterns dropped by the dying Scrags cast haphazard light here and there. He swiveled his head, examining the corpses scattered all over the chamber. The ancient stone floor was a charnelhouse of blood and ruin. Carrying their own lanterns, the Ballroom spread out and began moving slowly through the human wreckage, searching for survivors.

They found one still alive. His last sight was the tongue of his executioner.

Then, silence again.

Jeremy caught motion in the corner of his eye. He turned, raising a pistol, but lowered it at once. With his uncanny reflexes, of mind as much as body, he recognized the motion. A captain and a master of the martial arts, advancing slowly into the light.

The silence was broken, by a scream out of darkness. *"Daddy!"*

Motion anew, a girl's blurring feet. Racing across a field of carnage as if it were a meadow; skipping through havoc as easily as they would have skipped through grass.

"Daddy! Daddy! Daddy! Daddy!"

"It's an odd sort of place, this universe of ours," mused Jeremy. He smiled at the comrade at his side. "Don't you think?"

Donald X was cut from more solemn cloth, as befitted such a thick creature. F-67d-8455-2/5 he had been, once, bred for a life of heavy labor. "I dunno," he grunted, surveying the scene with stolid satisfaction.

"Master Tye! Master Tye!"

"Seems just about right to me."

Daughter struck father like a guided missile. Jeremy winced. "Good thing he's a gold medalist. Else that's a takedown for sure."

His eyes moved to a young man, standing alone in a lake of blood. The flechette gun was held limply in his hands. There was nothing in that face now but innocence, wondering.

"Odd," insisted Jeremy. "Galahad's not supposed to be a torturer."

Rafe

The first thing he recognized, as he faded back in, was a voice. Everything else was meaningless. Some part of him understood that his eyes were open. But the part of him that *saw* did not.

There was only the voice.

Your plan worked perfectly, Rafe. Beautiful! They'll make you a Hero of the Revolution. In private, of course. Just like they did with me.

Oddly, the first concrete bit of information that returned was the name. He felt a trickle of emotion re-entering a field of blankness. He hated being called "Rafe." He would not even tolerate Raphael.

Everyone knows that! There was less of anger in the thought than sullenness. The pout of an aggrieved boy.

Yeah, it was damned near as perfect an operation as I've ever seen—and I'll make sure to include that in my own supplemental report to Gironde's.

The name "Gironde" registered also. Gironde was a citizen major in the SS detachment on Terra. One of his own subordinates. Not close, though; not one of his inner sanctum. An "ops ape," Gironde was; not his kind at all.

You'll be glad to know that the Ballroom's sweep of the Loop seems to have damned near wiped out the Scrags completely. Lord, that was a stroke of genius on your part!

The word "Lord" was not supposed to be used. He remembered that. And remembered, also, that it was his responsibility to see to it that it wasn't.

Between the confusion caused by the rally at Soldier Field—all those people crowding through the streets and alleys—and their own efforts to catch the girl, the Scrags all came out of their hideyholes. Well . . . No doubt there's a few left. Not many.

The next sound he recognized as laughter. No, more like a dry chuckle. Very dry. Very cold. Then, more sounds. Someone, he understood vaguely, had pushed back a chair and risen from it.

Oh, yeah. You're a genius, Rafe. Just like you planned, the Ballroom wiped out the Scrags in one day. And the girl's safe, of course, so you got us out of that mess. Can you imagine? The nerve of those Manpower bastards! Trying to set us up as the patsy, figuring everybody would believe anything about Peeps now that Parnell's arriving.

That was the sound of a man pacing, he realized. And then, suddenly, understood that he was *seeing* the man. His optic nerves had been working all along, but something in his brain must have suddenly switched on. He had been looking sightlessly. Now he was seeing.

He arrives today, you know. Just after the Mesan assassination squad gets arrested by the Sollies we tipped off. You tipped off, I should say. Credit where credit is due.

Another harsh, dry laugh. He remembered that laugh. Remembered how much he detested it.

Remembered, even, how much he detested the man who laughed in that manner.

But he couldn't remember the man's name. Odd. Irritating.

Like a bird, his mind fluttered in that direction. Irritation was an emotion. He was beginning to remember emotions too.

The man who laughed—very big, he was, especially standing in the center of a room looking down at him—laughed again. When he spoke, the words came like actual words instead of thoughts.

"Of course, there isn't the horde of newscasters waiting at the dock for him that everyone expected. Plenty of them still, needless to say. But half of the Sollie casters are in the Loop, covering what they're already calling the Second Valentine's Day Massacre. Good move, Rafe! Everything about your plan was brilliant."

Usher. That was the man's name.

He remembered how much he detested that grin. More, even, than the man's way of laughing.

"Yeah, brilliant. And after the final masterstroke, which—" The man glanced at the door. "—should be coming any moment now, you'll go down in history as one of the great ops of all time."

He had been drugged, he suddenly realized. And with that realization came another. He knew the drug itself. He couldn't remember its technical name, although he knew that it was called the "zombie drug." It was so easy to use as an aerosol. He remembered thinking that his office had grown a bit muggy, and that he'd intended to speak sharply to the maintenance people. Highly illegal, that drug. As much because it left no traces in a dead body as because of its effects. It broke down extremely rapidly in the absence of oxygenated blood.

There was a knock on the door. Very rapid, very urgent. He heard another voice, speaking through the door. Very rapidly, very urgently.

"Now! They're about to blow the entrance!" Footsteps, scampering away.

Again, that hated grin.

"Well, there it is, Rafe. Time for you to put the capstone on your career. Just like you foresaw, Manpower saved its real pros for the attack on the embassy. Here they are, raring to go. 'Course, we got Bergren out already, so they're walking into a massacre. Just like you planned."

An instant later, he was being lifted like a doll by huge and powerful hands. Now that he was on his feet, he could see the Marines lining the far wall. All of them in battle armor, with pulse rifles ready to hand.

"Such a damn pity that you insisted on leading the ambush yourself, instead of leaving it to the professional soldiers. But you always were a field man at heart. Weren't you, Rafe?"

He was being propelled to the door. Usher was forcing something into his hand. A gun, he realized. He tried to remember how to use it.

That effort jarred loose his first clear thought.

"Don't call me Rafe!"

The building was suddenly shaken by a loud explosion and then, a split-second later, by the sound of debris smashing against walls. The shock jarred loose more memories.

This was exactly how I planned it. Except—

Usher was opening the door with one hand, while he shifted his grip onto—

Durkheim! My name's Durkheim! Citizen General *Durkheim!*

He heard Manpower's professionals pouring into the embassy's great vestibule. He could see the vestibule through the opening door.

There's not supposed to be anybody here, except Bergren and a squad of Marines. Newbie recruits.

The huge hand holding him by the scruff of the neck tightened. He could sense the powerful muscles tensing, ready to hurl him into the room beyond.

"Don't call me Rafe!"

"Hero of the Revolution! Posthumous, of course."

He was sailing into the vestibule. He landed on his feet and stumbled. He stared at the Manpower professionals swinging their pulse rifles. Call them mercenary goons if you would, they were still trained soldiers. Ex-commandos. Hair-trigger reactions.

He was still trying to remember how to use the gun when the hailstorm of darts disintegrated him.

THEREAFTER

The admiral and the ambassador

Sitting behind his desk, Admiral Edwin Young glared up at the captain standing at attention in front of it.

"You're dead meat, Zilwicki," the admiral snarled. He waved the chip in his hand. "You see this? It's my report to the Judge Advocate General's office."

Young laid the chip down, with a delicate and precise motion. The gesture exuded grim satisfaction. *"Dead—stinking—meat.* You'll be lucky if you just get cashiered. I estimate a ten-year sentence, myself."

Standing at the window with his hands clasped

behind his back, Ambassador Hendricks added his own growling words.

"By your insubordinate and irresponsible behavior, Captain Zilwicki, you have managed to half-wreck what should have been our greatest propaganda triumph in the Solarian League *ever*." Glumly, the ambassador stared down at the teeming streets and passageways over a mile beneath his vantage point. "Of course, it'll blow over eventually. And Parnell will be giving his testimony to the Sollie Human Rights Commission for months. But still—"

He turned away, adding his own fierce glare to the admiral's. The stocky officer who was the object of that hot scrutiny did not seem notably abashed. Zilwicki's face was expressionless.

"*Still!*" Hendricks took a deep breath. "We should have been able to start the whole thing with a flourish. Instead—" He waved angrily at the window.

Young leaned forward across his desk, tapping the disk. "Instead, all everyone's talking about is the so-called Peep–Manpower War. Who wants to watch testimony in a chamber, when the casters can show you a half-wrecked Peep embassy and a *completely* wrecked Manpower headquarters?" He snorted. "Not to mention the so-called"—his next words came hissing—"'*drama*' of Mesa's slave revenge. With most of their pros gone, Manpower was a sitting duck. Especially with that terrorist Jeremy X on the loose. Christ, they didn't leave anyone alive over there."

For the first time since he'd entered the admiral's office, Captain Zilwicki spoke.

"None of the secretaries in Manpower's HQ were so much as scratched. Your Lordship."

The glares were hot, hot. But, still, the officer seemed unconcerned.

"Dead—stinking—meat," Young repeated, emphasizing each word. He straightened up. The next words came briskly.

"You are relieved of your duties and ordered to report directly to Navy headquarters in the Star Kingdom to account for your actions. *Technically*, you are not under arrest, but that's purely a formality. You will remain in your private quarters until such time as the next courier ship is ready to depart. In the meantime—"

"I'll be leaving immediately, Your Lordship. I've already made the arrangements."

The admiral stumbled to a halt, staring at Zilwicki.

That moment, the admiral's secretary stuck his head through the door. The admiral had deliberately left the door open, so that the entire staff could overhear his dealings with Zilwicki.

The secretary's face was a mixture of concern and bewilderment.

"Excuse me for interrupting, Your Lordship, but Lady Catherine Montaigne is here and insists on seeing you immediately."

The admiral's frown was one of pure confusion. From the side, the ambassador gave a start of surprise.

"*Montaigne?*" he demanded. "What in the hell does *that* lunatic want?"

His answer came from the lunatic herself. The Lady Catherine Montaigne trotted past the secretary and into the room. She bestowed a sunny smile on the ambassador. Her cheerful peasant face clashed a bit with her very expensive clothing.

"Please, Lord Hendricks! A certain courtesy is expected between Peers of the Realm. In private, at least."

She removed the absurdly elaborate hat perched

on her head and fluttered it. "In public, of course, you're welcome to call me whatever you want." The smile grew very sunny indeed. "Now that I think about it, I believe I once referred to you as a horse's ass in one of my speeches."

The smile was transferred onto Admiral Young and grew positively radiant. "And I am *quite* certain that I've publicly labeled the entire Young clan as a herd of swine. Oh, on any number of occasions! Although—" Here the smile quirked an apologetic corner. "I can't recall if I ever singled you out in particular, Eddie. But I assure you I will make good the lack at the very first opportunity. Of which I expect to have any number, since I'm planning a speaking tour immediately upon my return."

It took a moment for the last few words to penetrate the indignation of the ambassador and the admiral.

Hendricks frowned. "Return? Return *where?*"

"To the Star Kingdom, of course. Where else? I feel a sudden overwhelming impulse to revisit my native land. Thinking of moving back permanently, in fact."

She glanced at her watch. The timepiece seemed more like a mass of precious gems than a utilitarian object. It quite overwhelmed her slender wrist. "My private yacht departs within the hour."

The smile was now bestowed on Captain Zilwicki. And what had been a radiant expression took on warmth as well.

"Are you ready, Captain?"

Zilwicki's square head jerked a nod. "I believe so, Lady Catherine." He peered at the admiral. "I think the admiral is finished with me. His instructions were quite clear and precise."

Young gaped at him.

Zilwicki's shoulders twitched in a minute shrug. "Apparently so. With your permission then, Your Lordships, I will do as I am commanded. Immediately."

Young was still gaping. Hendricks found his voice.

"Zilwicki, are you *mad?* You're in enough trouble already!" The ambassador goggled the tall and slender noblewoman. "If you return to Manticore in the company of *this*—this—"

"Peer of the Realm," Lady Catherine drawled. "In case you'd forgotten."

The smile made no pretense, any longer, of disguising its contempt. "And—in case you'd forgotten— I am thereby required to provide Her Majesty's armed forces with my assistance whenever possible. That *is* the law, Lord Hendricks, even if that herd of Young swine and your own brood of suckling piglets choose to ignore it at your convenience."

She laid a slim-fingered hand on the shoulder of the captain. As broad and short as he was, they made an odd looking pair. She was a good six inches taller than he. Yet, somehow, Zilwicki did not seem to shrink in the contrast. It seemed more as if Lady Catherine was in orbit around him.

"So—I must see to it that Captain Zilwicki is brought before the Judge Advocate General as soon as possible, to face the serious charges laid against him. And since I was leaving at once anyway, because of my *other* pressing responsibility to the Crown, I would be remiss in my duty as a peer if I did not provide the captain with transport."

Again, it took a moment for the words to register.

Admiral Young finally stopped gaping. "What 'other' responsibility?" he demanded.

Lady Catherine's eyes grew a bit round. "Oh, you hadn't heard? It seems that the self-destruct mechanism in Manpower's vault failed to operate properly. When those savage Ballroom terrorists wreaked their havoc on Manpower's headquarters, they were able to salvage most of the records from the computers. I received a copy, sent by an anonymous party."

She planted the hat back on her head. "I haven't had time to study it fully, of course—such *voluminous* records—but it didn't take me more than a minute to realize that the information needs to be presented to the Queen as soon as possible. You all know how much Elizabeth *detests* genetic slavery. She's said so in public—oh, I can't keep track of all the times! And in private, her opinion is even more volcanic." She shook her head sadly. "Such a hot-tempered woman. I worry about her health, sometimes."

The smile was back. "Elizabeth and I were childhood friends, you know. Did I fail to mention that? Oh, yes. Very close, at one time. Our relations have been strained for years, naturally, due to political differences. But I'm quite certain she'll want to speak to me on *this* subject. And Lady Harrington also, of course. I've never met her personally, but my butler Isaac is an old acquaintance."

She'd left them completely befuddled, now. The smile widened. "You didn't know? How odd, I thought everyone did. Isaac was one of the slaves Lady Harrington freed—well, she wasn't a peer in those days, of course, just another commoner naval officer—when she smashed up the depot at Casimir. I'm sure she'd agree to see him again, to allow him to present his overdue thanks. Along with a copy of these records. Quite certain of it."

Her hand squeezed Zilwicki's shoulder. "Captain?"

"Your servant, Lady Catherine."

A moment later, they were gone. The two men remaining in the room stared at each other. Their faces were already growing pale.

"Records?" choked Hendricks.

The admiral ignored him. He was already scrabbling for the communicator. In the minutes which followed, while Hendricks paced out his agitation, Young simply sat there. Listening to his chief legal officer explain to him, over and again, that he had neither the legal grounds—nor, more to the point here on Terra, the police authority—to detain a Manticoran Peer of the Realm engaged in the Queen's business.

Victor

As he leaned over the railing on the upper level of the terminal, studying the small party below getting ready to enter the embarkment area, Victor had mixed emotions. Which, sad to say, seemed destined to be his normal state. He almost felt regret for past simplicities and certitudes.

Almost. Not quite.

He heard a chuckle. The big man standing next to him, with the very pretty woman nestled under his arm, had—as usual—read his mind. Victor was almost getting tired of that also.

Almost. Not quite.

"Grotesque, isn't it?" mused Usher. "All that obscene wealth, in the hands of a single person? You could feed a small town for a year on what a private yacht like that costs."

Victor said nothing. He had learned that much, at least. *One thing at a time.* He didn't want to hear the lecture again.

"What do you think he's saying to her?" he asked.

Usher's eyes moved, focusing on the girl below. She was giving a fierce hug to the small man who had accompanied the party to the terminal.

"Well, let's see. He's probably stopped chiding her for using the Owl By Night. And he's probably already told her exactly which schools to investigate, once she gets to Manticore." A large hand came up and rubbed his jaw. "So I imagine he's simply telling her the kind of things which she really needs to know. Things from the heart, so to speak."

Below, the embrace ended. With the quick motions of someone steadying loss with new determination, Helen Zilwicki marched her entire party to the gate. There were six people in the party. Her father and Lady Catherine and Isaac brought up the rear. In the front, nestled under Helen's wings, her new brother and sister advanced toward a new life. Master Tye alone remained behind, simply staring.

Usher turned away from the railing. "And that's that. Come on, Victor. It's time for Ginny and me to introduce you to a new vice."

Victor followed obediently. He didn't even grimace at the gibe.

"Good lad," murmured Usher. "You'll like it, I promise. And if the elitism bothers you, just use the plebe word for it. *Movies.*"

He leaned over, smiling at his wife. "Which one, d'you think?"

"*Casablanca,*" came the immediate reply.

"Good choice!" Kevin draped his other arm over

Victor. "I do believe this is the beginning of a beautiful friendship."

Helen

On the second night of their journey home, her father didn't return to their suite on the yacht. Once she was sure he wasn't going to, Helen made up her bed on the couch in the small salon. It took her a while to settle Lars and Berry for the night, in the stateroom which she was sharing with them. Partly, because something of her own good cheer seemed to infuse them. But mostly it was because they were afraid of sleeping without her.

"Come on!" she snapped. "We aren't going to be sharing a bed forever, you know." She eyed the huge and luxurious piece of furniture. "Not one like this, anyway. Not with Daddy on half-pay, at best."

She did not seem noticeably upset at the prospect of future poverty. Lars and Berry, of course, were not upset at all. Their new father's "half" pay was a fortune to them.

"Get to sleep!" Helen commanded. She turned off the lights. "Tonight belongs to Daddy. And tomorrow morning too."

In the time which followed, Helen set her clever alarms. She did the work with the same enthusiasm with which she had spent the evening designing them.

But, in the event, the alarms proved unnecessary. She never managed to sleep herself. So, when she heard her father coming through the outer doors, early in the morning, she had time to disengage them before he entered. She even had time to perch herself back on the couch. Grinning from ear to ear.

The door to the salon opened and her father tip-toed in. He spotted her and froze. Helen fought to restrain her giggles. *Talk about role reversal.*

"So!" she piped. "How was she?"

Her father flushed. Helen laughed and clapped her hands with glee. She had *never* managed to do that!

Her father straightened, glared at her, and then managed a laugh himself.

"Rascal," he growled. But the growl came with a rueful smile, and he padded over to the couch. The moment he sat down next to her, Helen scrambled into his lap.

Surprise crossed her father's face. Helen had not sat in his lap for years. Too undignified; too childish.

The look of surprise vanished, replaced by something very warm. A film of tears came into his eyes. A moment later, Helen felt herself crushed against him, by those powerful wrestler's arms. Her own vision was a bit blurry.

She wiped away the tears. *Whimsy, dammit!*

"I bet she snores." She'd planned that sentence for *hours.* She thought it came out just right.

Again, her father growled. "Rascal." Silence, for a moment, while he pressed her close, kissing her hair. Then:

"Yeah, she does."

"Oh, good," whispered Helen. The whimsical humor she'd planned for that remark was absent, however. There was nothing in it but satisfaction. "I *like* that."

Her father chuckled. "So do I, oddly enough. So do I." He stroked and stroked her hair. "Any prob-lem with it, sugar?"

Helen shook her head firmly. "Nope. Not any." She pressed her head against her father's chest, as if listening to his heartbeat. "I want you full again."

"So do I, sugar." Stroked and stroked her hair. "So do I."

Nightfall

David Weber

"Citizen General Fontein is here, Sir."

Oscar Saint-Just looked up as Sean Caminetti, his private secretary, ushered a colorless, wizened little man into his office. No one could have looked less like the popular conception of a brilliant and ruthless security agent than Erasmus Fontein. Except, perhaps for Saint-Just himself.

"Thank you, Sean." He nodded permission for the secretary to withdraw, and then turned his attention fully to his guest. Unlike most people summoned to Saint-Just's inner sanctum, Fontein calmly walked across to his favorite chair, lowered himself into it with neither hesitation or any sign of trepidation, waited while its surface adjusted to the contours of his body, then cocked his head at his chief.

"You wanted to see me?" he inquired, and Saint-Just snorted.

"I wouldn't put it quite that way. Not," he added, "that I'm not always happy to visit with you, of course. We have so few opportunities to spend quality time together." Fontein smiled faintly at the humor Saint-Just allowed so few people to see, but the smile faded as the Citizen Secretary for State Security went on in a much more serious tone.

"Actually, as I'm sure you've guessed, I called you in to discuss McQueen."

"I had guessed," Fontein admitted. "It wasn't hard, especially given how unhappy she was to move ahead on Operation Bagration."

"That's because you're a clever and insightful fellow who knows how much your boss is worried and what he worries about."

"Yes, I do," Fontein said, and leaned slightly forward. "And because I know, I've been trying very hard not to let the suspicions I know you have push me into reading something that isn't there into her actions."

"And?" Saint-Just prompted when he paused.

"And I just don't know." Fontein pursed his lips, looking uncharacteristically uncertain. It was Saint-Just's turn to incline his head, silently commanding him to explain, and the citizen general sighed.

"I've sat in on almost all of her strategy discussions at the Octagon, and the few I wasn't physically present for, I listened to on chip. I know the woman is a fiendishly good actress who can scheme and dissemble with the best. God knows I won't forget anytime soon how she out-foxed me before the

Leveler business! But for all that, I think her concerns over the possibility of new Manty weapons are genuine, Oscar. She's been too consistent in the arguments she's made for those concerns to be feigned." He shook his head. "She's worried about moving so aggressively onto the offensive. A lot more worried, I think, than she lets herself appear at Committee meetings, where she knows she has to project a confident front. And," he added unhappily, "I think that because she's really worried, she's also very, very pissed off with you for pushing her so hard against her own better judgment."

"Um." Saint-Just rubbed his chin thoughtfully. Erasmus Fontein was, with the possible exception of Eloise Pritchart, the most insightful of StateSec's commissioners. He didn't look it, which was one of the more potent weapons in his arsenal, but he had a cold, keenly logical mind and, in his own way, he was just as merciless as Oscar Saint-Just. More than that, he'd been Esther McQueen's watchdog for the better part of eight years. She'd fooled him once, but he knew her moves better than anyone else . . . and he was a hard man for the same person to fool twice. Which meant Saint-Just had to listen to anything he had to say. But even so . . .

"Just because she's genuinely concerned doesn't mean she's *right*," he said testily, and Fontein very carefully didn't allow his surprise at his superior's acid tone to show.

It was very unlike Saint-Just to reveal that sort of irritation, and the citizen general felt a sudden chill. One thing which made Saint-Just so effective was his ability to think coldly and dispassionately about a problem. If personal anger was beginning to corrode that dispassion in Esther McQueen's case, her time

could be far shorter than she guessed. Worse, Fontein
wasn't at all sure *he* was prepared to dismiss her concerns, whatever Saint-Just thought. He'd had too many
opportunities to see her in action, knew how tough
minded she was. And, he admitted, had seen her
physical and moral courage much too close-up for
comfort during the Leveler revolt. He might not trust
her, and he certainly didn't like her, but he did *respect*
her. And if there was any basis to her fears, then
however rosy things looked at this moment, the
People's Republic might find in the next few months
that it needed her worse than ever.

"I didn't say she was right, Oscar." Fontein was
careful to keep his voice even. "I only said I think
most of her concern is genuine. You asked me if I'm
suspicious of her and a part of my answer is that I
think a lot of her reluctance to charge ahead with
Bagration was unfeigned."

"All right." Saint-Just puffed air through his lips,
then shook himself. "All right," he said more naturally. "Point taken. Go on."

"Beyond her apparently genuine concerns over her
orders, I really can't say she's given me much to work
with," Fontein said honestly. "She staked out her claim
to authority in purely military affairs the day she took
over the Octagon, and she works her staff, and herself, so hard that even I can't manage to sit in on
all the meetings she has with planners and analysts
and logistics people and com specialists. She works
best one-to-one, and no one could fault the energy
she brings to the job, but she's definitely got a firm
grip on the military side of her shop. You probably
know that even better than I do." *Since*, he did not
add aloud, *you were the one who told me I had to
let *her* get a grip on it*. "I don't like it, and I never

did. Nor have I made any secret about how much I don't like it. At the same time, she has a point about the need for a single source of authority in a military chain of command, and the results she's produced certainly seem to have justified the decision to bring her in in the first place.

"I don't *think* she's been able to sneak anything past me, but I can't rule it out. As I say, no one could possibly keep pace with a schedule as frenetic as hers. There've probably been opportunities for side discussions I don't know anything about . . . and I still haven't figured out how she made her initial contacts before the Leveler business, when all's said. I have a few suspicions, but even knowing where to look—assuming I'm right and I am looking in the right places—I haven't been able to come up with any hard evidence. That being the case, I'm in no position to state unequivocally that she hasn't managed to do the same thing again at the Octagon.

"And let's face it, Oscar, she's charismatic as hell. I've watched her in action for years now, and I'm no closer to understanding how she does it than in the beginning. It's like she uses black magic. Or maybe it's a special kind of charisma that only works with military people. But it *does* work. She had Bukato out of his shell within weeks of taking over, and the rest of the Octagon's senior officers followed right behind him. And she managed to send Giscard and Tourville out ready to take on pseudogrizzlies with their bare hands, even though you and I both know from Eloise's reports that Giscard was suspicious as hell of her reputation for personal ambition. If anyone could inspire one of her subordinates to risk trying to do an end run around me to set up some clandestine line of communication, she's the one. I haven't seen a single trace of that, or I'd already've been in here bending your ear about it, but we can't afford to take anything for granted with a woman like her."

"I know." Saint-Just sighed and tipped his chair all the way back. "I was never happy about bringing her in and giving her such a long leash, but, damn it, Rob was right. We needed her, and however dangerous she may be, she produced. She certainly produced. But now—"

He broke off, pinching the bridge of his nose, and Fontein could almost feel the intensity of his thoughts. Unlike almost anyone else in State Security, Fontein had read the doctored dossier Saint-Just had constructed when McQueen was brought in as Secretary of War. He knew exactly how that file had been manicured to make McQueen look like the greatest traitor since Amos Parnell—indeed, to brand her as a previously undetected junior partner in the "Parnell Plot"—if it became necessary to remove her. Unfortunately, Parnell was back among the living after Harrington's escape from Cerberus and spilling his guts to the Solly Assembly's Committee on Human Rights, and—

The rhythm of Fontein's thoughts broke as a sudden insight struck him. Parnell. Was his escape from Cerberus an even larger factor in Saint-Just's intensified suspicions of McQueen than the commissioner had previously guessed? The ex-CNO's return to life had definitely shaken a lot of the old officer corps. They'd been careful about what they said and who they said it around, but that much was obvious. And after the victories Twelfth Fleet had produced under her orders, McQueen, for all the Navy's original wariness about her ambition, was almost as popular with, and certainly as respected by, its officers as

Parnell had been. She must seem like some sort of ghost of Parnell to Saint-Just, and the neutralization of her edited dossier had hit him hard.

It was ironic, really. When the time bombs had been planted in that dossier, they'd been seen as little more than window dressing. There'd been no real need for anyone to justify her removal when StateSec had been shooting admirals in job lots for years, since no one in the Navy would have dared raise even a minor objection. The entire purpose had been to provide Cordelia Ransom's Propagandists with ammunition to dress up the decision and be sure the Republic's public opinion was pointed in the right direction. But now that McQueen had become so popular with both the public and the Navy, that sort of justification for removing her had become genuinely vital. And just when it had, Parnell had escaped from Cerberus and discredited everything in it.

Saint-Just's weapon had been knocked from his hand when he most feared he needed it, and perhaps that, as much as his frustration over her refusal to agree with his analysts, helped explain the way in which his habitual self control had frayed in this instance.

"She produced," Saint-Just went on at last, "but I think she's become too dangerous for us to keep around. Someone else—like Theisman—can go on producing now that she's gotten the Navy turned around. And we won't have to worry about someone like Theisman trying to overthrow the Committee."

"Does that mean you and the Citizen Chairman have decided to remove her?" Fontein asked carefully.

"No," Saint-Just replied. "Rob is less convinced she's a danger. Or, rather, he's less convinced we can afford to get rid of her *because* of the danger she represents. He may even be right, and whether he is or not, he's still Chairman of the Committee . . . and my boss. So if he says we wait until we either know we don't need her or we find clear proof she's actively plotting, we wait. Especially since Bukato will have to go right along with her. Probably most of her other senior staffers, too, which makes it particularly imperative that we be certain the Manties are really on the run before we dislocate our command structure so severely. But I expect Bagration to pick right up where Scylla left off, and if it does, then I think we *will* have proof we don't need to hang on to a sword so sharp it's liable to cut our own heads off. Not when we've got other swords to choose from. And in that case, I expect Rob to green-light her removal."

"I see." Despite himself, Fontein felt an inner qualm. For all his own reservations about McQueen, he'd worked closely with her for so long that the announcement that she was a dead woman, one way or the other, within months hit him hard.

"I don't want to rock the boat," Saint-Just went on. "Not now that Bagration is just kicking off, and certainly not before Theisman gets here and gives us someone reliable to hand Capital Fleet to. And above all, I don't want to do anything that will make her realize her time is running out. But I think it's time we started building a dossier to replace the one we can't use anymore. I want a nice, clean, convincing paper trail to 'prove' she was a traitor before she gets shot resisting arrest, and we can't throw that kind of thing together at the last minute. So I want you to sit down with Citizen Colonel Cleary and begin putting one together now."

"Of course." Fontein nodded. There was no chance in the world that Saint-Just would take overt action against McQueen until Pierre authorized it. The StateSec CO's mind simply didn't work that way. But it was very like him to attempt to anticipate and put the groundwork in place ahead of time. The collapse of the original "proof" of McQueen's "treason against the People" only made him more determined than usual.

"Remember," Saint-Just said firmly, unwittingly echoing Fontein's own thoughts, "this is only a preliminary. Rob hasn't authorized me to do a thing, and that means *you're* not authorized to do anything except gather information and begin assembling a file. I don't want any mistakes or unauthorized enthusiasm that gets out of hand, Erasmus!"

"Of course not, Oscar," Fontein replied just a bit cooly. Saint-Just gave a small nod in response, one with a hint of apology. One reason (among many) Fontein had been chosen for his position was that he would no more act against McQueen without Saint-Just's specific order to do so, except in a case of dire emergency, than Saint-Just would have had her arrested or shot without clearance from Pierre.

"I know I can rely on you, Erasmus," he said, "and that's more important to me and to Rob right now than ever before. It's just that waiting for the coin to drop with McQueen has stretched my patience a lot thinner than I ought to have let it. I have to keep reining myself in where she's concerned, and some of it just spilled over onto you."

"I understand, Oscar. Don't worry. Cleary and I will put together exactly the sort of file you need, and that's *all* we'll do until you tell us otherwise."

"Good," Saint-Just said more cheerfully, and shoved up out of his chair with a smile. He walked around his desk to escort his visitor out and, in a rare physical show of affection, draped one arm around Fontein's narrow shoulders.

"Rob and I won't forget this, Erasmus," he said as the door from his private office to its waiting room opened and Caminetti looked up from his own desk. The secretary started to rise, but Saint-Just waved him back into his chair and personally escorted Fontein to the door.

"Remember," he said, pausing for one last word before Fontein left the waiting room for the public corridor beyond. "It has to be *solid*, Erasmus. When we shoot someone like McQueen, we can't leave any loose ends. Not this time. Especially not when we're going to have to make such a clean sweep at the Octagon along with her."

"I understand, Oscar," Fontein replied quietly. "Don't worry. I'll get it done."

Esther McQueen was working late—again—when the door chime sounded.

She glanced at the date-time display on her desk and grinned wryly. This late at night, it had to be Bukato. No one else worked quite the hours she did, and of those who might work this late, anyone else would go through her appointments yeoman. Now what, she wondered, would Ivan have to discuss with her tonight? Something about Bagration, no doubt. Or perhaps about Tom Theisman's impending arrival to take over the reorganized Capital Fleet.

She pressed the admittance button, and her eyebrows rose as the door opened. It wasn't Bukato. In fact, it was her junior com officer, a mere citizen lieutenant. Citizen commodores and citizen admirals were a centicredit a dozen around the Octagon. No one paid all that much attention to the gold braid and stars walking past them in the halls, and a mere citizen lieutenant was literally invisible.

"Excuse me, Citizen Secretary," the young man said. "I just finished those signals Citizen Commodore Justin gave me this afternoon. I was on my way to his office with them when I realized you were still here, and it occurred to me that you might want to take a look at them before I hand them to his yeoman."

"Why, thank you, Kevin." McQueen's voice was completely calm, without even a trace of surprise, but her green eyes sharpened as she held out her hand for the citizen lieutenant's memo board. Despite his own conversational tone, the young man's features were drawn for just a moment as their eyes met, and McQueen's breathing faltered for the briefest instant as she saw the flimsy strip of paper he passed her with the board.

She nodded to him, laid the board on her desk, keyed its display, and bent over it. Had anyone happened to walk into her office at that moment, all they would have seen was the Citizen Secretary of War scanning the message traffic her staffer had brought her. They would never have noticed the strip of paper which slipped from the memo board's touchpad to her blotter and lay hidden beyond the holo of its display. And because they would not have noticed it, they would never have read the brief, terse words it bore.

"S says EF authorized to move by SJ," it said. Only that much, but Esther McQueen felt as if a pulser dart had just hit her in the belly.

She'd known it was coming. It had been obvious for months that Saint-Just's suspicion had overcome his belief that they needed her skills, but she'd believed Pierre was wiser than that . . . at least where the military situation was concerned.

But maybe I only needed *to believe that because I wasn't ready.* The thought was unnaturally calm. *I needed more time, because we're* still *not ready. Just a couple of more weeks—a month at the outside—would have done it. But it looks like waiting is a luxury I've just run out of.*

She drew a deep breath as she hit the advance button and her eyes appeared to scan the display. Her free hand gathered up the thin paper, crushing it into a tiny pellet, and she reached up to rub her chin . . . and popped the pellet into her mouth. She swallowed the evidence and hit the advance button again.

Thirty percent. That was her current estimate of the chance of success. A one-third chance was hardly something she would willingly have risked her life upon, or asked others to risk their lives on with her, if she'd had an option. But if Saint-Just had authorized Fontein to move, she *didn't* have an option, and thirty percent was one hell of a lot better than no chance at all. Which was what she'd have if she waited until *they* pulled the trigger.

She paged through to the final message in the board, then nodded and held it out to the citizen lieutenant. Incomplete though her plans were, she'd been careful to craft each layer independently of the layers to follow it. And she could activate her entire strategy—such as it was and what there was of it at this stage—with a single com call. She wouldn't even have to say anything, for the combination she would punch into her com differed from Ivan Bukato's voice mail number only in the transposition of two digits. It was a combination she'd never used before and would never use again, but the person at the other end of it would recognize her face. All she had to do was apologize for mistakenly screening a stranger so late at night, and the activation order would be passed.

"Thank you, Kevin," she said again. "Those all look fine. I'm sure Citizen Commodore Justin will want to look them over as well, of course, but they seem to cover everything I was concerned about. I appreciate it." Her voice was still casual, but the glow in her green eyes was anything but as they met the com officer's squarely.

"You're welcome, Ma'am," Citizen Lieutenant Kevin Caminetti said, and the younger brother of Oscar Saint-Just's personal secretary tucked the memo board under his arm, saluted sharply, and marched out of Esther McQueen's office.

Behind him, she reached for her com's touchpad with a rock-steady hand.

Citizen Lieutenant Mikis Tsakakis sighed mentally as he followed Citizen Secretary Saint-Just down the hallway from the lift shaft. By tradition, the night security assignment for any public figure was supposed to be less demanding than the task of protecting the same individual during normal business hours. And Tsakakis supposed that there had to be some basis for that traditional belief, even though his own experience scarcely supported it.

All of Oscar Saint-Just's personal security team knew that the Citizen Secretary for State Security liked to work late. Unfortunately, he also liked to work early. In fact, he had an uncomfortable habit of going in to his office at utterly unpredictable hours, especially when some particular crisis or concern hovered in the background.

No one could fault the hours that he put in, and none of his subordinates were about to criticize the work habits of the second most powerful man in the People's Republic of Haven. But that didn't mean that Tsakakis and his people liked it. Unlike Saint-Just, some of them actually preferred a semi-regular schedule with comfortable chunks of time allotted to such mundane concerns as sleep, or perhaps a modicum of a social life. A little time with a wife or husband on some sort of predictable basis wouldn't have come amiss, either.

Not that any of them would ever consider complaining about their charge's schedule. That would have been . . . unwise. Even more to the point, it would have been a quick way to get themselves removed from the citizen secretary's protective detail, and for all its worries and inconvenience, there was fierce competition for that position. Outsiders might have been surprised to discover that, yet it was true. It wasn't so much that StateSec's personnel loved their commander, because in truth he wasn't a particularly lovable person. But they did respect him, and however the rest of the universe might see him, he was normally unfailingly polite to the people who worked for him. Besides, the only State Security assignment which offered greater responsibility or prestige—or chance of promotion—was the Citizen Chairman's personal detail.

Still, protecting the most hated man in the entire People's Republic was scarcely a tension-free vocation. Only a lunatic would think he had even the most remote chance of penetrating Saint-Just's security screen, but historically speaking, lunatics had an unfortunate track record of success. Or of at least taking out the odd bodyguard in the attempt. All of which tended to keep one on one's toes.

It also helped Tsakakis to take his boss's unpredictable and inconvenient work schedule with a certain philosophical acceptance. Yes, it made his life difficult. But it also made it even more difficult for a potential assassin to predict the citizen secretary's movements with any degree of confidence. And if his principal's habit of disordering all of the citizen lieutenant's carefully worked out schedules without warning kept his entire team off balance, it also prevented them from settling into a comfortable, overconfident rut.

Tsakakis reminded himself firmly that staying out of a rut was a good thing, but it was unusually difficult at the moment. He had no idea what could have inspired the citizen secretary to get up four hours early, but it would have been helpful if he'd mentioned the possibility that he might do so before he turned in for the night. If he had, Tsakakis and the normal daytime security commander could have coordinated their schedules properly. As it was, the citizen lieutenant had been forced to screen Citizen Captain Russell—again—to alert her to the fact that Citizen Secretary Saint-Just would not, in fact, be at home where she expected to find him when she and her people reported for duty. The citizen captain was as accustomed as Tsakakis himself to such sudden and unpredictable alterations, but that didn't make her any happier about being awakened at two in the morning so that she could start waking up all of the rest of her people, as well. It hadn't made her any less grumpy, either, and even though she'd known it wasn't Tsakakis' fault, she'd torn a strip off his hide just to relieve her own irritability.

Tsakakis grinned at the memory of Russell's inspired vituperation and pithy comments on his probable ancestry. The citizen captain had been a Marine sergeant before the overthrow of the Harris Government, and her tongue's roughness was renowned throughout State Security. Tsakakis had enjoyed more opportunities to observe her style and vocabulary than most, and some of those opportunities had been less than pleasant, but he'd always recognized that he was in the presence of an artist, and he wished that he'd had his com unit on record to capture this morning's effort for posterity. He wasn't certain, but he didn't believe that she'd repeated herself even once.

They reached the citizen secretary's private office, and Tsakakis wiped the grin off of his face and assumed his on-duty expression as Saint-Just disappeared into his inner sanctum. The citizen lieutenant took a few seconds to inspect the positioning of the rest of his seven-man detail in the public corridor and the outer office assigned to Saint-Just's personal secretary, then opened a discreetly ordinary door and stepped through it. He crossed the floor of the cramped room beyond, seated himself before the surveillance panel, and brought the system online.

As public figures went, Oscar Saint-Just was more willing than most to accommodate the desires of his bodyguards. A lifetime as a security professional in his own right had a tendency to help a man appreciate the difficulties of his security staff's duties. And the fact that no more than a few trillion people would have liked to kill him gave a certain added point to his responsiveness. But there were one or two places where he drew the line, and one of those was his steadfast refusal to permit an armed bodyguard actually in his office. Tsakakis would have been happier if he'd been allowed to stand his post where he could keep the citizen secretary directly under his own eye, but he knew how fortunate he was not to have to put up with the sort of eccentric whims and all too frequent temper tantrums that came out of someone like Citizen Secretary Farley. And at least Saint-Just didn't raise any fuss over electronic surveillance.

Tsakakis unsealed his uniform tunic and hung it over the back of another chair, drew a cup of coffee from the urn in the corner, and settled himself comfortably for another thankfully dull, boring watch.

Major Alina Gricou swore with silent venom. *Damn* the man! They'd known he had a penchant for unpredictable movements, but why in hell had he had to pick *this* night, of all nights, to suffer from workaholic insomnia?

She forced her temper back under control, but it was hard. Her strike team packed the cargo compartment of the unmarked civilian air van claustrophobically, and she found herself longing for a proper assault shuttle's com systems with an almost physically painful intensity. She could feel her people's tension like an extension of her own. Every one of them knew the official plan as well as she did, which meant that all of them also knew that the operation's carefully choreographed timing had gone straight down the crapper.

Gricou didn't know why the execution code had been sent now, with so little warning—there hadn't been time for neat, orderly briefings—but she suspected that she wouldn't have liked the reasons if she had known what they were. All of the ones which occurred to her had to do with things like security breaches, and the thought that their targets' SS

security teams might be waiting for them had not
been a palatable one.

And now this.

She closed her eyes and forced herself to think
things through. If she absolutely had to, she could
use her battle armor's internal com to contact General Conflans, but that had to be a last-ditch option.
She wasn't particularly concerned about the security
of the encrypted transmissions, but StateSec maintained a round-the-clock listening watch, and any
military-band transmissions from unmarked civilian
vans hovering just outside the residential tower which
the commander of State Security called home were
likely to arouse all sorts of suspicions.

All right. If he wasn't here, there was only one
other place he could be. And maybe that was actually a good thing. Gricou had never truly been happy
about going after Saint-Just at home. Killing civilians
in job lots was what StateSec did, not what she did,
but she'd known going in that collateral civilian
casualties would be unavoidable if she and her strike
team met any organized resistance in a residential
tower. But if he'd gone into the office early, there
wouldn't be any civilians around. Or not any innocent ones, at any rate. Of course, the downside was
that StateSec HQ was scarcely what someone might
call a soft target. But at three in the morning, the
on-site security people's guard was bound to be down
at least a little, and she had what was supposed to
be the complete, current blueprint of the tower in
her armor's computers. Best of all, no one would
expect for a moment that anyone could be insane
enough to go after the ogre in his own lair.

Getting *in* shouldn't be a problem, she concluded.
Getting out again might be another matter, but if they

succeeded in taking Saint-Just alive, they'd have an extremely persuasive spokesman to get them past the defenses. And if they didn't succeed in taking him alive—or at least in killing him—then they and all the members of their families were extremely unlikely to survive the scorched earth purges which were certain to follow. Nausea churned at the thought, but she didn't have time for that. The operation had been planned to send her team in after Saint-Just and Captain Wicklow's in after Rob Pierre, simultaneously and before anyone else moved, in order to get them in before any general alarm could be raised, and Wicklow had no way to know that Saint-Just had picked this morning to be elsewhere. Which meant she had to make her decision quickly.

She turned to the pilot.

"Turn us around, Pete. It looks like we're going calling on the Citizen Secretary at his office, after all." She bared her teeth in a predatory grin. "I hope he won't be too upset that we didn't call ahead for an appointment."

Mikis Tsakakis yawned and stretched, then grimaced and reached for his coffee cup once more. Few things were more boring than watching someone else sit at a desk and do paperwork. But boring was good. Any bodyguard would unhesitatingly agree with that sentiment, he reflected, then snorted in mild amusement at his own thoughts and took a sip of coffee.

He glanced at a side display that monitored traffic around the tower. What happened outside was neither his concern nor his responsibility, but at this motherless hour any distraction was welcome.

Not that there was very much to see. StateSec's critical departments worked around the clock, of course, but the population of the tower was less than half as large for the night shift, and the air car parking garages were correspondingly sparsely occupied. He skimmed idly through the various levels, and grimaced again. There was no real difference in the light levels within the vast internal caverns, yet somehow they seemed dimmer and more deserted at such an early hour.

He watched a civilian air van ease in through one of the automated security portals and quirked an eyebrow. The van was unmarked, but then, a lot of SS vehicles were unmarked, and he wondered what covert operation this one was assigned to.

Alina Gricou very carefully did not sigh in relief as the security systems accepted the admittance code. General Conflans had assured her that they'd managed to get their hands on valid perimeter security codes, and she trusted the general with her life, or she wouldn't have been here in the first place. But she was also a veteran who had learned the First Law of Combat decades ago: Shit Happens. She made it a point to assume that any intelligence briefing would be full of crap, because that way any surprises would be pleasant ones.

Unfortunately, she'd had very few surprises in that particular regard.

This time looked like an exception, however, and she watched the schematic in her visor HUD as her pilot worked his carefully casual way towards the proper parking stall.

The sound of explosions woke him.

He didn't realize at once that they *were* explosions. He hadn't slept well in years, but he'd managed to sleep far more deeply tonight than usual, and at first, he thought it was simply a distant thunderstorm. But as he roused from sound sleep to groggy wakefulness he realized that it couldn't be thunder. The Chairman's Suite lay at the very heart of the People's Tower, and it was far too well soundproofed for mere thunder to disturb its occupant.

He roused further and sat up quickly in bed, and his pulse quickened as more explosions sounded. They were coming closer, and he rolled out of bed and fumbled his bare feet into a pair of shoes even as his hand darted under the pillow and came out with a heavy, military-issue pulser.

The door to his bedroom flew open, and he spun in a half-crouch, pulser rising. The man in the sudden opening flung his arms up, and Rob Pierre just barely managed not to squeeze the firing stud as he recognized one of his bodyguards.

"We've got to get you out of here, Sir!" the StateSec sergeant exclaimed.

"What's going on?" Pierre demanded. "Where's Citizen Lieutenant Adamson?"

"Sir, I don't *know*." The bodyguard's voice was tight with tension, and the words slurred as they tripped over one another with the clumsiness of panic restrained only by the iron rigor of training. "They're coming at us from the roof and from below, and they've got heavier weapons than we do. *Please*, Sir! There's no time for questions—you've *got* to go now, or—"

Pierre was already hurrying towards the door. The fact that the citizen sergeant didn't even know where Adamson, the commander of his personal security detail for over two T-years, was said terrifying things about what must be happening outside his bedroom.

But the man who had made himself master of the People's Republic of Haven was not the sort to stand paralyzed, like an Old Earth rabbit caught in a ground car's headlights, in an emergency. The StateSec sergeant's shoulders relaxed ever so slightly as the man he was responsible for protecting with his own life began to move, and he turned and stepped back out into the hallway first.

Pierre was almost surprised by the power of his own fear as the entire tower seemed to quiver to the fury of explosions and approaching combat. He'd thought that after so many death warrants, so much blood, he and Death were old friends. But they weren't, and he was astounded to discover that despite all his weariness and all the times he had wished there were some way—anyway—to dismount from the tiger of the People's Republic, he wanted desperately to live.

A haze of smoke and dust hung in the luxuriously carpeted passageway, and he could hear the wailing warble of fire alarms as temperature sensors responded to the inferno ripping its way towards his suite. The citizen sergeant had been joined by three other StateSec troopers. One had a light tribarrel, but the other three carried only pulse rifles, and, aside from the citizen sergeant, not one of them was from his regular detail. But the obviously scratch-built team seemed to know exactly what they were doing, and with the citizen sergeant directly behind them, they formed a flying wedge, moving down the corridor at a half-run. Pierre knew they were headed for the emergency dropshaft hidden in his private conference room, and he spared a moment to pray that whoever was behind this attack didn't know about the shaft or where it emerged.

And then, suddenly, it didn't matter whether they knew or not. Pierre felt the overpressure on his back as another explosion, louder than any of the others, roared behind him. The citizen sergeant spun around to face him, right hand bringing up his pulser while his left reached out, grabbed the Citizen Chairman by the collar of his pajamas and literally flung him further up the passage. Pierre's feet left the floor, and he sailed forward like some ungainly bird, until one of the pulse rifle-armed StateSec men caught him and slammed him to the floor.

Citizen Chairman Rob Pierre felt the StateSec trooper's weight come down on him. Knew the bodyguard was protecting him with his own body. Saw the citizen sergeant go down on one knee, raising his pulser in the two-handed grip of a man on a pistol range. Heard the tribarrel wine and hiss as a chainsaw of darts sizzled back up the passage. The citizen sergeant was firing now, full auto, filling the air with death, and none of it mattered at all. The figures striding through the smoke and newborn flame where the explosive charge had breached the corridor wall loomed up out of the inferno like ungainly trolls, swollen and misshapen in the soot-black of battle armor. The hurricane of pulser darts sparkled and flashed with spiteful beauty as they ricocheted from that armor, but not even the tribarrel was heavy enough to penetrate it. The ricochets were a lethal cloud, rebounding from the armored figures to lacerate what was left of the corridor walls, and Pierre knew that every one of his bodyguards must realize that they had no chance at all against Marine battle armor.

Yet all four of them stood their ground, pouring their futile fire back down the passageway, and then one of the armored attackers raised a grenade launcher. The launcher steadied, and the last thing Citizen Chairman Rob Pierre ever saw was the way the StateSec citizen sergeant flew backwards as the grenade impacted directly on his chest before it detonated.

The shrill sound of the alarm took Tsakakis completely by surprise.

For a moment, he didn't even recognize which one it was, but then he saw the flashing light on his com panel, and his heart seemed to stop. Sheer disbelief held him paralyzed for perhaps two breaths, and then the heel of his hand slammed down on the outside line's acceptance button.

"They're coming right over us! We never saw them on the way in, and—"

Explosions and the sound of weapons fire formed a hideous backdrop for the desperate voice, and then a final, louder explosion chopped it off with dreadful finality, and Mikis Tsakakis went white. He hadn't recognized the frantic voice, but he was certain he'd known the speaker. He knew *every* member of the Citizen Chairman's personal security detail.

His brain seemed to be frozen by the sheer impossibility of what must have happened. Thought was momentarily beyond him, but training substituted for it. His left hand hit his own alarm key as if it belonged to someone else, and his right hand had already drawn his pulser before he was even fully out of his chair.

The strident howl of the alarms was almost enough to drown out the thunderous roar of chemical explosives as the passengers from the unmarked civilian van triggered their breaching charges.

❖   ❖   ❖

Major Gricou led the way through the shattered security door. Properly, she knew, she should have let Sergeant Jackson take point, but that was a lesson she'd always had just a little bit of difficulty learning. Besides, in this situation out in front was where she needed to be, so Jackson could just keep himself busy watching her back.

The sudden clangor of alarms had taken her by surprise, but only for a moment, and she congratulated herself on her timing. She knew what had to have alerted whoever had sounded them. It couldn't have been the detection of her own team, because not even StateSec was stupid enough to warn a hostile assault force by setting off alarms all over the frigging building before their response teams were in position to strike. Which meant something else must have caused it, and she knew what that something else had to be. But although the news that someone had attacked Pierre was bound to throw SS HQ into a tizzy and send their security personnel to a higher state of alert, there wouldn't be enough time for it to do them any good. In fact, the confusion which rumor and counter-rumor must inevitably engender would actually help her.

She couldn't expect that confusion to last for long. Whatever she might think of StateSec's morals, its personnel were too well trained for that. But for at least the next few minutes, all the training in the world wouldn't be enough to offset the sheer stunning surprise of the discovery that a coup attempt was underway. And while the surprise lasted . . .

She stepped through the breach, turned to her left, and sent a screaming pattern of death howling down the corridor from her flechette gun. The SS file clerk who'd stood gawking at the night-black troll emerging from the cloud of dust and rubble didn't even have time to scream.

Tsakakis' team members reacted almost as quickly as he had. They were already opening the special wall lockers for the heavy weapons stored in them and assembling in the secretary's outer office by the time he made it out of the surveillance room. But just like him, their reaction was one of trained reflex and guard dog instinct which scarcely consulted their forebrains at all. They had no idea at all what was happening.

"Someone just attacked Citizen Chairman Pierre!" he barked, and saw his own shock in their expressions. "I don't know what's happening at that end," he went on tersely, "but it didn't sound good. And if this is some kind of coup attempt, the Citizen Secretary has to be on the same list, so—"

The office door flew open, and half a dozen weapons swung towards it. The uniformed citizen sergeant who'd opened it flung out his hands to show they were empty just in time, but he scarcely seemed to notice that he had just come within a few grams of trigger pressure of dying.

"They're coming up from the garage!" he gasped. "Don't know how many. They blew their way in. At least a dozen of them—in battle armor! Not more than one level away!"

The door to Saint-Just's inner office opened, and the citizen secretary stood in the opening, a long-barreled military style pulser in his right hand, but Tsakakis barely glanced at him.

"John! You and Hannah are right here on the Citizen Secretary. Al, you, Steve, and Mariano take the lift shafts. I want Isabela and Janos on the emergency stairs. *Nobody* gets through without my personal authorization—is that clear?"

Heads nodded, and taut-faced bodyguards dashed for their assigned positions.

"What about me, Sir?" the citizen sergeant demanded.

"If they're in battle armor, you need a bigger gun, Sarge," Tsakakis told him with a grim smile, and reached back into the locker for a plasma carbine. "You checked out on this thing?"

"Not in the last nine or ten months, Sir. But I guess it'll come back to me in a hurry, won't it?"

"It better, Sarge. It damned well better."

Gricou forged ahead down the hallway. Somehow, Jackson had managed to get in front of her anyway, and her armor audio pickups brought her the whining thunder of the sergeant's flechette gun as he spun to fire a short, professional burst down a cross corridor.

A thin haze of smoke eddied down the hall, and she heard the sound of small arms fire from behind, as well. So far there was nothing dangerous behind her, but she didn't begin to have enough people to hold open a line of retreat to the parking garage, so she wasn't trying to. Her rearguard's job was just to keep the lightly armed regular security types off her back until she got her hands on Saint-Just. Once they had him, they'd have the only door key they needed. But if they didn't get him . . .

She checked her HUD schematic again, and grunted in satisfaction. Less than three minutes since they'd detonated the breaching charges, and they were only one floor below their objective.

Ahead of her, Jackson charged the lift doors. A

stream of pulser darts cascaded off his battle armor, but he turned straight into them and triggered his flechette gun. Someone shrieked in agony, and the pulser fire chopped off abruptly. The sergeant started to punch the lift button, but Gricou's sharply barked command stopped him.

"We're taking the direct route!" she told him, and beckoned for Corporal Taylor and her demolition charges.

Tsakakis checked the charge on his plasma rifle again, and then scrubbed sweat from his forehead. Was he making the right call? Or was his decision to fort up the worst one he could have made? It had been automatic, made without any true consideration at the conscious level, but that didn't necessarily make it wrong.

One set of instincts screamed at him to get the citizen secretary the hell out of here. No one seemed to have a clue about what was truly happening, and the earbug of his personal com brought him only confusion and panic while State Security's duty personnel tried frantically to somehow bring order out of chaos. The only things he knew for certain were that someone had attacked the head of state and that other attackers were actually here, inside the building. That should have made putting distance between them and his charge his number one priority. But he didn't know where *else* there might be attackers, and he did know that there was nowhere else on the planet where there were more StateSec reinforcements than right here in this building. All he had to do was keep Oscar Saint-Just alive until those reinforcements could arrive.

❖   ❖   ❖

Corporal Taylor's charges exploded, and the ceiling of the corridor disappeared. Flame and debris erupted out of the sudden breach, and one of Tsakakis' team members became a mangled corpse. But two others were waiting, and Sergeant Amos Jackson died instantly as two plasma bolts slammed into his armor almost simultaneously.

Alina Gricou swore harshly as what was left of the sergeant fell back through the hole. Pulser darts and flechettes were no threat to battle armor; plasma rifles certainly were, and what the *hell* were they doing here?

Fresh alarms wailed as the thermal bloom of the plasma which had killed Jackson started fires, both here and on the floor above, but that was the least of her worries. It would take more than a fire to inconvenience someone in battle armor, but if there were plasma rifles waiting up there, then things were about to turn really ugly.

"Taylor, Bensen, Yuan! Grenades—*now!*"

Tsakakis recognized the sound of exploding grenades, and his jaw clenched. They were coming from the lift shafts. He'd been afraid of that, and a sharp spasm of grief twisted him. StateSec's institutional paranoia over its commander's security meant his people were probably more heavily armed than their attackers had anticipated, but aside from the limited protection from the anti-ballistic fabric of their tunics, they were completely unarmored.

More grenades exploded, and he heard someone screaming endlessly, terribly over the team's dedicated channel.

"John! Take Hannah and get out there and back up Al!"

Citizen Corporal John Stillman nodded curtly and jerked his head at Citizen Private Flanders, and the two of them headed out into the smoke.

"Now!" Gricou barked, and another pair of Marines vaulted up to the next floor. Even in a planetary gravity, their armor's exoskeletons made it a trivial feat. What was *not* trivial were the acquired gymnastic skills which made it possible for them to twist like bipedal cats in midair to bring their weapons to bear. Their flechette guns whined and thundered, belching death, but it took precious instants for their armor sensors to find a target. They tried to compensate by laying down suppressing fire, but the sole surviving bodyguard covering the waiting area around the lift shaft wasn't where they'd expected him to be. Their flechettes blew corridor walls into fragments and dust, and one of them saw him and swung his weapon towards him in the same instant that he pressed the firing stud.

The Marine died a fragment of a second before him . . . but only because plasma bolts traveled at near light-speed and flechettes didn't.

John Stillman and Hannah Flanders raced past the uniformed citizen sergeant and flung themselves to their bellies with their plasma rifles trained down the hallway. Neither of them liked lying in the middle of the corridor that way, but without battle armor, they had to respect the danger zone of their own weapons. The thermal bloom from a plasma rifle was vicious, which meant neither dared to get in front of the other, and that they couldn't get too close in against the walls. It also explained why having a citizen sergeant they didn't know and had never trained with behind them was one more worry. The last thing they needed was to have him start blasting away over them with his plasma carbine!

But then the citizen sergeant suddenly became a very minor concern. Stillman just glimpsed the vague loom of a figure through the wavefront of smoke rolling down the passage towards him, and raised his heavy weapon. Unfortunately, he was dependent upon the unaided human eye, while the Marine headed towards him had the full capabilities of her armor's sensors. She "saw" him—and Flanders—before he'd even realized she was there, and the blast of flechettes tore both of them apart.

The Marine shouted in triumph and headed down the corridor, but even her sensors couldn't see through solid walls, and the StateSec citizen sergeant who suddenly rolled out of a side passage ahead of her with his plasma carbine ready came as a complete surprise.

"Get up here, Isabela and Janos!" Tsakakis barked into his com. "They're coming up the lifts, not the stairs!"

He heard the sergeant whose name he didn't even know open fire out in the corridor, and his instincts screamed at him to get out there and help him. But cold intellect kept him where he was even as the last two members of his team obeyed his command. He loathed himself for it, but he did it.

Alina Gricou followed Corporal Taylor down the hall, and she felt Death's hot breath on the nape of her neck. It was taking too long. They had to get to Saint-Just's office before his bodyguards had time to regroup and realize they had to get him out of here, and these unarmored maniacs and their plasma guns were screwing her mission profile all to hell. They didn't have a chance against battle-armored Marines, but they didn't seem to care. Why in the name of God were they so willing to die to protect a butcher like Oscar Saint-Just?

Another StateSec noncom loomed up in the smoke and dust. Even through the crackle flames and the background noise of the grenade explosions and pulser fire from her two remaining rearguards, she could hear the unarmored man coughing and wheezing, but that didn't make his plasma carbine any less deadly. Taylor went down as the lethal bolt seared its way through her armor, and Gricou screamed a curse as she dropped to one knee and her flechette gun ripped the corporal's killer apart.

Private Krueger charged past her, and she hurled herself back to her feet to follow him. She and Krueger were all that was left now, aside from the two men fighting frantically to cover their rear, but they were less than thirty meters from Saint-Just's office. Krueger was as aware of the need for haste as she was, and he'd opened the distance between them while she was still rising from her firing crouch. He was almost at the door to Saint-Just's outer office—a door that gaped ominously open—when the plasma bolt came screaming down the corridor and cut him in half.

Gricou didn't waste the energy to curse this time. She only returned fire, hosing the passage with flechettes. Someone went down ahead of her, then someone else, and she charged forward, praying that neither of the bodies had been Saint-Just. The chance of getting out of this alive had become miniscule whatever happened, but if she'd killed *him* there was no chance at all. Yet somehow the near certainty of her own death had become secondary, almost—not quite, but *almost*—unimportant, as long as she could know that Oscar Saint-Just was already dead. And if he wasn't, then she had to catch up with them before the bodyguards ahead of her could get him to safety.

Mikis Tsakakis knew he would never forgive himself, but it had worked. The last two members of his team, people he had worked and trained with for over three T-years, were dead, and he'd used them as *bait*. He had *deliberately* recalled them, knowing they would run directly into the attackers, and they'd done just that.

And just as he'd hoped, the attackers had assumed that the two of them must be the rearguard of the security detail trying to get the Citizen Secretary to safety. It was the only answer that made sense, because surely no unarmored bodyguard would have been so stupid as to charge to meet someone in battle armor, no matter *what* they were armed with. Coupled with the open office door and the total lack of fire from it, all the attackers could conclude was that they were too late. That the Citizen Secretary was already gone . . . and that their only chance for success was to overtake him before he got away.

The citizen lieutenant made himself wait two seconds longer, and then he stepped out into the corridor.

There was only one of them left, a corner of his brain noted with near-clinical detachment, and from the sounds of combat coming from behind him, whoever they'd left to cover their rear was in serious trouble as the StateSec reserves converged upon them. Which made the battle armored figure moving rapidly away from him the only real remaining threat.

He brought the plasma rifle up into firing position, and everything seemed to be moving in slow motion. He had time to realize that for some reason he didn't even hate the person he was about to kill. He ought to, but he didn't. Perhaps it was because at that moment he hated *himself* too much to spare any hatred for another.

But whatever the reason was, it didn't matter.

Alina Gricou had one instant to realize she'd been fooled.

Her sensors detected the lone figure behind her the instant it stepped out into the corridor, but that wasn't soon enough. She was still trying frantically to turn when the plasma bolt struck her squarely in the small of the back.

Esther McQueen looked up from the tactical holo display in front of her as a Marine captain and two corporals ushered two more "guests" into the Octagon Work Room. The cavernous chamber, with its huge holo displays, plots, and communications consoles, made a perfect CP for her, although she rather suspected that her lords and masters on the Committee of Public Safety couldn't be too pleased at the use to which she was currently putting it. Citizen secretaries Avram Turner and Wanda Farley certainly weren't, at any rate—not to judge by their half-murderous, half-terrified expressions. They made as mismatched a pair as ever, and the furious, frightened glares they turned upon her indicated that they were anything but glad to see her, but McQueen was delighted to see *them*. At least that part of her plans had gone off as scheduled. Aside from Oscar Saint-Just and Pierre himself, her commando teams had made a clean sweep of the entire Committee. She had all of its members, now, and she allowed herself to feel a faint glow of hope that she might just pull this off after all.

Might.

If only they'd managed to take Saint-Just out cleanly! Or at least to take Pierre alive. Esther McQueen had never understood the underlying dynamic which allowed a man like Saint-Just to feel personal friendship for anyone, yet she'd seen ample proof of the StateSec commander's personal devotion to Rob Pierre. If she'd had Pierre in her hands, Saint-Just would have dealt. She *knew* he would have. But the Citizen Chairman's bodyguards had put up too good a fight, and her people had been too rushed for time to avoid collateral damage. The Chairman's Guard whose members mounted the normal sentries outside the People's Tower were much too lightly armed to seriously threaten battle armored Marine Raiders, but the heavy StateSec intervention battalions were another matter entirely. That was why her planning had stressed the imperative need for speed, not numbers— for forces small and agile enough to get in and out again before the intervention battalions could arrive— from the outset. And that, in turn, was how Rob Pierre had wound up caught in the crossfire.

McQueen regretted that as she had regretted very few things in her life. Not because of any great love for the Citizen Chairman, and certainly not because she'd intended to spare him indefinitely. If one thing in the universe had been certain, it was that she would have had no choice but to stand him up against a convenient wall eventually, and probably sooner rather than later. Which was a pity, in many ways, because for all of his failings, Pierre truly had managed to turn the corner on the fundamental structural reforms the People's Republic's economy had needed so desperately. But he would simply have been too dangerous to be allowed to live, and having profited from that sort of mistaken judgment on the part of the Committee's master, Esther McQueen would not make the error of extending it to anyone else.

Saint-Just would undoubtedly have realized that, but McQueen felt certain that he would have at least paused to negotiate if she'd managed to sweep up Pierre in her net. Not that anyone would ever know if she'd been right.

"Have we heard anything from Admiral Graveson?" she asked.

"No, Ma'am," Lieutenant Caminetti replied. The young man looked remarkably calm, under the circumstances, but she could see the fear for his brother in his eyes. "She hasn't responded at all."

"She may not even have gotten the heads-up signal, Ma'am," Ivan Bukato pointed out. "We never had an opportunity to test that com link."

"I know. I know," she agreed unhappily. *And if Amanda didn't get the word ahead of time, she almost certainly didn't have time to warn anyone else before the shit hit the fan.* Damn *Saint-Just and his purges! All I needed was one more week, and Amanda would have known ahead of time.*

"If Graveson didn't get the word, then we can't count on Capital Fleet at all," she said aloud. "It's almost certain that Saint-Just got the word to his SS units before anyone else in the Fleet realized what was happening. And if they're just sitting there, cleared for action and ready to shoot, nobody could possibly come out on our side without being blown out of space before they even got their sidewalls up."

"But at least they don't seem to be coming in on Saint-Just's side, either," one of her other staffers pointed out.

"Of course not!" McQueen snorted. "You think anyone in StateSec is going to be crazy enough to let regular Navy units clear for action at a time like this? If they ever did manage to get their wedges and walls up, it's a better than even bet that whoever they wound up shooting at, it wouldn't be *us*!"

"Agreed." Bukato nodded, but his face was tight with worry. "But it may not matter what the Fleet does. I don't like the reports coming in from the western part of the city, Ma'am."

"They're not too good," McQueen agreed, "but they're actually better than I was afraid they might be." She turned back to Caminetti. "What do we hear from General Conflans?"

"His last report was that all three battalions from the spaceport have come over, Ma'am," the lieutenant replied quickly. "One of them is on its way here to reinforce the Octagon perimeter. The general is personally leading the other two to support Brigadier Henderson."

"We just got word from Colonel Yazov, Admiral McQueen!"

McQueen turned towards the commander who had just entered the conference room, and despite the thick haze of tension hovering about her, she felt an undeniable urge to smile in satisfaction. One way or the other, no one in this room would ever use that stupid, sycophantic "Citizen" crap again, and it felt unspeakably good to put on the persona of an *admiral* once more instead of wearing the ill-fitting, quasi-civilian mask of secretary of war.

"The Colonel estimates that at least a third of the

atmospheric defense units are coming over to our side," the commander went on. "He says he thinks we can swing still more of them if we keep hammering away at our message. For now, he feels confident that he can at least keep any of the satellite bases from getting organized strike elements into the capital's airspace."

"And the units already in capital airspace that *haven't* come over?" Bukato asked with poison dryness.

"Those the defensive grid will just have to handle," McQueen told him. "And at least the bastards haven't started lobbing nukes at us yet."

"Yet," Bukato agreed. "But do you really think Saint-Just won't use them if he figures the situation is going south on him?"

"If he could get them through to the Octagon without major collateral damage, yes," McQueen said. "I think he'd use them in a heartbeat under those circumstances. But as long as the grid is up, he's not going to get through it with anything short of a saturation strike, and that would rip hell out of the entire city. After what happened last time, I don't think he'll dare take that chance. Our isolated neighborhood, yes; *that* he'd nuke. But not the city in general. After all, it won't do him any good to kill all of us if the way he does it outrages the rest of the Fleet so badly that they'll turn on him regardless of what his SS goons do. And it would, you know, Ivan."

Bukato grunted. The sound could have indicated disagreement, but it didn't. No one could be absolutely certain how the People's Navy would respond to yet another, even more massive use of nuclear weapons in Nouveau Paris, but the admiral was almost positive that McQueen was correct. Too many millions of civilians had already been killed, and with all of the Committee except Saint-Just in McQueen's hands, *someone* in the Fleet was virtually certain to take his chances on survival if he could only get a clean shot at the StateSec commander if Saint-Just was stupid enough to destroy another huge chunk of the capital.

"All right," McQueen said crisply. "So far, except for Capital Fleet and the fact that we didn't get Pierre or Saint-Just in our initial strikes, things seem to be going pretty much to plan. Ivan, I want you and Commodore Tillotson to stay in close communication with Conflans and Yazov. Captain Rubin, you're in charge of the Octagon defense grid. If they don't have our transponder codes, then they don't cross the threshold into our airspace, understood?"

"Understood, Ma'am," Rubin replied grimly.

"Major Adams, you're in charge of coordinating our garrison units with the grid. Stay close to Captain Rubin and see to it that your man-portable air defense units are put in the best places to back up the grid."

"Aye, Ma'am!" the Marine major barked.

"Ivan," McQueen turned back to Bukato, "where did we stick Fontein?"

"We've got him under guard in your office, Ma'am."

"My, how appropriate," McQueen murmured, and even here, even now, one or two people surprised themselves by laughing aloud at her wicked smile. She grinned back at them, then gave her head a little toss. "I think we can safely say that friend Erasmus is a realist and a practical man," she told Bukato. "He really does support the Revolution, but once he knows Pierre is gone, I suspect that we can swing him over to our side if we can convince him that Saint-Just is going down, too. Or at least into *pretending* that he's come over to our side, which would be almost as good in the short term. If I can talk him into endorsing our broadcasts, we should be able to split StateSec between him and Saint-Just. At least, it would certainly hamper Saint-Just's ability to deploy his damned intervention battalions!"

"I can't fault that, Ma'am," Bukato said, "but I'm afraid he may be just a bit harder to turn than that."

"You may be right," she replied much more grimly. "On the other hand, if I screw the muzzle of a pulser far enough into his ear, I think I can convince him to follow me anywhere."

She smiled at her followers again, and this time there was no humor at all in her expression.

Oscar Saint-Just's habitually expressionless face was carved granite as he sat in the office just off his emergency HQ and listened to the latest reports.

"Sir, the troops are getting worried!" a citizen brigadier half-blurted as he burst into the Citizen Secretary's office. "They're hearing rumors that the Citizen Chairman is—well—"

Saint-Just turned his head, and the panicky report slithered to a sudden stop as the citizen brigadier quailed before those icy, basilisk eyes. The officer swallowed hard, and Saint-Just let him sweat for perhaps fifteen seconds while he held him pinned under his pitiless gaze. Then he spoke, very coldly and precisely.

"The troops will do what they're told to do, Citizen Brigadier. As will their officers. *All* of their officers. We are now operating under Case Horatius. You will so inform all unit commanders, and you will also inform them that any measures of summary justice they may feel are necessary are approved in advance. *Is that clear?*"

"Y-Yes, Sir," the citizen brigadier said quickly. He turned on his heel and hurried out of the office even more rapidly than he had entered it, and Saint-Just permitted himself a faint, bleak, death's head grin. The citizen brigadier was an idiot if he hadn't already figured out that Case Horatius was in effect. Although, in fairness, it might be shock rather than stupidity, for Esther McQueen had managed to take them all by surprise . . . again.

Saint-Just closed out the background chatter of combat reports and frantic requests for orders and rubbed his eyes with the heels of his hands. What in God's name had kicked the woman off *now*? Surely she had to have realized Rob wasn't about to have her shot before he knew that the Manties and their allies really were on the ropes! Was it simply that she'd hoped to achieve surprise? If so, she'd succeeded, but for all the ferocious efficiency with which the first stage of her coup had been executed, it was obvious to Saint-Just that the follow-up stages were far less solid.

Not that they have *to be all that solid*, he admitted grimly to himself. *The bitch got Rob.* A fresh pain of purely personal anguish stabbed at him, and he suppressed it sternly. There was no time for that. Not now. *And she's got all the rest of the Committee in the Octagon with her. If she can get them to sign off on her actions, then—*

A buzzer sounded the distinctive signal which informed him that the communication staff manning the secret, hidden command center which Tsakakis and Citizen Captain Russell had hustled him off to had just picked up a transmission they felt had sufficient priority to interrupt whatever else he might be doing. He grimaced at the thought of fresh tidings of still more disaster, but he also lowered his hands and reached out to stab one of the keys on his communications panel. The combat chatter vanished instantly, and his mouth tightened as Esther McQueen's voice replaced it.

"To all loyal members of the People's military! This is Citizen Secretary of War McQueen. The Revolution has been betrayed! I have received positive confirmation that Citizen Chairman Pierre has been *murdered*—murdered by his own State Security 'bodyguards' at the direct orders of Oscar Saint-Just! The reports available to me are still unclear as to what could have prompted the Secretary for State Security to commit this heinous crime, but the simultaneous attempt to take myself and all other members of the Committee into custody clearly indicates the existence of a far-reaching and dangerous organization of traitors within State Security. I call upon all loyal members of StateSec to remember that your oaths of loyalty are to the Revolution, the Committee, and to the Citizen Chairman, and *not* to the personal ambition of a man who has betrayed all of them! I call upon you to resist his illegal orders and his treasonous attempt to seize complete, personal power from the legitimately designated organs of government. Refuse to assist him in this despicable act of treachery and betrayal!

"To the regular branches of the People's military, I say this. State Security is not your enemy! Only those individuals within it who choose to serve the purposes of a would-be tyrant and dictator are your foes! As you have so valiantly defended the People and the Revolution against outside enemies, so now

you must defend them against *internal* enemies—
enemies who are far more deadly than the
Manticorans and their puppets because they strike
from the shadows like assassins. I call upon you to
honor your oath to the service of the People and the
Committee of Public Safety!

"This is not a struggle in which ships of the wall
have a place. Whatever Oscar Saint-Just may choose
to do, we of the legitimate Committee of Public Safety
refuse to turn Nouveau Paris into a wasteland of
wreckage and bodies. We hold the Octagon, and we
will defend it by whatever means are necessary, but
we neither request nor will we tolerate nuclear or
kinetic strikes within the area of the Capital! Should
you be ordered by Saint-Just or his minions to carry
out such strikes, you are instructed to refuse those
orders, no matter what threats may accompany them.

"What the Committee most urgently requires at this
time are additional loyal ground and atmospheric combat troops. I need not tell any of you how powerful
the State Security intervention forces in and around
Nouveau Paris are. I hope and believe that many of
the personnel of those intervention battalions will
remember their oaths to the Committee and refuse
to participate in this naked effort to suppress and
destroy all that Citizen Chairman Pierre fought so
long and so hard to accomplish. But it must be
anticipated that many others in those battalions will
accept the illegal orders of those officers who have
allied themselves with the traitor Saint-Just. The
defenses of the Octagon are strong, but we cannot
resist a mass attack out of our own resources for an
extended period. It is essential to the survival of the
Committee that loyal forces relieve the Octagon and
escort the civilian members of the Committee to

safety. I therefore call upon all Marine and Planetary Defense officers and charge you, as Secretary of War and in the name of the legitimate members of the Committee of Public Safety, to move at once to the relief of the Octagon and the suppression of any and all forces loyal to the traitor Oscar Saint-Just! In this moment of—"

Saint-Just stabbed the communications button again, and this time his expression was a vicious snarl as McQueen's voice died.

She was good, he admitted. Every word vibrated with sincerity, passion, and outrage. He wouldn't be at all surprised if even some of his own StateSec people believed her, and he had no doubt at all that a large majority of the regular military would *want* to believe her. How could they want anything else, when she was the one who had led them to victory and *he* was the one who had ordered countless of their fellows and their fellows' families executed? And with Rob dead, they could believe her if they so chose. However senior to her his membership on the Committee might be, both of them were simply "citizen secretaries." She had as great a claim to legitimacy as he did . . . at least for anyone looking from the outside into the chaos and confusion which she had sown across Nouveau Paris. Worse, she did indeed have every surviving member of the Committee in the Octagon with her, and he and Rob had spent years stamping out any hint of defiance among the Committee's membership. Now McQueen had physical control of all those sheep, and Saint-Just had no doubt at all that she could . . . *convince* at least the majority of them into signing off on her version of what had happened. As for any of them who declined, he was sure it would turn out that they had been tragically murdered by traitorous StateSec units before McQueen could rescue them from his murderous minions.

And that bit about forbidding any nuclear or kinetic strikes on the capital—*that* was downright brilliant! It snatched the moral high ground right out from under his feet, and at the same time it posed a threat which was almost certain to hold his own SS-crewed warships at bay. Citizen Commodore Helft had already destroyed two superdreadnoughts which had looked like moving to support McQueen, and at the moment, the rest of Capital Fleet's ships were under the guns of Helft's battle squadron. He could undoubtedly destroy dozens of them before they could bring up their sidewalls, but there were too many of them for him to count on getting all of them before the survivors got *him*. And thanks to McQueen's orders, it was virtually certain that at least some of them would try to stop him from bombarding the capital, even at the risk of their own near-certain destruction. And once he started killing them in large numbers, their consorts would almost certainly react, for how could they know where Helft would stop if *they* didn't stop *him*.

Someone else knocked on the frame of his open office door, and he looked up to see a citizen colonel whose name he could not recall.

"Yes?"

"Sir, we just got another report from Citizen General Bouchard." The citizen colonel paused, and cleared his throat. "Sir, the Citizen General says that his attack has been stopped. I'm . . . afraid they took heavy casualties, Sir."

"How heavy?" Saint-Just's expressionless tone never wavered, and the citizen colonel cleared his throat again.

"Very heavy, I understand, Sir. Citizen General Bouchard reports that both of his lead battalions are falling back in disorder." The citizen colonel inhaled deeply, and straightened his back. "Sir, it sounds to me like what he really means is that they're running like hell."

"I see." Saint-Just regarded the citizen colonel with a sharper edge of interest. "What actions would you recommend, Citizen Colonel?" he asked after a moment, and the officer met his eyes squarely.

"I don't have any firsthand information, Sir." The citizen colonel spoke with much less hesitation, as if what he'd already said had broken some inner reserve. "From the reports I've seen here, though, I don't think Citizen General Bouchard is going to get through on the ground. They've got too much manpower and fire-power, and, frankly, Sir, they're much better trained for this sort of standup, toe-to-toe fight than we are."

"I see," Saint-Just repeated in a somewhat colder tone. "Nonetheless, Citizen Colonel," he went on, "and notwithstanding the inferiority of our own troops, this mutiny must be suppressed. Don't you agree?"

"Of course I do, Sir! All I'm saying is that if we keep hammering straight down the same approaches into their teeth, we're going to take insupportable casualties and fail to achieve our objective, anyway. At the same time, Sir, it looks to me as if they can't have much of a central reserve within the Octagon itself—not of ground troops, anyway. They've got more forces moving towards them from half a dozen Marine and Navy commands, but their reinforcements aren't there yet. I believe that the organized units we retain on the ground in the vicinity would be better occupied throwing a cordon around the Octagon to keep additional mutinous units from reaching it.

While they do that, we should move Citizen Brigadier Tome's brigade up to support Citizen General Bouchard while we bring in reinforcements from outside the capital. If we have to, we can put in a frontal assault once we have the manpower to carry through with it despite our losses. In the meantime, Sir, I would recommend that we keep as much pressure on them with air attacks as we can, but without committing ourselves to a serious attack and the losses it would inevitably entail."

Saint-Just regarded the other man thoughtfully. No doubt there was a great deal of military logic to what the citizen colonel had just said. Unfortunately, this was as much a political confrontation as a military one, and every hour that McQueen continued to pour her appeals into the listening ears of the regular military units in the Haven System moved the political balance further in her favor.

"I appreciate your candor, Citizen Colonel . . . Jurgens," he said, squinting a bit as he read the name off of Jurgens' name patch. "And if Bouchard's people are falling back anyway, then no doubt ordering them to assume a defensive stance, at least temporarily, makes sense. But there are other factors to consider here, as well."

The citizen secretary rubbed his forehead—the equivalent in him of another man's raging tantrum—then shrugged.

"Please pass my instructions to Citizen General Bouchard to hold his positions and use his reserves to seal the approaches to the Octagon while he reorganizes," he went on after a moment. "Then ask Citizen Brigadier Mahoney to step back in here."

"Yes, Sir! At once!"

❖   ❖   ❖

"General Conflans reports that his forces have linked up with Brigadier Henderson's and that the enemy has broken off the attack!"

Someone in the War Room raised a half-cheer at the news before he could stop himself, but McQueen only nodded calmly. A part of her wanted to cheer herself, for Conflans' report was the best news she'd gotten since the last of the Committee's members had been rounded up. His attempt to take the StateSec intervention battalions in the flank must have succeeded, and that meant that the ground forces immediately available to Saint-Just had been effectively neutralized.

She glanced at her chrono. Strange. Time had felt as if it were dragging past with glacial slowness, yet over five hours had passed since her commando teams kicked off the operation.

Five hours, and I'm still alive. Now that I've gotten this far, I guess I can admit to myself that I hadn't expected to be alive by now. But if Gerard is right and Bouchard really is pulling back, then it sounds as if the momentum is by God slipping over to our side after all!

She recognized a familiar danger sign, and made herself step back from her own enthusiasm.

Careful, woman! Get yourself all overconfident and stupid, and Saint-Just will put your head on a pike in the People's Square by evening!

She turned to Bukato.

"Tell Gerard to turn over to Henderson the moment he feels sufficiently confident to do so, and to get himself back here to the Octagon," she said crisply. "And tell him to bring as big a reinforcement with him as he thinks he can without weakening Henderson dangerously."

"Of course, Ma'am," Bukato replied. "You think it's time to begin thinking about planning an offensive of our own?"

"No," she said grimly. "I think it's time that we reinforced the Octagon's ground forces as much as we can." Bukato's eyes widened in surprise, and she laughed harshly. "If Gerard and his people have convinced him he can't get through on the ground, Ivan, then he's going to try something else. He has to, because the clock is on our side."

"But that's crazy, Ma'am," Bukato objected, less like a man who thought she was wrong than like one who truly believed she was. "The defense grid would blow them apart!"

"You know that, and I know that, but does *Saint-Just* know that?" she returned with a shark-like grin. "And even if he does know, does he *care?* Bottom line, Ivan, he still has a hell of a lot more firepower planetwide to draw upon than we do. I don't think he could get through the grid, either, but we might both be wrong, and he only has to get lucky once. Besides, they're only people, and he's got plenty more where they came from if he breaks this lot."

Bukato looked at her for a moment longer, as if he wished that he could disagree with her assessment, then nodded.

"Yes, Ma'am. I'll pass those orders right away."

"We've got the airstrike and assault echelon organized, Citizen Secretary."

Saint-Just looked up as another of his senior staffers stepped through the office door to make the report.

"They've been fully briefed?" the citizen secretary asked.

"Yes, Sir."

"Then send them in."

"Immediately, Sir!"

The staffer hurried away, and Saint-Just looked down at his desk and its sophisticated communications panel once more. He hoped the assault shuttles and sting ships he was about to commit to battle could do the job, just as he hoped their pilots truly accepted that they had no choice but to fire on the other members of the Committee of Public Safety. Whatever happened, the integrity of the state must be maintained. He was in a fight for his own personal survival, for Esther McQueen could never afford to leave him alive after this, any more than he could have afforded to leave *her* alive. But there was more at stake here than mere survival. McQueen might well prove as effective as a political leader as she had proven as a military leader. In the judgment of history, it was entirely possible that she would be considered a far better head of state than Oscar Saint-Just could ever hope to be. But that didn't matter. What *mattered* was that she had killed Rob Pierre. That wherever she might lead the People's Republic, it would not be to the destination Pierre had chosen, and Rob Pierre had been not simply Saint-Just's friend, but his chieftain.

Perhaps Esther McQueen had never fully understood that, but it would have changed nothing if she had. For all of his blandness, all of his famous lack of emotion, Oscar Saint-Just had the soul of a feudal clansman, and he *would* have his vengeance.

"Tango Flight, this is Tango One Lead. The mission is a go. I say again, we are go for the attack."

Citizen Lieutenant Angelica Constantine closed her eyes in pain as the strike leader's voice came over the com. She couldn't believe it. No, that wasn't right. She *could* believe it; she simply didn't want to.

She opened her eyes once more and watched her HUD as the icons began to shift and change. Forty StateSec atmospheric sting ships just like her own formed the true heart of the strike's power, although a dozen pinnaces would lead the way. She didn't envy the flight crews of those lead ships. They were individually far more capable—and dangerous—than any sting ship, but that scarcely mattered, because there was virtually no chance that any of them could survive to penetrate the Octagon's defenses, and their crews knew it. Their true function was simply to draw the defenses' fire. To distract and confuse the tracking and fire control crews in hopes that a handful of the despised sting ships might get through.

Constantine knew all about the attack plan, and she gave it no more than a twenty percent chance of success. And even that estimate, she knew, might well be wildly over optimistic. The attack had been ordered and organized with ruthless, reckless haste in a desperate effort to get it in while McQueen and her accomplices might still be in the process of securing control of the grid. If they hadn't gotten control of it, or if their control was still less than complete, then at least some of the attackers might manage to get through. But if they did have full control of it . . .

Not even the Levelers had dared to challenge the Octagon's on-site defenses, and she wondered now why Citizen Secretary Saint-Just had never had the defense grid disabled or at least placed under SS control. A lot of people, all too probably including Angelica Constantine, were about to die because he hadn't, and fear flickered and simmered in her mind like some dark fire.

Yet however frightened she might be, fear explained only a part of the knot of despair resting in her chest like a lump of cold iron. Her husband, Gregory, was also State Security . . . and assigned to the Octagon security staff. She had no idea if he was even still alive, but whether he was or not wouldn't change a thing. And it probably didn't much matter either way. Not really. The Legislaturalists had built the Octagon like a fortress, because that was precisely what it was: the command nexus for all of the Republic's armed forces, and the central facility charged with the air defense of the Republic's capital, as well. Tango Flight would do its best to break through and disable at least some of the defense grid's fire stations with precision guided munitions in hopes of opening a hole for follow-on assault shuttle waves to exploit. Success was unlikely at best, but now that Citizen General Bouchard's hastily mounted ground assault had turned into a bloody shambles, it would take hours—possibly days—to organize a proper assault out of the wreckage, and God only knew how the situation could change in that much time. McQueen's coup attempt had to be crushed before still more of the regular armed forces rallied to her, and if this attempt failed, the only way to stop her was to flatten the Octagon around her ears. Which would also mean burying Gregory in the rubble right along with her.

The only redeeming factor was that Angelica would probably be dead even before him.

"Tango Flight, execute!" Tango One Lead barked.

"Here they come, Ma'am."

Esther McQueen's raised hand interrupted the latest report from Lieutenant Caminetti, and she turned quickly to the huge main plot at Captain Rubin's announcement.

Normally, that plot was used to display the locations and status of every unit of the vast web of fortifications and fleet units stationed to protect the Haven System from any foreign attack. Now it showed something which very few of the people in the War Room had ever seen on it, even in drills: a detailed holographic map of the City of Nouveau Paris and a hundred-kilometer radius around it. The map was scabrous with the red blotches of identified threats and a thinner scattering of green friendly units, and she felt a familiar stab of tight-mouthed tension as a deadly cluster of tiny crimson arrowheads appeared upon it.

Her trained gaze identified each of the plot's icons as readily as someone else might have read a newsfax, and her eyes narrowed.

"Those poor bastards."

She glanced to her right at the soft regretful murmur, and Ivan Bukato shook his head as her eyes met his.

"We have lock," someone announced, and McQueen turned her attention back to the plot as sighting circles reached out to entrap the arrowheads.

"They must know they don't have a prayer," Bukato said quietly, and she shrugged.

"Of course they don't," she agreed absently. "And whoever ordered them in knows it, too. But she might be wrong, so she's spending them to find out for sure whether or not we managed to secure the grid before some StateSec loyalist could disable it. Or possibly in an effort to distract us from something else."

Bukato's eyes flicked once from the plot to the unyielding, almost serene profile of the diminutive woman beside him, and then he returned them to the display with a tiny shiver.

An angry war god smashed his palms together, and the mangled wreckage of a pinnace spewed itself across the smoke-tinged blue skies of Nouveau Paris.

It was not alone. The battle steel hatches of massively armored ground emplacements flicked open like striking serpents, and mass-drivers hurled anti-air missiles out of them at four times the speed of sound. The missiles' impeller wedges flashed to life as soon as they cleared their launchers, and they howled in on their targets like vengeful demons. The pinnaces leading Oscar Saint-Just's airstrike never had a chance, and then it was the sting ships' turn.

The transatmospheric craft had come in high, but the pure air-breathers lacked both their ceiling and their speed. The best that they could manage was little more than mach three, but they compensated by coming in in terrain-riding mode. They shrieked in barely two hundred meters above the ground, weaving their ways between the ceramacrete mesas of the People's Republic's capital city's administrative and residential towers, and fresh missiles streaked to meet them.

Not impeller wedge missiles this time, because hardwired software imperatives made it impossible for the defense grid to fire such weapons at any targets at less than five hundred meters' altitude. A hit by one of those weapons on any tower would inflict catastrophic damage, and so, as if in some bizarre effort to level the playing field, the slower and lower sting ships could be engaged only with less capable old-fashioned reaction drive missiles.

But if the field had been leveled slightly, it

remained uncompromisingly tilted in the defense grid's favor. The system's designers might have denied the grid the use of impeller wedge missiles, but it had scores of launch stations, and at least ten missiles targeted each of the incoming attackers.

It wasn't a battle. It wasn't even a massacre. Not one of the attackers survived to reach its own launch range of the Octagon, and fireballs and explosions rocked the heart of Nouveau Paris as bits and pieces of men and women and once sleek attack craft thundered down from the heavens.

"My God," someone blurted. *"Assault shuttles?"*

McQueen didn't even turn her head to see who it was. It didn't matter, and even if it had, she could not have taken her eyes from the plot as a fresh wave of icons appeared. There were dozens of them, each a StateSec assault shuttle with up to two hundred fifty men and women aboard, and they streaked straight towards the Octagon as if their pilots actually believed that the sacrifice of the sting ships might have somehow distracted the tracking systems from their own approach. She watched them come, and an ancient phrase out of the history of Old Earth whispered in the back of her brain.

"C'est magnifque, mais ce n'est pas la guerre," she said very softly.

"Dear God in Heaven."

Oscar Saint-Just didn't even turn his head, and his stonelike expression never wavered. He felt certain that the staffer didn't realize that he'd whispered his half-prayer aloud. But even if the man had, and even if he'd been foolish enough to mean it as a criticism of Saint-Just as the man who had ordered the mission, the citizen secretary would have chosen, just this once, to ignore it.

His eyes never flickered as he watched the icons of the troop-laden second-wave assault shuttles streak into the teeth of the Octagon's defensive fire. They came in at just over mach three, but they had come in higher than the sting ships had, and the impeller wedge missiles slashed into them with lethal efficiency. They had better ECM than the sting ships, but nowhere near enough of it to make any real difference, and the missiles ripped them apart effortlessly. Only two of them got close enough for the energy weapons on the Octagon's roof to engage them directly.

The last assault shuttle went down, taking its embarked company of StateSec ground force troopers with it, and the silence in Saint-Just's office could have been chipped with a knife. The SS commander watched the displays tally the horrendous casualty numbers with an unyielding basilisk gaze, then gave a tiny shrug.

I had to try. Badly as it turned out, my other options were even worse. And now, bad as they are, they're all I have left.

He inhaled, and turned away from the displays to seat himself once more behind his desk.

"And now Citizen Secretary Saint-Just knows for certain who controls the grid," Esther McQueen murmured softly, turning from the main plot to survey the direct view screens. Fires and secondary explosions filled them, and for all the serenity of her tone, her eyes were cold. "I do hope that whoever passed on the order for this attack survives to be captured," she went on in a nearly conversational voice.

"I'd like to . . . discuss his choice of tactics with him myself, Ma'am," Bukato agreed.

"I agree that they never had a chance of breaking through, Ma'am," Captain Rubin said respectfully, "but as you yourself pointed out, I don't see that they had any real choice but to try."

"I realize that, Captain," McQueen said after a moment. "But it was a forlorn hope from the beginning, and whoever actually ordered those shuttles in should have realized that the instant we mowed down the sting ships. And if she did, and if she'd had an ounce of moral courage, she would have told Saint-Just that sending those shuttles into the same defenses was nothing but an act of murder. It never had any real chance of succeeding as a serious attack, and if it was only a probe, he'd already drawn the response that should have told him everything he needed to know with just the sting ships. There was absolutely no point in taking the additional casualties."

"Which doesn't even consider how many civilians must've been killed or injured when the wreckage landed," Bukato pointed out grimly.

"No, it doesn't," McQueen acknowledged. "But we can't really get too sanctimonious about those casualties, Ivan. We're the ones who fired the missiles that brought them down, after all. And I suppose that in the ultimate sense, we're at least as responsible as Saint-Just for any civilians that got killed. If we hadn't made our move, he would just have had us quietly rounded up and shot and none of this would have happened."

"I know that, Ma'am. But at least we're *trying* to minimize collateral casualties."

"True, and it's also true that Saint-Just and Pierre between them have killed more of the Republic's citizens than the entire Manty Alliance put together, so replacing them as the new management has to be an improvement any way you slice it. But we *do* have a certain selfish interest at stake here, as well, don't we?"

She smiled thinly, and to his own immense surprise, Ivan Bukato actually chuckled.

"What's the latest status report from the port?"

Saint-Just's conversational voice had the impact of a screamed obscenity in the silent, lingering aftermath of the destruction of Citizen Brigadier Tome's entire brigade. All eyes snapped to him, and then a staffer shook herself and cleared her throat.

"I'm . . . afraid the news isn't good, Sir," she admitted. "We've got a little more information now, and it looks like McQueen managed to get Citizen General Conflans slipped into the spaceport garrison's chain of command without our noticing. The latest estimate is that virtually the entire garrison went over to him in the first twenty minutes—that's where they got the manpower to stop Citizen General Bouchard's attack." The staffer paused, then drew a deep breath. "And I'm afraid that's not all, Sir," she went on in a slow but determined tone. "Communications reports that Citizen General Maitland has just joined Citizen Colonel Yazov in announcing his open support for the mutineers."

"I see."

Saint-Just refused to allow his voice to show it, but the news about Maitland and Yazov hit him hard. Yazov had been the first StateSec officer to declare his support for McQueen. A mere citizen colonel might not seem all that significant in the great scheme of things, but no one knew better than Saint-Just how

much success or failure at a moment like this hinged
on perceptions and the reactions of frightened, confused human beings *to* those perceptions. And that
had made Yazov's defection a body blow. The citizen
colonel had been handpicked for his apparent loyalty and devotion, as much as for his capability, when
he was assigned to be in Nouveau Paris spaceport as
the competent executive officer that the political
appointee who officially commanded the capital city's
primary space-to-ground link required. As such, his
defection raised frightening questions about what
other "handpicked" officers McQueen might have
reached.

That was bad enough, but now Yazov seemed to
have convinced his titular CO to join him, and their
joint public endorsement of McQueen's version of
what was happening was even worse. If even StateSec
officers claimed to believe that *Saint-Just* was truly
the traitor and that McQueen represented the legitimate Committee and its interests, then the steady,
ultimately fatal erosion of his position would become
inevitable.

They're driving me to it, he thought almost calmly.
*They're not going to leave me any choice. And if I
do it . . .*

He closed his eyes for a moment and made himself face the implications of the decision rumbling
down upon him with the inexorable power of Jug-
gernaut. It represented what was probably his only
hope of crushing McQueen before the balance of
power slid too far in her favor. He dared not wait
while even more of the regular armed forces stationed
here in Nouveau Paris went over to her, and especially not if more of his own StateSec personnel began
to follow Yazov's example.

This thing had to be settled *now*, before it got completely out of control. In a worst-case scenario, the fighting could drag on for days or weeks, and every hour would increase the odds that still more of the Navy and Marines would throw their allegiance to the Octagon. Even if they didn't go over to McQueen, other officers might began to get ideas of their own. An ambitious man might very well see an opportunity to carve out a power base of his own while Saint-Just and McQueen were locked in a death grapple which would prevent either of them from dealing with him. And even if that didn't happen immediately, and even if Saint-Just managed ultimately to suppress McQueen's rebellion, the damage would still have been done as far as any hope for his own legitimacy was concerned. The longer this dragged out, the more people would be tempted to believe her version of what had happened. Some of that was going to happen whatever he did, but at least a rapid and ruthless resolution might help to minimize the damage.

And what happens when everyone realizes just how far you're prepared to go, Oscar? Will it frighten them into behaving themselves? Or will they wonder just how much they really have to lose with you in charge?

Oscar Saint-Just stared into the pitiless unknown of the future, and if a man with so much blood already on his hands had dared to believe in God, he would have prayed to be spared what he saw there.

"I may be overly optimistic, Ma'am," Ivan Bukato said, "but I believe we may just have turned the corner."

He and McQueen stood side-by-side, gazing into an immense viewscreen that showed a panoramic view of the smoke and wreckage strewn about the Octagon's approaches. Morning had given way to afternoon. Now afternoon was slowly yielding to a red-tinged and bloody evening lit by the pyres of two more waves of assault shuttles and strike aircraft. They had been blown apart by the defense grid just as efficiently as their predecessors, and General Conflans had cut his way through the confusion to the Octagon with the equivalent of almost a complete Marine regiment.

"I think the timing of Maitland's announcement may have been decisive," the admiral went on. He waved one hand at the main plot, where the spaceport now showed a solid, friendly green, then jabbed a finger at another block of green. This one indicated one of the neighboring administrative towers, and it had been the blood red of State Security less than five minutes before. "When an entire SS intervention HQ decides to 'support the legitimate members of the Committee' against its own commander, it actually begins to look like we'll pull this off after all."

"I'd hesitate to start making any long-term retirement plans just yet," McQueen said with a wry smile, "but it does look as if the momentum is slipping over to our side. Maybe I should go have another discussion with Fontein."

"All joking aside, Ma'am, that might not be a bad idea," Bukato said seriously. "Like you, I expected him to cave in sooner than this, but now that rank and file StateSec people are coming over to us, maybe you could convince him that endorsing your position is the best way to minimize the ultimate bloodshed."

"You may have a point," McQueen conceded. "Erasmus and I are never going to feel all warm and fuzzy about each other, but I believe the man is genuinely committed to stability and the minimization of wholesale destruction. And I think he's hard-headed enough to recognize the inevitable when it looks him right in the eye."

"I'm afraid I'm a bit more cynical about his ultimate motivations, Ma'am. But it's beginning to look to me like the tide is coming in, and whatever his commitments may be, I don't think he wants to drown."

"You could be right to be cynical. And the bottom line is that it doesn't matter whether he signs on with us out of principle or out of self-preservation, now does it?"

"No, Ma'am, it doesn't. Not in the short term, at least."

"In that case, I think I *will* go have another little chat with him. Mind the store for me, Ivan."

"Yes, Ma'am."

"Get me Citizen General Speer on a maximum security line," Saint-Just said. His voice was almost as emotionless as it had been at the very beginning, but only almost, and one or two of the taut-faced, anxious officers staffing his HQ glanced at one another.

"Yes, Sir," his com officer said quickly. "Where would you like to take it?"

"At my desk," the citizen secretary replied, and his chief of staff quickly gathered up the other officers with his eyes and shooed them all down to the far end of the room.

Saint-Just hardly noticed. He sat square-shouldered behind his desk, and waited while the communications system connected him to the woman who commanded every State Security trooper in the city of

Nouveau Paris. It didn't take very long, but the small handful of seconds seemed endless and yet all too fleeting. Then his com's display blinked alive with Rachel Speer's strong-boned face.

The pickup at Speer's end was adjusted for wide focus. He could see the hustle and bustle of her own staff in the background, and even now, one corner of his mouth tried to quirk into a smile. There was no chance at all that she'd simply forgotten to narrow the field of view. She wanted him to see all of that energetic effort . . . and to remember it when the time came to assign blame for this unpleasant afternoon.

"Citizen Secretary," she greeted him. "I'd like to say it was a pleasure to see you, Sir. Under the circumstances, however, I doubt that you'd believe me if I did say it."

"As ever, Rachel, you remain a mistress of understatement." Saint-Just's voice was poison dry, and Speer's face went instantly blank. There were several different ways his reply could have been taken, and it was obvious that she didn't much care for most of them.

Saint-Just let her worry about it for a moment, but he didn't really have time for such minor matters, and he cleared his throat. The small, harsh sound wasn't loud, but Speer's eyes narrowed as she heard it.

"The reason I'm screening you," the citizen secretary said flatly, "is that I've decided that we cannot permit this situation to drag out any further. Citizen Colonel Yazov and Citizen General Maitland's defections were bad enough, but now Citizen Brigadier Azhari has gone over to McQueen, as well . . . and he appears to have taken his entire HQ with him."

"Sir, I assure you that I had absolutely no reason

to suspect that Azhari was even considering such a betrayal!" Speer broke in. "I'll have his family picked up immediately, and—"

"I didn't say it was your fault, Rachel," Saint-Just said flatly, "and assuming that you and I both survive, there will be time to deal with his actions later. I only mentioned them to make the point that we can't afford to delay any longer. So I am authorizing and directing you to execute Bank Shot immediately."

Citizen General Speer's expression tightened, and her eyes widened ever so slightly. Saint-Just watched her reaction carefully, and he was rather reassured by what he saw. He'd been half-afraid that she might object or argue, but she'd obviously had time enough to realize that Bank Shot was a possibility from the outset. And it was equally obvious that whatever she thought of the notion, she was not about to risk anything which might be construed as less than total loyalty at this particular moment in the history of the People's Republic. Still . . .

"Sir, have you considered warning McQueen about the possibility of Bank Shot?" she asked very carefully.

"I have. And rejected it," Saint-Just said flatly. He held her eyes unflinchingly, then waved one hand in a small gesture. "The woman is a realist, Rachel, so you might be right; if we tell her what we can do to her, she might at least try to negotiate some settlement. But we'd also have to tell her *how* Bank Shot works if we expected her to believe us, and we can't risk the possibility of her stalling just long enough to locate the hole in her defenses and plug it."

Speer was silent for another ten seconds, then nodded.

"Yes, Sir. I understand," she said after only the

briefest pause. "I'll begin the evacuation at once, and—"

"I don't think you *did* understand me fully, Citizen General," Saint-Just interrupted in a voice whose tone of icy calm surprised even him. "I am instructing you to execute Bank Shot *immediately*. There will be no evacuation."

"But, Sir! I mean, I realize the situation is critical, but we're talking about—"

Speer failed to keep the consternation out of her expression, and Saint-Just saw something very like horror in her eyes, but he cut her off brusquely.

"I understand precisely what we're talking about, Citizen General," he said, still in that icy voice. "As I just pointed out, however, whatever else she may be, McQueen is no fool. If she sees us evacuating any towers outside the immediate vicinity of the Octagon, she's entirely capable of realizing what's coming just as if we'd warned her intentionally. Which would put the ball in her court, if she chose to go back on the air. What if she figures it out and appeals to Capital Fleet to prevent it?" He shook his head. "No. There's no way of knowing where things might go, so I will repeat myself once, and once only. *There will be no evacuation.* Is that understood, Citizen General Speer?"

Rachel Speer opened her mouth, then closed it again. For perhaps three seconds, she said nothing at all, but then she nodded.

"Yes, Sir, Citizen Secretary. I understand."

"—so I believe it's time that you reconsider your position, Citizen Commissioner," Esther McQueen said calmly. She sipped coffee from the Navy cup in her hand and smiled ever so slightly as Erasmus

Fontein drank from a matching cup. She found herself forced to genuinely admire the people's commissioner's air of calm composure, and she was determined to appear just as composed.

"You manage to make it sound so reasonable, Citizen Secretary," the StateSec man observed after a moment. "Unfortunately, Citizen Secretary Saint-Just might not find it quite so sensible of me."

"Oh, come now!" McQueen chided. "You know as well as I do how little legitimacy Saint-Just can command on his own. I have all of the rest of the Committee here in the Octagon, and two-thirds of them have already agreed to publicly support me. StateSec officers are even beginning to come over—not in enormous numbers yet, perhaps, but to come over. More to the point, perhaps, Capital Fleet hasn't made a move. They may not have opened fire on their StateSec watchdogs, but Saint-Just hasn't been able to get them to fire on *us*, either, and you know what that means as well as I do. It's been over fifteen hours now, and he hasn't been able to suppress us, and he's the one whose support base is eroding out from under him. When the rest of the Committee comes in on my side, he's finished."

Fontein sipped more coffee, buying time to think before he responded, and she was content to let him. Both of them knew how critical it was for Saint-Just to defeat the challenge she represented quickly. That would have been vital under any circumstances, but with Rob Pierre dead it became even more crucial to Saint-Just's hope of survival to crush any challenge to his own authority quickly. As the Revolution's watchdog, Oscar Saint-Just was undoubtedly the most hated single individual in the entire People's Republic of Haven. If any alternative to him even looked as if it *might* be viable, his hold on power would become far worse than merely precarious.

Fontein lowered his cup and stared into it for several seconds, then raised his head and looked squarely into McQueen's eyes.

"You might be right about that," he said finally. "But Oscar may just surprise you yet. And even if he doesn't, even if you actually manage to pull it off, what in God's name pushed you into *trying* it in the first place? My God, woman! You may pull it off, but you had to be insane to risk everything on one throw of the dice this way! And *please* don't try to tell me that you were 'ready' for all of this. I've been assigned to you too long not to recognize when you're improvising as you go along."

"Of course I'm improvising," she told him. "I didn't have much choice when you and Saint-Just decided I had to go, but I won't pretend that I had all of my own plans firmly in place." She shook her head. "I never thought Pierre would authorize my removal before we knew for certain that the Manties were on the ropes."

"What are you talking about?" Fontein demanded, and McQueen's eyebrows rose at the genuine surprise in his voice.

"Please, Citizen Commissioner," she said. "I won't pretend I was happy to learn that Saint-Just had authorized you to move against me, but I decided that I should consider that was only business, not personal. Under the circumstances, it's hardly necessary for you to try to pretend he hadn't, though."

"But he—" Fontein began, then cut himself off. He stared at her for several seconds, and then chuckled with absolutely no humor at all.

"I don't know why you think Oscar was planning

to remove you any time soon," he told her, then waved one hand in the air as he saw her expression of disbelief. "Oh, I'm not saying that he hadn't decided you had to go, Citizen Secretary. I'm only saying that anything he and I discussed was at a very preliminary stage. The, ah, *evidence preparing* stage, one might say. In point of fact, I was instructed *not* to act against you in any other way without his specific authorization, because the Citizen Chairman hadn't authorized *him* to act."

It was McQueen's turn to be surprised. Almost against her will, she found that she actually believed him, and she began to chuckle herself.

"It would have been much simpler all around if you could have just told me that, Citizen Commissioner," she said after a moment. "If I'd had just two more weeks to put things together, Saint-Just never would have known what hit him, much less had time to respond! Still, I suppose all's well that ends well."

"I still believe that congratulating yourself on victory could be a bit premature," Fontein said. "On the other hand, you're right about Oscar's failure to suppress your little mutiny quickly. And if you truly do have the rest of the Committee in your pocket, I suppose the odds are that you really will manage to pull it off in the end. I trust you won't think any less of me if I admit that I would prefer to survive rather than to die a principled but useless death. I don't suppose you'd care to troll any offers of high office under the new regime under my nose to entice me to shift allegiance, would you?"

"I can if you want me to," McQueen replied. "Of course, you're not stupid enough to believe me if I do. No, Citizen Commissioner. I don't believe I trust your cupidity enough to attempt to bribe you with the offer of a platform from which to intrigue against me in turn. What I'm offering you is a chance to sign on for the record, with the understanding that afterward you will be provided the opportunity to slip away into quiet and obscure retirement on some nice Solarian planet of your choice with a comfortable pension tucked away in some Solarian bank. I believe you know me well enough to know that I'll keep my word about allowing you to retire . . . as long as you *do* retire. And that if you *don't* retire, I won't make the mistake Saint-Just did and leave you alive to make problems in the future."

She smiled pleasantly at her people's commissioner, and as if against his will, Fontein smiled back.

"Such candor is rather refreshing," he observed. "And I suspect that I can legitimately convince myself that lending you my public support is actually my duty on the grounds that anything which brings the fighting to a close quickly will reduce both the civilian casualty count and the probability of long-term instability for whatever regime replaces Citizen Chairman Pierre's."

"So you'll publicly endorse my authority?" McQueen pressed.

"Let's just say that I'm inclining in that direction. I would, however, like the opportunity to speak with the members of the Committee who are currently your . . . guests first. Both to assure myself that they really *are* your guests, and also that you're not, ah, *exaggerating* the level of support you enjoy from them."

"I believe that can be arranged, Citizen Commissioner."

Esther McQueen stepped back into the War Room. Bukato looked up from a conversation with Captain

466   *Changer of Worlds*

Rubin and General Conflans and started to walk
across to her, but she waved him back to his conference. It looked like they were discussing something
important, and good as her news was, it would keep.

She folded her hands behind her, and turned back
to the visual display of the smoke and flames litter-
ing the Octagon's approaches. Lights were coming on
in the residential towers outside the actual defense
grid perimeter, and she shook her head.

Look at that, she thought. *A goddamned war going
on less than three kilometers away, and I'll bet two-
thirds of them are just sitting there watching out their
windows while we kill each other! What a hell of a
thing when the citizens of the capital city of what's
supposed to be a civilized star nation have seen so
much bloodshed that they don't even head for the hills
when it starts up all over again.*

She shook her head again and watched the red disk
of the setting sun dropping behind the tops of the
towers to the west of the Octagon.

*Maybe I should decide to take it as a compliment—
a sort of comment on their faith in the accuracy of
our fire control!* She snorted. *They probably figure
one bunch of politicos is as bad as another. God knows
I would, in their place, by now. I wonder if they
really care which of us wins, or if they'd just prefer
for us to finish one another off for good and get it
over with?*

She gazed at the setting sun a moment longer, then
drew a sharp breath, and turned briskly back to the
War Room. There were things to do and people to
talk to, and she had a lot to accomplish yet.

I didn't really expect to make it to noon, she told
herself. *But I did, and however hard I work at
restraining Ivan's optimism, I really do think he's*

right. We've got the bastard. He needed to nail us by nightfall, and he hasn't.

"Sir, you have a com request from Citizen General Speer."

This time, Oscar Saint-Just didn't even acknowledge the information. He only reached out and pressed the stud to accept the call.

"Citizen General." He nodded to the woman on the display, and she nodded back.

"Citizen Chairman." Saint-Just's face tightened ever so slightly as someone applied that title to him for the first time. There was a subtle message in Speer's choice of words, and he wondered if perhaps she might have more of a point than he realized . . . or chose to admit to himself, at least.

Just how badly do I want Rob's job? I know that I've always told myself that only a madman would want it, but did I really mean it? And if I did, then why aren't I on the com to McQueen right now, trying to work out some sort of compromise to end this thing without killing any more people? Vengeance for Rob is all well and good, but isn't it just possible that there's something else at work here, as well?

Not that it mattered.

"I am ready to proceed with Bank Shot," Speer went on formally, and Saint-Just nodded once more.

"Then do so," he said calmly, and fifteen kilometers away from his office, Citizen General Rachel Speer pushed a button in her own command room. A signal flashed out from that button over a secure landline connection that no one outside the innermost circles of State Security had ever even suspected existed. It reached a relay hidden in a subbasement of the Octagon, and from there it flicked to its final destination.

The fifty kiloton nuclear demolition charge whose presence not even Erasmus Fontein had known about detonated, and the Octagon, Fontein, the entire surviving membership of the Committee of Public Safety, Ivan Bukato, and Esther McQueen and her entire staff became an expanding ball of flame in the heart of Nouveau Paris.

The thermal pulse flashed outward, followed moments later by the blast front itself, and the towers around the Octagon took the full fury of their impact with absolutely no warning. Many of the inhabitants of those towers had fled hours before; the majority had not. They had taken cover, but the towers were over a kilometer in height and half a kilometer in diameter. Their mass and bulk had seemed sufficient to protect those sheltering deep at their cores, and so they had been . . . so long as the combatants restricted themselves to chemical explosives.

They were not proof against the cataclysmic eruption of fusion-born plasma in their very midst, and the fireball of the Octagon's destruction enveloped them like the fiery breath of Hell itself.

At least those man-made mountains of ceramacrete were tough enough and huge enough to channel the blast. They acted like a breakwater, protecting the city beyond them with their own deaths, and their sacrifice was not in vain, for "only" one-point-three million citizens of Nouveau Paris perished with them.

Oscar Saint-Just's office was two-thirds of the way across the city from the Octagon, and the office itself lay at the very heart of its own tower. Not even the eye-tearing brilliance of a nuclear detonation could penetrate that much alloy and ceramacrete, but the entire stupendous edifice trembled as if in terror as

the shockwave rolled over it. The deeply buried
landlines of the government's secure communications
system were fully hardened against the EMP of the
explosion, and Rachel Speer's image on his com display didn't even flicker.

Nor did her gaze, as she looked out of the display
into his eyes.

"Detonation confirmed . . . Citizen Chairman," she
said softly.